GRIPPING TALES OF ADVENTURE AND DANGER IN A LAND WITHOUT LAW

✦ ✦ ✦

The Man from Shadow Ridge

Tom Dawson thought he'd left everything behind two years ago, when he fled to his brother's ranch in California. Then one terrible tragedy, and the fate of a young boy, brings the turmoil back . . . in the midst of the raging Civil War.

Cannons of the Comstock

When a secret Confederate society conspires to raise and equip an army that would engulf California in the Civil War and break the Union blockade that strangles the South, only peace-loving Tom Dawson and Montgomery James, a former slave child, can expose the conspiracy.

Riders of the Silver Rim

A tragic accident sends blacksmith Joshua Roberts west, through the merciless desert, to find peace. But what he finds in a lawless silver mining town in the Sierras is raw trouble . . . greedy, unscrupulous enemies who are a far greater threat than his dark secret.

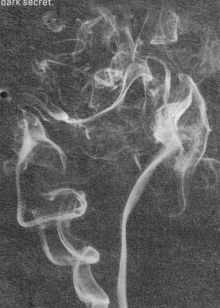

LEGENDS OF THE WEST

VOLUME FOUR

The Man from Shadow Ridge

Cannons of the Comstock

Riders of the Silver Rim

BROCK & BODIE THOENE

TYNDALE HOUSE PUBLISHERS, INC., CAROL STREAM, ILLINOIS

Visit Tyndale's exciting Web site at www.tyndale.com

For further information on Thoene titles, visit www.thoenebooks.com and www.familyaudiolibrary.com

TYNDALE and Tyndale's quill logo are registered trademarks of Tyndale House Publishers, Inc.

Legends of the West, Volume Four first printing by Tyndale House Publishers, Inc., in 2008.

Designed by Stephen Vosloo

Edited by Ramona Cramer Tucker

This novel is a work of fiction. Names, characters, places, and incidents either are the product of the authors' imaginations or are used fictitiously. Any resemblance to actual events, locales, organization, or persons living or dead is entirely coincidental and beyond the intent of either the authors or the publisher.

Library of Congress Cataloging-in-Publication Data

Thoene, Brock, date.
  Legends of the West / Brock and Bodie Thoene.
    p. cm.
  ISBN-13: 978-1-4143-0113-6
  ISBN-10: 1-4143-0113-8
  I. Thoene, Bodie, date. II. Title.
  PS3570.H463L44 2007
  813'.54—dc22   2006039065

Printed in the United States of America

14 13 12 11 10 09 08
 7   6   5   4   3   2   1

JOHN WAYNE, LEGEND OF THE WEST*

The movies of John Wayne rank right up at the top of my very first memories. When Papa and Mama would load us four kids up and head for the 99 Drive-in Theater, we knew we were in for a treat. Going to see the latest John Wayne film was always our most exciting family outing. His movies were so influential in my life, in fact, that I can even identify the years of my childhood based on what movie we saw.

From the beginning, I was drawn to, and into, John Wayne's world. The heroes he portrayed were very much like my own father. They believed in God, Family, and Country. They never told a lie. Their word and a handshake was the best contract. They stood firm against the bad guys, even if it cost them everything, because that was the right thing to do. They believed that good character mattered

---

* For more "John Wayne, Legend of the West" stories, see Legends of the West series introductions for Volumes One, Two, and Three, by Brock and Bodie Thoene. For further information visit: www.thoenebooks.com and www.familyaudiolibrary.com.

more than any other trait since it seemed to cover all the bases. If you had good character, people could count on you to get the job done.

These were the principles of personal integrity, portrayed by Duke on screen in *reel* life. These same principles were also lived out before me in *real* life—both as a child, in my own home, and when Brock and I began working with Duke at Batjac Productions.

We first met John Wayne when we were just starting in our careers as writers. He generously provided us with the opportunity to learn the craft of storytelling from the best American writers.

Having watched every movie he'd ever made, I knew what was expected of me the first day I walked into his office at Batjac. His high expectations were familiar and comfortable, because I'd already seen them displayed on the big screen.

I truly loved working for John Wayne—his firm character, his wit, his sense of humor, his no-nonsense straightforwardness, his deep integrity. Brock and I were honored to not only work *with* him, but to call him friend . . . and to have him call us friends in return. Duke was truly a man who lived and breathed honor and steadfastness in a chaotic world.

The last film John Wayne made was *The Shootist,* in 1976. It was filmed mostly in Carson City, Nevada, less than forty-five minutes from our home.

The story was set after the turn of the twentieth century and dealt with an aging gunfighter named J.B. Books, who was dying of cancer. The Old West had died out, and the modern world had finally caught up with Books. The legendary gunfighter and his way of life were a thing of the past.

In retrospect, the themes in *The Shootist* seemed ideally suited to be Duke's last movie. Duke was a straight-shooter—much like J.B. Books. In the chaos of Vietnam and the rise of the drug culture, the world around Duke had turned aside from the straight and narrow. Situational ethics had become the norm.

About the same time that America legalized on-demand abortion, the motion-picture industry enacted a rating system. The ratings program destroyed family values that had been an integral part of the movie business. By then the truly great filmmakers were dying off. The motivation to create movies that could be viewed by anyone was fading. By 1976, movies were laced with profanity, nudity, and explicit sexuality and were identified with letters to warn parents what should and should not be viewed by their children. Duke personally believed that the rating system was among the worst things to ever happen in the motion-picture industry. No longer could a mom and dad load up their kids and go to a movie, confident that it would convey family values and positive lessons in the story.

In response to the motion-picture rating code, Duke said, "Morally, this will prove to be among the worst things to ever happen in America . . . [it] has opened a door to darkness which will only open wider and darker with every passing year."

Nearly forty years later we see how right John Wayne's predictions were. What is on screen in movie theaters now simply grows more violent, more explicit, more evil with every passing year. The immorality depicted on the big screen has now become commonplace on television and, by extension, in video games. The pornographic downward spiral in film, drama, music, and literature is unprecedented. As far as portraying explicit sex on screen, Duke had this to say: "Sex is a participation sport. It is NOT a spectator sport."

Like movies, popular fiction is now written down to appeal to the lowest common denominator. There are no limits in profanity, sexual content, and violence that have not been violated. All moral boundaries have been smashed.

While working for Duke, Brock and I were expected to set boundaries in what we wrote, while *never* sacrificing the depth of meaning or literary value. He expected that the stories we wrote would be enjoyed by readers of any age. He expected that our written words would inspire folks to live out the principles of truth and carry a message that "right will triumph over evil in the end."

Now, many years later, our Legends of the West are based on those same values. Within every story are biblical truths, set in the American West . . . as John Wayne saw it. As he taught us to see it.

In all our writing we have tried to honor the creative, moral, and spiritual ideals of the man who gave us our start as writers. We sometimes felt, as we worked with Duke, that we were catching the tail of a bright, shooting star as it brushed the earth. Indeed, John Wayne *was* a Shooting Star. . . .

It is our hope that these stories, the Legends of the West, will enlighten the path of your life . . . and also reveal the Truth that John Wayne believed in so wholeheartedly.

BODIE THOENE, 2008

The Man from Shadow Ridge

The Civil War rages on in the East,
but the remote mountains of California
are still untouched by the struggle.
Two years ago, in 1861,
Tom Dawson left Missouri and
fled to his brother Jesse's ranch
beneath Shadow Ridge. Life
has been good—peaceful, happy.
Then a stagecoach is robbed, and
six people are murdered. The
turmoil of Tom's past returns in a
flash . . . with the fate of a young
child hanging in the balance. . . .

To the men of the Thoene clan—
Papa Gil, brother Jess,
sons Jacob and Luke—
who share with us a love of the West, past and present,
and to Talon Zachary,
whose timely appearance, like that of this book,
foretells great things to come.

✳ CHAPTER 1 ✳

Harness leather groaned as the weary horses leaned into the last steep climb before Granite Station. The wagon was heavily loaded with flour, beans, salt, and seed. Two sleeping boys and a bolt of calico cloth completed the freight.

Tom Dawson looked like a man more at ease on the back of a green-broke Indian pony than holding the lines of a team of farm horses. His rugged, sun-browned face was creviced from the weather like the landscape. His dark brown eyes matched the color of the hair that straggled across his forehead from beneath a black broad-brimmed hat. His features had the lean, angular look of a man by no means settled into an easy life, but the small wrinkles at the corners of his eyes betrayed the fact that he smiled on occasion, too.

It was late, past dark already. Tom had expected to reach his stop for the night hours before. The army quartermaster sergeant who was to have met Tom early that morning had not arrived until midafternoon. The sergeant had sent Tom off with the warning that the stagecoach from Keyesville had been robbed. All five passengers and the driver had been brutally murdered.

Now Tom wished he had camped on the flat along the banks of Poso Creek with other travelers who had stopped for the night. His wagonload of goods might be just as tempting as gold to outlaws hiding out in the lower reaches of the Sierras. Tom's Colt Navy revolver and his Sharps carbine lay within easy reach beside him on the wagon seat.

The lights of Granite Station finally appeared atop the rise. Their friendly glow could not come too soon to suit Tom; he urged the horses to quicken their pace the last mile up the hill.

Granite boulders lined the road. The full moon cast sharp shadows from the rocky outcroppings, every one suggesting a cavernous skull. The steep ascent forced travelers to slow down; it was a natural place for an ambush. Tom knew that blood had been spilled here before.

The treeless slopes around Granite Station marked the dividing line between the oak-covered foothills of the Sierras and the grassy plains of the valley below. What thin grass grew among the boulders hissed in a fitful east wind—the dry breeze of Indian summer that promised no rain to relieve the parched earth but foretold winter's approach just the same. Over the rustle, Tom could just make out the tinny sound of a banjo and an occasional raucous laugh.

A rustling closer at hand startled Tom out of his reverie. Turning, he saw his older nephew, Jed, blinking at him from a tangled pile of calico.

"Hold on, boy. Don't wrestle that cloth. Your ma will skin us both," Tom scolded.

"I'm sorry, Tom. I thought I was home to bed an' got to reachin' for a blanket," the sleepy voice replied.

"Just lay still a mite longer; we're almost to Granite."

From the long sigh that responded, Tom knew that Jed had already rejoined his brother, Nathan, in slumber.

Good boys, both of them, eager to go with Tom on this three-day trip—and not complainers either. But the long delay and the dusty trip from town had worn them out.

At last the team crested the hill overlooking the little stage stop nestled below. The horses drew the wagon up and stopped across the dusty roadway from the small clapboard building that served as restaurant, saloon, and hotel of dubious accommodations. Tom planned only to grain the horses and buy a meal for himself and the boys. They would sleep on their cargo under the stars and start on at first light.

Tom could hear voices and an artlessly strummed banjo from the saloon, but no one appeared from the barn to assist Tom with

the harness. He decided to let the boys sleep until he had obtained
their supper, so he chocked the wheels of the wagon with two rocks
that lay near for the purpose and unhitched the team. He turned
them into the common corral, noting the presence of the station
keeper's chestnut gelding and three other saddle horses unknown to
him. Stowing the harness on a rack in the barn, Tom strode across
the road.

The stage stop appeared to lean over him as he approached. Tom
reflected that even in daylight it seemed to be bracing itself away
from the downhill slope on which it perched.

The music stopped abruptly with a cry of "More whiskey!" just as
Tom pushed open the door.

Three men sat playing cards at a table at the far end of the room.
The station keeper propped his banjo against the stone fireplace and
scurried behind the mahogany bar to oblige the demand for liquor.

"Howdy, Tom." The station keeper, a slightly built, balding man
in his early sixties, addressed him by name. "You jest up from town?"

"Yup, Charlie. Running late and almost too tired to be hungry."
The enticing aroma of a pot of beans simmering on a cast-iron hook
in the fireplace made Tom's stomach rumble, giving the lie to his
words. "Reckon I will have some beans. And the boys will be waking
up, now that their cradle's quit rocking."

"Heh! Cradle quit rockin'; that's a good one!" Charlie's wheezy
laugh was interrupted by a growl from one of the cardplayers.

"Whar's the whiskey? You old coot, ya gonna jabber all night?"

Tom's attention swung around to the three men at the table. The
one who had just spoken was a stout, florid-faced man who mopped
his forehead with a stained bandanna.

The two who flanked the speaker exchanged a furtive glance
across the table; it went unnoticed by the red-faced man. One of
these was lean and drawn-looking. His clothes, a faded, nondescript
shade of gray, matched his hair. Even his face had an ashen cast. He
watched the others with intense, dark eyes, saying nothing.

The remaining member of the group was the only one Tom
knew. It was Byrd Guidett. A rough, loud bully of a man, Byrd was
built like a miner—as thick through his chest as he was wide, with

an enormous neck and massive shoulders. He wore his curly red hair long, and his reddish beard was untrimmed.

Byrd Guidett still claimed to be living by prospecting for gold in the high reaches on the Kern, but it was said that he more likely worked the left side of the law rather than the left side of a sluice box. A mining partner of Guidett's had disappeared in a mysterious accident, and since then respectable folks had tried to walk the long way around Byrd.

"Drink up, ol' cuss," Byrd said. "Maybe yer luck will change." This was addressed to the stout man who had poured two fingers of rotgut into his glass and the other two on the table.

Charlie scampered back to the fire and, taking three none-too-clean tin plates off a sideboard, dished up three helpings of beans. He added a handful of corn dodgers to each plate and passed the lot to Tom.

"What do I owe you?" asked Tom.

"Did ya bring my coffee?" asked Charlie. At Tom's nod, he said, "Well, if ya don't charge for freightin' my Arbuckle, I reckon a few beans and 'pone is free."

"Well, much obliged and welcome to boot." Tom started out, then stopped short at a movement in the corner behind the cardplayers. He had been wrong about there being only four occupants of the dimly lit room, for crouched on the floor near the sweaty-browed gambler was a small Negro boy.

At Tom's sudden stare, Charlie's gaze also moved to the boy. Catching Tom's eye, Charlie shook his head slowly as a warning to say nothing. "I'll come out directly to see to yer team," he said.

With a slight narrowing of his eyes and a quick nod, Tom left with supper for him and the boys.

The boys roused themselves and eagerly lit into the beans. Because they were still nine parts tired, their usual banter was absent, and they ate in silence.

Presently, the saloon door opened, and Charlie joined them. The flickering light that came out through the wavy glass panes was pale.

"I'm glad you said nothin', Tom. That's two powerful mean men in there. Byrd you know of, an' that fat Missouri fella's been yellin' at me since he an' the boy came."

When Tom made no reply, he went on. "Byrd an' that gray-lookin' fella rode in about sundown. The Missourian was already pretty likkered up, an' they got this game goin' right away like they was anxious to get started."

"How do you know the one's from Missouri?" asked Tom.

"Well, he tol' me he come from there with his chattel. I ain't seen no cows, an' then he says he mean the little colored—" At Tom's sharp jerk of the head toward the boys, Charlie left the word unfinished.

"A black man? Can we see 'im?" the boys asked.

"No, boys, it isn't our affair. And anyway, it's just a child."

Charlie resumed. "So them three been playin', with the pike drinkin' an' losin' an' Byrd winnin', an' the slim fella jest watchin'."

"Obliged for the beans and the word," said Tom. "Guess we'll turn in now."

Jed and Nathan started a groan of protest but fell silent at a look from their uncle.

Tom handed the plates over to the station keeper. "I'll put out some grain for my team if it's all right."

"Help yerself, Tom, an' g'night to y'all." Charlie moved back across the road, dropping a tin plate in the process. He appeared to inspect it briefly by the window's glow. Then, wiping it on the seat of his denim pants, he seemed to find it satisfactory and went in.

✵ ✵ ✵

The shot and the crashing noise came just before dawn. Tom's mind instantly sprang awake. Grabbing the Colt Navy, he ordered, "Jed! Nathan! Get in the barn and stay there!"

Crouched beside the wagon, he waited till the boys had sprung over the side and run into the barn's opening. For a moment he thought an extra shadow ran after them, but the moon had set and he shook his head to clear his vision. His attention was turned to the saloon as the door burst open and Byrd thrust himself out.

"Whar's 'at nigger? He's mine now. Whar'd he go?" Byrd moved forward as if to cross the street and enter the barn. "I'll bet he run in here!"

The click of Tom's .36 caliber as he cocked it was loud enough to be heard in the moment Byrd paused for breath. He froze in his tracks, as did the gray man who had appeared in the doorway behind him. Slowly Byrd turned to face Tom.

"What's this all about?" Tom asked quietly but with an unmistakable edge to his voice.

"I won 'im fair an' square, an' that hunk of lard called me a cheat an' made to draw on me!"

"So you shot him," said Tom.

"It was a fair fight, wasn't it, Yance?" This last was addressed over his shoulder to the man in the doorway.

"Yup, I seen it all."

"So move outta my way," ordered Byrd with a new burst of bravado. "He's mine, an' I aim to fetch him!"

"California's free territory," replied Tom softly, "so you can't *own* him. Anyway, I was right here and I didn't see him go into the barn."

"I mean to look—," Byrd began, then stopped as Tom raised the pistol to point directly at Byrd's chest.

"Nope," Tom said. "He's probably scared and still running over these hills. Besides, if you were to find him, he'd have to be held for the inquest."

Yancey started, then said, "Byrd, we don't need no inquest."

"Shut up!" Byrd snorted. Facing Tom, he added, "Yer prob'ly right about the kid. He lit a shuck out the door, an' he's maybe halfway back to Missouri by now." Raising his hands, open palms toward Tom, he began to back slowly toward the saloon. "We've wasted enough time here already. If a deputy wants a statement, he can look us up. *Charlie* will say what happened, won't ya, *Charlie?*"

The old station keeper cleared his throat nervously from inside the doorway.

Taking this noise to mean *yes,* Byrd said, "Bring our winnin's, Yance. I'll get the horses."

Tom watched in silence without uncocking the revolver as Byrd retrieved two bridles from the corral posts and caught his and Yancey's horses.

Charlie came out and, at a nod from Tom, entered the barn to return with two saddles and blankets.

Moments later, Byrd and Yancey were mounted. As they settled into their high-cantled saddles, Byrd rode slowly over to Tom. "I won't forget ya, Tom Dawson."

Then he and Yancey spun their horses and loped up the road to the northeast.

✦CHAPTER 2✦

Tom stood watching the two ride out of sight. He thought it wise not to let down his guard too quickly, so he called out, "Charlie, do you still have that shotgun in back of the bar?"

"Why, sure I do, Tom!"

"You'd best bring it out here."

It was only after Charlie had returned with an ancient but serviceable double-barreled shotgun that Tom allowed his attention to turn from the knoll over which Byrd and Yancey had ridden.

"You'd better keep watch till full light," Tom directed the station keeper.

"'Deed I will! This here load o' buck is good for polecats an' other varmints—even birds!"

Tom entered the dark stable softly. "Jed, Nathan, come out now; it's all over."

A rustling of hay greeted his ears; then two tousled and straw-covered heads appeared from under the haymow.

"We heard it, Uncle Tom."

"But we was real still."

"I know, boys. You did real well."

"Can *he* come out now, too?" asked Jed.

"What? He who?"

"You know, the little black'un!"

So there really had been a third boy-sized shape that had darted into the barn! In protecting his own nephews, Tom had aided the child in staying out of Byrd's clutches as well.

"Come out and show yourself, boy. No one will harm you now."

A further rustling and a third hay-strewn head poked up. Only the outline of a round dark shape could be seen.

Tom stepped to a post and took down the lantern; then, reaching into his pocket, he extracted a lucifer match and proceeded to light the lamp. "Come on out, boy. Let's have a look at you."

At this further reassurance, the child stood, brushed himself off, and took a place beside Nathan. The boys were almost identical in size. Both wore overalls, but the black child wore no shirt, and his clothing was ragged, here and there inexpertly mended. Both boys were barefoot.

Tom stooped to nine-year-old height and asked gently, "Do you have a name, child?"

"Yassuh, massah. I be Montgomery James," he said with a shy grin.

"Well, Montgomery, you need not call me massah—nor anyone else. California is a free state."

The boy's eyes grew round with wonder. "Please, suh, where does I go den?"

"Well, now, where are you from? Do you have family or kin?"

The boy looked troubled. His grin faltered. "I reckon not, suh. Mistuh James, he the one what was shot, taken me off'n de farm when I was real small. I disremember any folks—"

"How do you come to be in California?"

"Mistuh James, he be a Missouri man. After order eleben come, he in trouble wid de sol'jers, an' we come away real sudden-like."

"All right, Montgomery, that will do for now. Let's get you three some breakfast. It will soon be light enough to travel, and I'm anxious to be home."

While the boys hastily washed their hands and faces in the horse trough, Charlie set down the shotgun long enough to bring out more cornbread cakes and a clay jug of buttermilk. By this time the first rays of dawn had risen over the eastern hillside above the little stage stop.

The boys ate while Tom and Charlie held a conference over the Missourian's body.

"I'll help you bury him, Charlie."

"Obliged to ya, Tom. I'll fetch the shovels."

Tom leaned over the dead gambler and absently poked through his pockets. He found a handful of silver coins, a handkerchief, and a single cuff link engraved *J. D.* Tom straightened as Charlie entered the room carrying two shovels.

"Hadn't we best bury him outside, Charlie?" suggested Tom dryly.

"Laws, yes! K-killin's fluster me so," Charlie stammered. "Here, hold these." He threw the shovels to Tom.

In the moment's confusion, Tom put the handkerchief and coins on the bar but slipped the cuff link into his pocket. Leaning the shovels against a wall, Tom grasped the feet and Charlie the arms of the corpse as they half carried, half dragged it outside. Wrapped in an old canvas slicker, the body soon lay beside four other earthen mounds on the slope a short distance below the stage stop.

"You don't worry about planting them too deep, do you?" remarked Tom.

"Naw, some kin may want to claim 'em, an' then I'd jest have to dig 'em up again."

The two men walked back up the hill to where Jed and Nathan had harnessed the team and hitched them to Tom's wagon. The boys had already rejoined the freight in the wagon bed, but Montgomery James stood uncertainly alongside the rear chestnut's flank.

"What'll ya do with the child, Tom?" inquired Charlie.

"Me?" asked Tom, startled. "I thought you'd keep him here with you."

"Naw, Tom, naw. I've got to send word to the sheriff about the killin' by the afternoon coach. I can't watch him, less'n he run off. He's a witness, ya know, an' contraband to boot."

"Charlie, he has no place to run *to*. Besides, I thought I left all that contraband talk behind when I left . . ." Here Tom's voice trailed off as if he had gotten dangerously close to a topic better left alone.

"Please, Uncle," begged Jed, "let's take him home with us. Ma will look after him, and he won't run away from us, will you, Mont?"

"Now, boys, I don't want to impose on your mother without asking."

Charlie interrupted this objection by saying, "Why, sure. What's one more young'un, more or less? He won't eat much, an' I can tell the sheriff whar to find him."

Tom gazed down at the tight black curls and fearful eyes upturned to search his face and sighed. "All right, child. Climb aboard."

"Oh no, suh. I nevuh rides *wid* no white folks—I jes' walks alongside."

"Well, Montgomery, if you are to be staying with us for a time, you'd best get in. We don't make our *guests* walk, whatever color they may be."

Urged on by the boys already seated in the wagon, Montgomery climbed over the tailgate and sat down on a flour sack. An unexpected smile broke over his face as though he had just seen a glimpse of heaven.

Tom climbed up, and with a nod to the gnarled station keeper to unblock the wheels, he slipped the brake lever and clucked to the team.

"Be seein' ya, Tom—best be right wary now," the old man urged.

Without a reply except a pull on the brim of his hat to acknowledge the advice, Tom started the wagon out of Granite Station and over the hill toward home.

The journey was a familiar one to the team, and they needed little direction, confident that their home pasture lay at the end of one more day's pull. The ease of travel allowed Tom to review the night's events. He did this with a part of his mind while at the same time remaining vigilant. He thought it unlikely that Byrd would seek vengeance openly on an obviously prepared foe, but the possibility of an ambush remained. Byrd's personality ran to open force if he clearly had the upper hand . . . but to treachery if he didn't.

Tom mused that the Missourian's destiny to die by gunfire seemed foreordained. If it was true that he had recently left his native state, then he could have only just escaped the same fate as at the station. The Missouri-Kansas border was on fire. Pro-slavery and abolitionist factions raided each other's settlements with bloody results.

In fact, the bloodiest of all these clashes had recently occurred in August in the sleepy little Kansas town of Lawrence. Quantrill's Confederates had swept into Lawrence, overpowered its inhabitants, and slaughtered three hundred men and boys while putting much of the town to the torch.

The reports of such sickening atrocities carried out against innocent civilians had accelerated since the outbreak of the Civil War, but the turmoil had existed since the early 1850s. Pro-slavery elements from Missouri had sought to force their views on the newly organized Kansas territory. Abolitionist leaders like John Brown had responded with "an eye for an eye." And so it had gone.

The eastern half of the nation was embroiled in war, to be sure, but Kansas and Missouri seemed to be engaged in a blood feud, a duel to the death liable to end only with the destruction of *all* the participants.

Tom pivoted around to look at the boys in the wagon bed. Montgomery seemed to have overcome his shyness. All three boys were talking animatedly and—glory be—comparing skin colors! He was pleased that Jed and Nathan showed a frank and open curiosity in welcoming their guest.

Montgomery was elaborating on his departure from Missouri. "An' den gen'rl, he says dat de country is lousy wid rebs. So he give out wid order 'leben. Ever'body got two days to move! Ever'body in a tizzy, throwin' things out de windas into dere wagons an' such. But Mistuh James, he catch wind dat de sol'jers comin' to arrest him. So we dasn't wait but lit out!"

Tom resumed his thoughts. Just such turmoil had caused him to leave Missouri himself two years before. In 1861, he had been a member of the Marion Rangers, a Missouri regiment. The regiment's pro-Southern loyalty asserted itself, and the Rangers decided to join the Confederacy. Tom had no stomach to fight on behalf of slavery, but to reenlist in a Union outfit would force him into battle against former friends and neighbors. Maybe he had been wrong not to stand up for his belief in the Union, but he had been grateful when word had come from his brother, Jesse.

Tom had mixed feelings about joining Jesse; after all, other issues were involved. . . . But at last he had decided to go.

For two years, things had been peaceful in California; the war was only a distant, tragic noise. Others from the Ranger group had made the same choice to come west. Tom had even had a letter from a former comrade-in-arms, Sam Clemens, late of Missouri, now living in Virginia City, Nevada Territory.

Tom sighed. Despite what the quartermaster sergeant had said, he hoped the raid on the gold shipment was only robbery and murder and the connection to the rebel cause just a ruse. He didn't want to think this peaceful countryside would experience the horror of civil war, even though he knew there were Southern sympathizers among the hill folk.

The wagon was rounding an oak-covered hillside on the last level stretch before the climb up Pruitt's Hill when Tom saw a flash ahead and just to the right of the wagon road. A gun barrel?

Tom slowed the team and cautioned the boys to be ready to jump behind a nearby clump of rocks if need be. He checked the loads in the Sharps and the Colt, then carefully watched the spot where he had seen the flash. There it was again, nearer the road this time. It appeared to be on the fork in the trail that led eastward to Poso Flat and the goldfields beyond.

The ears of the chestnuts were pricked forward, standing at attention.

In the next moment, horses and driver relaxed as approaching sounds indicated that their maker had no sinister purpose. Riding muleback, with sunlight flashing from his spectacles, and singing "Old Hundred," Parson Swift rode into view. "Hello, Tom," he called.

"Hello, Parson," Tom returned as he waited for the man of God to approach.

"Well, hello to you also, boys, and—saints alive, who's this?"

Briefly Tom explained Montgomery James' presence and the events of the shooting.

Parson Swift nodded gravely. "That explains why Byrd passed me by without a word a while back. He and a man I didn't know were riding down into Poso Flat just as I was starting up the grade. I'm heading down into the valley for a spell. I'll stop by Granite and say a few words over the man."

"I'm sure his family, if he had any, would be grateful," said Tom. Then he added, "And I'm glad Byrd's heading off east away from our track. I didn't want to see these youngsters involved in a gun battle."

"Amen, and you remember, young Tom Dawson, those that live by the sword will die that way." The lanky parson started his mule toward the valley, and the four in the wagon made their way home in the drowsy afternoon.

✵ ✵ ✵

When the fork in the road leading to the town of Greenville appeared, Tom urged the team past it and on toward home. Shortly thereafter, they came to the ford of the Poso known as Lavers Crossing.

Shadow Ridge, which now loomed directly ahead, was aptly named. Its chaparral- and oak-covered sides never appeared distinct to the eye but were always hazy, as though enveloped in thin, blue smoke. Local Indian lore had it that the mountain was sacred; some said haunted. It was called a "ghost mountain" because it was a perfect mirror image of the Sierra Nevada peak some ten miles due east.

While the eastern range reached up to cedars and pines, it was crisply outlined against the sky. Shadow Ridge, though real enough, had a miragelike quality. The Tuolomne elders maintained that Shadow Ridge was home to "shadow animals" and other spirits—counterparts of the real deer and grizzly bears that made their homes in the Sierras. All the tales made good storytelling material for gusty nights around a crackling fire. The trails of the Tuolomnes and Yokuts skirted the base of the peak without venturing into its precincts, but their fear had not bothered Tom's brother, Jesse, at all.

Jesse had brought his wife and two young sons to the property he homesteaded on the eastern slope of Shadow Ridge. His land ran from a lower ridge down to the fertile plain watered by Poso Creek.

Quail and gooseberries flourished in abundance on the hillside, while the bottom land furnished feed for cattle and good soil for planting.

Jesse's Missouri upbringing made him feel more at home as a farmer than a rancher, and his expertise soon paid off. With the army's presence at Fort Tejon and the San Joaquin Valley too swampy and malarial for farming, he rightly judged that in his corner of this mountain valley, potatoes would grow well—and travel well, too.

He had made enough money to pay for sawed cedar to build a fine home for his family, and his success with the army contract had prompted him to invite his brother to join him.

The team turned into the lane heading to the barn. Jed and Nathan jumped off before it had completely stopped and ran to where their mother was tending her pumpkin vines in the little kitchen garden.

"Ma, can Montgomery stay with us?"

"He doesn't have any kin, but now he's free!"

"We don't have to send him away, do we?"

"Now, boys, what's all this about?" Emily asked, waiting for the flow of words to slow and a coherent explanation to emerge.

Tom lifted Montgomery down from the wagon bed. The child trailed behind as Tom left the team standing patiently and walked over to his sister-in-law.

"'Lo, Emily," Tom began. He felt shy in approaching, not because he doubted her kind heart, but because he was always cautious to be extra polite to his brother's wife. Tom and Jesse had been rivals for Emily's attention in Missouri. Jesse had pressed his suit and won because he had been able to present his plan for a home, a farm, and a life, while Tom had still been devil-may-care—attractive as a dashing beau but not serious enough for a prospective husband. Tom believed that Emily cherished him still, but their affection was of the purest and deepest kind now.

She stood in her garden, dressed in dark blue calico, with her fine honey blonde hair escaping the bonnet she wore to protect her face. The afternoon sun lit up her pert nose and creamy skin.

Tom began again. "Montgomery here—" he turned to beckon the child to come and stand beside him—"is an orphan. He was brought to California by a Mister James, who got himself killed by Byrd Guidett last night. Byrd was going to take him away, but Montgomery, well, Mont doesn't need to *belong* to anyone now. Anyway, can he stay on the place for a time?" he concluded lamely.

"Of course he can, and he's welcome! Byrd Guidett is nothing but a cutthroat and a thief. Come here, Montgomery."

Emily's beauty and easy manner won the child's heart in an instant, and he crossed to stand beside Nathan.

"Will you look at that? You two boys are the same size. Montgomery, I'll bet we can find some of Nathan's clothes that will fit you, and I'm sure he'd enjoy your assistance with his chores."

"Yessum. I'se a hard worker an' don' eat much," responded Montgomery.

"You shall eat your fill, for we've plenty and to spare. *After* you wash up," she said firmly to the three youngsters. "I declare, you've brought home another forty acres on your faces."

"C'mon, Mont. I'll race you to the pump!" shouted Nathan as the three raced off around the corner of the house.

"Mind, now, wash those arms and necks, too," she called after them.

"Yes, Ma" and "yessum" blended together, floating back over their retreating forms.

She turned to regard Tom with an upraised eyebrow. "Was there trouble for you?"

"Not to speak of. Byrd and his partner backed down pretty easy. I thought there might be mischief on the road, but Parson Swift said he saw them headed down Poso Flat way. Anyway, Byrd wasn't anxious to wait around for an inquest into the shooting." He continued, "Is Jesse around?"

"No, but I expect him back most anytime. He finished the work on the barn roof and went off to hunt some quail. You should wash up, too; supper's almost ready."

"I'll just unload the wagon and see to the team, and then I'll be along."

They parted toward barn and house—the slim, wiry, dark man and the slender, fair woman.

Jesse appeared in the barn just as Tom was hanging up the harness. The family resemblance could be seen in their faces, but Jesse was broader and a shade taller. His serious face showed lines of concern. "Byrd Guidett again?"

"Yes, and a killing this time." Tom related the story to his brother, then went on. "What's more, the stage was robbed south of Wheeler Ridge early yesterday. Everybody was gunned down."

"Did they try to make a fight of it?"

"No, and that's the worst. They were lined up beside the road and shot down in cold blood. The army thinks it's the work of reb agents who would be recognized hereabouts."

"Could that be Byrd's doing, too?" asked Jesse.

"He's capable of it. Charlie said Byrd and his partner seemed anxious to settle into a card game, like they'd nothing better to do and no hurry to be elsewhere."

Jesse added, "They could have stashed the gold somewhere, then wanted to throw off suspicion by being purposefully seen a good distance from the killing."

"If that's so, Byrd's greed and temper may have messed up his plan. If he had the drop on that James fellow, he should have left off without another killing."

"I was thinking that very thing. If we ride over to Greenville tomorrow, maybe Deputy Pettibone will be around to listen."

19

✶ CHAPTER 3 ✶

The Dawson brothers had done well in their sale of the potato crop to the Union soldiers of Fort Tejon. A neat stack of twenty double eagle gold pieces glistened on the table between them.

"When you're done admiring the profits," Emily joked, "I'll deposit those in the bank if you don't mind."

The Dawson "bank" consisted of a loose stone in the fireplace and a quart canning jar half full of assorted coins and a few gold nuggets that served as small reminders that Jesse had once dreamed of striking it rich in the goldfields. But he and Emily had long since found contentment in the wealth of healthy sons, a good crop, plenty to eat, and an occasional bolt of calico. It was *enough*. Jesse had come to believe that a man who wasn't satisfied with enough would never have enough to be satisfied.

Tom had dreamed of a different kind of gold mine, a different way to strike it rich. Now, as Emily scooped the meager stack of gold coins into the jar, Tom's eyes glistened with amusement. "Wait a minute," he said, raising a hand laconically. "That's not all."

"Not all?" Jesse leaned forward. "That's more than I expected."

Tom nodded. "For the potatoes, yes." He reached into the deep pocket of his jacket and pulled out a leather bag that seemed to bulge at the seams. He hefted it twice for the effect of its weight.

Emily blinked in astonishment and looked from Tom to Jesse, then back to Tom again.

"The horses?" Jesse croaked.

Tom grinned broadly and nodded, tossing the bag onto the table with a heavy thud. "In advance."

"But they're not even broke yet!" Emily exclaimed.

"It doesn't matter." Tom took the jar from her and placed it beside the leather lump on the table. "It seems Mister Lincoln's army is desperate for our horses."

"But they're only a scruffy bunch of mustangs," Jesse protested.

"Doesn't matter to the army anymore. I told you, for every man that falls in that cursed war, ten horses go down. Some to rifle fire, some to artillery, some to the stewpot of hungry men. North and South, the armies are all afoot now."

Emily furrowed her brow. "And they should stay afoot, too, if it makes it harder for them to kill one another."

In reply, Tom upended the sack, letting a heap of gold coins clatter to the tabletop among the cups and saucers. "That is not the opinion of the Union army, Emily."

She gasped at the sight. "If Mister Lincoln would pay that in advance for wild, hook-nosed creatures that his officers have never seen, then he is a fool indeed!"

"The South would pay that much for them as well." Tom shrugged. "Maybe more."

Jesse picked up a double eagle and held it to the light. "Then Jefferson Davis is a fool, too."

"I won't argue with that." Tom scooped up a handful of coins. "Two thousand dollars here." He paused for effect. "And this is only half of it. Another two thousand when we deliver forty green-broke horses to the Union army at Fort Tejon."

Jesse gave a low whistle. "A hundred a head?"

Tom produced a neatly folded paper, emblazoned with the official seal of the Union army. "I wasn't expecting more than twenty apiece."

Emily leaned over her husband's shoulder and scanned the document. "They want the horses in a month! But you haven't even started to break them!"

There had been nearly fifty horses corralled in five makeshift corrals since mid-July. Two journeys into the Mojave Desert had yielded the half-starved mustangs for Jesse and Tom. Emily had shook her head in disapproval at the sight of the bunch and had proclaimed that no one in his right mind would mount an animal so homely, let alone spend good dollars to buy one. She had resented the feed that had disappeared down their ungrateful gullets, but after a month of good Dawson hay, she admitted that they looked a bit healthier.

"Only a month, you say?" Jesse clutched Emily's hand and winked. "Why, I tamed wilder things in half a day."

She blushed and turned toward the stack of dishes on the kitchen counter. "Not *forty* mustangs!"

"You'll have to get a bigger jar for the bank, Emily," Jesse chided. "And have a little faith."

"Just don't go get yourselves all busted up. You're not eighteen anymore, you know."

Tom leaned back in his chair with the casual air of a man who had won a great victory. "We're not going to break 'em. We'll put Jed and Nathan and Montgomery to the chore."

Emily narrowed her eyes and threatened him with a swat from her dishcloth if he talked any more nonsense. "Food for the stomachs of Union soldiers. And now food for Southern cannons! I thought we were supposed to be far away from this war."

✳ ✳ ✳

Dinner that night was a sumptuous affair, planned as a celebration for the successful sale of the potato crop to the army.

Emily had prepared a turkey, shot by Jed and proudly carried back to the farm by him from a manzanita thicket. She had stuffed it with cornbread and sunflower-seed dressing, lightly spiced with fragrant sage. For the cornbread that accompanied the turkey there were gooseberry preserves and honey from their own hives of bees. A bowl of boiled potatoes brought good-natured groans from the table, but with a topping of fresh butter, salt, and a dash of red pepper, they disappeared as quickly as the rest.

Montgomery had to be coaxed to join them at the table, but once in place, he began to eat with as much enthusiasm as the others.

The conversation was of the most pleasant variety. They talked of how the money would be spent—so much for staples, so much for a new three-row cultivator, some for household furnishings and "frippery," as Jesse joked with Emily.

"That quartermaster sergeant said that next year they could take as many more loads as we could send," said Tom.

"That so? Well, it sounds like we'll need that cultivator real soon. We can open up that lower quarter section a year sooner than I expected," Jesse mused aloud.

"The sergeant told me they were getting another complement of troops to patrol the desert country clear to the Colorado."

Jed spoke up. "Yes, and he said they'd be riding camels, just like the wise men did—you know, for crossing the sand."

Nathan broke in, "With one big hump and a long snaky neck. The sergeant said they can spit tobacco juice fifty yards right in a fella's eye!"

"Now, boys," Jesse admonished, "you mustn't believe all you hear. That man was just funning with you."

"Yes, sir, Pa," replied Jed.

Nathan still looked stubbornly committed to the truth of his tale. "But he said we'd see 'em."

"That will be enough, Nathan," Emily reproved. "Mustn't argue with your father." Then, hastening to make sure no one felt too chastised, she asked, "Who's ready for pie?"

Vigorous nods went around the table.

Emily retreated to the kitchen and returned moments later with a fresh-baked apple pie, its flaky crust laced with sugar and cinnamon. "Now, just wait till I give you some more coffee, and then I'll dish it up."

All the males rose, even Montgomery, who after a moment's uncertainty grabbed his glass of milk, as did Jed and Nathan.

"To Emily," said Jesse and Tom.

"To Ma," echoed Jed and Nathan.

"To Missy," added Montgomery.

Emily blushed and smiled, obviously pleased at the tribute.

As they seated themselves again and Emily began passing the pie around, Jesse observed, "Yes sir, Tom, right here's what a man works for. A fine family and the means to feed and shelter them. A fine wife who makes a man look forward to coming home to supper. You know, Tom, you need to get married. There's nothing like it in the whole world."

❋ ❋ ❋

After the meal the men sat smoking their pipes while Emily knitted. They had drawn their chairs up to the fireplace more for sociability than for warmth. The oak log glowed pleasantly. The three boys could be heard talking and occasionally laughing in the kitchen. Presently they finished washing the dinner dishes and came to stand in a row beside the scrubbed oak dining table.

Tom leaned forward to knock the dottle out of his pipe into the stone fireplace and stood. "Mont, I expect you can bunk with me. Emily, that was as fine a meal and as enjoyable an evening as could be found anywhere. Good night, Jesse, Jed, Nathan."

"G'night, Missy; I nevuh et bettah," added Montgomery.

"You are most welcome, both of you. Montgomery, we are pleased to have you stay with us. You must remember in your prayers to thank God for your deliverance. And you, boys," addressing Jed and Nathan, "be sure to tell Him thank you for sending you a companion."

A chorus of yessums responded; then Jed and Nathan went to the loft they shared, while Tom and Montgomery exited to the barn. Tom's room was actually the tack room of the barn, but it served him well, and a second cot was quickly set up for Montgomery. Soon all were fast asleep.

✴CHAPTER 4✴

Deputy Pettibone was a rather small man with an enormous mustache. His graying hair was thinning on top—an observation that could not be made of his upper lip. Wiry as a bottle brush and still golden in color, the mustache seemed to precede Pettibone into rooms as if it had a presence all its own.

He was proud of that mustache and proud of his hometown of Greenville as well. From Tommy Fitzgerald's fur trading post in 1845, Greenville had grown to a population of over five thousand in less than twenty years. It boasted not one but two churches, a school, four hotels, and assorted smithies, livery stables, and saloons.

For all the commerce, though, there was only one general store. Occupying the most prominent site at the juncture of the road to Lavers Crossing and the stage route to the valley, Mullins' store represented civilization and its attendant comforts to the citizens of Greenville.

Replete with food items, cookstoves, yard goods, farm implements, the latest in weapons and ammunition, Mullins supplied the needs of the community. Through him one could order seed from Iowa, a machine from Chicago to plant it, or a mahogany casket with real silver handles from far-off New York for a person to be planted in. Robert Mullins' boast was that he could arrange to have anything one could imagine delivered in only six short months.

Mullins the man was as expansive as the horizons his store featured. Standing three inches shy of six feet, he nevertheless tipped the scales at three hundred pounds. The apparent absence of a neck seemed not to bother him at all; indeed, the compensation of having three chins seemed more than adequate. His hands, which were like lumps of bread dough, were never idle. He constantly fidgeted with his merchandise, especially the candy jars arrayed on a shelf behind his counter, or with his watch chain that stretched across his front like the trace chain of a four-up team.

Deputy Pettibone, like others in these mountains, saw in Mullins a man of the world, knowledgeable and prosperous. As such his advice was often sought and his presence on school board and church council accepted as his natural due.

"And when I got the news, I came up from Tailholt pronto," Deputy Pettibone was saying. "Do you think we should get up a posse and get after Byrd?"

"Well now, Sheriff, you know that if Byrd has faded back into those hills, he'll be next to impossible to dig out. What's more, like it or not, it appears that the stranger made the first move. Even if you could locate Mister Guidett and compel him to come in, he'd just get acquitted."

"But shouldn't we at least dig up that feller and hold an inquest?"

"Sheriff, you do as you think best," Mullins said, "but unless you intend to bring in the perpetrator—and I think we agree that's unreasonable—what's the point? The man is undeniably dead; he had no connections in this country, and apparently he deserved what he got—even your station keeper Charlie admitted that, and he's the only witness."

"Well, not exactly. There was a small black child who saw it."

Mullins turned from the peppermint candy jar, which his sausagelike fingers had been exploring, and leaned across a case displaying bottles of Robin's Milk Cascara pills and Chicago Pharmaceutical's Diastalin tablets. "A black child, you say? Did that dim-witted hostler know anything about the dead man other than he came from Missouri?"

"Naw. He showed me a pitiful handful of stuff. 'Course Byrd had all his money. One strange thing: he had no letters, nor any papers telling who he was."

"You don't say? Well, perhaps he was a fugitive himself. Tell me, where is the child now?"

"Tom Dawson stopped there for the night. Byrd was for taking the black child away with him after the shooting, but Tom faced him down and then took the boy home."

"Did anyone think to see if the child had stolen anything?"

"No. No, least I don't think they checked. But here's Tom now; we can ask him."

Tom and Jesse entered Mullins' store and approached Deputy Pettibone.

"Hello, Jesse. Say, I was just fillin' Mister Mullins in on what happened at Granite Station. We—" here he drew himself up to his full height— "*we* think it's mighty peculiar that fella didn't have no name, nor any papers."

"The child he had along said the man's name was James—likely enough for a Missourian—and the boy had heard that name used for as long as he could remember," Tom explained.

"But was there no indication of the man's business?" This came from an attentive Mullins.

"No," Tom continued, "but there are many folk leaving that county who might not wish to bring any record of their past along."

"Quite, quite. And for a man who couldn't drink or gamble successfully, it's a wonder his lack of skill with guns wasn't discovered sooner also."

Deputy Pettibone felt the need to reassert his interrogation, so he asked, "Tom, are you certain that the child carried nothing away with him?"

Tom laughed. "No, Mike, that child barely had rags to cover himself. Fact is, he still thought he was a slave, and—say, there was one thing!" He slapped his pockets. "Yep, it's still here. When we went to bury that stranger, I must've slipped this in my pocket." Tom extracted the silver cuff link and laid it on the counter.

Before Deputy Pettibone could respond, Mullins' agitated fingers had grasped the jewelry and brought it close to his face. Just as quickly he laid it down again and commented, "It's nothing. Cheap workmanship. He probably lost the mate to it somewhere."

Jesse spoke up. "Didn't you say his name was James? Looks to me like this *J* is in the wrong spot. Who do you suppose J. D. could be, anyhow?"

"Ah, the man was a gambler, gentlemen. Most likely he won *some* of the time. Perhaps this J. D.—whoever he was—was even unlucky enough to lose his cuff link to the unfortunate Mister James."

Pettibone scratched his head doubtfully and made as if to reach for the cuff link.

But Mullins opened a drawer below the countertop and dropped it in. "I'm sure it's nothing, but if I have time perhaps I can examine it further for a jeweler's mark—something to tell us of its origin."

Pettibone's mouth began to work, then shut with a snap, as did the drawer when Mullins threw his girth against it.

"Mike, Jesse and I want to talk to you about Byrd anyhow. Can we visit with you a bit?"

"Shore, Tom, come on to my place."

"No need to move, gentlemen," Mullins interjected. "Just pull up a couple of chairs here. Sheriff Pettibone was here seeking my advice about Guidett, so I'm sure he wouldn't mind if I listened to your opinions. Would you, Sheriff?"

Tom and Jesse looked at each other, but Deputy Pettibone had apparently made up his mind, and he started arranging three chairs and an empty crate of Weaver's soap flakes around the fireless pot-belly cast-iron stove.

Jesse began. "Mike, you know that stage holdup?"

"Yes, terrible thing. So cold-blooded and all. The army's out lookin' into that right now, but I hear tell whoever did it covered their tracks right smart."

"Tom and I figure that Byrd and his partner could have done it, stashed the gold, and then, by hard riding, made Granite in time to throw off the scent."

"Especially if they circled around to the northwest and came in over Shadow Ridge," Tom added.

"Gentlemen, gentlemen!" Mullins interrupted. "Byrd Guidett had neither the brains nor the ambition to challenge the army for a gold shipment. He's a poor desperado at best."

Pettibone addressed Tom. "Now I came up from Tailholt by the only trail anywhere near Shadow Ridge, and comin' that way, they couldn't have made Granite by afternoon if they rode like the wind."

"I wasn't thinking of the Tailholt trace, Mike. Jesse has heard talk of some older Indian trails—back in old Spanish days and even before. Why, even the old Yokut chief Split Reed says that the mountain is haunted by the spirits of the ancient ones. Could be Byrd has found a lost trail across the south slope."

Robert Mullins' bulk obscured the ladder-back chair he occupied, but his words were anything but obscure. "Sheriff Pettibone, you know as well as I do that the south face of Shadow Ridge is a mass of deadfalls and brambles. Undoubtedly, the Indians regard it as haunted because any of their number who ventured there came to grief with a cliff or a rattlesnake. No, gentlemen, this is idle speculation. I certainly would not support endangering the lives of a posse of fine citizens for such a preposterous notion."

Tom's eyes flashed, but his brother laid a restraining hand on his arm. They both looked to the deputy for comment.

Pettibone's mustache worked vigorously as if chewing on what had been said. Finally, he spoke. "Naw, boys, I'm glad you mentioned your idea, but it won't wash. Like Mister Mullins here says, there ain't no way around the south slope of old Shadow. Shucks, even pickin' his way along, Byrd would probably break his neck, let alone ridin' fast. Byrd's overdue for hangin', but this slaughter ain't his doin'."

Tom shook off Jesse's hand and stood up. "So that's it, huh? 'Thank you, Mister Dawson, but *this* time Byrd didn't kill anybody worth bothering about'? Listen to me, Pettibone, if you ever want to be *Sheriff,* as Mullins here keeps calling you, you'd better start thinking for yourself."

With that Tom and Jesse walked out, leaving a puzzled Deputy Pettibone and a complacent Mullins.

The store owner remarked, "The mark of a conscientious public servant is that he avoids irresponsible behavior. Bravo, Sheriff Pettibone, bravo."

The mustache puffed out proudly.

✵ ✵ ✵

The dusty streets of Greenville were mostly deserted. The afternoon was hot and still. Tom's buckskin and Jesse's sorrel stood idly at the rail outside Mullins', their heads dropped and their eyes half closed. Even their tails were unmoving, as though the oppressive heat had caused all the flies to seek shade.

"I guess that's that," Jesse commented. "You satisfied?"

"You know I'm not, but what else is there to do? What should we do with Mont?"

"He can stay, far as I'm concerned, but let's give him the choice. I'm sure Parson Swift could find a home for him, but he seems good-natured, and the boys are taken with him. Maybe he'll want to stay on."

"Before we head back, I want to get Matt to tighten that loose shoe—and maybe I can see what he thinks about old trails around Shadow Ridge."

30

"Good idea. If Tommy's at home, I can do the same with him. He knows most everything about this country as well as the Indians—better'n most."

✵ ✵ ✵

Matt Green's blacksmith shop stood beneath a huge water oak just down the hill from Mullins' store. Green had taken the liberty of naming the town for himself, even though Tommy Fitzgerald had been the area's first white resident. Tommy had an Indian's outlook on land; he had never considered it something to be owned.

Matt was a wiry sixty-year-old, as crusty and taciturn when sober as he was loudly abrasive when not. His face was framed by a gray beard that, together with his bushy eyebrows and craggy face, made him resemble Abraham Lincoln—until he opened his mouth. Matt seemed to have teeth only where they would meet the other jaw unopposed.

It was just as well that the likeness to Lincoln was not complete, because Matt was drunkenly outspoken in favor of the South. Not that he favored slavery, but he believed the Southern states should be allowed to depart in peace.

Tom's friendly "howdy" produced no more than a grunt of response from Matt.

The blacksmith was pulling on the wooden handle of a bellows suspended from the ceiling. With each pull the glowing coals of his forge cast a shower of sparks upward. Matt's grizzled face was streaked with grime, as though scorched by the flight of the escaping cinders. The bar of iron barely visible amid the flames was already cherry red. With a last heave on the bellows handle, Matt grasped a pair of tongs with his left hand and pulled the iron from the fire, laying it across his anvil. A few deft strokes of his short-handled hammer bent it into a rough U-shape; then back into the fire it went.

This process of alternately heating and hammering continued until with a convulsive last stroke, Matt thrust the now-recognizable mule shoe into the tempering bucket, producing an explosive blast of steam. "Now, what can I do for ya, Dawson?" Matt's manner was gruff but no more than usual for him.

"Buck's fixing to throw a shoe. I thought maybe you'd tighten it for me."

"Le's see; he was jest shod two weeks ago. Musta caught it on somethin'."

The two men walked out to where the buckskin stood, and Tom watched as Matt examined the right front hoof.

"Yup, I can clench it up some. Lemme finish this batch of mule shoes so's I can let the forge go out. It's too hot for this work today."

"That's fine," Tom agreed. "Mind if I watch? I need to visit with you about something, anyway."

The blacksmith's eyes narrowed with suspicion. "What about?"

Tom began slowly. "Jesse and I have been talking about Shadow Ridge. In all the time I've been here, I never heard tell of any trail around the south slope."

"'Cause there ain't none!" Even from one as crusty as Matt Green, the vehemence with which this was uttered was surprising.

"Why, surely there must be an old Indian trail or two—"

Matt interrupted Tom. "It's naught but a death trap—pits and slide rock! Don't you be messin' thereabouts, see!"

"You don't believe it's haunted, do you?"

"Mebbe I do and mebbe I don't, but there can't nobody get round thataway, and that's all there's to it!"

Matt lapsed into a stony silence as he returned to work the bellows, leaving Tom to hope that his brother was having better success with the old mountain man Tommy Fitzgerald.

✷ ✷ ✷

"Light and set, boy, light and set." Tommy's reception of Jesse was as warm and genuine as he was old. It was said that even Tommy didn't know what his age was.

He had crossed the plains with Walker's expedition, surviving attacks by Shoshone and later Paiute war parties and living through a near drowning. When he reached the high pass through the Sierras near a place now called Greenhorn, he stood amazed with the first group of Anglo explorers to see the great central valley of California.

Tommy had hunted tule elk in the swamplands of the valley, but he always returned to this mountain home located on, as he said, "the first level spot I set my foot on west of the mountains."

When the Mexican alcaldes held sway over the Southern California ranchos, when the Russian bear's presence was still felt in the North, and San Francisco was just a miserable Hudson Bay outpost called "Yerba Buena," Tommy already had a thriving fur-trading business.

Because of ample water and abundant acorns, the Yokuts had made their fall and spring home in these mountains. They were a nomadic people, moving their camp to the valley floor in winter and to the high mountains in the summer. Tommy located his home at their crossroads, built an adobe cabin, and began to trade.

The Yokuts were not an aggressive people, and because game and fowl were so readily available, the tribe never lacked food. Nor did they feel any need of horses since they didn't depend on buffalo as their brothers of the Great Plains did. There had never been much cause for fighting, so they accepted Tommy's presence gratefully, as he gave them access to iron tools. They especially prized the white man's knives, having used only obsidian blades before.

The area, with its narrow, fast-flowing streams, was not suited for beaver, but the Yokuts traded in fox furs—both gray and red—and deer and elk hides.

Tommy had watched their numbers dwindle, mostly because of white man's diseases like cholera, until after forty years, very few remained. None came to trade with Tommy anymore, and now he sat outside the crude one-room adobe with his long white hair and beard, lost in his thoughts and occasionally taunted by Greenville schoolchildren.

At Tommy's invitation, Jesse dismounted and joined the old man in the shade of a gigantic water oak.

"How stands the Union, boy?" This was Tommy's standard greeting and called for no particular acknowledgment.

But today Jesse replied to the question. "I guess it's on shaky ground these days. From what I hear tell, it's taken some hard knocks lately."

"Ya don't say? But, boy, we can lick the Mex. For all their trumpets, they can't match our long rifles, not by a long shot."

Jesse shook his head sadly. "No, Tommy, that Mexican war's been done these twenty years already. I mean this war between the states over slavery and all."

"Oh, I remember somethin' o' that now. I reckon I was back a ways there."

"That's all right. I want you to remember back even further than that for me—back to old Injun days and before."

"What d'ya mean, boy?"

"Tommy, I know you know these hills like the back of your hand. Why, I bet you know every trail and blaze in them."

"'Deed I do, boy, 'deed I do! Why, I come through here afore Fremont was a pup! I know'd Adams and Carson—all them folks. I recollect one time Kit and me was—"

"Whoa up," Jesse interrupted, for he saw that he had to jump in quickly before Tommy Fitzgerald had gotten completely wrapped up in his tale. "I want to hear you tell about these parts, especially the old trails around the south side of Shadow Ridge."

"Old Shadow? Why, that mountain's haunted for sure. Plenty of good men lost their way, and ain't none of 'em come back—white or Injun—neither."

"Think, Tommy, think. Weren't you ever on the south face?"

"Only oncet an' that were enough!"

Jesse leaned forward. "Tell me about that time."

Tommy closed his eyes for a moment as if collecting his thoughts; then with one hand gathering his beard and the other holding his forehead, he began. "My pard, Matthews, him that's buried in Oak Grove next to the cedar stump, died up on ol' Shadow. One day he says to me, 'Tommy, I've shot a grizzly and let him get away. First light I'm goin' to track him round Shadow Ridge.'

"I says to him, 'Give it up, Frank; ya won't never find him.' And Matthews, he says, 'I cain't leave him go. If he lives he'll be rogue for sure.'

"So I said I'd go with him, and next morning we set out. Well, sir, we pushed round that south slope with the deer shrub and chaparral gettin' thicker an' thicker. We found a gob o' blood, and we could foller that humpback real easy where he crashed through. When the track give up sudden-like, Matthews, he said to me, 'Be right canny now, Tommy; he's close.'

"An' jest as he said them words, all at once there riz up the biggest silver tip I ever seed—right under his feet 'most like. Matthews tried to draw a bead, but that bear clubbed him jest as he shot. I believe Frank was dead afore he ever hit the ground.

"The bear never stopped to bother Matthews—jest come straight for me. I throw'd down on him and shot him in the eye—no further than from me to where you're sittin' now—but he never slowed down nor turned. I know'd I was a goner, but I drew my toothpick and run up the hill with that bear 'most on me.

"Do you know, I come on a path! Real faint—no more'n a trace, but goin' round the slope. I'm thinkin' maybe I'll distance this twice-shot bear when all at oncet I run plumb into a stone wall!

"I turned an' faced that there bear with jest my knife and him agrowlin' an snarlin' real fierce an' lookin' horrible with his one eye blowed all over his head. I was abackin' toward a clump of manzanita close by when it happened."

"What, Tommy? What happened?"

"I crashed into that manzanita, and next thing I was fallin'. Then crash, my head hit, an' I didn't know no more. I come to with a cracked skull an' a busted elbow an' some busted-up ribs, but I was livin'. It was dark, so I laid real still to see if that grizzly was still nosin' about. I laid there clear to daybreak, hurtin' an' real scared.

"Come dawn I got the biggest scare yet, 'cause right over my head, leanin' down at me, was the grizz'! But he was stone dead! Yes, sir, he died right on the edge of that cave, an' me knocked out jest fifteen feet below him!"

"A *cave*? You're sure it wasn't just a pit you'd fallen into?"

"Naw, boy, naw. When I came to myself, I seed a stream of water an' a black hole a-runnin' way back in the mountain. Some Indian signs, too, boy—paintin's on the rocks, real old an' all. I clumb up a rubble pile an' bless me if I didn't have to climb over that bear a-gettin' out!

"It took me 'most two days to get down out o' there, what with bein' busted up. I drug poor ol' Frank down to where we'd tied the horses, an' then I couldn't load him! I finally had to leave him an' ride for help. The Injuns brought him out an' buried him, an' they tended me through a ragin' fever.

"Well, sir, those Injuns said it was a good thing I'd drug Frank as far as I did 'cause they wouldn't have set foot on the mountain proper. I said to myself, 'That's good enough for me. I ain't goin' back!' An' I ain't never been back neither!"

"Didn't you ever tell this story to anyone else?"

"No, I didn't. There wasn't nobody but the Injuns to tell it to at first; then later on I was afeared someone would get killed if they went lookin' for the cave, so I jest kept close till lately."

"Lately? You mean, just now?"

"Someone else asked me about the trail round ol' Shadow about a year ago. Said they'd heard Injuns talkin' about such. Well, I told 'em my story but cautioned 'em not to try an' find it—jest like I'm a-tellin' you now!"

"But who was it, Tommy? Who else asked about the trail?"

The old mountain man scratched his head for a moment, and his eyes seemed momentarily glazed. "What was that? What did ya ask me?"

"I said, who else asked about Shadow Ridge?"

"I'm powerful sorry, boy. I can't remember. But say, did I ever tell ya about the grizzly I killed up on the Truckee? Say, that there was a bear! Why, that bear was a-trackin' me!"

"Thank you, Tommy, but I'll have to hear that story another time," replied Jesse, standing up to go.

"Anytime, boy, anytime." The old man's head dropped, and he fell silent—but whether in sleep or deep thought, Jesse couldn't tell.

✷ ✷ ✷

Riding back home, Jesse and Tom compared notes.

"I got nothin' from Matt at all—practically bit my head off for asking."

Jesse recounted Fitzgerald's story, bringing an exclamation from Tom. "A trail *and* a cave—why, Jesse, that means that not only is there a way around but maybe even a place to keep fresh mounts!"

"Ease up, Tom. Remember, Tommy's an old man and liable to get mixed up. I was excited, too, till I noticed that he likes to tell bear stories an awful lot and I remembered that he couldn't recall what year it is!"

"But at least we should go check it out, shouldn't we?"

"Well, I suppose so, but we needn't rush off tomorrow. We've got plenty to do around the place with those horses, and it's for certain that we'll get no one to go with us—not on the strength of old Tommy's recollections. Pettibone's mind is altogether made up for him by Mullins, so we'll be on our own. Anyway, they're probably right. How could a trail exist and no one even know about it? And even if there were such a patch and Byrd could have used it, that doesn't prove that he did."

"There you go," snorted Tom, "just like you always do. You find out that something's possible but maybe a little chancy, and you start backin' up. How'd you ever get up your nerve to move out here, anyway?"

"I knew I had to be able to offer Em something mighty special to win her away from you, old son—it was worth the risk. Now just let be till we get all our projects caught up; then I'll go with you if you still think it's so all-fired important."

✶ CHAPTER 5 ✶

The cabin showed no signs of having been lived in for years. Its squared timber had once been mortared, but the chinking had been allowed to fall into such disrepair that more spaces than mortar appeared.

The windows were gaping holes only partially covered by ragged flaps of cowhide, and the wood-plank door hung crookedly from a torn leather hinge. Set in a side canyon through which flowed a seasonal tributary of Cedar Creek, the site was the graveyard of some long-gone miner's hopes for wealth.

Mullins stopped to lean against a gnarled buckeye that stood at the edge of the cabin's clearing. Panting for breath after his hike up the canyon from where he had left his rig hidden just off the main road to Greenville, he peered through the clumps of elderberry bushes and mopped his face.

Inwardly he swore and muttered to himself at the apparent emptiness of the scene; then he heaved his bulk forward a few more steps. He stopped short at a movement in the doorway and looked through squinted, piglike eyes as Byrd Guidett strolled out.

"I know'd it was you. I heerd ya wheezin' and crashin' through the brush a mile off."

"Shut up, you fool, and get back inside!" snarled Mullins. "Where's Yancey?"

"Here." A voice at Mullins' elbow made him jump and caused even more sweat to pour down his florid face. Yancey stepped out from behind a brush-obscured boulder, replacing a gleaming knife into his boot top as he did so.

The three moved into the cabin. Yancey and Byrd stood on either side of the crumbling stone fireplace. On the oak beam mantel lay Byrd's rifle. The room was otherwise bare except for a rough bench on which Mullins seated himself.

"We done it!" boasted Byrd. "The strongbox is hid, and no one left to mark us for the law! We come over slick as ya please and made as though we hadn't a care except to play some cards. 'Course, we had a little set-to at Granite, but we came off none the worse for it."

Mullins exploded. "You fool! None the worse? Do you know who it was you killed? That Missourian was Colonel James. He'd been working undercover since the secession. He was here to deliver my commission from President Davis personally and to take charge of raising the army of the Pacific!"

"What? That ol' drunk a colonel?"

Yancey spoke up, his gray face more animated than one would have thought possible. "He didn't give no recognition sign. How was we supposed to know?"

Mullins turned on him, his jowls quivering with rage. "Did you expect him to announce himself to any cutthroat brigand he came across? He was on his way to meet with me. The gold you stole was to be used to purchase arms and train our fighting force to lead California out of the Union! *He* had the names of our contacts for making the purchases!"

"But, boss," said Byrd, "we got the gold. Cain't we jest buy the guns ourselves?"

"Do you think we can go to any arms dealer in San Francisco and say, 'Please, sir, we'd like to buy three hundred rifles'? We'd be in Fort Alcatraz before you could cry 'Pinkerton' and hanged shortly after!"

A somewhat subdued Byrd lapsed into silence, and after a moment Yancey asked, "What's to be done?"

"The talk is that James had no papers on him—in fact, nothing but the cuff link, which I very fortunately got into my possession before anyone asked too many questions. That must mean that he had hidden the papers somewhere until after he made contact with me. Perhaps he felt that he was being followed or might be searched."

"But, boss, there's ten miles of boulders around Granite Station! How'll we ever find 'em?"

Mullins calmed down a little and looked thoughtful. "Maybe that nigger boy can show us where they stopped before Granite. Or maybe Colonel James even gave the papers to the boy to carry."

"I know'd I should've catched that boy! See, Yancey, I told ya we shoulda had him!"

Yancey replied dryly, "I seem to recall you not wantin' to press the issue with Tom Dawson and Mister Colt's child."

Byrd glared at Yancey, but Mullins silenced any reply by saying, "Enough of this! Colonel James' death was an unfortunate accident, which luckily for you, Byrd Guidett, is reported to be not entirely your fault."

"Not entirely my fault! Why, he—"

"Shut up, I tell you! Now listen; it's clear what must be done. We must eliminate any curiosity about Shadow Ridge. There must be no snooping anywhere near the quartz ledge. Secondly, we must have that child!"

✷ ✷ ✷

Tom and Jesse had chosen half a dozen of the stoutest old oak trees around the place to tie the broncos to. Saddled and cinched, the first six horses in the string were tied high and tight to the strongest limb of a tree. Cotton rope hobbled their legs, and another rope wound around the rib cage and up through the forelegs, then through the halter to create a harness that would squeeze hard whenever the animal fought to pull away from the tree where it had been tied.

A critter what won't stand polite at a hitchin' rail is gonna come over backward an' kill hisself an' maybe somebody else! That had been the first rule Tom and Jesse had learned from their Missouri horse-trader father. In the years since, the brothers had seen enough spoiled horses fighting a hitching rail to know the fact for themselves.

Even though there were a hundred ways to break a mustang, the brothers started by letting each animal teach itself a few manners.

Some fought the rope and the tree branch more than others, jumping back and straining until they almost sat down on their hind legs, then lunging forward to relieve the pressure of the taut rope around their girth. Other horses learned to stand still after only one or two halfhearted battles. One thing was certain: They all learned sooner or later that it was easier to stand politely, regardless of the commotion around them, than to fight the rope.

It was the job of Jed, Nathan, and Montgomery—Mont as he soon came to be called—to wave flour sacks and holler like Indians within view of the tied horses but safely out of range of flying hooves and the thrashing of bodies of a thousand pounds of unhappy horseflesh. *Sacking the horse* was the term Tom gave this process. After a while, the horses stopped quivering and totally ignored the bellowing of the small ranch hands.

Seven of the more stubborn animals fought for days. One powerful young bay stood sweating beneath the saddle for nearly a week, receiving from the hand of his tormentor food and a bucket of water twice a day until at last the brawny animal nickered happily at the sight of the man who had trussed him up like a prisoner. Tom chose this horse for his own. He had spirit and a will, and once Tom had tamed the spirit and turned the will into a desire to please, the big bay had the promise of being a fine mount.

Except for his strength and size, the animal was anything but handsome. His large head had a curve like a Roman nose. The lower lip protruded slightly and moved incessantly as though he were trying to speak. His legs were black and blended into four iron-hard black hooves. The black hooves were an attribute that pleased Tom. An animal with white stockings meant soft, white feet, which were less likely to hold up in the harsh mountain terrain.

"This fella will go from here to the Atlantic and never need to be shod," Tom commented as he picked up the foot and examined it. "Let them have their pretty horses. I'll take good legs any day."

Emily overheard Tom's proud mumbling as she walked by with a basket of laundry in her arms. "Well, he is anything *but* pretty." She laughed. "It is lucky for us that the Union Calvary is buying these creatures by the head. They certainly have the biggest heads of any horses I have ever seen!"

"I'm keeping this fella." Tom hefted a heavy sack of feed onto the saddle of the still-tied animal. "Jugheaded though he is."

Emily nodded. "Then name him Duncan!" she said, not missing a beat. "As a personal favor to me." She smiled brightly.

"Duncan?" Tom scratched his head. "Why Duncan?"

She continued to the house with her basket, still giggling at her secret joke. *"Duncan!"* she called over her shoulder.

Tom shrugged and patted the thick neck of the bay. "I christen thee Duncan. Whoever he was, he must have been as ugly as a mongrel dog!"

As if in agreement, the newly named Duncan nickered.

✳ ✳ ✳

Jed, Nathan, and Mont were ready for school the morning the first twenty of the army's horses were gathered for delivery to Fort Tejon.

Tom mounted his big bay horse, then hefted Mont up for a proud ride around the barn. Duncan had learned quickly when Tom had begun to ride him in the round pen. Now, while the rest of the rough string of mustangs was still reining reluctantly, Duncan moved easily to the leg pressure of his rider.

Emily had packed more than enough for the four-day journey. She kissed Jesse good-bye and stepped back as he swung the pack over the saddle and mounted. "Be careful, won't you?" She looked worried for a moment, then added, "'He shall give His angels charge over thee, to keep thee in all thy ways!'"

Jesse sounded a gruff "Amen" in response before leaning down to kiss her farewell once again.

Tom looked away at their embrace. It was obvious that Jesse did not want to leave Emily for even a short journey.

Tom issued a spate of orders to the boys. Feeding and milking and other chores would have to continue even with the men gone.

A chorus of eager assurance came from Jed and Nathan and Mont, who now seemed to fit into the family as easily as the others.

Tom was surprised when Emily reached up and briefly took his hand in her own. "Look after my Jesse, now," she whispered.

Tom cleared his throat and pushed his hat back on his head. "He's always been the one looking after me; you know that." Something in her eyes made him uncomfortable. He looked away, staring between the ears of the big bay horse. "When are you going to tell me why I'm calling this horse Duncan, anyway? Here I am taking him to a fort full of Union soldiers; this horse is ugly enough to draw fire. Someone is gonna ask me, Emily, why I've named this jug head *Duncan!*"

"Tell us, Emily!" Jesse urged jokingly. "Just think, if we were ambushed by Indians you'd have to live with the fact that we never knew."

Her eyes flashed with anger. "No such talk now, Jesse Dawson! But if you must know, I've named him for an old black preacher who, whenever he was asked to pray, would say, 'De Lawd *done can* do it, suh! Ah knows de Lawd *done can!*'"

Mont blinked, as if surprised by her dialect, looked at the horse, and said loudly, "Well, I'd say de Lawd *done can* do 'bout anything He want to! He done he'ped get dem hosses broke, and now He *done can* bring Mistuh Jesse an' Mistuh Tom home safe-like!"

There was a burst of laughter all around.

Mont patted the muscled shoulder of the horse. "Duncan!" he said with finality.

With a whistle, Jesse and Tom began to move the herd down the lane.

✳ ✳ ✳

"Hee-yah!" shouted Jesse.

"Whoop! Whoop!" urged Tom as the last of the string of twenty green-broke mustangs were turned into the stock pens at Fort Tejon.

The steps of the adobe buildings were lined with spectators, civilians, and off-duty soldiers alike. The drive from the range in Linns Valley had taken four days, but now it was successfully concluded.

The cavalry captain who gestured for the gate to be closed behind the last horse nodded with satisfaction at the sight. "They look fine, gentlemen, just fine," he called to Tom and Jesse, who sat their horses flanking the gate. "Who would have thought that you could take wild and scrawny horseflesh and turn it into such sleek appearance in a short span of time?"

"Well, Captain," commented Jesse, "all we did was catch this bunch at a watering hole up Mojave way inside a box canyon. We drifted out the ones we didn't want, and we kept the others fenced away from water for a few days, only givin' them to eat and drink by our own hand. After about a week they got mostly docile."

Here Tom took up the tale. "Well, sir, next we got a rope on that lead mare over yonder." He pointed out a tall bay horse with a white blaze on her face that ran up into one blue eye. "When we started for home, she led real easy, and the rest of the herd just followed along."

Jesse resumed describing the route back to the ranch by explaining how they had gone over Walker Pass, forded the Kern River, and then followed the Bull Road across the Sierra to home.

"After crossing the river, these horses were in feed like they'd never seen out in the desert. They didn't have any more reason to run away, and with this mare leading the way, the rest came on pretty easy."

"As for sleek," Tom said, "all they needed was a few weeks of good feed. When we were culling the herd, we took care to pick only the sound ones that showed their ancestry back to the granddaddy horses brought to this country by the Spanish folk. Blood will tell, given time and opportunity, and this bunch has shaped up real well."

"Of course, gentlemen, how well they shape up as cavalry mounts remains to be seen," pointed out the captain. "Well fed they may be and able to be driven, but green broke to the colonel's satisfaction is another matter."

"I thought you might be interested in that, Captain," remarked Tom. "So I'd like you to look at Duncan here."

"I can already tell that you didn't select this animal for his beauty, Mister Dawson. Perhaps you should tell me why I'm to pay attention to him."

"You see, Captain, Duncan here came out of that same herd at the same time as the rest. Now he's had a little extra work put on him by me special, but nothing your boys couldn't do with their mounts. Watch this."

Tom spun Duncan around on his hind legs and galloped off toward the large oak tree under which explorer Peter Lebec had been killed by a grizzly. Duncan flashed around it, turning so close as to enable Tom to reach upward in passing and grasp a handful of leaves from a low branch. Halfway back across the parade ground, Tom jerked the horse to a sudden stop, and Duncan almost skidded as he sat back on his haunches.

Tom next worked the horse in a tight series of circles and figure eights, then trotted him back over to the watching crowd. Drawing rein before the grinning captain, Tom slid from Duncan's back to stand beside the bay as if to say, *See, nothing to it at all.*

"Excellent! Just excellent. And you say the rest of the string can come as far in as little time?"

"There's no doubt about it, Captain. After all, this one is not only jugheaded to look at; he's the most pigheaded and stubborn one of the bunch."

"And you say you can have the remaining twenty here in short order?"

"Absolutely," promised Jesse, "and there's more where these came from, too."

"Well, then, get them to us just as quickly as possible, and perhaps we'll be doing business in a regular way. Why don't we go into my office and see about your payment?"

"Suits us," said Jesse with a smile. "Then we'll be startin' back to get to work on the next batch."

As they walked up the steps, a portly quartermaster sergeant called out to Tom, "Hey, Dawson, this here crop's livelier than potatoes, huh?"

To the roar of laughter which erupted, Tom waved good-naturedly and replied, "Yes, and you'd best be careful, Sergeant. Fork one of these spuds wrong, and you'll be the one gettin' peeled!"

✳ ✳ ✳

The young lieutenant leading the detail of four troopers was preparing to leave at the same time as the Dawson brothers, so they all rode together as far as the crossing of Cottonwood Creek.

"We'll be turning west there toward the ranch of Colonel Thomas Baker," the lieutenant remarked, raising his eyebrows significantly.

When neither brother reacted to this announcement, he continued, "Baker is being arrested for interfering with recruiting efforts for the Union army. He has been very open about his pro-rebel sentiments but has recently gone too far."

"Isn't Baker some kind of government man himself?" inquired Tom.

"Yes, he's a state senator, and he's been using his political opportunities to ridicule the Union army and describe in detail the defeats we have experienced at rebel hands. He's even gone so far as to say that the war is no concern of Californians, and boys from here ought not go off to fight in it. He stops just short of treason by pretending to favor a peaceful settlement to the conflict, but we believe that he privately favors pulling California out of the Union. Anyway," the lieutenant concluded, "he's to be arrested on the recruiting charge, and that should interrupt his little schemes for a while."

45

✶CHAPTER 6✶

Byrd crouched behind a cottonwood tree that grew up from the creek bed. He was peering through its leaves toward the mouth of the canyon out of which the stage would have to emerge. Dust devils chased each other across the intervening plain. Byrd scrutinized each one to see if it would resolve itself into the coach and four that he was expecting, but for over an hour each round of wind had been a false alarm.

He was annoyed that the coach was late. The dust from the dry creek bed caught at his throat and irritated his eyes. For a time he amused himself by plucking cottonwood leaves and dropping them one by one at his feet, but he soon grew tired of this and drew the stained bandanna from around his neck and mopped his forehead.

He turned the bandanna over briefly in his hands, considering whether to tie it around his face. He glanced toward the stage road, looked upward at the sun, and threw the bandanna down on the ground in disgust.

Nervous at this delay, he decided to check his Walker Colt to make sure it was loaded properly. He reached for the four-pound pistol he wore tied down and drew its nine-inch length carefully from the holster and regarded it with squinted eyes.

Someone had once remarked that the only thing Byrd cared about in all the world besides himself was the six-shooter. Byrd would never have thought to express that observation in just that way, but it was nevertheless true and with good reason. He earned his livelihood by his ability with the Walker's faithful performance, and it had saved his life on more than one occasion. Of course, it had not been able to save the Texas Ranger from whom Byrd had obtained it.

The weapon was loaded and capped as it had been the two earlier times Byrd had checked, and he swore at himself for this apparent nervousness. He was, he decided, tired of waiting. Being tired made him grouchy, like a petulant child in need of a nap.

He had just returned the Colt to its holster when he heard Yancey's signal—a low, whistled quail call that sounded like "Chicago, Chicago."

Byrd's head snapped up, the revolver again in his hand.

Yancey would nag him later for not spotting the coach first. This thought only served to increase his irritation. Sure enough, out from the canyon a moving black shape appeared, throwing a trail of dust behind.

On through the sagebrush it came, presently moving near enough for the form of the coach to be seen. A little closer and the team of mules drawing it could be made out; shortly after, Byrd could see the driver and a shotgun messenger perched on the box.

Any nervousness Byrd might have felt vanished. Now he was all business. He stooped over and retrieved the bandanna, but his eyes never left the approaching stage. With his left hand he drew the cloth around his neck and swore at the awkwardness of trying to knot it one-handed. He replaced the .44 momentarily, just long enough to tie the kerchief and pull its folds over his nose. His bushy red beard pushed the mask out from his face.

He looked down the draw to where Yancey squatted, similarly masked and armed. Byrd had a moment to sneer at Yancey's choice of weapon. It was a .36 caliber Allen, a pepperbox—good for a hide-out weapon but not a man's gun, in Byrd's opinion.

His attention returned to the stage, now less than four hundred yards away. Their plan was simple. Since the seldom wet creek bed had no bridge, the stage drivers were in the habit of pitching violently down one bank and back up the other without even slackening speed. Just below the rim of the bank nearest the stage, Byrd and Yancey had laid the trunk of a cottonwood. This unexpected obstacle should cause the lead mules to balk, and in the confusion Byrd and

Yancey would have the opportunity to get the drop on the driver and guard.

Byrd could see the pair of men clearly now. The driver was leaning forward, skillfully working the lines, getting the utmost speed out of the surging team. The guard was leaning back, bracing himself against the expected swoop into the gully. Sunlight glinted dully on the barrels of the shotgun he carried.

As expected, the coach didn't even slow as it passed the crest of the creek bank. Over it came, the team dipping below the rim so rapidly that the wagon appeared to be propelled straight across the wash for a space before dropping to follow the contour. In front of the leaders was the tree, its branches right in their startled faces.

The driver had no chance to halt the suddenly pitching team, for as the leaders attempted to swerve, the abrupt loss of rhythm caught the wheelers off guard, slewing the coach violently to the left, then turning it over on its side with a rending crash. The driver flew off the box after the team, and the guard pitched over the tree trunk in the direction of the tumbling coach, which finally came to rest on its side, surrounded by a great cloud of dust.

As the dust began to clear, low moans could be heard coming from the coach's interior. One wheel made a mournful creaking as it continued to revolve lazily on its now vertical axle.

Byrd straightened and pushed his hat off his forehead in astonishment. He glanced to where Yancey also was taking in the scene of wreckage with an amazed look on his face. They had expected to stop the stage's headlong rush but nothing like this.

Anticipating no resistance from the destruction that presented itself, both men put away their weapons, Yancey thrusting the pepperbox into his waistband.

They converged on the coach from opposite sides. Byrd wore a whimsical grin as if he wished he could always conduct a robbery in such a spectacular manner.

Yancey, normally silent, was moved to what was for him garrulous speech. "Did ya see that, Byrd? I'll be a suck-aig mule if that weren't the most horrific crash. Them fellers didn't have no chance at all."

Byrd studied the scene with a proprietary air, noting with satisfaction that the guard's neck was bent at an impossible angle; he was dead. Then Byrd spoke. "Where'd that driver get off to? Last I seen, he was sailin' after them mules. Well, no matter, he musta fetched up in the next county in so many little pieces, they'll have to pick 'em up with a dustpan and a broom."

That whoever was in the coach still lived was evidenced by an occasional groaning. Even though there appeared to be little chance of fight left in anyone who had experienced the crash, Yancey pulled his pistol again before stepping up on the useless thoroughbrace and peering down into the interior.

"Thar's only one in here, and he looks busted up bad," called Yancey.

"Leave 'im then, and let's get to business."

The two undid the boot and found the expected strongbox. It had not broken open in the crash, but the hinges were bent.

Byrd soon was able to pry the hasp and lock off the case. Inside was a sheaf of official-looking documents, which Byrd thrust into his shirt unread. As a matter of fact, he couldn't have read them, anyway. Beneath the papers was the gold—about ten thousand dollars' worth.

Byrd hefted the box to his shoulder and turned to slog through the sand to where they had tethered the horses. Yancey trudged alongside.

An arresting pair of clicks brought them to a sudden halt. Beside the body of the guard stood the driver. His bloodless face was drawn with pain, and his left arm dangled limply at his side.

But Byrd's attention was centered on the man's right side, where he cradled the guard's shotgun under the crook of his arm and had just thumbed back the hammers.

In a halting voice he ordered, "Throw down that box and your weapons."

Byrd and Yancey complied, each fingering his pistol gently in the face of the double-barreled threat.

"Now raise your hands and keep 'em up."

With a glance at each other, Byrd and Yancey did so while moving slightly apart. The driver's strength was failing; he had difficulty keeping the shotgun's muzzle elevated.

"Listen, mister, yer stove up bad, and so's yer passenger. Now ya'd best let us ride outta here, an' we'll send back some help."

"Shut up, you two. I need to think," mumbled the driver.

"But yer man here, he needs help now—cain't ya hear 'im?"

As if on cue a frightened moan came from the coach. In the instant that the driver's attention wavered, Yancey's hand flashed downward toward his shirt collar and upward again with the knife that had hung between his shoulders.

The shotgun discharged both barrels into the ground with a roar, but the blade that now quivered in the man's stomach occupied all his attention.

Byrd scooped up his .44, but it wasn't needed.

A moment of startled disbelief crossed the driver's face, and he swayed forward once, then pitched face-first into the sand.

Byrd and Yancey rode off, laughing at how easy it had been.

Seven men rode downward out of the narrow pass guarded by Fort Tejon, through a rocky sagebrush-covered ravine, and out onto the gentler slope that led to the floor of the San Joaquin Valley.

The dusty haze of Indian summer obscured their view up the valley, but even so it was a magnificent sight. Stretching some three hundred miles from where they rode to the San Francisco Bay and beyond, the great central valley was crisscrossed with waterways, swamps, and marshes. Here and there herds of tule elk roamed.

As they rode, Tom caught more than one of the troopers casting admiring looks at Duncan. Homely he might be, but they could tell at a glance that he had heart. These hardened men knew the value of a reliable horse. Patrolling the reaches of the great desert as they did, there had to exist implicit trust between man and beast. In the previous year's campaign against the Mojave Indians, the lieutenant himself had been saved from an agonizing death by his mount's ability to locate water when the tank they were depending on had turned out unexpectedly empty.

So when Duncan snorted and pricked his ears forward, not only Tom but Jesse and the whole party took note. They were just approaching the intersection of their northward-bound track and the road that led westward from the mines. The breeze was blowing toward them, and suddenly all their animals gave evidence of uneasiness.

The lieutenant called a halt and stood in his stirrups, craning his neck and peering forward. "I see something in the bed of the creek yonder. Jones, you and Brown go forward and reconnoiter."

"Aye, sir," the troopers responded and galloped away.

A few moments later one of them returned at high speed.

"All right, Trooper Brown, report."

An ashen-faced Brown burst out, "They're all dead, sir! I mean, it's the stage, and it's been wrecked!"

"An accident, Trooper?"

"Yes, sir . . . I mean, no, sir—that is, we thought it was, with the coach all busted up. The guard, he's got a busted neck. And the passenger, he's dead, too."

"Well, what makes you think it isn't an accident?"

"It's the driver. He—"

"Speak up, Brown. What is it?"

"It's the driver. . . . He's got six inches of knife stuck in him!"

✳ ✳ ✳

An investigation of the area revealed in short order how the holdup had been accomplished. They could see where the outlaws had waited to surprise the stage and how successful they had been. From the position of the driver's body and the discharged shotgun lying beside it, it was even possible to reconstruct how he had met his fate.

"How could this happen?" began Jesse. "After that other holdup with everyone murdered, why wasn't this stage escorted?"

"Great scott, man!" returned the lieutenant testily. "Don't you know how shorthanded we're running here? This patrol is half its normal strength and on top of that has twice its usual assignment to patrol!"

"Look, Lieutenant," Jesse replied, "we know you've got your problems, but this can't be allowed to continue. Pretty soon no one will feel safe traveling through the valley. Already folks are starting to talk about the need to form a California militia to mount our own patrols. People are saying that if the army can't or won't protect us, then we'll have to do it ourselves."

"May I warn you, Mister Dawson, that kind of talk is precisely what the so-called *Colonel* Baker is being arrested for!"

"Listen," broke in Tom, "we're not talking politics here; we're talking the safety of our families. Whether this is some rebel plot or plain old highway robbery makes precious little difference to folks who lose their lives or their loved ones!"

The lieutenant looked subdued for a moment before he spoke. "Of course you're right, and the ones who did this and the other holdup must be brought to justice as quickly as possible. We still believe that this is all linked with the plot to introduce rebel elements into the control of California gold. There may even be a bigger conspiracy afoot than you or I can imagine."

"I know," added Jesse, "that there are those in the mountains who have no use for the government in Washington; they just want to be left alone. But that doesn't necessarily make them favor the Southern cause nor get them involved in robbery and murder!"

"I'm aware of that, Mister Dawson, but you can certainly see we need help if this situation is to be remedied. Suppose we were to make an appearance in Greenville and other communities, pledging our increased attention to the problem, while at the same time requesting the cooperation of all the citizens in locating those who have done this?"

Jesse turned to Tom. "What do you think? Would that help matters any?"

"I don't know, Jesse. It's certain that once the news of this holdup gets out, there's going to be a real uproar. I'm not trying to tell the army its business, but it seems to me that if they'd admit we've got a problem and work together with us to solve the situation, it would be the right approach."

Tom continued to address the officer. "Don't expect any of the mountain folk to come up with information about rebel sympathizers among their friends and neighbors. They won't tolerate thieves and murderers, but they believe a man's politics are his own business—at least as far as his thoughts are concerned."

"Very well, gentlemen, I'll communicate your views to my commanding officer. I feel certain he'll agree that some immediate action will be required. Meanwhile, if you see the local deputy—what's his name, the one with the enormous mustache?"

"Pettibone?"

"That's the one. Would you inform him about what's happened and ask him to communicate it to the sheriff and others? We'll try to pass along any helpful information just as soon as we can."

✳ ✳ ✳

The scene of the wrecked stagecoach and murdered men was still vivid in the minds of Tom and Jesse as they rode the final mile into Greenville. Neither had spoken for hours. Anger at the first sight of such a violent crime had finally dissipated into helpless frustration. Whoever had done this thing was long gone—vanished without leaving so much as a single track on the stony paths that led from the scene.

Tom and Jesse would inform Deputy Pettibone that once again the gold destined for the Union coffers had been stolen. But there was little that could be done, and hardly an ounce of sentiment would be spared for the stolen Yankee gold. Wasn't there a war on, after all? Didn't people get hurt in wars, even here in California?

Tom had seen this sort of thing a hundred times in Missouri. Senseless killing. Murder in the name of a cause. Somehow people here needed to understand that there was something else at issue. Something crueler than war. What was it? He had tried to figure it out before. How could he put a name to the cold chill that had coursed through him at the grisly sight he had seen?

As if reading his thoughts, Jesse turned to him. "Whoever did that enjoyed killing. There was an evil love of death."

Tom did not need to reply. Yes. That was it. That was what he had seen on the Kansas–Missouri border. He had even glimpsed that evil in his own soul. Now, as if to escape the landslide of emotions and memories that engulfed him, he spurred Duncan into a gentle lope up the last hill before reaching town.

At the top of the rise, a cloud of dust rose from the schoolyard, and a new sound greeted him. Boys shouted and little girls shrieked as two dozen children pressed in for a better view of a miniature battle.

"Get 'im!"

"Wallop that nigger, Sam!"

"Hit 'im in the face!"

"Kill them Yankee lovers!"

Tom stood slightly in his stirrups and tapped Duncan, who raced toward the schoolyard.

So it came here as well. Even among the children, who mimicked their parents.

✶ CHAPTER 7 ✶

aw pieces of beefsteak. Just the thing for black eyes." Jesse handed out the evening's uncooked supper to each of the three boys. "Just hold it there over your shiner. I reckon it will still make a good meal after you're done using it." Jesse winked at Emily in an effort to lighten her mood. She had not smiled since her first look at the dusty, battered boys.

Mont bit his lip and glanced at Jesse through swollen eyes. He had taken the worst beating, and now Jesse wondered how the child could see. "Um, Mistuh Jesse . . ." He looked at the meat in his hand and held it timidly as though he were afraid to put it to his bruised eye.

"Yes. What is it, Mont?" Jesse knelt and put his hands on the boy's shoulders. He was keenly aware what young Mont must be feeling. After all, hadn't the fight been over the color of his skin? That and the sale of horses to the Yankees?

"Well, suh . . ." He continued to gaze at the meat. "Should ah be puttin' dis here meat on my eyes, too?"

"Of course, Mont!" Emily chimed in. "It's only a bit of beefsteak, and there's plenty more where that came from. You must not worry about that!"

"Yessum. Ah mean . . . no, ma'am." He still looked uneasy. "What ah means is, if'n dis is gonna take away my black eyes . . . it ain't gonna make white round my eyes . . . is it? It'd be plumb awful if I was to go back to school all spotted like!"

Suppressing a laugh, Jesse reassured him that the beefsteak would simply take away the welts.

Emily guided Mont's hand up to his swollen face and then sat him down firmly at the kitchen table next to Jed and Nathan.

With a solemn shake of her head, she led Jesse to the door and stepped out onto the porch. "What next?" She wrung her hands distractedly.

Jesse lifted her chin gently and looked into her eyes. "How about a kiss hello?" he asked, pulling her close and brushing her lips with his.

"Oh, Jesse!" She leaned heavily against her husband. "I'm so worried. We had so hoped to be spared from this terrible war. But even *here* . . . people are so—" She did not finish.

Jesse was stroking her hair as if she were a child to be comforted. "It was only a kids' schoolyard fight. Nothing to fret over."

"No." She began to weep softly. "It's more than that. Not just Mont. Children can be so cruel! But . . . Jesse, Mrs. Burton had harsh words for me at church, and—"

"Mrs. Burton? At church, no less. Emily, you can't—"

"Listen to me, Jesse!" Emily stepped back and held the face of her husband in her hands. "I'm *frightened*! People don't take kindly to you and Tom breaking horses for the army. When I got home from church yesterday, someone had opened a gate! Five horses were turned loose! Five of the best. I thought it was just a malicious prank at first, but then I got to thinking about what Mrs. Burton said about how *many* folks are angry about those horses! I could scarcely sleep last night for thinking about it. And now today the boys get into it. Not only that, you come back with word that there's been another robbery—men killed and Union gold stolen. . . ." She looked fiercely away at the setting sun. "I thought we would be free from this sort of thing here in California. The promised land. Free from war and killing and prejudice."

Jesse sighed and leaned against the porch railing as he followed her gaze to Shadow Ridge. "It wouldn't matter where we lived, Emily," he said softly as weariness crept into his voice. "You know that. Folks are always finding some reason to make trouble, to stir things up. You know it's not just the war between Yankees and rebels that has people riled up." He put his arm around her. "It's a different war. The war is inside men's hearts. Fierce and mean. And I don't suppose it's any different anywhere. No better or worse. Folks just love to hate."

The sky darkened, and the trill of crickets filled the cool evening air. Neither Emily nor Jesse spoke for a long time.

At last, when the corralled horses nickered for their supper, Emily said quietly, "The boys and I managed to round up three of those jughead horses of yours. Two are still out there wandering around Shadow Ridge, I suppose."

"Be careful how you speak of those jugheads. They are money in the bank—pure gold beneath those scruffy hides. Tom and I will go find those two."

"Jesse!" She began to protest, but he had already gone to find Tom.

✻ ✻ ✻

Colonel Mason was trying his best to keep his temper under control. He knew if he responded emotionally to what he was hearing, he would lose the attention of the meeting. It wasn't easy, though, given what Matt Green had been saying.

"Yer bunch of blue-bellied scoundrels couldn't track a black bear on a snow-covered hillside! You ain't up here to try and catch no robbers; ye're jest makin' up stories so's to get folks to rat on their neighbors!"

"Now that's not all true, Mister Green; we have reason—"

"I'll give you reason! I'll give you reason! You can't catch no holdup men no more'n all the Yankee gen'rls that was ever spawned can catch the likes of Jubal Early or Robert E. Lee! You ain't showed nothin' to me, 'cept that now you got an excuse to go off a-chasin' poor folks what don't want to fight no Yankee war!"

There were muttered growls of approval at these sentiments.

"If I may be allowed to respond—"

"Here's my ree-spond!" Matt made as if to spit but caught himself just in time. "Sorry, Parson, I disremembered where we was."

"Thank you for recollecting that this is a church, Mister Green. Now perhaps we should allow the colonel to continue."

Matt subsided, muttering to himself.

"Thank you, Parson Swift. Here is the situation from the army's point of view," Colonel Mason said. "Gold belonging to the United States government has been stolen. That makes the affair our concern. Civilians have been killed in those same attacks. That makes it a case for the civilian authorities as well. Now, whether or not you believe that the robberies are politically motivated, the fact remains that such attacks cannot be allowed to continue.

"As much as it pains me to admit it, thus far Mister Green is correct. All our efforts to date have not apprehended the culprits, which is what brings us to the point of today's meeting. Contrary to what Mister Green thinks, we are not here to pursue draft dodgers or deserters or to inquire into anyone's personal beliefs."

Here Colonel Mason looked Matt Green squarely in the eye before continuing. "It is necessary for us to pursue whatever information we possess, and that information is that these robberies are linked to a conspiracy to promote the rebel cause.

"Now, we are prepared to see that every stage has an armed escort and to mount regular patrols of the highways in order to prevent further occurrences. What we want from you good people is a report of any suspicious activities, any strangers in town, or known outlaws whose movements seem questionable."

Matt Green burst out with another interruption. "There, ya see what I'm a-tellin' ya? Who's an outlaw far's the army is concerned? What's sur-spicious?"

He seemed disposed to continue his tirade, but at the front corner of the room Robert Mullins rose, smiling graciously. "With all due respect, Mister Green, I think that the colonel has made it very clear that it is up to us as good citizens to determine what is reported and what is not. It will be on each of our consciences to come forward with information that might prove helpful. After all, we want the army to participate in defending the citizenry from this wanton depredation until such time as our own capable sheriff, Mister Pettibone here, can lay the perpetrators by the heels."

Mullins paused and glanced around the room. "What about this as a workable compromise? So long as the army demonstrates that they can, in fact, improve the protection of the public highways, we should have no objection to cooperation. Further, let a committee of responsible citizens be formed to whom reports can be made of suspicious actions. This committee can then pass judgment on the merits of each report before deciding whether to bring the information to the army's attention. This should satisfy Mister Green's concern about harassment of private citizens, while at the same time filtering information so that the army's valuable time is not wasted in wild-goose chases.

"What do you say, Sheriff Pettibone? Is this a workable solution?"

Pettibone stood up next to Mullins, but given their difference in size, he appeared to be more dwarfed than ever when standing next to the storekeeper. He tugged on one end of his mustache reflectively and then commented, "It seems to me that's a real workable answer, provided a' course that the right men be on that committee. What say you serve as the chairman, Mister Mullins?"

Tom looked at his brother and raised his eyebrows as a low chorus of "'At's right; Mullins'll keep 'em straight" and "Good idear" came from around the packed sanctuary.

Seeming flustered, Mullins clasped his hands in front of him and bobbed his massive head up and down as his jowls quivered. "Why, I don't know what to say. I never considered . . . but if you think I should serve, why naturally . . ."

Matt Green spoke again. "I say put the parson on that committee. He's a man of sense, an' he don't talk so much!"

Parson Swift stood to acknowledge the nomination. "Thank you, Matt. I believe you all know that I can be trusted to keep your private thoughts private, but I do agree that something needs to be done to bring the murderers to justice."

"Who else?" someone said. "We need one more."

"Don't nobody suggest Matt!" another voice added.

Finally the parson said, "I'd like to recommend Jesse Dawson. He is a member of this community with a fine reputation. He has seen firsthand the awful results of the crimes we're discussing, and he has a business relationship with the army, which should make him acceptable to them. What do you say, Colonel?"

"A fine choice, Parson Swift, and a good solution all around. May I take it that the matter is settled, then?"

There were nods of agreement mixed with some grunts of disapproval from around the room.

Deputy Pettibone frowned.

Noting his look, Mullins pointed out, "And naturally, Sheriff Pettibone's official capacity means that he will automatically be part of the committee's discussion as we share information."

Pettibone looked pleased.

The only other markedly unsatisfied individual was still sitting next to his brother as the men began to file out of the church. Tom leaned over and whispered to Jesse, "I can tell this committee isn't your cup of tea. Why didn't you decline the *honor*?"

"I'm not sure I can explain why I let it stand. The parson's a good, levelheaded man, but with Mullins being on the church board and all, I was thinking Mullins might be able to throw his weight around." He grinned maliciously. "But maybe the parson and I can balance him some."

"You don't really think that committee will do any good, do you?"

"Maybe not, but the parson's right about one thing: I won't be forgetting the sight of that driver anytime soon. Survived the wreck of the coach and then stuck like a pig and left to bleed to death!"

Byrd motioned for Yancey to hurry.

Yancey, far more adept and quiet at slipping through brush than Byrd, had no difficulty keeping up.

The two were slipping up on the Dawson home in obedience to Mullins' instructions to kidnap Mont. Guidett agreed wholeheartedly with the plan since he saw it as a chance to recover what he believed was his rightful property. Yancey had some misgivings. He expressed to Robert Mullins his doubts that any information Mont had would be valuable to them, and kidnapping a child would arouse the countryside into a protracted search.

Mullins had snorted his derision. "For an orphan nigger boy? Nobody'll give him so much as a thought, much less try to search for him. And if you do this correctly, everyone will believe the boy is a runaway and not kidnapped at all."

So Byrd and Yancey were now creeping down the Poso Creek draw, having left their horses about half a mile from the Dawson place. They had selected this night by watching for several evenings in a row from a hilltop overlooking the farm until what they were hoping for had occurred. Tom and Jesse Dawson had left together at the end of the workday to ride into Greenville, leaving Emily and the three boys home alone.

It was all well and good for Mullins to say that they could make it look as if Mont had run away, but if they were discovered, they wanted to avoid a gun battle or any possibility of pursuit.

The gathering gloom cast pools of shadows under the scrub oaks. Twice, coveys of quail flew out of the dust with a clatter of wings as they sought to escape the night prowlers by nesting in the tree branches. Overhead the bats darted in and out of the open spaces between the oaks.

At each disturbance, Byrd and Yancey stopped short and listened. No sound came from the direction of the farm except for the nicker of a horse accepting his supper.

Even Byrd began to walk more cautiously. He made an effort to avoid the piles of brittle buckeye leaves that the breeze had gathered into heaps.

They had circled behind the Dawson place so as to approach it from the uphill side. From the rising land to the west they could look down on the barn, which was completely dark, and on the house, where only a gleam of light was visible.

Byrd motioned for Yancey to squat down beside him as they prepared to observe for a while.

Almost immediately they were rewarded as they saw the door open and Mont walk out alone. He went across the dusty yard to the tack-room door of the barn and went in. A moment later, a light peeked through the cracks in the door to show that Mont had lit a lantern or a candle.

Byrd turned to Yancey and whispered, "Looks pretty easy, don't it? Yancey, you circle the long way around to the far side of the barn while I creep up on the corral side closest to us." He added a few more instructions, and then Yancey disappeared from view.

Byrd thought he saw movement behind the corral, but he wasn't sure. Minutes passed. Then he saw Yancey moving stealthily toward the far corner of the barn. "So far, so good," Byrd said under his breath.

The plan was simple. Yancey would approach the tack-room door and tap on it lightly as though he were Emily coming for a goodnight word. As Mont opened the door, Byrd would grab him. Yancey was placed to block any bolt the boy might make away from Byrd's grasp. While Byrd held the child, Yancey would make a quick grab for Mont's meager possessions to complete the illusion that he had run off. Then they would ride back to the hideout.

Byrd began his stalk. First to the tree trunk nearest the corral, then to the corral's corner. From post to post he moved, a hulking shape of sinister intent.

At the corner of the barn he stopped. The next move was the most exposed since the front of the barn had no cover and was in full view of the house. Byrd noted with satisfaction that the barn door was ajar, giving him a halfway point to each.

As he left his last concealment and made for the barn door, Byrd felt a rising excitement. It was all going so well. He'd have the boy *and* he'd show Mullins what he was capable of.

In the midst of his self-exaltation, he heard the front door of the house open. Someone was coming out. Instinctively his hand dropped to the butt of his gun, but he forced himself to jump into the crack of the barn opening and pull the door shut behind him. He pressed himself into the shadows in the hinged corner of the crack and waited with bated breath.

It was Emily, and she was coming straight for the barn! Byrd examined her thoughtfully. As she reached the tack-room door and opened it, a light from within fell on her. Byrd could see her shape clearly. He liked what he saw.

Byrd licked his lips. *What a woman. Wouldn't I like—*His gaze lingered on her. *She's too good for the old clod kicker she's married to; she'd prob'bly appreciate a man like me.*

Byrd's lust began to overcome his caution. *Who's to know? Thar she is, not ten feet away.*

He had actually begun to move toward the door when he remembered Mullins' last command: "No one must know that anyone has the slightest interest in the child. If you cannot get away cleanly, wait for another occasion."

Byrd paused, his eyes narrowed, nearly deciding to disregard Mullins' orders.

Then he heard Emily speaking. "That's right, Mont. I've given the boys permission to stay up until their father and uncle return. They'd like you to join them and play some checkers. Would you like to?"

"Oh, yessum, Miss Emily."

"Well, come on then."

Byrd shrank back against the wall. *Blast it! We'll have to wait for another time,* he decided. *Then I'll grab the boy, get Mullins off my back, and have the woman, too.*

A moment more, and the door of the house opened and shut again as Emily and Mont went inside.

Byrd whistled softly to Yancey, and together they retraced their steps to where they had tied their horses.

When they reported their failed attempt to Mullins, he swore softly but seemed relieved that there had been no disturbance.

Byrd naturally didn't divulge any of his thoughts but privately made his own plans for "another time."

✣ CHAPTER 8 ✣

Tom and Jesse planned to look into Tommy Fitzgerald's tale of an old track around Shadow Ridge and the possibility of a cave there, but the farm delayed their exploration.

Mont worked eagerly alongside Nathan and Jed, helping with the haying and the digging of an additional root cellar to lay up potatoes, pumpkins, and squash.

The boys were inseparable companions. They went exploring along the sandy banks of the level stretches of Poso Creek. Sent out to gather quail eggs and to search for late gooseberries, they would return just as often with a new variety of lizard or an unusually colorful feather.

Finally the day came when Jesse and Tom felt free to go exploring. The boys asked to accompany them, but permission was denied.

"Boys, it's as rough a country as you'll ever see, even if it isn't haunted. Besides being steep and treacherous, it's a natural place for rattlesnakes and mountain lions." Jesse addressed his elder son firmly. "Jed, I expect you to see that the littler ones don't act foolish or come to grief by being where they ought not be."

"Yes, Pa."

"Besides," added his uncle, who was tightening the girth of his saddle as he spoke, "there probably isn't a grain of truth to the story anyway—more'n likely this will be a wasted trip."

"Boys, look after your ma while we're gone. Don't run off without fetching the water for the house and seeing that the wood box is filled. We won't be gone over two days at most."

Tom went into his room in the barn and returned with his rifle. He thrust it into the leather scabbard hanging from his saddle, then went back for a powder flask and bedroll.

Jesse stepped away from his packed horse to where Emily stood in the doorway of their home. "We'll be back soon, Emily. We'll just take a quick look around to see if what Tommy said was fact."

"I'll be praying for a safe and quick return for both of you," promised Emily, clasping Jesse's hands and looking into his eyes.

"You aren't afraid, are you?" Jesse asked quietly.

"Not afraid exactly, no. It's more an uneasiness. If Byrd Guidett used a hidden trail like you think, then he murdered five people in cold blood."

"Emily, Tom and I aren't looking for a gun battle, and we'll go real watchful. I thought maybe you were believing the spook stories," he teased.

"Oh, hush and get on out of here! The sooner you two get this notion out of your systems, the sooner I get my new chicken coop built and the winter's wood split."

A quick embrace and a parting kiss, and Jesse swept into his saddle.

Tom mounted Duncan. "So long, Emily. See you, boys."

With a last look and a wave they were gone, up the slope toward Shadow Ridge, angling around its southeastern rim.

They rode easily at first, walking their horses up a hillside covered with scrub oak. Soon the gooseberry and manzanita patches grew larger and closer together.

Tom watched the ground for signs of a trail or even the marks that another rider had recently passed this way. He saw nothing to indicate the presence of anyone. The ground was thickly carpeted with decaying oak leaves, and he noted the clear impressions of deer tracks and once where a bear had crushed the undergrowth.

Tom looked ahead to where his brother rode and thought—not for the first time—what a fortunate man Jesse was. Tom admired him for what he had built, had carved out for himself. Emily had chosen well; Jesse was a fine provider and father for their family.

Only lately had Tom discovered in himself a desire to build. Always before, his thoughts had run toward roving, seeing sights not seen before. Now he felt that the time had come to put down some roots.

Jesse turned in his saddle. "Don't you think we're wasting our time?"

Tom pulled his horse to a halt and pushed his hat back. "It sure appears so. Nobody's been on this stretch of hill in a hundred years, seems like." Then squinting upward he added, "What do you say we split up and circle that granite face yonder? I'll try to work around the top, and you push through that low spot."

"Even if we strike a path up there, that still won't explain how anyone could make their way down this slope without leaving so much as a trace. And to get down off this slope to the Poso Creek trail, they'd have to come through here someplace."

"You're probably right, Jesse, but since we're too late to head back tonight, let's camp in the saddle anyhow and head back tomorrow."

Jesse examined the height of the sun above Shadow Ridge's rim and nodded.

The two rode together for about a quarter of a mile; then Jesse turned his mount to pick his way down the slope, while Tom urged his horse up and around a sheer rock face.

✴ ✴ ✴

Jesse's travel was strewn with boulders—some as big as wagon boxes—that had fallen from the granite wall. Bushy thickets had grown about the rock falls, causing him to backtrack often and look for a way around. Several times he found himself moving into what appeared to be an open space, only to find his line abruptly blocked and impenetrable.

Worse yet, the ground underfoot became treacherous, the soft earth giving place to shale rock, with only a thin layer of soil covering it. Jesse's mount began to pick its way along. Jesse didn't urge it to any great speed, preferring to trust its sense of safe footing. This was a mountain-bred horse, no stranger to hillside trails. It had been called upon before to chase deer over rocky ledges and had gone down into and out of deep mountain canyons.

The horse plainly didn't like what it saw and felt on this stretch of Shadow Ridge. Gingerly stepping around a gooseberry patch that seemed to grow out of solid rock, the mount paused after each step to test its footing.

✷ ✷ ✷

Tom was having his own share of difficulty. On the first two places he approached, the upper slope yielded dead ends against sheer granite outcroppings, and each time he had to turn farther back the way they had come in order to proceed.

"At this rate I'll be home before we ever see the top of this ridge," Tom addressed his horse.

Duncan pricked his ears to listen, then seemed almost to nod in agreement.

Rounding a house-sized boulder, Tom was surprised to find a fairly open route up the face of the cliff.

Gaining the top of the granite escarpment in about half an hour, he halted on top of a sheer drop to view the countryside. Behind him the manzanita closed in, completely covering the saddle between the two nearest peaks. It was apparent that no route over Shadow Ridge could be found from this approach.

On three sides of him the land fell away, dropping several hundred feet to the slope up which he and Jesse had ridden, then less sharply down to Poso Creek.

Tom could not see Jesse's ranch from this vantage point, but he could identify the hill behind which it lay and the bend of the Poso that contained Lavers Crossing.

"Good lookout," he noted aloud, "or a place to signal from."

Far below stretched chaparral and rockslides as far as the eye could see. Tom mentally reviewed the possible travel and concluded again that no trails were visible, nor did any routes present themselves. Indeed, only one rock-filled canyon cut through the mountainside, and it provided no opportunity for travelers.

Tom observed that the canyon did intersect a bend in the path of Poso Creek but at a point where the main trail lay a few hundred yards away from the stream behind a little oak-covered knoll.

"You know, Duncan, if a body could get down from here to that canyon's mouth, he'd cut off miles of trail and come out where he could choose his moment to set out on the road to Granite."

A further study of the canyon, however, indicated the impossibility of that thought since the gorge was both deep and narrow, except near its juncture with Poso.

"Now's when we could use Tommy's cave," Tom remarked. "Some way down past these slides and . . . say—"

He stood in his stirrups for a better view. A trick of light caused by the westering sun allowed something to appear to his eye that had not been there before. Right at the bottom of the gorge, only one bend of river from the Poso Creek intersection, was a large black shadow. A cave? A moment more and the hillside reverted to its previous appearance of gooseberry thickets and fallen buckeye branches.

Tom rubbed his eyes thoughtfully, but the shadow did not reappear, or rather, the lengthening shadows of the ridge swallowed up the canyon's mouth in gloom, eliminating the momentary contrast.

At that instant Tom heard a shot, followed by a shout. As if the mountain itself were falling, a roaring crash rose, gaining momentum like peal after peal of thunder.

The horse snorted and pranced sideways as though fearful that the rock ledge underfoot would give way.

Tom stepped from the saddle, shucking the rifle from its scabbard. "Jesse! Jesse!" he called, even though he knew his voice would not carry over the echoing rumble that coursed down the mountainside and rebounded off the canyon walls.

Tom could see a rising cloud of dust against the evening sky just where the rockslide had occurred. After two or three minutes that felt like hours to Tom, the crashing reverberations stilled, replaced by a soft sighing, as if the mountain were settling itself. An occasional thumping crunch was heard as dislodged boulders bounded down the slope to find new resting places against the oaks far below. In another moment, all was silent.

"Jesse, Jesse, where are you?" Tom called again.

But there was no answer, nor any further sound from that direction.

Catching the reins, Tom jumped back into his saddle and began plunging down the slope he had lately ridden up. As though sensing his rider's urgency, Duncan plunged faster downward, leaping over boulders in his way and skidding across shale-covered slide rock.

When Tom regained the point at which he and Jesse had parted, he realized that picking his way around rocks and thickets would lengthen his travel, so he abandoned Duncan and followed Jesse's trail by foot.

Hurrying furiously, he scrambled over rockfalls in his path. A new rubble field lay at the bottom of the cliff, covering chaparral and manzanita thickets that had previously blocked forward progress at the cliff's base.

Rounding a corner of the granite outcropping, Tom tore through the thicket that remained, heedless of the barbed branches grabbing at his hands and arms, even piercing the leather chaps he wore.

Finally one more wrench free and Tom was in the open. He stopped abruptly. There, at the cliff's base, lay his brother. Beside his outstretched hand lay his Colt revolver.

Tom rushed to his brother's side. Jesse was on his back, his face turned to the side. His clothes were not torn, not even disheveled. His hat was nowhere to be seen, but the hair across his forehead looked unmussed.

Tom knelt beside his brother. "Jesse, are you hurt?"

There was no reply, and as Tom gently turned his brother's face toward him, he saw the reason: the right side of Jesse's skull was crushed; he was dead.

Tom found Jesse's horse tangled in a thicket so that it could go neither forward nor back. From its location and that of Jesse's body, Tom surmised that the horse had bolted uphill, thus avoiding being buried by the slide but unable to prevent the first falling rock from striking and killing Jesse.

❊ ❊ ❊

The lengthening western shadows were countered from the east by a rising wind, but the sickly breeze did nothing to hold back the blackness.

Soon only the peaks of the Sierras held patches of sunlight on their heights. One by one even these tall candles were snuffed out.

Tom sat in the gathering gloom, cradling his brother's head in his lap. Tom's shoulders slumped and his neck bowed. He was overcome with incredible weariness.

Twice he started with a sensation of startled joy in the mistaken belief that his brother lived. Each time it was only a trick of his tear-blurred eyes that suggested movement—a ruse of the blood pounding in his ears that counterfeited breath.

A man cannot live long in the West without knowing death and its forms—sometimes peaceful, but more often sudden and frequently violent. Tom accepted the reality of his brother's death much the same way as the night fell—a few moments of lingering hope, then black certainty.

He gave no thought to building a fire, having no energy to gather wood. He could hear the horses stamping nervously around, so he got up and unsaddled them, leaving them to graze. Then he returned to his lonely vigil.

The stars began to appear overhead, at first a handful, then hundreds and later uncountable numbers as the Milky Way brightened into view. It was a moonless night, and the hazy starshine made all but the nearest bushes and rocks indistinguishable from the black hillside. Without the brightness of the moon, the stars appeared with more clarity and distinctness, distant as they were, than anything as near as the earth.

Tom's thoughts went back to his earliest memories of his brother. Mostly he and Jesse had fought. Jesse, the cautious, the thoughtful and never-in-trouble one, and Tom, whom everyone thought first to blame when any mischief was discovered. Yet there was always a deep-rooted affection between them, a sort of mutual admiration for the qualities the other possessed.

A night bird called from the brush, seemingly close by. The horses had settled down to cropping what dry grass they could find, and Tom knew their natural caution on the steep slope would keep them from wandering far.

Tom was not by nature a fearful person, nor did the wild countryside at night hold any terror for him. Even the nearness of death made no impression of fear on him, yet the night had an edge to it. An uneasiness penetrated his dulled senses, as if part of his mind were keeping watch and sensing something amiss.

He tried to lay the blame for his jumpiness on his grief and his apprehension at the sorrow he would carry back down the mountain to Emily and the boys, but he was not entirely successful. His mind tried to reconstruct what had happened. He reviewed what he had seen of the rock face—the treacherous ground, the sudden crashing, the accidental discharge of Jesse's gun, and his shout.

Something about the gunshot bothered Tom—something he couldn't quite put his finger on. Every time he tried to recapture the moment that perplexed him, his thoughts jumped to the tragic conclusion, and the ache he felt inside interfered with his reason.

He felt a rising anger, directed first at himself. Why were they on this godforsaken mountain, anyway? There wasn't any trail and never had been. What was he trying to prove, and why had he dragged his brother along? Jesse, who lay dead on these stones, had never been adventurous, never courted danger. He should never have been overtaken by disaster. Why should he be dead while Tom still lived?

What would Emily do now? How could she raise the boys and keep the farm? The work was too much for one man, but they couldn't afford to pay a hired hand, so Jesse had sent for Tom.

What's more, Tom knew he couldn't stand to stay around. Emily would hate him, would hate the sight of him as a constant reminder that Tom had caused her loss. She and his nephews would sell the place and go live with her family back in Missouri.

And Tom? He'd been wrong to think of settling down. He'd never be one to build anything or to own anything more valuable than his horse. He'd go back to drifting through the mining camps, or maybe he'd join one of the cattle ranches on the coast.

71

✷ CHAPTER 9 ✷

It was altogether too fitting that the sky was a leaden gray with the first storm of the rainy season. The trees that stood guard over Oak Grove Cemetery still wore their leaves, but without sunlight to reflect from their surfaces, they appeared drab and subdued. Grayish green moss hung in formless folds from their branches as if nature itself had put on a crepe of mourning.

The little group gathered around the mound of earth and the raw wound of a grave over which the pine coffin rested. The people in their black coats and black shawls stood silent and still, like an awkward group of statues.

All around were the graves of earlier settlers and their families. Some had reached this place of rest in ripe old age and some in the bloom of youth. Their granite markers and lovingly tended plots mingled with rude patches of earth with dimly lettered wooden signs. These latter graves held mute testimony to strangers who had chanced to die or be killed in the hills; their epitaph was the sober phrase: *Known only to God.*

Tom stood, hat in hand, beside Emily and opposite Parson Swift. The brothers braced their mother on either side, while Mont hung back. Behind him stood a little knot of townspeople.

The parson reminded his listeners, "'We have this treasure in earthen vessels, that . . . the power may be of God, and not of us. . . . We know that if our earthly house . . . were dissolved, we have . . . a house not made with hands, eternal in the heavens.'"

He went on to explain that because Jesse was a Christian, the parting that had taken place and the sorrow they felt, however strong and painful, were only temporary. He urged them to look around at the withered grass and remember that the same God who returned the green of spring each year would reunite them in new and glorious bodies that never felt pain or suffered death.

He prayed simply but with a firm voice for the Lord to help them through their grief and asked that all present would be reminded of the fleeting nature of life and the need to "walk uprightly before their Maker."

When he concluded with a final "amen" and a chorus of murmured "amens" replied, Parson Swift moved around the grave to take both of Emily's hands in his. Looking at her with his kind blue eyes, he said, "Emily, Jesse was a fine man. God has called him to some great purpose we don't see just yet, but I know your faith will bear you up—one day at a time."

She nodded, unable to speak.

At a gesture from Parson Swift, his wife came up from the group of mourners to take Emily's elbow and turn her from the casket toward those waiting to offer condolences.

Tom drew apart, standing alone now at the head of his brother's grave. A seething mass of emotions boiled inside him. Grief mingled with his sense of guilt was compounded by his swelling bitterness.

Parson Swift turned aside to speak with him, but before he opened his mouth, Tom burst out, "Don't hand me any of your pious sayings, Parson! This needn't have happened. I don't care what you say about great purposes; Jesse's family needed him here!"

"Tom, don't you think God understands what you're feeling right now? Haven't we all felt at times like shaking our fist in God's face and demanding an explanation? But what other statement can He make than what He gave to Job: 'Where were you when I laid the foundations of the earth?'"

"That may be so, Parson, but if God caused this to happen, then I don't want any part of your God!"

"Tom, I won't pretend to have an answer that will satisfy you— but I know that God does, and I'll pray that He'll let you find it."

Tom didn't respond; he couldn't respond at that moment. All he could see was Emily, now a grieving widow, surrounded by the women of the community.

Miss Peavy, the schoolmarm, expressed her sympathy, then drew Jed and Nathan to her and knelt to their height. "Boys, you must be very strong and brave for your mother. Jed, you must be manly and look after your younger brother."

"And Mont, too?" added Nathan.

Miss Peavy looked perplexed for a moment, then turned to find a wide-eyed Mont James watching her fearfully. "Well, I don't know. Now perhaps Mont will need to . . . Your mother may not be able to . . . what I mean is—"

"Noooo!" shouted Nathan. "Mont's *got* to stay with us, doesn't he, Ma?"

Emily looked around from where she was being embraced by Mary Davis, the livery stable owner's wife. "Of course Mont will stay on with us. Why should he leave now?"

"But, Emily, you'll have your hands full with your two boys and taking care of your place."

"Yes, and land sakes, Emily," added Victoria Burton, wife of the hotel's proprietor, "how will it look, your raising this black child as your own—I mean, well, he *is* black."

Emily looked confused. "But what difference can that make?"

"You're just not thinking clearly, Emily," said Mrs. Davis. "This child is part of that dreadful business about Byrd Guidett. Why, Jesse would be alive today if he hadn't gone off after that foolishness about Shadow Ridge."

"No, Ma, no!" insisted Jed and Nathan. "Mont didn't do anything wrong. Don't make him go away."

Tom could stand no more. He burst into their discussion. Over his shoulder he called savagely to the parson, "Is this part of your fine God's plan, too, blaming Jesse's death on this small boy?"

"No, it's certainly not," the parson said sternly. "Ladies, it is very unchristian and uncalled for at a time like this—"

"You have to talk like that, Reverend, but we all know what bad luck these . . . you know what I mean . . . are. Just look at this war going on now! Why didn't we just leave them in their place?"

Tom was preparing for another outburst when a soft, oily sort of voice interrupted. "I think that our emotions are a little raw right now, don't you, Parson?" Robert Mullins' carefully modulated tones dripped over his listeners. "I'm sure that Mrs. Davis is just express-ing the frustration everyone feels at the *Eastern* war. Why, all of us have lost relatives in Mister Lincoln's conflict, and this present tragic occurrence, accompanied by this Negro child, seems to bring us into that maelstrom somehow. Mrs. Davis certainly meant nothing personal. She was merely trying to suggest that the child's presence would be an unpleasant reminder. Perhaps it would be best if he stayed elsewhere for a time. With me perhaps. I could use some assis-tance around my store."

"Thank you, but no," replied Emily. "Mont will continue to stay with us for now. I'm sure he realizes that we don't hold him in any way responsible for what happened."

She gathered the three boys, and the group moved off toward the waiting buggies. She could not move quickly enough to escape the sound of the clods of earth falling on Jesse's coffin.

❅ ❅ ❅

Each man stepped up to the graveside to take a turn wielding one of the shovels. After a moment of silently turning the dirt, a nearby hand would reach out to take the shovel from its user before passing it on to another.

As Mullins reached out to take the shovel from Tom's hand, the man murmured, "Terrible, terrible."

❅ ❅ ❅

The service was over. The ladies of the church had prepared a meal for the family and friends to share back at the Dawson home. Each of the families separated at the gate of the cemetery to go to their respective homes, there to bundle up the savory meats and fragrant pies to offer as consolation to the bereaved.

Robert Mullins, the senior elder present, was in charge of locking the gate of the Oak Grove Cemetery. The last to leave, he paid his respects again to the family, shook hands all around with the other church members, and even had a moment's word with Parson Swift about taking up a collection to provide a fine headstone for their recently departed brother Jesse Dawson.

Nodding solemnly to each family as the buggies departed, Mullins looked the picture of respectability and Christian concern. He watched them disappear from sight around a curve of the road, then raised his voice above its previous obsequious level and called, "All right, you two—you can come out now."

From behind a clump of brush on the knoll overlooking the burial ground stepped Byrd and Yancey. They walked down to meet Mullins, where he stood beside the grave.

"Well, well. Once again a job half done. In case you didn't notice, there are *two* Dawson brothers, and one of them is still alive!"

As though he had been expecting this criticism, Byrd kept silent and let Yancey put forth their practiced defense.

"Now, boss, it's like this. When they split up on the hill up yonder, we know'd we could take one with the rockslide, see, and make it look like an accident. As it is, ain't nobody thinks anything about ol' Shadow 'cept maybe it's haunted for true, and anyway it's powerful bad medicine. If we'd hauled off and shot that other one, somebody woulda gone to find 'em. Only then it weren't possible to make it be no accident—"

"You pitiful fools! Couldn't you have disposed of them in the tunnel where nobody would've been the wiser? Why should anyone have found the bodies at all?"

Byrd and Yancey looked guiltily at each other. Mullins had spotted the flaw in their excuse immediately.

"See, it was gettin' on to dark," Byrd tried, "and we wasn't gonna take no chance at lettin' Tom Dawson get away. But we figured it'd be worse to give away where we was for an uncertain finish than to send him down thinkin' it was an accident. We can finish 'im later."

Mullins rubbed his face thoughtfully. "Why, Byrd, Yancey, you astonish me! I'd never have given you credit for coming to such careful restraint. This may work out for the best after all. Now there's clearly no reason for anyone to explore Shadow Ridge any further."

Byrd looked pleased with himself. Completely ignoring the shake of Yancey's head, which was intended to mean *leave well enough alone,* he resumed explaining. "Yes, sir, we know'd Tom Dawson would be comin' right wary, after that shot and all, and we—"

"What!" Mullins produced an almost piglike squeal. "What shot? I thought you said it entirely appeared to be an accident!"

"Now, jest calm yourself. The dead 'un only got off one round. We figger Tom'll put it down to a misfire when his brother's horse throw'd 'im. 'Course, it woulda been different if he'd nicked Yancey and we'd had trouble gettin' outta there our ownselves, but as it was—"

Mullins' voice and manner were icy. "You mean to say that Jesse Dawson saw you on the ledge about to push over the rocks and had time to get off a shot at you? You idiots! What if Tom figures out that it was no accidental discharge? What if the brother lived long enough to say something to him? You've already said it was near dark. How can you know for certain? Now we've got to eliminate Tom Dawson—and the sooner the better—before he has a chance to do any more thinking or to share his suspicions with anyone else."

"Cain't we jest dry-gulch 'im? Pettibone's no great shakes as a tracker. We could hole up on the ledge for a piece after."

"And have people start to question how it happens that two brothers both die so close together? We're trying to eliminate curiosity, not create more of it. Besides, have you forgotten about the black child? I can't afford to have you two in hiding for now—not after I've spent time leading Pettibone to think that the shooting of Colonel James was entirely self-defense."

Mullins paused, breathing heavily. "No, I've got a better idea. Let's go about this completely open. Everyone knows there's bad blood between you and Dawson over the nigger boy. What about if we set up another "self-defense" situation? Why, I'll bet I could even get awarded temporary legal custody of the child after such an unfortunate accident. Yes, broad daylight, that's the way of it." He rubbed his hands together gleefully, as though contemplating stacks of gold coins in his office safe.

Byrd's eyes narrowed, and he ground out a question. "Ya want me to kill Dawson in front of witnesses and stand trial for it? You must be nuts. I ain't aimin' to get my neck stretched for nobody."

"There won't be a trial, you fool. Now listen; here's how we'll work it. . . ."

✦ CHAPTER 10 ✦

The house was quiet now. *Too quiet,* Tom thought as he wiped his muddy boots and knocked timidly on the frame of the screen door. Behind him on the porch dry leaves scudded forlornly over the planks, then swirled away across the empty yard, where only two weeks before Jesse had wrestled playfully with the boys as Tom and Emily had howled with laughter. Tom stared hard at the place where they had tumbled down, and the memory almost made him smile again. But the vision was only a memory. The laughter and the moment would never return, and that thought made Tom's smile die even as it reached his lips.

Mercifully, the boys had school to keep them occupied. Reading and writing, the mysterious world of ciphers, and childhood games could ease their pain a bit. But Tom and Emily had no such escape. The absence of the children only seemed to emphasize the terrible silence that had come to the ranch since the death of Jesse. That first dull ache of shock and disbelief was now honed into a sharp blade of grief that managed to pierce their hearts every time they turned around.

A thousand times a day Tom found a thought on his lips, but Jesse was not there to answer. Talk about the crops, the stock, the weather, and the war in the East was now frozen into a silent monologue. *What would Jesse think? What would Jesse do?* Those two questions had helped Tom reason his way through a maze of confused emotions over the last days. Jesse would want him to stay here as long as Emily needed help. He would expect Tom to see her and the boys safely back to Missouri.

Tom raised his fist and knocked again. He would tell Emily that. He would let her know he planned to do his duty by her and the children. For the sake of Jesse, he would see to it that they arrived in St. Louis safe and sound beneath her parents' roof. Emily's father was a wealthy man. He would see to it that his young, widowed daughter was well cared for.

Emily was never meant to live a hard life in the West. She would fit in again easily with St. Louis society. *Yes,* he thought, *she will fit.* North and South, the country was now filled with widows as husbands clad in blue or gray shared common graves in places like Gettysburg. Wasn't that why Jesse had remained in the West long after the goldfields had begun to play out? Hadn't he remained here in California just so he would not be forced to fight against friends and neighbors in this terrible war, so Emily would never have to wear black or sleep alone in an empty bed or call his name in the dark?

They had come west to escape the mindless destruction, and somehow death had followed them even here. How pointless it all seemed! How unjust and harsh that the hand of God had swept across the face of the mountain, and—

The door opened. Emily's face was pale with grief but seemed to radiate an inner peace. "Why, Tom! What are you doing standing out there on the porch with your hat in your hand?" She smiled and held the door open for him.

He could not bring himself to look at her. Her black mourning dress had become the uniform that united the nation's women. It did not matter which cause their husbands, sons, or brothers had died for. Tom had never expected to see that uniform on Emily, however, nor could he have imagined that she would still be so beautiful even with the gingham and calico put away.

"I thought maybe we might need to talk a bit," he said haltingly.

"Yes. I was just going through—" Her gaze moved toward a neatly folded stack of Jesse's clothes on the dining-room table. "You and Jesse are . . . were . . . close to the same size, and I was wondering . . . Jesse would like you to . . ." Tears clouded her eyes.

Tom remained in the center of the room, toying nervously with his hat. He could not think of wearing his brother's clothes any more than filling his brother's boots. He cleared his throat. "No. No, thank you, Emily. I . . . it might be hard for the boys to see me in their father's gear." He did not add that it would also be difficult for Emily.

She seemed relieved by his reply. "You're right. Silly of me. Then perhaps you could take them to Pastor Swift when you go to town? He'll see that they are put to good use."

Tom nodded, wondering how he could best broach the subject of selling the ranch and returning to the East. He glanced toward the desk where Jesse kept his journals and had spent hours long into the night deep in his accounts. "Jesse would want me to stay . . . I think . . . to help you." He cleared his throat again and scratched his head. "That is, if you would like me to, until—"

"Of course, Tom," she said softly, interrupting his words.

"We'll need to sell the place and then get you and the boys back home."

She drew in her breath sharply and glared at Tom as though he had slapped her across the face. "*Sell?* Back . . . you mean Missouri? Thomas Dawson! You can't mean that you think I would take my sons back to Missouri!"

Tom was instantly sorry that he had spoken. He had not meant to upset her, but he was in it up to his neck now. "Back . . . *home,* Emily. Your folks. Your family."

She raised her chin defiantly. "*This* is my home! This is where Jesse is buried, and one day I will be buried beside him!"

Tom ran his fingers through his hair. He should not have opened his mouth. He should have let her bring it up. She always was a strong-minded woman. "You can't stay here."

"You honestly believe that Jesse would want me to take our sons back to Missouri? Of all men, Thomas, I can't believe that you have forgotten that there is a war on! I have lost two cousins who fought for Georgia and another who died fighting for Lincoln! Not only is the country divided, but my own family is torn in two by this conflict. Missouri is a border state! Jesse had only just said to me how relieved he was that we are so far away from all that! How glad he was that the hand of God had brought us here to Shadow Ridge to raise our boys in safety and peace!"

Tears began to flow now as the words *safety* and *peace* echoed hollowly in the empty house. Tom saw her turn toward the pile of overalls and shirts sewn from flour sacks. He knew that Jesse had refused to exchange his mended denim for the uniform of a soldier. While others had turned in their plows for the weapons of destruction, Jesse had neither condemned nor joined them. When Tom had turned his back on the fighting and appeared at the ranch with tales of childhood friends firing from the opposite sides of a riverbank, Jesse had taken him in without a word of condemnation.

"When this war ends, Emily," he answered quietly, "I'll see to it you get back to St. Louis."

"Don't be such a fool, Thomas Dawson!" She whirled around to face him. "It doesn't matter who wins this war as far as you are concerned! If you go back to Missouri, you'll be hanged! And now you're telling me you're going back there!"

"Just to make sure . . ."

"To make sure there's still a price on your head? To make sure that both of the Dawson brothers die young?" Her fists were clenched as she hurled the absurdity of his thought back at him. "You don't have to go back to Missouri if you want to die young! Go back on that mountain! Back on the cursed mountain!" She began to sob and sank onto the settee. Blonde hair fell in wisps around her face as she cried into her hands. "Do you really think this helps? Go away! Just get out, Tom. Let me be awhile!"

Stricken, Tom stared at her in horror. What a fool he was! It was too soon to bring any of this up. Too soon! He backed toward the door. "I'm sorry, Emily," he said as he slipped out onto the porch.

The dry leaves swirled around his legs and followed him back to his cot in the barn.

✳ ✳ ✳

Each member of the Dawson family chose a different way of dealing with grief. After Tom's unfortunate attempt to discuss relocating to Missouri, he took to finding reasons to go into town.

Jed alternately comforted and was comforted by his mother. He carried himself with a manly dignity and did his chores without being told. But when his mother brought him his father's pocket watch and said that it was right for him to have it now, he had to fight back tears and bite his lip. Emily found him later, sitting on the corral fence staring at Shadow Ridge, the watch clutched in his fist.

Emily threw herself into housework. Given the excuse that many of their friends and neighbors would be dropping by to call, she found that the house could never be clean enough to suit her. She swept and scrubbed the wood-plank floors until they shone, then was still able to locate imaginary crumbs to pick up. Alone at night in the empty bed, she couldn't sleep, so she took to rising at four o'clock in the morning, starting in again on chores that she had completed at midnight the night before.

Nathan, on the other hand, seemed to feel the weight of Jesse's absence the hardest—sobbing one minute, then becoming bitterly angry the next. Once when Tom returned from town, he happened to walk in and catch Nathan unawares. Nathan glanced at his uncle, and the resemblance to his father was so great that the boy started up; then realizing the deception, he ran crying from the room. Tom turned around and without a word to anyone rode back to town.

Nathan soon stopped playing with Mont. He did not intentionally ignore his friend, but he was unable to believe that his life would ever be the same again. With Jesse gone, there was no room for play.

So no one noticed how Mont was reacting to Jesse's death. He appeared at mealtimes, but they were such silent and unhappy affairs that he retreated immediately afterward to his quarters in the tack room.

✳ ✳ ✳

Daylight had begun to fade, and Emily was busying herself in the kitchen preparing a meal of cornbread and fried chicken. Tom had not yet returned from town, but supper was nearing completion, so Emily sent Jed out to the springhouse for a jug of buttermilk and dispatched Nathan to fetch Mont.

"Mont. Hey, Mont! Ma says come to eat," called Nathan.

There was no reply.

"Mont, don'tcha hear me? It's time to eat." Nathan pushed open the tack-room door, a long creak of the hinges announcing his entrance. He expected to see Mont perched on the edge of his cot or seated in the middle of the floor repairing a piece of harness, but Mont was nowhere to be seen.

Maybe he's gone into the barn, Nathan thought, so he walked around the corner into the barn, calling for Mont all the while. A quick inspection of the stalls still gave no evidence of the black child's whereabouts.

Raising his voice to a shout, Nathan called out, "Mont James, come down from that hayloft! I don't want to play, and Ma's waitin' supper!"

When there was no answer, he marched over to the ladder that led upward to the fragrant hay storage, the scene of many pleasant hours in happier days. Still no Mont.

Nathan was not worried, but he was perplexed and growing angry. It was not like Mont to be absent at mealtimes. But then Nathan couldn't remember having seen Mont at all since noon.

On the way back to the house, Nathan made a short loop past the corrals, the water pump, and the garden patch. No Mont.

I'll bet he slipped around and went into the house when I was lookin' out here for him, reasoned Nathan. "Ma," he said upon entering the house, "is Mont in here with you?"

Emily looked up from where she was filling a platter with pieces of chicken. "Why, no, Nate. Didn't you find him?"

"No, Ma, an' he's not in the barn nor any place around."

"Perhaps he went with Jed down to the springhouse." No sooner were the words out of her mouth than Jed returned, carrying the jug of buttermilk, and without Mont.

"He wasn't with me," added Jed, having overheard their words. "And where's Uncle Tom?"

"Mercy me!" exclaimed Emily. "That must be the answer. He must have gone with Tom to town. They'll both be returning most anytime now. You know, boys, we must not forget about Mont no matter how bad we feel. We have each other to lean on, but poor Mont has no family except us, and we must not shut him out.

"We all feel terrible just now," she went on, "and I know that I haven't given you the attention I should have." She waved aside their protests. "But I looked around at the house tonight, and I think it's clean enough, don't you?"

This brought small grins to the faces of the boys.

"Let's make a pledge to start seeing—really seeing—each other again, and that includes Mont." She might have added *and your uncle,* but she didn't.

They were interrupted by the sound of Tom's horse outside but were so confident that Mont was with Tom that no one stepped out. A couple of moments elapsed while he unsaddled and turned Duncan into the corral.

When he entered the house, he was alone. "What's for sup—? What are you all staring at? Is anything wrong?"

They all began to talk at once. "Isn't Mont with you?"

"We can't find him."

"Didn't he go with . . . ?"

When the din subsided, Tom looked to Emily for an explanation.

"Tom, it seems that Mont is gone. I sent Nathan to bring him in to supper, and he's nowhere around. The last time anyone saw him was at dinner today, and we thought perhaps he'd ridden over with you."

"Why, no, Emily, I haven't seen him since this morning. You may remember I left before noon. The last I saw of him, he was sittin' on his cot by himself."

"Oh, Tom, that's just what the boys and I have been talking about! I'm afraid we've been neglecting each other—and Mont in particular. You don't suppose he's run away, do you?"

"Now, Emily, don't get all riled up. I'm sure he's around here someplace and hasn't come to any harm. The boys and I will go look for him right now. Okay, boys?"

The boys nodded vigorously, and soon all three had lit lanterns and gathered behind the house.

"Listen carefully, Jed, Nathan. I want you two to go together.

Head north to where Sandy Creek joins up with the Poso; if you haven't found Mont by then, each of you get on either side of the creek and come down to Lavers Crossing. Don't get farther away than you can see each other's lanterns clearly. Don't go past the crossing; just turn and go back to the house. I'll meet you back there."

"Which way will you go, Uncle?" asked Jed.

"I'll head up Shadow Ridge way."

✳ ✳ ✳

Tom needn't have worried that the brothers would become widely separated. In fact, they traveled so closely together that one lantern would have been adequate.

The night was full of sounds—the familiar rustle of the long-tailed mice scurrying through the fallen leaves, the whisper-soft swoop of an owl's wings. Later on the mournful cries of the coyotes echoed from the summit of Carver Peak. The boys had no difficulty finding the juncture of the Sandy and Poso Creeks, nor did they have any difficulty staying together. But they were not successful in finding Mont.

The lengthening search and the deepening night combined to stretch their imaginations. "Do ya s'pose he got snake bit?" wondered Nathan.

"Maybe—" Jed nodded gravely—"or took off by Injuns more likely."

"Could be a mountain lion got 'im or a great big ol' bear."

The same threat seemed to occur to them simultaneously. "You don't think . . . Byrd Guidett . . ."

✳ ✳ ✳

Tom's search was all uphill. He moved in an arc, zigzagging back and forth across the slope and gaining a few yards of elevation with each swing. He tried not to think about his last trip down this hillside with the body of his brother or how much he was coming to believe in the mountain's evil reputation. Of course, the more he tried to avoid these thoughts, the stronger they kept returning.

God, he thought, *aren't* You *supposed to be running things around here? First Jesse and now this poor boy? Can't You make a better job of things than this? Here I am trying to get things settled at this ranch so I can take off and not be such a constant reminder to Emily of her sorrow, yet things seem to get more unsettled all the time!*

He was so lost in these thoughts that he almost missed exploring the little hollow formed by granite boulders and the fallen buckeye trunk.

Tom could never say later what it was that caught his eye. Surely no movement or flash of light—just the small dark clump that turned out to be Mont against the larger darkness. Tom jumped on the buckeye log and raced into the rocky depression, calling out Mont's name. He began to fear the worst, saw himself carrying another corpse down to Emily—this time a slight little form. "God," he begged, "not again."

And at that moment a very sleepy and bewildered Mont sat up and rubbed his eyes. "Where is I? Mistuh Tom, is I gonna get beat?"

"Oh no, Mont. I'm so glad you're all right. You are all right, aren't you?"

"Yassuh, I'se fine."

"How come you're way up here on this mountain?"

"Well, suh, you and Miss Emily done been so kind to me an' all, an' now you is so sad. Ain't no time to be a lookin' after a no-'count like me. Anyways, I heard dem friends of Missy's say dat it weren't right for me to be livin' wid her no more, an' dat I'se de reason Mistuh Jesse got hisself killed. Anyways, I figgered she'd be better off if'n I went off . . . Maybe a-lookin' at me makes her sad mos' likely."

"Mont, nothing could be further from the truth. We all like having you around and don't want you ever to go away. Why, Nathan and Jed are out in the dark right now trying to find you."

"Is dat for true? Y'all wants me to stay?"

"I promise you, it's the truth. But say, weren't you awful scared here by yourself tonight?"

"Oh, naw, suh! I wasn't 'lone nohow."

"What do you mean, not alone?"

"You know, Mistuh Tom, Massa Jesus, He be right here beside me, so I'se got no cause to be scared."

There was a thoughtful pause; then Tom said slowly, "Mont, I want you to be my partner from now on. It seems that there are some things we can teach each other. For now, let's go home. We don't want to worry Miss Emily anymore, and I expect she's been keeping our supper warm for us."

✦ CHAPTER 11 ✦

The Bella Union Hotel was not a fancy establishment, but neither was it a cheap saloon. A two-story affair that boasted decent food and clean beds for weary stagecoach travelers, it also attracted the business of some of the local families. Miners and cowboys, whose interests were more enticed by cheap liquor in less clean surroundings, would usually gather at the Diamondback or down at the Richbar.

So it was with some surprise that Alex McKenna noted the arrival of Byrd Guidett and Yancey into his place of business. They had been seen around town for the past few days and seemed to be minding their own business. An inquiry to Deputy Pettibone had brought the response that there was nothing Byrd could be charged with; if he caused no trouble, he was as free a citizen as the next man.

Byrd and Yancey went into the bar on the left side of the downstairs hallway, opposite the restaurant that opened on the right. McKenna watched from his place behind the counter but made no move to interfere or question their presence. He produced whiskey and glasses without comment.

✦ ✦ ✦

Tom Dawson walked into Bella Union, closely followed by Mont James. Tom and Mont had ridden over together to deliver Jesse's clothes to Parson Swift, and Tom intended to stop in for a drink before heading back. In deference to Emily's request, he sent Mont into the dining room for a lemonade rather than having the boy accompany him into the saloon.

Tom noted Byrd and Yancey seated at a table near the back of the bar, but he chose to ignore them. Instead, he stepped up and ordered his beer.

McKenna, like the name of his operation, was avowedly pro-Union. He and Tom fell to discussing the recent war news. Since the battle of Chickamauga, in which the casualties totaled almost forty thousand, the war had come to a virtual standstill. There had even been time to plan memorial services for those who had fought and died at Gettysburg. The dedication of the cemetery adjacent to the sleepy little Pennsylvania town was to have been scheduled for mid-October, but a conflict had arisen for the planned featured orator, Edward Everett, so the ceremony was postponed until November.

Neither man paid attention when Yancey got up from the table and went out the back door.

A minute later Byrd rose and walked to the front window. "Hey, Dawson, 'pears to me yer horse is loose. Didn't anybody learn ya to tie a knot?"

Tom looked over. Sure enough, Duncan was trotting off down the street as if he had been shooed away from the rail. Tom knew the horse had been securely tied. Grimacing at McKenna, he went to retrieve Duncan, stopping by the dining room long enough to tell Mont to remain there till he returned. Tom figured that the horse would make his way down the street as far as the first livery stable, where he would stop in expectation of a handful of grain.

✵ ✵ ✵

Byrd had remained at the window. When he saw Tom going down the street to retrieve his horse, Byrd turned and entered the dining room. "Come here a minute," he called harshly to Mont.

Mont looked scared and said nothing.

"Are ya deaf? I said come here, an' this is a white man talkin'."

Mont still hadn't found his speech, but he could find his feet. He jumped up and ran for the back door of the Bella Union, then skidded to a stop as Yancey appeared in the doorway. Turning around,

Mont tried to duck Byrd, who had followed close behind him. But Guidett grabbed the boy by the collar, picking him completely off the floor, and carried him into the saloon.

"Here, now," began McKenna, "what's this about? What'er ye aimin' to do with the boy?"

"Jest mind yer own business. This boy was s'posed to belong to me, and I aim to get some work outta him."

"Suppose ya get down there and shine my boots." With this he gave Mont a hard thrust to the floor. "What, no shine rag? I 'spect this'll do." He jerked Mont's shirt upward, ripping it apart and popping the buttons, then threw the cloth at the boy. "What? Nothin' to shine 'em with?"

Mont made as if to lick the cloth and apply it to Guidett's boot.

Byrd kicked him in the stomach and chest, propelling him across the floor so fast he skidded into a brass spittoon, where he lay breathing in short, pained gasps. "How could ya even *think* such a thing, boy? Nigger spit on a white man's boot? You'd best think again. Now, a white man's spit'd be proper for a white man's boots. Go on, reach on down in thar and get a big slug, then crawl over here and get to shinin'."

McKenna started to protest, but Byrd whirled around. "Jest keep yer mouth shut and yer hands on the bar. I'm collectin' on some winnin's, and I aim to get paid in full."

"Paid in full sounds like a lot to expect from a small boy, Byrd Guidett. Perhaps your account would get settled more to your satisfaction with me." Tom Dawson had returned and stood in the door of the saloon. He had taken in the scene at a glance, and his hand hovered near the Colt that hung at his side.

"Are ya fixin' to draw against me, Tom Dawson? Takin' the part of a nigger against a white man—why some folks'd be callin' you a nigger lover."

"Call me anything you like, Guidett, but touch that boy one more time and they'll be calling you dead."

Yancey moved crablike around the side wall till he was even with Byrd on the other side of the room and also facing Tom.

Byrd made as if to step forward and kick Mont again. His expectation was that this would goad Tom into drawing, and Byrd believed himself to be the better gunman. He also knew that McKenna could truthfully report Tom's threat, and in this community of largely pro-Southern sentiment, a verdict of self-defense would easily be obtained.

What he did not expect was that a very determined small boy would see the kick coming. Grabbing the spittoon, Mont hurled it and the contents into Byrd's face.

"What the—?" Byrd clawed at the slimy goo that clung to his face and beard. He dared not lash out now or attempt to draw, for he could only dimly see through the tobacco juice that burned his eyes.

Tom had indeed drawn his gun, but he swung it to cover Yancey, who put both hands up slowly and backed against the wall.

"Mister McKenna, will you be so kind as to remove Mister Guidett's weapon? Thank you. Now if you'll please hold it on his friend over there. I wouldn't want anything to interfere with Mister Guidett's receiving a full accounting of what he is owed."

So saying, Tom released the hammer of his own gun and, calling Mont to him, gave it to the boy to hold.

A wild look of delight spread over Byrd's face as he guessed Tom's intention. "I'll break you in two!" he shouted and lunged at Tom.

Tom sidestepped the jump easily, and Byrd plowed past him like a runaway locomotive, crashing into a table. Whirling around, Byrd made as if to jump at Tom again, but this time as Tom moved to one side, Byrd also pivoted and grabbed Tom's arm.

Pinning Tom's arms to his sides, Guidett lifted his adversary off the floor in a massive bear hug. This was known to be Byrd's favorite move. With it he had crushed men's ribs and made them cry for mercy before he allowed them to crumple to the floor.

But he had not reckoned with the wiry strength of Tom's arms and shoulders as he flexed his muscles and pushed Byrd's embrace away. In the slack thus obtained, Tom leaned his body backward in Byrd's grasp and bent forward suddenly, ducking his head. He drove the top of his forehead directly into Guidett's nose.

With a scream of infuriated pain, Byrd dropped his hold and grabbed his face with his hands. His nose was gushing blood.

Tom followed up his advantage by driving his right fist into

Byrd's midsection. This blow made Byrd back up a step, but as Tom closed in, Byrd raised his own clasped hands over his head, striking Tom over the left ear so hard he staggered back.

Byrd gave a wild cry, his face a fearful mask of gore and tobacco juice, and brought both his fists together on either side of Tom's head. Tom stumbled, his head spinning. Byrd closed in, clearly intending to apply his crushing hug again.

Tom knew he couldn't escape that clutch as easily this time, so he moved to step in toward Byrd at the moment when the cutthroat's arms were outstretched to encircle. Byrd was unprepared to ward off the blow from Tom's left. It worked even better than Tom anticipated, for as Byrd raised his head to apply his press, Tom's fist caught him in the throat.

Byrd backed up, gasping. His eyes were swelling shut. Again he threw himself at Tom, and this time Tom was unable to avoid the rush. Byrd's force hurled him back savagely against the counter of the bar, making him cry out at the stabbing pain from a breaking rib.

He tried to slip under Byrd's grasp, but Guidett followed him down to the floor, then jumped up for a leap that would land both his knees and all his weight on Tom's chest.

In that split second, sensing Byrd's gathering force preparing to spring, Tom reached out wildly with his arms and encountered the spittoon lying where it had rolled after being thrown by Mont. Tom's fingers closed over the rim, and in the next instant he drove it with all his remaining strength against the side of Byrd's head.

The impact snapped Byrd's head against the bar, sending a shower of blood through the air. The force of this strike was not great, but it was enough. Guidett had had difficulty breathing since the blow to his throat, and now he collapsed on top of Tom.

For a moment neither moved. Mont was crouched on the floor, biting his lip to keep from whimpering, Yancey slouched against the far wall, casting wishful glances toward the exit—a thought that McKenna discouraged with a negligent wave of the gun.

Finally, Byrd Guidett stirred, and a muffled voice underneath croaked, "Get this stinking mess off me—I'm about to be crushed!"

"Remove Guidett," directed McKenna to Yancey, "and mind that ye drag him faceup, so ye get no more blood on me floor!"

Yancey instantly obeyed, pulling the ugly heap away.

By the time Yancey had dragged Byrd to the front porch, he began to revive. Yancey helped Byrd to his feet. Then the two staggered outside, where Yancey doused Byrd's swollen face in the nearest horse trough.

Inside the saloon, McKenna insisted on helping Tom personally. The barman made Tom sit in a chair while he rubbed a towel soaked in whiskey over cuts on Tom's ears, forehead, and knuckles, while muttering to himself, "This is better than that nasty carbolic and smells nicer, too."

Tom tried to rise, but a stabbing pain in his back made him gasp and sit back down.

McKenna helped Tom remove his shirt, then bent him forward gently. "Aye, he's broke one o' yer short ribs, lad. 'Tis a good thing ye're as strong as an ox, or he would have crushed yer whole rib cage like an eggshell. As it is, ye'll be mighty tender for a spell, but ye'll soon be right as rain. Here, boy—" this was addressed to Mont— "run upstairs to me room, 'tis the one jist at the top, and bring a sheet off me bed."

Mont looked first to Tom for permission, and at his nod, ran upstairs.

✳ ✳ ✳

Mont wasn't sure what drew him to the window, but stepping past McKenna's rumpled bed, Mont looked down into the street. What he saw puzzled him, for he noticed a most unlikely conference. Mont saw Byrd get up from the horse trough and shake his head like a dog shakes water from its body. Then he turned as if to reenter Bella Union, violently throwing off Yancey's restraining hand.

Next Mont saw the two seemingly being addressed by someone on the boardwalk in front of the hotel. It looked as if Byrd started to argue, placed a boot on the step, then stopped. A moment later, Byrd and Yancey turned to walk down the dusty street leading out of town, with Byrd turning back twice and Yancey urging him along. But the one who had apparently ordered them out of town stayed out of Mont's view.

✳ ✳ ✳

When Mont returned with the sheet, McKenna tore a strip from it and, directing Tom to hold it under his arm, proceeded to wrap it around and around until, in Tom's words, he was "trussed up like a turkey."

"Do you have to make this so tight?" Tom complained. "I was having enough trouble breathing as it was."

"Aye, lad, 'tis for yer own good. We can't have that bone wanderin' around in ye. Give this but a week or so to knit, and ye can unwind it. Then ye'll be ready to fight again . . . and what a fight it was! I know of no man who's stood up to Byrd Guidett and lived." McKenna picked up the spittoon, now completely concave where it had connected with Byrd's skull, and shook his head ruefully. "A perfectly good spittoon ruined, and him still alive after, more's the pity."

"Yes, well, I only wanted him to leave Mont alone. I'm glad I didn't have to kill him to teach him that."

"Ye may regret it later. Byrd's head is hard in more ways than one, and he'll not like bein' bested in a fight. Ye'd best watch yer back trail, and keep yer wits aboot ye."

✳CHAPTER 12✳

Byrd waited until he judged that the last of the late arrivals had come. The hillside from which he watched not only overlooked the church but also gave him a view in both directions through town.

It was a frosty morning; his breath, as well as that of the bay horse on which he sat, was visible in ragged, steamy puffs. A fitful, lusterless sun was trying unsuccessfully to break through the overcast. It contributed no warmth to the day, only the promise that it would stay just above freezing.

The horses in the churchyard stood huddled together in little clumps for warmth, even normally fractious ones subdued in spirit. A row of horses still hitched to buggies and wagons stood in a row, tethered to a cable strung between two iron bolts in adjacent oaks.

I'll show those crackers how it is, Byrd thought, feeling his battered nose.

Occasionally he could hear the pump organ straining to produce a hymn, but with the doors and windows tightly shut against the cold, the sound was muffled. Byrd could not be sure that all the occupants of the church building were unarmed, bundled up as they were in heavy coats, but he considered it unlikely that any carried firearms.

"Too bad for them if'n they do," he muttered sarcastically.

He couldn't see Yancey from where he waited, but he knew Yancey was watching him. "I'm not gonna freeze my tail out here any

longer," he mumbled to his horse. "Let's get this show on the road."
He stood in his stirrups and waved his arm three times over his head.

Yancey broke from the cover of the creek bed next to the church property and covered the small slope to the building in a stiff lope. Both men knew that Yancey's approach could not be seen from any of the church's windows. Yancey waited to the side of the church's front doors and at the bottom of the steps, where he could duck around the corner and out of sight if anyone unexpectedly appeared.

Now! Byrd thought, adjusting his mask and drawing his Colt. He urged the horse down the hillside until at the bottom it was in direct line with the church door. "Eyowhh!" he yelled and drove his spurs into the bay's sides.

The startled horse leaped forward, bolting across the road, while Byrd fired three shots. His first went into the air, but his second and third bullets went through the upper panes of two of the tall church windows.

He was at the steps, where Yancey had already flung open the doors and ducked back to the side. Byrd's excited horse never even hesitated but jumped to the entrance in one bound, then past the doors and into the building itself. Byrd had to duck to keep from getting knocked off by the doorframe, but he came up shooting; everyone else in the building ducked, too, crying with fear as they dived for cover.

His next shot took out another window; then, in a flash of devilish inspiration, he took deliberate aim at the smokestack of the potbelly stove standing in the center of the twenty-by-thirty room. With a crash and a clang, the pipe parted at the joint nearest the ceiling, showering soot on everything. The pipe folded up on itself as if exhausted from having stood so long and collapsed into the center aisle. Grayish brown smoke poured from the stove into the little room. Only the high ceiling prevented the scene from being instantly obscured.

Byrd next turned his attention toward the pump organ at the left front of the room, where a slight, gray-haired lady had been playing. He shot the last bullet in the revolver directly through the side of the instrument, which erupted in a clatter of keys and stops, then gave the groan of a dying cow. The organist leaped backward off the organ bench. There she cowered—a rumpled heap of skirts and wounded dignity.

Byrd transferred the empty weapon to his holster and drew another from his belt. Circling the prancing horse in the space between the door and the ruined stovepipe, he noted with satisfaction that all the women were huddled down between the pews, covering the heads of small children, and not a few of the men had ducked under cover as well.

In this first moment of shocked silence, Parson Swift, who had been seated on the small platform behind the pulpit, rose. "What's the meaning of this outrage?"

"Shut up and sit down, you old Bible-thumper! I'm here to deliver a message, an' it won't hurt my feelin's none to shoot you first!" So saying, Byrd cocked the pistol and leveled it at the preacher's chest. "An' that goes for any of the rest of you what feels like interruptin' me!" His voice croaked awkwardly.

"This here message is to any folk what feels like lickin' them Yankee soldier boys' boots. Don't do it! They may think they got a lock on this state, but they got another think comin'! We aim to make them Yankees think that their hides'd be a whole lot safer outta these hills for good, an' that goes for any other nigger lovers in these here parts! An' don't count on no blue bellies to protect ya; they cain't even protect their own selves!"

Looking right into the muzzle of the gun, the parson said calmly, "Are you quite through?"

Byrd's pistol remained pointed at the parson for an instant longer. Then, whirling his horse around, he galloped out the door and down the steps, firing three more times as he did so.

✢ ✢ ✢

The waters of the little cove were so deep that the dark blue color of the Pacific Ocean did not lighten at all as it swept against the rocky headland. The small peninsula was covered with cypress trees, which further sheltered the south-facing bay from storms.

Onshore a fire was burning, producing a thick, greasy plume that reached into the afternoon sky. Beached in the cove was half a carcass of a gray whale, the other half having already been drawn up the short slope to the try-pots. The teams of mules that pulled the fifty-foot-long strips of blubber balked when first introduced to the smells and sights of the whaling station, but they soon discovered that the footing was more sure and the loads easier to move than the cinnabar ore they had lately been hauling on steep mountain paths.

Robert Mullins didn't believe he could ever get used to the whaling station. The oily film that covered everything in the area disgusted him, and the view of the partially stripped whale with its ribs exposed and its blood coagulating in little pools on the shore was obscene.

And this rube of a captain is not cooperating either, thought Mullins.

"Captain Alexander," Mullins tried again, "I really need your assistance. You have been recommended to me as a trustworthy individual whose sympathies are correct. Surely you can see that the transportation of arms from San Francisco could be accomplished much more easily and safely from this point on the coast to the central mountains than overland past the many forts of the valley."

"I'm certain that what you say is correct, Mister Miller," replied the captain, unaware of Mullins' real name. "But why come to me at all? I merely operate this whaling station for Mister George Hearst, who owns this ranch. I'm not an arms merchant, nor a shipper of arms. I came to this coast to get away from the war and ply my trade in peace. As you can see," he said with a sweep of his hand, "I only make war on whales."

Mullins replied calmly enough, although inside he fumed like the try-pots, "I've shown you the cuff links and explained how I came to have both of them. I've also shown you that I can pay. What more do you need?"

Alexander pulled his hat down over his forehead until its brim almost touched his hawklike nose, and he gazed sternly down at Mullins. "I've heard your story, all right, and I concede that your tale about one of your hirelings having mistakenly killed Mister James in a drunken brawl is too wild for any pea-brained Yankee to have concocted.

"Nevertheless," he continued, "Mister James should have had in his possession certain information that would confirm your status and sustain your worthiness to be privy to the name of my associate in San Francisco."

"I've already explained that we know how to locate the papers. It's merely a matter of doing so in a way that will avoid unnecessary interest on the part of federal agents."

"I applaud your caution, Mister Miller, but its very fact should help you to understand my position. You say that you want to arm some miners who will seize the gold production for the Confederacy and then throw the Unionists out of the valley. Even if such a program were of interest to me, you must understand that there are larger wheels turning in the world than your little machinery. Plans are at work to deny the Northern oppressors the use of any ports on the Pacific Coast. Do you catch my drift?"

"Indeed I do, Captain, indeed. But can we not begin now to work toward that glorious day and the inclusion of California in its rightful place under the Stars and Bars?"

"Not without your papers, Mister Miller. You must have those papers!"

✳ ✳ ✳

The two boys darted eagerly from tree to tree in their play, swooping and turning like a pair of swallows in flight. The morning was perfect for play—clear and crisp after the first snow of the year had left only an inch or two of pure white powder on the ground. The snow would not remain past noon; indeed, it had already slipped from the tree branches, but right now was a good time to practice tracking skills, mingled with a rousing game of hide-and-seek.

Nathan and Mont might have missed having Jed around if they'd stopped to think about it. But for the time being they were having too much fun to regret that the older boy, who was usually their leader, was home with the measles.

"He must rest quietly, boys, and he can't do that with you whooping around the place, so off you go. Besides, if you catch the measles, you'll have to be quiet soon enough yourselves, so get out and get to playing," Emily instructed.

They hadn't needed much urging.

"Look here, Mont. This is a rabbit's track. An' over here, slippin' up alongside Mister Rabbit, is an ol' fox."

"I hopes Mister Rabbit done made it home safe," commented Mont.

"Me too. An' lookit, see where this deer went by. Let's see, he stood right here nibblin' on this bush. Then somethin' musta spooked him; look at the jump he made. Clean over here, and then off he run!"

They moved from discovery to discovery throughout the morning as if the world were newly created for their enjoyment. At the juncture of Sandy Creek, they turned to follow its course mountainward into newer and less familiar territory.

Presently they came to a gooseberry thicket, where a few little runways already imprinted in the snow gave evidence of the passage of a flock of quail. From the center of the thicket a soft clucking, churring sound could be heard.

"My pa always says, said, he . . ." Nathan choked.

"Go on," urged his friend gently. "What he done said?"

Nathan drew himself up proudly. "My pa said that on cold mornin's or right after a snow, the quail family always stays close to home. See, they get right in the middle of their patch of berry thorns; they keep each other warm, and they stay good and safe that way."

"Your pa was sure enough a smart man an' a kind one," observed Mont, "an' he made me feel right at home wid you'uns. Jes' like the li'l quail mus' feel in de middle of his fambly."

Nathan nodded sadly. "I miss him somethin' fierce, Mont. Sometimes I forget that he's gone, and I think of somethin' I want to run and show him, and then I remember and . . . Anyways, I like rememberin' things he taught me. When I tell 'em to you, it makes me feel better somehow, almost like he was here himself.

"Say—" Nathan brightened—"I'm gettin' hungry. How 'bout you? Ma packed us some lunch, but I reckon that we could have part of it now and save the rest for later."

"Sounds mighty fine to me. What we got?"

Nathan rummaged through the burlap potato sack he had been carrying slung over his shoulder. "Let's see. Here's some cold chicken

101

and a piece of cheese each an' some crackers. An' here—" he paused for effect—"here's provision for us mighty trackers. Brown sugar and butter sandwiches!"

The two boys sat back-to-back on a boulder at the head of the gooseberry patch, where they could see partway down the valley that was their home. The fresh-baked bread was thickly sliced and spread with home-churned butter. The brown sugar filling made a crunching sound in the still morning air, and the delicious sweet taste complemented their camaraderie.

When they finished eating, Nathan suggested they get their game of hide-and-seek under way. "Now, we need some boundaries."

"What's a bound'ree?" inquired Mont.

"You know, markers to show how far you can go to hide so's the game is fair. Like, let's make this rock the farthest up the hill you can go, and the creek down yonder is the bottom. On the east side we'll say—" he studied the terrain with a judicious eye—"that there big cedar tree and on the west that pile of rocks yonder."

"What's safe?"

Nathan carefully inspected again. "It needs to be somewhere's right in the middle. I know. You see that bunch of ol' buckeye trees twisted around together? Right in the middle of that."

"Who's gonna be 'it' first?" asked Mont as they walked down the hill toward the clump of buckeyes.

"Let's peg for it. First one as can stick this barlow knife in that buckeye trunk gets to choose."

Nathan produced his pocketknife, and the two took turns trying to make it stick in the twisted wood.

On his third try, Nathan succeeded. "All right, you hide first an' I'll seek. We'll leave that knife there to mark home. I'll count to fifty, an' then I'll come lookin' for you."

"Make it a hunnert," begged Mont. "I wants to hide real good!"

"All right, a hundred it is," replied Nathan. So saying, he turned his face to the tree trunk and began counting loudly: "One, two, three . . ."

"Count slower!" Mont yelled back over his shoulder as he circled around the clearing, hoping to confuse his pursuer before striking out to the west as quietly as the scrunching snow permitted. Once he stopped to throw a rock back into the middle of a brush pile; then he turned to run, chuckling quietly to himself at the trick he was playing on his friend.

Mont knew exactly where he was headed—for the westernmost "boundary" of rock had attracted his attention while they were eating. Directly in front of the heap of boulders an oak tree had fallen across a buckeye, and the two trees had crashed to the ground together. The gnarled buckeye, being all twists and turns, would not lie flat but made a little archway over which the branches of the oak spread a partial cover.

As he approached his chosen hiding place, he slowed, even though behind him he heard, ". . . eighty-five, eighty-six . . ."

Mont selected his path carefully now, leaping from a rock to a pile of brush and from the brush to a clump of gooseberries and from there to the oak's trunk, then down behind it into the space left vacant by the buckeye's fall.

Mont stood for a moment, noting with satisfaction that he could see no footprint nor any other sign of his passing in the last hundred or so feet of his path. *'Spec that'll pause 'im some,* he thought as he settled down to wait.

Nathan was just finishing his count. "Ninety-nine, one hundred! Ready or not, here I come!" So saying, he took off directly east, toward the sound made when Mont had thrown the rock. Since Mont had circled around that way before taking off west, Nathan was supported in his choice by the sight of Mont's footprints in the snow.

I'm hot on his trail already, thought Nathan. He jumped on a chunk of granite to survey the scene for possible hiding places. South and east he noticed a clump of brush that looked promising and set off in that direction. He remembered to watch over his shoulder in case he was wrong and Mont broke from cover to run for "home."

Nathan skidded to a stop in front of the brush pile. Carefully he circled it, looking for Mont's tracks before his own had obscured the trail. All around the suspected hiding place the ground was clear and covered with a blanket of unmarked snow. Nathan stopped to scratch his head in thought. *He can't have come this way unless he flew.* He spotted a nearby scrubby oak with a fork about eight feet off the ground and decided to try it as a new observation post.

✳ ✳ ✳

Mont poked his head ever so carefully up from behind the buckeye and heard Nathan moving off to the east. He had just about decided to risk a dash toward the embedded knife when he saw Nathan climb the oak, and from his perch in the cleft of the tree, begin a slow scan of the countryside. Mont ducked back down.

✳ ✳ ✳

Nathan had noticed the jumble of buckeye and oak, but from his angle there didn't appear to be any space that offered a hiding place. Instead, he decided that a growth of manzanita near the cedar that marked the eastern edge of their game looked promising. He jumped clear of the tree into a little pile of snow at its base and ran off to investigate the new possibility.

✳ ✳ ✳

Mont remained hidden. He couldn't tell if Nathan had left his lookout or not, but he didn't want to offer any movement as a target. He amused himself by making a little pile of stones behind the log, all the while listening carefully for the sounds that would indicate his friend was approaching. Presently, he heard them. There was the crunch of boots on snow and the sharp crack of a branch breaking underfoot. Mont huddled down into the hillside, trying to breathe even quieter and willing his pursuer to go away. Mont strained his ears but no longer could hear Nathan's footsteps. Had he succeeded in fooling his friend?

Mont eased his cramped legs just a little and thought about raising up once more to survey the hill. At that moment, a sound from behind him made him freeze.

Then right over his head a booming voice exclaimed, "Wal' what's this here? If it ain't a runaway nigger, catched at last!" A brawny hand grasped Mont's coat collar and lifted him out of concealment, then turned him around in midair, bringing him face-to-face with Byrd Guidett!

Mont kicked and struggled and tried to scream, but a huge hand clamped over his mouth, and all his efforts only got him a clout over the ear with another heavy fist.

✳ ✳ ✳

Nathan had explored the area around the eastern boundary. He thought about climbing another tree, but none close by had branches near enough to the ground for this to be done easily. Remembering what he had seen of the fallen trees, he put his hands together in a gesture of anticipation. "Sure enough, he's fooled me! Why I bet he's fixin' to make a dash for home right now."

With this thought, Nathan began running as fast as he could back across the area of their play. When he reached the tree with his pocketknife stuck in it, he was pleased that Mont hadn't gotten there ahead of him, so he continued on toward the west.

Nathan rounded the end of the oak's stump at full speed and almost collided with Byrd, who was threatening Mont with another blow if he didn't stay still. Seeing Nathan he exclaimed, "What's this? Another one?"

"Let him go!" Nathan shouted at Byrd. "You let my friend go!"

"You jest come on over here to me, boy. I'm havin' a little talk with this nig . . . I mean, yer friend here. Whyn't ya join us?"

Mont twisted free for an instant and called out, "Run, Nathan, run!"

Nathan took one more look and decided that getting away to get help was the best he could do. He turned to make a run for his house, but he hadn't gone more than three steps when Yancey stepped out in his path with his boot knife in his hand. "You'd best do as the man says and walk on over thar nice and easy like. It ain't real comfortable tryin' to run with his here knife a-stickin' betwixt yer shoulders, so ya'd best walk nice and slow."

"My uncle is coming to get us. He should be here anytime now. You'd better let us go right now."

Nathan's attempted bluff was good, but it had the wrong effect.

105

Yancey looked at Byrd and raised his eyebrows. "Could be the boy's tellin' the truth. Stead of tyin' him up, what say I jest cut his throat and be done with it?"

Mont stiffened in horror in Byrd's grasp, and Nathan stood rooted to the spot, too frightened to run, when Byrd replied, "Naw. That'd raise the whole countryside after us. If we ain't got time to tie 'im to a tree, we'll jest have to take 'im along. There ain't nothin' here to show they was around anyways, so no one will know what's happened to 'em nohow."

Yancey's lips parted in a sinister grin. "We got 'em, Byrd. We finally got 'em."

✦ CHAPTER 13 ✦

Like a deer carcass across the saddlebow, Nathan hung head downward over the horse's withers. They were moving at a fast trot—deliberately, not in headlong flight. The bouncing motion with the saddle horn in his stomach made it hard for Nathan to breathe. Even if he hadn't been scared to death of Yancey's knife, he wouldn't have been able to yell for help. Nathan tried to concentrate on getting air into his tortured lungs and after that to pay attention to the direction of their travel. He could tell that they were skirting the edge of Carver Peak and moving along parallel to, but some distance from, the side of the trail that led to the mining town of Tailholt.

Nathan tried to think what would happen to them. He believed that his uncle would come in search of them if they weren't home by nightfall. But they hadn't left any word about which direction their play would take them. Nor had they been able to leave any sign showing where they had been. Even if Tom located the trail of the two horses, how was he to know that it had anything to do with the disappearance of the two boys? Nathan began to pray silently, *Dear God, help us!*

Mont, meanwhile, was unconscious. He had attempted to struggle in Byrd's grasp, then tried to persuade the outlaws to release Nathan. But all he got for his efforts was a gruff "shut up!" from Byrd and a clout alongside his ear that had knocked him senseless. Byrd's grip kept the boy from falling headfirst to the ground.

The two outlaws drew up at the head of the canyon that sloped down around the northern flank of Shadow Ridge toward Tailholt.

"Shall I kill 'em and dump 'em here?" asked Yancey, indicating the trembling Nathan.

"Naw, this is too close to our real track, an' anyways, Mullins may know of some use for the brat. Jest you be sure of this—" Byrd addressed Nathan by sidling his horse close and yanking Nathan's head up by the hair—"if'n ya cause us any mite of trouble, ye're nothin' but crow bait. Is that right clear to ya, boy?"

Nathan gave the tiniest of nods at Byrd's scowling face, and then his head was flung back down to bounce off the horse's shoulder.

Yancey motioned to the trail. "What say we split up here, jest in case Dawson do get after us?"

Byrd felt his nose and head for a moment, then remarked, "Maybe I been lookin' at this thing all wrong. I got a real hankerin' to meet up with Tom Dawson again. Maybe I oughta go back an' make it easy for him to find me!"

For a moment Yancey looked genuinely worried that Byrd's temper and his desire for revenge would result in their getting caught. He thought for an instant, then replied carefully, "You could sure 'nuff do that, Byrd, but we better not wait on gettin' the boy to tell us where them papers is hid. You already know what an uproar Mullins is in. Jest hold on for a bit. You'll get yer chance soon."

Guidett looked as if he wanted to argue but apparently saw the wisdom of Yancey's advice. He indicated with a jerk of his head that Yancey should take the right side of the canyon, while he and the still unconscious Mont rode down the left.

Now Nathan was more confused than ever. *What papers?* he wondered miserably. And they were plotting to kill his uncle. An instant before, he had wanted nothing more in the whole world than for Tom to come riding up. Now he desperately wanted his uncle to stay away! And who was Mullins? The only Mullins he knew was the fat, self-important storekeeper. Surely *he* couldn't be mixed up in this—why, he was one of the church leaders! Of course, he reminded himself, his father had never cared for the man, said he "gave himself airs."

These thoughts ran through Nathan's mind as the jolting ride resumed. The trail they followed became narrower and steeper until the ground over which Nathan hung suspended had dropped away two hundred feet below! Now Nathan tried to hold his breath on purpose for fear that even inhaling might overbalance him and send him plummeting into the depths of the White River Canyon. He tried closing his eyes but immediately felt dizzy and sick to his stomach and in danger of losing his precarious perch.

Yancey remarked dryly, "Don't go to pukin' on me, boy, or I'll figger that this here canyon is a powerful good spot to drop ya inta!"

When the gorge finally bottomed out and widened as it neared the town of Tailholt, Yancey directed his horse down the remaining six feet of bank that separated the cliff face from the river bottom. The river was dry at this time of year but would soon enough be an outlet for the rains to find their way downward into the San Joaquin Valley.

Yancey's gelding moved silently through the soft sand toward the farther bank. There a dense thicket of cottonwoods obscured the view of the river from riders on the Tailholt road. The bay stopped of his own accord as if they had done this maneuver before. Yancey cocked his head first one direction and then the other as he listened for travelers before crossing the road.

Nathan felt a surge of hope. They must be close to the town where there was a little hotel and a few businesses. Tailholt was a rough mining camp, but there were surely some good people there who would help him escape from this killer. If only he could give some sign, let someone know! But there wasn't anyone around to hear if he yelled, and trussed up as he was, he couldn't hope to make a run for it.

A bellowing voice floating up toward their place of concealment froze Yancey's intended movement to urge his mount over the bank. Someone was coming up the road! As quickly as Nathan's spirits soared they were brought to earth again by the cold sharp pain of Yancey's knife pressing in behind his ear. In a threatening voice made all the more sinister by its hoarse whisper, Nathan heard Yancey murmur, "Not a peep, d'ya hear? I'd as soon stick ya as look at ya."

The bellowing voice grew louder, and then a creaking was heard and an intermittent popping—a bullwhacker and his team of oxen. "Curse your hides you ill-gotten sons of perdition." *Crack!* "Can't ya move any faster?" *Crack!* "I'll sell ya for hides and tallow right where ya stand!" *Crack!*

This fountain of curses and whip-cracking noises sounded as if it would pass by and go on up the hill, but all at once it stopped directly in front of Yancey and Nathan.

The drover could be heard exclaiming, "Well, how are ya, ya old horse thief?" This was apparently directed to someone whose approach down the road had been masked by the bullwhacker's carrying-on.

Whoever the second party was, he was considerably more soft-spoken than the drover, and so only half the conversation could be heard. "Ya don't say? Up Havilah way? I thought that was all played out years ago."

There was a pause, then, "Not me, hoss, not me. Why, these four-legged devils are sure enough like stone, but at least they move when I tickle 'em!" *Crack!* "Show me the hard rock mine that'll do that, and I'll join ya."

The unseen and unheard second party to this conversation must have been riding a horse, for it chose this moment to nicker, and quite unexpectedly, Yancey's gelding answered it!

Yancey immediately leaned forward over its neck to silence it with a restraining hand, and the point of his knife pressed deeper into Nathan's flesh. The boy gasped but remained still as a tiny trickle of blood began running down the side of his face and dripping off his nose. Both Yancey and Nathan held their breath—the one in fear of discovery and the other in fear of death.

A moment more and both released quiet sighs, for from the road they heard, "Jim Dobber is dead? Ol' 'Mud' Dobber hisself? Why, I'da thought he was indestructible. Measles, ya say?"

At last the bullwhacker announced, "Well, ol' cuss, we'd best be movin'. I want to top the grade afore sundown. Go along, ya useless lumps!" *Crack!* "Rattle your hocks afore I cut out your brand marks an' sell ya for strays!" *Crack!* "Be seein' ya, ol' cuss!"

A short while later Yancey crept up to the edge of the cut and noted that the road was clear in both directions. Occasionally a shouted curse and the pop of the drover's whip could still be heard echoing down the canyon, but it was getting fainter and farther away.

"Ya done real good, boy. You was right smart to set so quiet. That loudmouthed teamster may figger he can tickle his ox real clever with that fool whip, but jest you mind how good I can tickle with this little play-pretty of mine." So saying, he drew the flat of his knife across Nathan's neck once more for good measure, and then they rode on across the road.

✳ ✳ ✳

Mont was just beginning to come around. His head hurt, and his bound wrists and ankles ached. He had no idea where he was or where Byrd was taking him. But he was smart enough to realize that any movement or sound might get him clobbered again, so he remained still, pretending unconsciousness.

Byrd had chosen the easier side of the canyon for himself to travel, so Mont had awakened to the view of a gently sloping hillside below him. It seemed to him that they had been traveling forever. In fact, the afternoon was drawing to a chilly close when Byrd Guidett muttered, "Whoa" to his big bay horse, and they stopped in the shadows of the ridge's northwestern fringes.

Below them was the gold-mining community of Tailholt. Its thousand or so inhabitants were already indoors, away from the wind that had an increasing bite to it. In some of the windows the glow of lanterns was beginning to appear. Mont looked wistfully toward the warm, snug little homes.

"Awake finally, eh?" grunted Byrd. "You ain't the only one wishin' to get inside by a fire and hunker down with some decent food." Then, as if even this brief observation had betrayed too much gentleness, he shoved Mont roughly off the horse onto the hard ground with a thud. "Wal', we ain't goin' to no nice warm cabin, see? An' if'n ya don't tell us what we want to know and that right quick, I might jest tie you up to a rock and see how soon some bear comes to make a meal off'n ya, if'n ya don't freeze to death first."

Both man and boy were chilled and stiff by the time Yancey and Nathan rejoined them.

"Whar ya been?" Byrd said grumpily. "You musta stopped for supper, and me a-freezin' my rear off out here!"

"Get down off yer high horse, Byrd Guidett," Yancey threw back. "You know'd we had to take the long pull around Tailholt, besides pickin' our way down that canyon. An' then I had to wait near an hour to cross the road. Some bullwhacker freightin' to Keyesville met up with some'un comin' down, and they went to palaverin' right in front of me! An' what am I s'posed to do, ride on acrost sayin', 'Pardon me, boys, whilst I get to my hideout, an' pay no mind to this trussed-up brat here'?"

Even Byrd was taken aback by Yancey's tone. "They didn't see ya then?"

"'Course not! Now, are we gonna stay here shootin' off our mouths, or are we gonna get on the trail?"

When they had ridden into the hills some mile and a half, they came to a wide expanse of shale rock with no dirt covering. Carefully they began picking their way across the dangerous surface until at last they rode off onto broken ground about a half mile from where they had last made a track.

Yancey passed his reins to Byrd and slipped off his horse, leaving Nathan to balance across the gelding with even greater difficulty. As Byrd rode and led Yancey's mount, Yancey moved along behind, smoothing out the sign of their passing with a handful of brush. He did this for perhaps another four hundred yards until satisfied that even if someone were able to trace them as far as the shale, their path after that would be impossible to pick up.

Byrd paused long enough for Yancey to mount again; then both men urged their horses upward at a good pace.

✳ ✳ ✳

Nathan thought with a shudder that they were now climbing Shadow Ridge itself. Somewhere on these lonely heights his father had died. He also knew that somewhere to the east awaited his home and his mother, but this cold, inhospitable, and sinister mountain lay in between!

✳ ✳ ✳

The way the cave appeared was startling to Nathan. He was amazed at the suddenness with which the opening seemed to be right under-foot, where there had previously been solid granite mountainside.

The western rim had grown increasingly steep and barren for the last hour of the ride, with no features to attract anyone's atten-tion. No entrance of any kind was visible—no boulder-strewn lip, no telltale shadow. What existed was a slightly flattened area—no more than a bench on the slope and so near the tip that it seemed too small to contain anything worth investigating. Right inside this flattened space was the mouth of hell . . . or so it seemed. A gaping black hole, at first a vertical shaft, resolved itself into a sloping entryway down into the earth.

The level bench near the mountain's peak coincided with an outcropping of limestone. This slight declivity caught the runoff and snowmelt, which gradually melted away the limestone, leaving a near-perpendicular crater. Sometime later an earthquake had col-lapsed a portion of the edge, and that occurrence, combined with still later landslides, had provided access to the depths.

Byrd's horse sniffed the air over the opening as if to say, "This looks familiar, but I'm still not sure I like it." Then he stepped down-ward into the granite rubble that formed the ramp.

Once down the short slanting heap of debris, the cave's entrance disappeared almost immediately under a granite roof. Just inside this roof the cavern made a sharp turn to the right, so even though the crater was exposed to sunlight, very little reached the interior of the cave past the first few feet.

Byrd reached out toward the wall and grasped a lantern that sat on a rocky ledge just level with a man on horseback. Fishing around in his shirt pocket for an instant, he removed a match, which he struck on the rough wall and applied to the wick.

The warm yellow glow revealed a level floor of trampled gravel and a crude barricade of branches that blocked the entrance from the first bed of the tunnel. Across the rude fence were two more horses that whinnied a greeting to the two ridden by the outlaws.

Interested in spite of his aching muscles and his fear, Nathan raised up for a look. The horses may not have been signaling to their equine counterparts after all but reacting to the presence of Mont and Nathan. Nathan recognized both animals as having been stolen from their ranch!

Byrd and Yancey stepped from their mounts, and Yancey pulled aside two rails of the barricade. They led their horses in among the other two, with the boys still hanging over the saddles. Once through the opening Yancey replaced the fence, and Byrd yanked both children to the ground. With a pocketknife he slit the rope that tied their ankles but left their hands bound. "Get up," he growled roughly, gesturing for the two to precede him deeper into the cave.

Yancey lit a lantern and began to unsaddle the horses as Byrd led Mont and Nathan over another fence at the rear of the cavern. The glow from his lamp pushed back the darkness just far enough for them to see that the room they were leaving was as large as a small barn and obviously well suited for that purpose. Along one side of the passage was a channel in the rock that was filled with water like a cistern. The pool of rainwater that had formed this cave was still present, but its location was now below the surface. As the tunnel narrowed and angled downward, the pool's overflow continued down into the mountain, as it had for ages past, and formed the tunnel through which they walked.

Mont's feet had evidently been bound more tightly than Nathan's for he was having difficulty walking. His stumble to the fence had been managed clumsily, and now, just on the other side of it, he fell.

"My feet!" he exclaimed. "They's all needles!"

"Get up and move, ya little varmint! Do ya think I'm gonna carry ya?" With that Byrd grabbed Mont by the collar and jerked him to his feet. "Now walk!"

"Come on," encouraged Nathan. "Lean against me. I'll help you."

So saying, Mont stumbled next to Nathan, and the two lurched down the passageway.

The cave had become both narrower and lower after exiting the room for the horses; now it opened out again into a space of room-sized proportions. Byrd lifted his lantern as they entered; they had evidently arrived at the gang's living quarters. A crudely constructed fire pit stood along one wall, the surface completely blackened with soot. Black streaks ran upward until they disappeared into the shadows of the craggy ceiling, where a crevice leading to the surface provided natural ventilation.

A pile of supplies, cans of beans, and a flour barrel were jumbled together in one corner, while a heap of empty cans and other rubbish made up a garbage dump in another. Along two walls were bed frames with wooden sides and cross-laced webbing made of leather. These meager belongings and a small table with two chairs standing in the center of the open place comprised the entire furnishings of the room.

On the wall opposite the way they had entered were two dark holes that showed as exits. Into one ran the underground stream that had passed through this cavern along one wall and which could be heard gurgling into the passage beyond. The other opening was somewhat uphill from the rest of the cave—another stream of water had at one time flowed into this room, but it had since dried up.

Byrd gestured for the boys to sit down in the chairs, and he proceeded to light a fire in the fire pit, igniting some kindling that had been set there before. As this caught, he added small oak branches, and soon the air became noticeably warmer. He then scooped up a coffeepot full of water from the stream and set it on a flat rock next to the blaze.

Yancey came in from tending the horses just as Byrd dumped a double handful of ground coffee into the boiling water. He tossed a can of beans to Yancey, and both men deftly opened the tops with their knives and used the knife blades to eat with. Byrd poured himself a cup of coffee and then poured one for Yancey. All this fixing and eating and pouring had been done without a single word being spoken and without any acknowledgment of the boys.

Nathan endured the smell of the beans and the aroma of the coffee as long as he could, then remarked timidly, "Please, may we have some food, too?"

Byrd flung his now empty can onto the rubbish pile and towered menacingly over the boys. "You two are a hull mess o' trouble. We got little as it is, an' not to be wasted on the likes of *you*." He raised his arm as if to strike Nathan for asking.

But Yancey interrupted. "Hold on, Byrd. 'Member, they gotta be able to talk here directly, so we'd best feed 'em some."

Byrd looked as if he begrudged them so much as one mouthful, but he opened one more can of beans and unceremoniously dumped the contents on the table. After cutting their hands free, he remarked, "There it is. Now go ta eatin' an' don't waste one bean."

The boys scooped up the tiny supper and licked their fingers.

"Next I suppose you'll be wantin' milk to drink or some o' my coffee." As the two small friends looked up hopefully, Byrd concluded, "Well, ain't that jest too bad? Get on over an' lap up some water like the two scrawny curs you are."

Leaving one lighted lantern on the table, Byrd took the other in his meaty hand and growled at the boys to follow him. He led them over to the dry side passage. It was a space no bigger than a pantry, a shaft reaching upward and into the dark, out of reach of the lamplight.

Thrusting them inside, he gave them a warning. "Don't try to run off, see? You cain't get up the shaft, an' if'n I catch ya tryin', I'll give Yancey—" he jerked this thumb over his shoulder—"a chance to go to carvin' on ya with his toad sticker. Ya know, they say the Comanch can peel a man's hide like skinnin' a spud. Wal', Yance there will make ya *wish* them Injuns had you instead!" He left, taking the lantern with him and leaving the boys in total darkness and abject misery.

☀ CHAPTER 14 ☀

It was late afternoon before Emily noticed that the boys had been gone longer than she expected. She had been busy all day, alternating farm chores with household cleaning and stops to visit Jed in his sickroom. He was comfortable enough, but his fever came and went, and Emily spent much of the day sponging his forehead with cool water and bringing him cups of tea with sugar when the chills were on him. Near sundown, he slept, and Emily sank into the rocking chair near the fire, exhausted.

"Where can Nathan and Mont be?" she mused. "It's getting cold outside, and I can't imagine that the lunch I packed would keep them from coming home for supper." The thought of supper reminded her that she had a pot of soup simmering in the kitchen, and so with a resigned sigh she rose and went to check on it.

Through the kitchen window she heard hoofbeats and looked out to see Tom ride into the yard on Duncan. His hat was pushed back on his head in a jaunty manner, and he was grinning as he pulled saddle and bridle from the horse and gave it a good-natured swat to turn it into the corral. He disappeared for a moment as he walked to the front door of the house, and then, as she expected, she heard his knock and a shout: "Emily, it's me, Tom."

She called out, "Come on in, Tom," then returned to the front room to meet him.

"Emily," he began without preamble, "guess what? They paid me the whole amount in gold. And that cavalry officer they brought along to inspect the horses said—" he drew himself up in military fashion and puffed out his chest to support an imaginary load of medals—"'Son, these are the finest mounts I've seen this side of the Mississippi. We'll take as many more as you can deliver—and just as soon as you can have them ready.' 'Yes, sir, Colonel,' I said, 'we'll sure have them for you.' Where are the boys? I want to tell them how good we did."

"They aren't back from playing yet. I shooed them out of the house because Jed has come down with the measles. He's been in bed all day and been running a fever, but he's asleep now and doing all right, I think."

"Measles, eh? Say, that can be pretty serious. Have you ever had them?"

"Yes, when I was just a little girl. Have you ever had measles?"

"Same with me, I guess. I must have had them about Jed's or maybe Nathan's age. I felt pretty rotten for a week or so and broke out with a terrific set of spots, but then I got over it pretty quick. How about the other two? Any sign of them catching it?"

"No, not so far, although three children over at the school have had it, so I'm almost positive these three have had an equal chance. Really, the reason I sent them off today was so I could get some work done while it stayed quiet for Jed to rest. Then, too, if they are going to be cooped up with measles, I thought it would be better for them to run off a little excitement first."

"Do we need to get a doctor?"

"I did talk to Doc Welles, and he said Jed just needed rest and good food. He said kids seem to do all right as long as they keep warm and still and don't get pneumonia. He did say that it was a lot tougher on adults. But enough about measles; tell me more about your great horse trading!"

Tom paused as if gathering his thoughts before going on. Then he began in a halting voice and a more serious tone, "Emily, on the ride to Fort Tejon and back . . . well, on the trip I had a chance to do some thinkin'."

"Yes, Tom—thinking about what?"

"Well, you know I feel responsible for you and the boys and all. I mean, not that I mind or anything, but, you know, I want to see you taken care of. Do you understand what I'm saying?"

"No, Tom, I'm not sure that I do."

Flustered, Tom began to speak, stopped, then finally tried again. "You see, since we made out so well with the horses, and since it looks like we got a steady market, with the money being good and all, I was just thinkin' . . ."

"What, Tom? What are you trying to say?"

Tom drew a deep breath and plunged ahead. "It's this way. What with this sale and the prospects of more to come, there's plenty of gold put by for you and the boys to go back to Missouri now. You could go back and buy you a place of your own. Pay cash for it, too. I should have known you wouldn't want to be moving back in with your folks and imposing on them. Well, now you don't have to. You can get a nice house, and I can send back more money right along as I get more strings broke, and . . . why, Emily, whatever is the matter?" Tom stopped speaking when he noticed that Emily's expression had changed and she appeared ready to burst.

"Ooh, you, you *dunderhead*! Didn't I tell you before that this is my home now? I wouldn't want to go back to Missouri if I could go as the Queen of Sheba. Get a place of my own, indeed! I *have* a place of my own, Tom Dawson, and it's here, right here! And to think I thought you . . . you were—ooh!"

"What, Emily, you thought what?"

"Just never mind, Tom. There's some soup on the stove. Help yourself while I go check on Jed. Then you might go out and holler for the boys if you've still a mind to be *helpful*. It's getting dark and past suppertime."

✷ ✷ ✷

Tom went out to the kitchen, shaking his head and muttering as he went. Who could understand women? Everything he'd said was perfectly reasonable, even carefully thought out, and look how she'd reacted! And what else could she have possibly thought he meant to discuss? Unless, unless . . .

Tom shook his head again. No, it wasn't possible. It couldn't be, could it? He decided that he needed a little fresh air to clear his head more than he needed a bowl of soup right then, so he went out through the kitchen door.

It was getting late. The sun was already below the top of the mountain, and the wind had a nip to it. Even though the night was clear and the daytime sun had all but melted the snow, winter was definitely stirring. It might even freeze.

He began to call out, "Hey, Nathan! You, Mont! Suppertime!"

When there was no response, he started walking slowly north-ward toward the creek bottom where he knew the boys liked to play. When he reached the place, they weren't there. He called to them again but still got no answer. Tom began to walk along the creek in the direction he thought their games might have taken them; then he thought better of it and decided to go back for his coat and a lantern.

Emily was just coming out from checking on Jed. "Did you find them? I heard you calling."

"No," he replied. "And it's getting dark and cold outside. I think I'll grab a light from the barn and walk up the creek a ways." At Emily's worried frown he added, "Don't get upset. They probably were having such a fine time that they wandered farther away than they intended. But Nathan knows this valley real well. He can find his way back. I'll just go help them along a little."

Out in the tack room Tom put on a heavy fleece-lined coat and lit a lantern. He thought briefly about saddling a horse and riding out, but he figured that tracking two small boys at night was better on foot.

Tom was pleased to find that when he returned to the creek bed with lamp in hand, he could immediately pick up their tracks in the sand. He followed them along the stream's course, lost them briefly where they had turned aside to look at something, then picked them up again a hundred yards farther on where they had rejoined the creek's path.

When Tom arrived at the juncture of Poso Creek and Sandy Creek, he missed the trail where the boys had left the sand to strike out across the hillside, so he circled back until he found it. From the point at which they exited, he thought he could guess where they might have been headed. It was a large rock that stood partway up the hillside—a good lookout post for the upper end of the valley. Just the place two boys who were out exploring would want to visit. Tom himself had used it before to survey the countryside when he went deer hunting.

When he reached the spot, he could tell that Nathan and Mont had been here, but they were not here now; worse yet, they seemed to have milled around a lot, without giving a clear indication of which direction they had taken next.

Tom was heading back downhill when he came upon the other sets of tracks. The boot prints of two men appeared both coming and going on the hillside, and the outward bound set was pressed deeper into the earth as if the men had been carrying something. Tom's heart began to race. How could he be sure? He couldn't bring this kind of news to Emily without proof. After all, he didn't even know for certain that Nathan and Mont had been near the men. He decided to recross the area one more time to see if he could locate anything definite, any clue to the boys' presence.

✱ ✱ ✱

"Didn't you find them?" Emily asked when Tom returned to the house. At his negative response, she cried, "But where can they be? You don't think that someone could have . . . ?" A look of horror and grief came over her face. "Oh no, Tom, not Byrd Guidett! But you can't *know*! I mean, maybe you just haven't looked in the right place yet."

She followed Tom's glance downward to his right palm outstretched in front of her; then she sank onto a bench, and with her face in her hands, began to sob.

In Tom's hand, glistening in the firelight, lay Nathan's barlow knife, taken from the tree trunk that marked the spot where a day of fun had turned into a night of terror.

"Oh, Tom, what does it mean? Where are the boys? What could have happened to them?" gasped Emily. "Could they be lost, or was it . . . was it . . . a wild animal? But, no, they'd get up a tree, wouldn't they? Oh, where can they be?"

"Take it easy, Emily. Here, sit down," instructed Tom, grasping her arms and moving her toward the rocking chair.

"Sit down? We've got to look for them. Where's my other lantern and my shawl? Tom, you've got to ride to town for help! Why are you just standing there?"

Tom sighed heavily. "Now, Emily, you've got to get hold of yourself. I've got something to tell you, and it won't be easy."

"No, Tom, *no*! You can't mean—"

"Emily, calm down! I don't think they're dead. In fact, I don't think they're even hurt. Do you recall that Byrd Guidett wanted to take Mont with him as some winnings in that poker game when he killed the man?"

"Why, yes, of course. And you stopped him, and . . . oh, Tom, you don't think Byrd took him and Nathan!"

"Yes, I do think that's what happened. There were tracks of two men near where I found the knife and some sign of a scuffle with the boys. I followed their trail to where they had tied their horses; then I came back here to tell you. Now, Emily, there wasn't any blood nor any sign that the boys had been harmed. Byrd and that partner of his could have ki—hurt the boys right where they caught 'em if they'd intended to."

"But why take them away, Tom? What do they want?"

"I don't know the answer to that. Byrd may still be tryin' to get hold of Mont, but there must be more to it than that. Even the fight he and I had at the Bella Union didn't seem strictly due to Mont. It's more as if Byrd wants to get at me for something, or he thinks the boys know something. . . . I don't know what. . . ."

"But he must know he'll be tracked, trailed wherever he goes, and brought to jail!"

"Yes, I'm sure he does. And that means two things."

"What, Tom, what?"

"He's not gonna leave a trail that's easy to follow and whatever he thinks he can accomplish by taking the boys must be real important to him! Now, I'm riding to town to get help. You stay put and take care of Jed. I'll be back just as soon as I can."

✳ ✳ ✳

The first person Tom called on when he arrived in Greenville was Parson Swift. Even though awakened from a sound sleep, the parson came quickly to the door and admitted Tom to the parlor. As the minister listened attentively to Tom's story, Swift stoked the fire in a small chrome and cast-iron stove, his mind racing.

"Everything you say makes sense to me, Tom," he concluded. "I think we need to rouse the town and get started right away. The longer we wait, the farther ahead they'll be and the more chance for them to cover their tracks. Let's go over to the church."

So saying, he wrapped his robe tighter around him and retrieved a pair of worn slippers from his bedroom. "I explained things to Mrs. Swift," he said as they went out the door. "She'll be brewing some hot coffee for us."

Over the entryway of the little church was a narrow steeple containing one high-pitched bell. Parson Swift grasped the bell rope firmly and, with strong sweeps of his wiry arms, began pealing the alarm. Its clanging sounded unnaturally loud in the clear, crisp night air. Soon the interrupted silence was further broken by the barking of dogs and neighing of horses.

123

A few moments later lights began appearing in windows, and exclamations and slamming doors echoed off the hills around town.

Deputy Pettibone, to his credit, was the first to arrive, his night-shirt hanging down over his trousers. In one hand he was carrying his boots, and slung over his other arm was his gun belt. "Where's the fire, Parson? Is the church burning, or what?"

"It's not a fire, Deputy. It's—" Before the parson could complete his answer, the volunteer fire company arrived, hauling their pump cart by hand. The water wagon arrived next, pulled by a team of snorting draft horses that looked far more alert than their driver, who sawed at the reins while alternately blinking, yawning, and cursing.

"Come into the church, men; come in," called the parson, realizing that explanations would be futile until everyone was assembled and quiet.

Confusion ruled as newcomers inquired, "What's this about then? Ain't there a fire? No, it ain't, it's the livery stable. Naw, it's no fire at all; Jeff Davis has been captured!"

Pettibone stood and raised his hands for silence. Gradually it grew quiet in the room, and the deputy addressed Parson Swift in a somewhat squeaky voice. "Just what's this here alarm about, Parson? Is there a fire or ain't there?"

"Just quiet down, men; quiet down," instructed the preacher as the babble threatened to erupt again. "Yes, there is an emergency, and, no, it's not a fire. Tom Dawson here will explain."

Quickly Tom outlined the situation—how long the boys had been gone, what he had found and where, the tracks he had followed, and what he thought it all meant. "So you can see we need to get after them right away. There's no telling what they'll do to those boys. Guidett's already shown how he treats folks in this town."

Mutters of agreement and a general movement out the door were halted by a measured voice raising carefully chosen phrases at the rear of the room. "May I suggest that we not be hasty, gentlemen? The night, while cold, is not desperately so, and the great likelihood is that the two children have merely wandered too far from home and have curled up somewhere for the night." Robert Mullins paused, then continued. "Most probably they've found some warm spot to get into, one of our neighbors' barns or haylofts, and are now peacefully sleeping—even as we should be."

"Didn't you hear what I said, Mullins? I found my nephew's knife and the boot tracks of two men, even some sign of a struggle!" Tom burst out angrily.

The parson laid a restraining hand on his arm.

"Now, Mister Dawson, didn't you say that you discovered this 'evidence' after dark? How can you be certain what it means?"

"You gob of lard! I'm tellin' you my nephew and Mont James are in the clutches of that bloodthirsty killer *right now,* and you want to stand here jawing about proof?"

"Naturally, Mister Dawson, your emotions are running rather high just now, and I think we all understand that, don't we, men? But let's not be hasty."

"Now jest hold on a minute there, Mullins," began stocky Bill Gardell. "If it was my kid, I'd be out lookin' right now, an' I'd want my neighbors to be helpin'."

"Just so; just so, Mister Gardell. I wasn't suggesting that we not help. But if some sort of abduction has taken place as Mister Dawson believes, don't we stand a much better chance of tracking them by daylight? In fact, if all of us went up there now, wouldn't we obscure the marks and actually make it more difficult to proceed? Let's seek expert counsel on this. Sheriff Pettibone, what do you think?"

"Well, I . . . I don't rightly know. I mean, those is little kids an' all. Still, tracking by night is hard enough, an' if we was to trample the ground, well, then, where would we be?" Pettibone stopped as if not sure what point he'd just made.

On that his audience was in complete agreement, but Robert Mullins covered the awkward silence just as if Pettibone had offered a masterful summation. "Exactly right, Sheriff. And, friends, may we remember one thing? The Dawson boy, assuredly one of our *own,* is accompanied by the young Negro child, no stranger to being a runaway, I assure you. Isn't it likely that under his influence, even a fine child like young Nathan could be led astray?"

"You mean because he's black, we needn't worry if he has disappeared or been stolen? He's no concern of ours? And some of that *taint* has rubbed off on Nathan, too?" Tom said angrily. "Is this what all of you believe? Mullins, you no-good, lousy—"

"Now, Tom, no harsh words that you'd regret later," soothed the deputy. "I'm sure Mister Mullins meant nothin' mean about either child. He was just tryin' to keep us calm. Tell you what, we'll all go out in the mornin' at first light. Now what do you say to that?"

"I say I'm sorry I wasted my time comin' all the way over here to get help from my *neighbors.* Now get out of my way. Move over, I say, or I'll knock you down!" Tom shoved two men aside as he went up the aisle of the church and out the door.

"We'll join you at first light, Tom. You can count on us," called Pettibone after him.

Several men looked ashamed, but no one except the parson moved to follow Tom out of the building.

Parson Swift laid a hand on Tom's shoulder just as he was about to mount Duncan.

Tom whirled around, his right arm raised as if to strike. "Oh, it's you, Parson," he said, dropping his fist. "Sorry, I—"

"You needn't explain, Tom. I'm as disgusted as you with the

125

whole lot, especially Mullins and that spineless Pettibone." This was an astonishing comment since the soft-spoken preacher had never been heard to say a harsh word about anyone. "I'm not a woodsman nor any kind of tracker, but if you'll have me, I'd like to go with you."

Tom stared at the parson for a moment, then grasped his hand warmly. "Thank you, Reverend. If I don't burn this whole town to the ground, starting with Mullins' store, they'll have only you to thank. No, I'll go alone tonight. Come morning, some of these *neighbors* really might feel up to comin' to help, and they'll need someone to get 'em organized. Will you do that for me?"

"Of course I will, Tom, and I'll send my wife over to stay with Emily. I expect she's taking this pretty hard."

"You know she is. In fact, would you ask your wife to not say anything about this meeting to Emily? I'll just let her think there's folks who care in this town till maybe some of them wake up and find out they do!"

✦CHAPTER 15✦

At first light Tom stood again by the tree where he'd found the knife. He had little trouble picking up the tracks, though he frequently walked and led Duncan for fear of missing a turn. He reasoned that the two outlaws were carrying one child apiece and that sooner or later they would hole up. He had to believe, had to hope that he was doing the right thing. He had no other alternative.

As Tom searched, he thought often of Emily—so brave but so grief stricken. Would she be as insistent on making this land her home if she had seen the lack of concern among those she counted as friends? Could a return to war-torn Missouri have been any worse than this?

What was wrong with those people, anyway? Could they really abandon two children because they were afraid to get involved? Could the color of a child's skin mean that his fate was of no concern at all?

And what was Mullins' role in this? As a merchant and a church leader, one would think that he'd be strong against any lawlessness and have a heart full of compassion. "Mullins' heart must be as cold as the coins in his cash drawer," Tom muttered. Now, what was it about Mullins' cash drawer that stuck in Tom's mind? For some reason the image of Mullins standing over his counter stuck with Tom, but he couldn't for the life of him figure out why.

During the night another light snow had fallen on Shadow Ridge, and the trail petered out completely. Try as he might, Tom could find no place where the two tracks had exited the snowfield. Looking up the slope, with the morning sun behind him brightening the looming peak of the mountain, Tom could see no objective that any riders would have been trying to reach. There was no hideout, not even rocks big enough to conceal a horse.

They came up here purposely to lead me off, thought Tom. *Then they backtracked their own trail or rode down off this saddle somewhere and went toward Tailholt.* He was quite sure they would have avoided the main road only while it was light. Then when darkness had fallen, they could have returned to the highway. But how in the world could he figure out which direction or how far they had gone?

Turning his horse around, he wearily made his way back toward home. As he reached the place where he had begun to track, he came upon Parson Swift waiting for him.

The parson looked expectantly at Tom but said nothing.

Tom shook his head sadly, and the two rode back to the Dawson place, where Emily and the parson's wife had kept an all-night vigil.

✷ ✷ ✷

Mont and Nathan crouched together in their stony prison. They linked arms tightly, not only out of fear but out of relief at finally— if only briefly—escaping the threatening knifepoint and punishing fists.

As their eyes adjusted to the light seeping from the larger cavern into their grotto, Mont could make out Nathan's tear-stained face. Nathan made no sound as he cried, but he couldn't hold back the tears any longer.

Mont listened for a moment to the noisy sounds of self-congratulations that issued from the other room, then decided he would risk a whisper. "Is you all right, Nathan?"

The hoarse, choked reply was unable to cover the lie even as Nathan spoke it. "I guess so. I'm okay."

"Is you hurt anywheres?"

"He cut me, Mont! Right here!" Nathan's hand went up and gestured behind his ear. "He told me if I made a sound, I was dead! His blade was an inch from taking my life. When we stopped by the road for that wagon to pass, he stuck his knife in my neck, and the blood ran down over my nose. I wanted to call out for help or jump down and run away, but I couldn't. I couldn't, you see!"

Nathan sounded close to sobs, so Mont made little hushing sounds. "Shh now, Nathan, we's still alive, and we's got each other."

"But I want to go home! I want my ma. What are they gonna do with us?"

"I don' rightly know what dey're fixin' to do wid us, but you know what my ol' mammie tol' me?"

"Your mama, Mont? I didn't think you remembered her."

"I dasn't talk 'bout her much, 'cause it makes me real sad, but I 'member she tol' me 'bout Massa Jesus allus takin' care of me. She say, 'Mont, Massa Jesus, He see ever' sparrow where dey go. He see 'em when dey in de nest, an' He see 'em when de cat be a-fixin' to get 'em. I 'spects He can take care of a little blackbird like you.'"

"But what about the sparrow that the cat *does* get—what about that?"

"Den it goes up to heb'en an' fly free all de day long, I reckon. But you an' me, we'll tell Massa Jesus dat we ain't ready jes' yet. I has only jes' found out dat I is free right here. I means, dey may have catched us now, but I doesn't belong to nobody! Now we needs to pray an' den go to sleep."

✳ ✳ ✳

For a minute when he first woke up, Nathan didn't know where he was. As he realized the predicament, he felt a moment's panic when he couldn't see Mont. In trying to find some comfort on the hard floor of the cave, they had managed to squirm past each other and were on opposite sides from where they had fallen asleep.

It was impossible to tell how long they had slept. Light was still coming in from the larger tunnel, and since no outside light reached to this depth, Nathan didn't know if he'd slept ten minutes or ten hours. He felt rested, though, and hungry again, so he guessed that it must be morning.

There were no sounds coming from the other room. Nathan lay very still and listened, but all he could hear was the gurgling of water as it made its way through the cavern beyond and plunged downward into the mountain.

Could they have been left alone? Was it possible that the outlaws had gone away? Nathan glanced over at Mont, decided against waking him, and crept slowly and cautiously over to the chamber entrance.

Quietly he lifted himself up from his huddled position and peeked around the corner. The fire in the pit was out, burned to a small pile of ashes. The two outlaws were still present, both of them asleep on the rough cots.

Nathan backed up into the smaller space. He bent down and shook his friend gently to wake him, while keeping his other hand ready to clasp over Mont's mouth to stifle any sound.

Mont awoke with a start but didn't make any noise. His eyes opened wide, and he understood instantly when Nathan placed a finger across his lips and then gestured for Mont to follow him.

One step at a time, darting from bed to bed, the two boys tiptoed out into the room. Their advance was painfully slow. It was all Nathan could do to not make a run for it. They stole past the rough table, across the open space near the upward passage, then stopped abruptly.

"You'uns wouldn't be thinkin' of runnin' away now, would ya?" a raspy voice behind them drawled.

Both boys whirled around. Yancey was sitting up on his bed eyeing them with amusement. Nathan trembled as he noticed that Yancey already had his knife out in his hand.

"No, sir, we just needed to get a drink of water, an' we didn't want to wake you," offered Nathan.

"'Pears to me you went the long way round to get to the crick over thar, but go on now, help yerselves." Then as the boys actually did go to the tiny stream to get a drink, Yancey added in a lower, sinister tone, "I'm right glad you wasn't a-sneakin' off, 'cause I mighta had to stop ya. That coulda been real unpleasant for somebody." With these words he flipped his knife, faster than they could see his wrist move, hurling the blade into the table leg.

The sudden *thok* awakened Byrd, who sat up with a start.

Yancey continued speaking to the boys. "Now Byrd thar, he don't hardly wake for nothin', but me, I sleep like a rattlesnake. Do ya know how rattlesnakes sleep, boys?" When the children made no reply except to shudder, he went on. "They sleeps with one eye open, and when they strikes, they hits hard! Some'un 'most always dies."

Byrd sat rubbing his face and shaking his shaggy head. "Was they tryin' to sneak off?"

"Naw," replied Yancey. "They wouldn't even think of such a thing."

After the robbers had made coffee and fried some thick slices of bacon, they tossed a couple of biscuits to the boys, who were sitting at the table. The biscuits were hard as a rock, but nothing else was offered, and neither child had any desire to ask for more.

"When's that Mullins s'posed to get here?" Byrd asked.

"He cain't get here afore tonight. He won't know that we got hold o' these two till we don't show at the cabin at noon. He'll be along right smart after that," concluded Yancey dryly.

"An' what'er we s'posed to do with these two brats? Why don't we just find out 'bout them papers now an' be done with it?"

"Go right on ahead," commented Yancey. "Long as ya don't fix it so's nobody else can ask more questions later."

"All right, boy!" Byrd faced Mont, sticking his nose near his. "Where'd that master o' yours hide them papers?"

Mont gulped before answering. "What papers, suh? I don' know nothin' 'bout no papers."

A powerful backhand caught him on the side of the head and sent him sprawling to the floor.

"Ya see, Yancey, I tol' ya we'd have trouble with 'im. His memory ain't workin' too good, but I expect I can help 'im along some." He dragged Mont back roughly into the chair and continued. "Now 'bout them papers, boy. Didn't ya see that colonel you was with hide somethin'?"

At the shake of Mont's head, another cuff landed on his other ear and knocked him into the table.

Nathan jumped from his seat, shouting, "You leave my friend alone! He doesn't know anything about any old papers! Stop hitting him!"

Byrd had turned to grab Nathan by the throat when a voice from the lower outlet of the cave commented, "Yes, you'd best stop hitting him for now, Byrd. You might succeed in killing him before I find out what I want to know, and that would not make me happy." It was Robert Mullins!

"Boss, how'd ya get here so soon? I mean, how'd ya know already that we had 'em?"

"Apparently you two incompetents not only succeeded in making off with one child too many, but you left enough marks that the Dawson child's uncle could follow you in the dark! It took all my persuasion to see to it that there wasn't a posse on your trail last night!"

"But, Mister Mullins," Nathan blurted out with a shocked expression, "what are you doing here?"

"I might well ask the same thing of you, young master Dawson. But I think I'd be addressing the wrong person." He fixed his stare on Byrd.

"They was together. I mean, we didn't think it'd be smart—"

"Guidett, your problem is that you *never* think. At least for once you didn't leave a gory corpse behind to mark your passing. If you had, I don't think even I could prevent the fools who inhabit that miserable little town from tearing this mountain apart with their bare hands until they caught you."

Here he turned to address Mont and Nathan again. "Which is not to say that anyone would ever find two very small corpses if they were hidden inside this mountain. Perhaps you can persuade your little friend there to tell us what we want to know. What ails you, boy? Can't you sit up straight?"

"I . . . I . . . don't know. I feel real strange all of a sudden," said Nathan in a shaky voice.

"Come, come, you'll have to do better than that! Shall I let Mister Guidett resume his intended action at the moment I arrived?"

"No, please. I feel better now, just a little woozy is all. But please, sir, let Mont alone. He don't know anything about any papers."

"Is that so?"

"Yassuh. I din't see no papers, an' Colonel James, he din't tell me 'bout none, neither."

"Hmm. All right. Suppose for a minute that I believe you. Why don't you tell me where you stopped the night before Colonel James' unfortunate death?"

"I don' rightly 'member de man's name, suh. But it were a fine house next to a riber. Kinda on a island-like."

"What's that? You mean to say you stayed *with* someone? You weren't just camped?"

"Oh no, suh. Dere was even a fine barn for me to sleep in, an' dey give me a real nice supper."

"Think, boy, think! What was the name?"

"Shall I see if'n I can jog his memory some?" offered Byrd, but Mullins waved him back impatiently with his fleshy hand.

"I'se real sorry, suh. I 'spects I din't hear no names. Dis house was by a riber on one side, like I tol' you, an' had a slough on de other. An' jes' 'cross o' dat slough dere was a big field, an' folks was a-campin' dere fo' de night, but we—"

"Stop!" shouted Mullins. "That's Baker's house and his field. Listen carefully, boy. Did the man you saw there look like this?" He gave a brief description of Colonel Thomas Baker.

Mont's eyes brightened. "Yassuh, dat's de very man! Can we go home now?"

The storekeeper squinted his piglike eyes, and a most unpleasant expression crossed his face. Then it passed, and his usual ingratiating smile returned. "No, I'm afraid that won't be possible yet. You see, we have to recover something from that house that belongs to me, and just in case we have trouble locating it, I might want to ask you some more questions. You stay here as our guests for a while and behave yourselves, and I'm sure you'll be treated all right. Won't they, Yancey?"

A look went between the two men, but nothing was said.

"Guidett, you come with me. Take good care of our guests, Yancey. Even young Dawson may have some bargaining value."

Mullins and Byrd exited down the tunnel up which the fat man had lately come.

✻ CHAPTER 16 ✻

H ow could they be so spiteful?" questioned Emily. "Those two little boys out there alone—or worse. How can people be so small?"

"It isn't that they're altogether hateful, Emily," corrected Mrs. Swift gently. "You must remember that they're terribly afraid for their own families as well. Most of them have lost kinfolk in the war, and lots of people want to raise their families out here in peace, just like you. Now that peace is threatened. Byrd Guidett is simply a big bully, shooting up the church like he did, but he has made these folks see violence up close, and most of them would rather shut their eyes or run away. Still, may God forgive them for not going out to search at least. I'm praying that God will put a terrible weight on them until they do what's right."

"Can't we track the riders any farther?" the parson asked Tom, who was seated with his head bowed in sorrow and exhaustion.

"No, Parson, the little dab of snow we got last night was just enough to hide the tracks. If we had more help, maybe we could comb the whole canyon down to below the snow line and pick up the trail again, but I can't cover all that ground myself."

"Then what will we do?" sobbed Emily. "We can't leave Nathan and Mont and do nothing."

"I'll help you, Uncle Tom," suddenly voiced a pale, thin figure in a long nightshirt. Jed stood in the bedroom doorway looking weak but resolute.

"Bless you, Jed, but no, you get back to bed," Tom replied. "The best thing you can do is get your strength back and stay here and look after your ma."

"I'll go out with you, Tom," Parson Swift offered.

"All right, Parson. There's nothing else to do but try. Let me get some grub together and some bedrolls, and we'll go. Maybe we'll get lucky and run onto the trail easier than I expect."

"We can bring something with us more powerful than luck, Tom. God loves those boys—and you, Tom, Emily, and Jed. We need to hold on tight to our faith and expect God to lead, even when there isn't a trail we can see with our eyes."

Tom nodded solemnly, hoping the parson was right.

There was a knock at the door. When Emily rose to answer it, she swayed, overcome by fatigue and worry. The parson's wife gently but firmly seated her again and went to the door instead.

Standing on the porch was Alex McKenna, the barman of the Bella Union. "Is Tom Dawson nae aboot?" Then seeing Tom in the room, he addressed him. "I was nae in town last night or I would have been with ye sooner. When I heard what had happened, I coom straightaway. These others here have coom on, too."

"What others?" inquired Tom, coming to the door and peering out.

Outside in the yard, bundled up in heavy coats and looking sheepish, was a group of riders. Among them were Bill Gardell, Red Burton, Bob Davis, and a few others.

"Hello, Tom," began Gardell. "Me an' some o' the boys . . . well, we figgered we didn't do right by you last night, but we want to make amends."

"Tell him the whole truth, Bill," urged Red. "When we got home last night an' told our wives what went on at that meetin' an' how Mullins talked us into not doin' nothin', me an' Bill an' Bob here got lambasted real good. We was in Alex's havin' coffee this mornin' an' kinda comparin' bruises when Alex got the gist of what happened, an' he allowed as how he'd horsewhip us if we didn't get over here right smart. Ain't that the size of it, fellas?"

A chorus of "and how" and "you bet" chimed agreement.

Davis added, "Truth is, Tom, I didn't sleep too good last night anyways. I figger we let Byrd Guidett bully us jest far enough. An' as for Mullins an' his slick talk, well, you see neither him nor Pettibone is here now. We figgered we couldn't wait on them to lead no more, so here we is. That is, if you'll still have us."

"You bet I'll have you! Parson and I have just been sitting here trying to figure out how we could cover four hundred square miles between the two of us. Come in, fellows, and fill up your canteens with hot coffee; we've got some hard, cold riding to do."

They went out in pairs to scour the hillsides. They took a bearing on the approximate direction the tracks were heading when last seen, then fanned out in a half circle before riding down to the snow line, so as to give themselves the broadest possible chance to pick the trail up again.

It was late afternoon when Red Burton spotted the deep tracks that emerged from the snow on the gentler slope of the canyon side that led down toward Tailholt.

Three rifle shots fired in close succession brought Tom and the others riding over.

"Look here, Tom," said Red. "These tracks is fresh, an' they come out headin' in the right direction."

"But that's the track of only one horse. Where did his partner go?"

"We figger they split up at the head of the canyon, plannin' on meetin' later," replied Red. "An' Bob here agrees it's likely this one was up to no good, or else why'd he be ridin' over here on the hill with a good road no more'n a quarter mile away?"

"All right. It makes sense to me. Part of us'll follow this trail, but the others need to keep working their way down the opposite side, just in case the second rider turned off another way. Parson, you and Bob and Red come with me; Alex, if you don't mind, I'd like you to lead the other group."

"Whatever ye say, Tom. Coom on then, boys; we're nae followin' naught by sittin' here."

Tom's group followed the hoofprints down toward Tailholt without difficulty. They found where the rider had apparently waited for some time and saw marks on the ground to indicate that something had been thrown. Another set of tracks rejoined there, but Tom decided not to call the other group immediately, thinking they might come across some clue that would be helpful. He sent Bob and Red into Tailholt to ask if anyone had recently seen Byrd Guidett or two small boys.

By the time they returned with negative answers to both questions, Alex's group had completed their search and joined up again.

"They didn't leave the boys anywhere along the trail, and no one's seen them in Tailholt. Let's figure that they went on from here," Tom reasoned, "and we'll follow this track up Shadow Ridge."

✳ ✳ ✳

"They've hoodwinked us for sure," said Bill Gardell. "They rode on this shale, then doubled back, dustin' their tracks as they went. Shucks, if they come this far in daylight, they could've chanced goin' back on the road by night an' be most anywheres by now."

Tom rose in his stirrups and glanced anxiously at the mountain. "What about farther up? Couldn't they have crossed the slide rock and gone on up?"

"Naw, you can see for yourself there ain't nothin' there," remarked Red. "Why, even a squirrel would stand out, no more brush than there is up there. Besides, what'd they do up there anyway but come back down?"

McKenna turned to Tom in apology. "I ken he's right, Tom. We're wastin' time on a cold trail."

"Are you all for giving up, then?" asked Tom quietly.

"Nay, nay, dinna misunderstand. Let's split up again. Some will ride through Tailholt an' doon the mountain, inquirin' of all travelers if they've seen aught of two men and two young lads, and others to do likewise yon Jack Ranch way. Never ye fear—they canna stay hid for long."

Tom looked down at his saddle horn for a long moment before nodding slowly in agreement to this plan.

All the riders turned their mounts, making their way back down the hillside in single file.

Tom was the last to leave. He turned his horse around, then twisted in his saddle to look at the bleak summit of Shadow Ridge. He raised a clenched fist toward it in anguished helplessness. Something close to hatred was in his eyes as he turned again to follow the others.

✳ ✳ ✳

It was five days before Byrd returned to the cave. When he did he was in a foul mood, and Yancey as well as the two boys shrank from him. "Five days hidin' out in that stinkin' swamp in a cold camp. Not even coffee, that fat pig says, we don't want to give away our presence."

"What about them papers?"

"Who knows? We ain't even got inside the house yet."

"Why not? Don't them folks ever leave?"

"Naw, it's worse than that. He's got a mess of Yankee officers stayin' with 'im!"

"Yankees! What's we s'posed to do now?"

"Mullins went on back to his store—his nice, warm, dry store—an' left me to watch. 'Wait till day after tomorrow,' he says. 'If you haven't gained entry by then, go back and trade places with Yancey,' he says. 'I'd stay myself but my continued absence would be noticed.' That lousy, stinkin'—" Byrd indicated Nathan, then continued, "What's the matter with him?"

"Don't know exactly," Yancey said. "He's been actin' real poorly since right after you left. First I thought he was fakin', but I felt of him an' he's got the fever all right. Says his head hurts an' his throat, an' he's breakin' out in some rash or somethin'."

"Well, I ain't gonna wet-nurse no sick kid. Be just too bad if he hauls off'n dies, now wouldn't it? Save us the trouble."

"No! No! Home! Mama, Mama, Mama! Jed, look out . . ." Nathan's voice trailed off, but he continued to thrash around.

"Listen here, boy, you'd best keep yer friend quiet. I'm gettin' powerful tired of his carryin' on," ordered Byrd ominously.

"Yassuh," replied Mont. "But he's burnin' up wid de feber, an' now dem spots is 'most all over his body."

"Yeah, well, give him some more water, but keep him quiet!"

"Yassuh." Mont tried to get Nathan's attention but to no avail. Mont took off his own jacket and used it for an extra cover over Nathan's trembling limbs. He moistened his pocket handkerchief and used it to cool Nathan's fevered face.

Nathan continued to shiver all over as if he were in a freezing snowstorm without a stitch of clothing on.

Mont looked anxiously at his friend, and then, making up his mind, got all his courage together and went into the larger room to address Byrd. "Mistuh Byrd?"

"What is it now?"

"My frien', he need to be next de fire, an' he need some hot food."

"Why, ya little . . . I'll . . ."

"If'n he dies, Mistuh Mullins gonna be powerful upset. You'd best stop an' think on dat!"

Byrd laughed, as if surprised that such a small person could stand up to him so forcefully. "All right, then, fix him a place by the fire, an' let's see if ya can cook. I'm almighty tired of my own cookin' anyways."

Almost as soon as Mont assisted Nathan to stretch out by the fire, the sick boy began to calm down. His contorted muscles relaxed, and he ceased muttering to himself and fell into a peaceful sleep.

Mont used this break in his constant attention to his friend to fill the cleanest pot he could find with fresh water from the stream and put it on a hook over the fire. As it began to heat, he got grudging permission from Byrd to use a small pocketknife. With it he shaved pieces of jerky into small bits, which he dropped into the pot.

Byrd dipped himself a cupful of this soup as it began to boil, but Mont continued to heat and stir the mixture until it had reduced to about a third of its original volume.

Nathan began to show signs of awakening as Mont poured out a small amount into an empty tin can to cool. As Nathan's eyes opened and he looked around the room, Mont aided him in sitting up halfway and held the can to his lips.

At first Nathan sipped slowly, but little by little he ate more eagerly until he had consumed all that remained in the pot. He smiled gratefully at his friend, then lay down and returned to a relaxed sleep.

✳ ✳ ✳

"Nothin'—not a blessed sign of 'em!" reported Red. "Me an' Bob went clean to Tulare. We met up with drovers, an army patrol, an' even a band of Tuolomnes. None of 'em have seen Byrd or two men with two kids or even one black kid for that matter. You have any luck?"

"Yeah, tons of luck, an' all of it bad," said Bill Gardell. "McKenna an' me went to Jack Ranch, Sugarloaf, an' even busted our hump gettin' over Portagee Pass, an' nothin' to see nor nothin' to hear about. It's like they dropped off the world. One thing's certain, though: Byrd must be mixed up in this, else it's right strange of him to disappear at the same time as those two kids."

"Where's Tom and the parson?" asked Bob.

"Parson went back to check on Mrs. Dawson an' give 'em the report, such as it is."

"And Tom?"

Bill and the Scotsman exchanged rueful glances. "We couldna get him to coom back with us and rest a spell," said McKenna. "When we could nae mair ride nor walk, he made us give him the rest o' our kit, and he rode out Howling Gulch way."

"Howling Gulch? That windswept hole? There ain't even water nor wood for fires up that rock-choked gully. What'd he think to find thar?"

"Do ye nae ken, mon? Tom is near crazed with grief, and what's mair, he canna think on what will coom to Miss Emily if he canna find her lad."

"It's sure enough true what Alex here says," added Bill. "He's a-clutchin' at straws."

✳ ✳ ✳

Tom rode Duncan around a pile of rubble that had fallen from the heights of the narrow gorge into its narrow throat. The boulders and gravel completely filled the canyon to a reach of twenty feet up the walls. For the third time in the past hour Tom had to dismount Duncan and look for a way to scramble around a dusty obstacle.

The sides of the gully were treeless, even brushless, in their barren disarray. It appeared to Tom that the only thing growing there was a fine crop of decomposed granite that flowed down the walls as if determined to prevent even the tiniest plants from ever taking root. The bottom of the canyon was dry, a stranger to any regular flow of water, though it showed the unmistakable marks of flash flooding. The gorge was a tremendous runoff channel when the storm clouds broke over the heights of Sunday Peak, but the swift passage of water did no more than aid the crumbling rock avalanches in keeping the sides scoured clean.

But it was neither the sliding gravel flows nor the boulder-strewn gully nor the silent passage of a temporary river that gave the canyon its name. Howling Gulch took its designation from the fact that the tiniest gust of wind reverberated down the plummeting walls, shrieking in exit at the canyon's mouth like demons being cast into everlasting torment. And the wind blew all the time.

It was blowing particularly hard today. A week of fruitless searching had brought Tom to the point of being alone in the search, and the rising volume of the canyon's howling heralded the approach of another wintry storm that had mercifully held off through much of the search for the boys.

Gravel blew into Tom's face, assaulting his eyes like red-hot sparks from the blacksmith's forge. He ducked his head down to his chest and soon found that he could not lead Duncan and hold on to his hat with the other hand and keep his balance all at the same time. Leaving the horse to stand ground-tied for a moment, Tom made several attempts to fasten his bandanna over his hat's crown before he finally succeeded in bringing the ends together under his chin.

When he could next clear his vision, Tom studied the rockslide he was trying to lead Duncan around. This pile of rocks seemed even more jagged, heaped up higher and the canyon sides even steeper than those he had crossed to get to this point. Tom considered trying to retrace his steps to the bottom of the gorge and try the other wall, but momentary glimpses across the rubble showed no more promise than what he was already facing.

"I guess this is as far as you go, boy," he commented to Duncan. Tom retrieved a rifle from its scabbard on the horse and thrust a box of cartridges into the pocket of his heavy coat. He loosened Duncan's girth but left the saddle in place. He was glad Duncan could be trusted to remain ground-tethered, for there wasn't anything he could be tied to anyway. "Be seein' you," Tom remarked, to which the horse only made answer by turning about and placing his broad rump into the wind. *Fine send-off,* thought Tom with grim humor. *Even the horse turns his back on me.*

He struggled upward for the next twenty minutes before reaching the top of the rock dam. He was right to have left the horse behind, he reasoned, or he would not have made it this far at all. The wind was really howling now, a blast so fierce that Tom could not stand erect for fear of being blown back down the slope he had just climbed. The screeching increased, like a steam boiler about to explode.

Tom stumbled down the other side, heedless of the path he took—anything to get off the exposed ledge where he felt like a fly in the path of a descending fly swatter. Halfway down, his feet went out from under him on a patch of loose gravel. As his boots shot forward with increasing speed, Tom flung his arms out to the sides, grasping for anything that might offer a grip to stop his plunge. The rifle, against a quartz ledge to Tom's right, went off on impact, but its roar was completely masked by the wind.

Tom fell heavily on his side against a boulder; the ribs broken in the fight with Byrd cracked painfully. This time it felt as if an even greater fist had slammed into Tom's body, and his breath was expelled in an agonized "Ooof!" Tom lay still, panting, trying to draw air back into his lungs.

He looked around in a daze, unable to see the rifle from where he lay and anxious to locate it—not because of its firepower, but simply because he needed to lean on it in order to stand up. For the moment he had completely forgotten why he came to be in such a place. As he crawled up the side of the rock against which he had fallen, each breath was like a spike driven into his side. His face was raw and bleeding from the gravel driven into it by the force of the gale. His hands were stiff and aching, and when he looked to see why, he saw that on one hand three fingernails had been ripped out by his scramble to find a hold on the rock face. The palm of the other hand was bloody with fingernail marks where he had clenched his fist in the agony of bruising his ribs.

"God," he cried, "what am I doing out here? Why don't You help me?"

"We is climbin' Jacob's ladder, we is climbin' Jacob's ladder, we is climbin' Jacob's ladder, sol'jers of de cross," sang Mont to Nathan. The two were sitting in the small cave where they had been sent by Byrd while he went to feed the horses.

"An' don't even poke yer noses out till I get back an' tell ya to, un'erstan'?" Byrd had said.

So the boys sat in the dark, and Mont sang softly, much to the delight of his friend.

"Mont, how long have we been here, anyway?" asked Nathan.

"I don' rightly know" was the reply. "An' when you was mos' outta your head wid de feber, dem days did drag on so. Bes' I can figger, we done been here 'most ten days since we was catched."

"Do you think they'll let us go, or is anyone ever gonna find us?"

"Shore, we's gonna get outta here; you jes' wait'n see!"

They heard noises coming from the other cavern but thought only that it was Byrd returning from feeding. There was a shuffling, a pause, and then more shuffling. It sounded as if some heavy sack was being dragged across the floor of the tunnel. Mont stopped singing so they could listen, but neither boy made any move to go see what it was.

Presently they heard a flop, as if that same imagined sack had been carelessly thrown onto one of the cots. A long, drawn-out groan followed, then silence.

Their heightened senses anticipated Byrd's return from the upper tunnel even before they heard him enter the adjoining cave. When he did enter, they heard him say, "Yancey! When in thunder did you come? What ails ya, anyway?"

A hoarse croak that in no way resembled Yancey's voice replied, "It's the fever an' the pox. I'm like to die with it, Byrd. I couldn't watch no more, so I come up."

The boys heard and understood the clumping footsteps that followed this announcement. It was Byrd backing up rapidly away from Yancey's bed. "Well, ain't this fine! How're we s'posed to watch them kids an' Baker's if ye're a-layin' here sick?"

"I'm cold clean through, Byrd Guidett, an' I ain't been dry since I left here. I can still watch them brats. You get on out to Baker's an' leave me be!"

"All right, all right, jest don't let them put nothin' over on ya."

Sometime later there was no sound from the other room, and no one had come to tell the boys that they could come out or when it was time to eat. So they went silently to the juncture of the two passages and peered carefully around the corner. Yancey lay on his bed, breathing heavily. His hair hung in matted streaks across his face, and one arm trailed limply to the floor.

Mont and Nathan looked at each other, and each knew what the other was thinking. Remembering how quickly Yancey had awakened on their last escape attempt, the boys decided to test him.

Nathan called out softly, "Mister Yancey, is it time for supper?"

To their great disappointment, Yancey sat up immediately and regarded them with sunken, red-rimmed, bloodshot eyes. He stared at them, saying nothing and swaying slightly back and forth. "You two—," he began but got no further as a racking cough shook his whole frame, bending him almost in half with the spasm of it. When he could speak again, it was to gasp, "You two, get back an' keep still. Leave me alone!"

✳ ✳ ✳

How long Tom had been lying stretched out across the rocky ledge, he didn't know. What finally roused him from his stupor was no new pain or another moment of violent activity. Instead, his conscious mind struggled to awareness because of a lessening of the storm's frenzy, a gradual slackening of its voice.

Tom took stock of his injuries before trying to move. His hands were stiff but no longer bleeding. All his fingers worked, though unwillingly. His face felt burned as if polished by the wind, but his vision was clear and undamaged. As for his side, he drew a cautious breath and was almost surprised that no sharp pain resulted. He sat up carefully and noted with gratitude that his rifle lay where it had landed—just on the other side of the rock on which he was lying. He turned his gaze around to look at the gravel pile on which he had fallen in order to begin calculating a path around it, but it was not the marks his boot heels had made that drew his horrified attention. At the point where his side had been crushed against the rock, at the precise location where his next step would have taken him, there was an abrupt drop-off straight down into the gorge. Leaning out, Tom could barely see the bottom some hundred feet below.

He crept over to the rifle. It was undamaged. Tom used it to pull himself upright, where he stood, shakily surveying the canyon. "God," he said, "You are here with me. You were helping me even when I thought You'd left me alone. Wherever Nathan and Mont are right now, won't You hold on to their hands like You did mine? And Emily too, Lord. Help her see that You know all about lookin' for lost children."

When Tom had struggled painfully back to where he had left Duncan, he found the horse patiently waiting. Taking a canteen from his saddle, he drank a swallow, then poured some water into his hat for the grateful beast. With another handful he bathed his face; then he took another long swallow. "Let's go home," he said to Duncan.

✵ ✵ ✵

Not until late the next evening were Tom and Duncan able to get back down to the area of Greenville. Though exhausted and sore, Tom felt an unexplainable calm.

When he arrived back at the Dawson ranch, he was received with exclamations of joy and made to sit next to the fire, while Emily tenderly bathed his face and hands and put ointment on the deep scrapes.

Tom listened as she related to him that all the other searchers had again reported in, with no greater success than when Tom had last seen them. In turn, he told her what he had experienced. He didn't try to conceal his disappointment at not being able to locate Nathan nor the extent of his anger and frustration that had driven him to Howling Gulch.

"But, Emily," he added, "something happened to me up there. I haven't found the boys yet, but I know we're going to. And this isn't just false hope to make you feel better. I really believe God promised me He'd bring them home if I'd only trust Him."

"I know, Tom," she responded. "I've been praying for your safe return, and look what God brought you back from. Everyone has been here praying for you and the boys, especially Victoria Burton. She stayed with me last night."

"God bless 'em," he replied. "Now I just need some sleep; then I can go out lookin' again."

She brushed her lips against his. "I know you will, Tom, and God will be leading you every moment."

Back in his room in the barn, Tom fell instantly into a deep sleep. He awakened once to drink a bit of soup, then slept again clear into the next night.

Tom was having a confused dream. In it he was trying to swim up a rockslide. He heard a shot and then a shout. It was his brother's voice. No, it was Nathan's high treble. Something was pulling him down. The air was thick like mud as he tried to come to the surface of Shadow Ridge, but the syrupy air didn't slow the rocks and boulders that went bounding past him—each one narrowly missing his head. Another shot and another shout.

What was holding him back? He squirmed around to see. It was a silver chain, its links twined around his legs. The links glinted dully in a shadowy afternoon light. The chain wound around his boot tops and tightened around the cuffs of his trousers, the end of the chain dropping off down the hill. Someone was tugging on it, but Tom couldn't see who. Then came a shot followed by an agonized shout!

Tom sat bolt upright, covered with sweat. He rubbed his hand over his face and shook his head. What a nightmare! He had relived

147

his brother's death, but with himself as the intended victim, and the unknown fate of his nephew thrown in as well. How vivid that gunshot, how lifelike the scream—

Tom stopped himself in midthought. Deliberately he forced himself to reexamine the confused scenes. What was it that bothered him so about the two sounds that were so deeply implanted in his consciousness? Tom forced his mind to return to the actual scene on the mountainside that tragic afternoon, comparing its events to his dream.

There was no sudden flash, no leap to an instantaneous understanding, but rather a gradual realization. Tom thought it through carefully, tested his conclusion, found it sound. He remarked out loud, "The shot came before the shout. That means Jesse's gun didn't go off in the fall; he was shooting at something before he was struck. Something or *someone*. If that's true, then somebody wanted his death to *look* like an accident. They wanted to keep us from finding something, but they didn't want to let on that there was anything anybody would want to find."

He debated whether he should wait until morning to tell Emily, but he couldn't sleep, so he dressed quickly, deciding that he would walk around a little and think.

When he got outside, he noticed a thin sliver of light coming from under the window shade in Emily's room. Perhaps she was still awake. He went to the front door and tapped gently, not wanting to disturb her yet willing her to be awake.

His quiet knock was rewarded with a shuffling noise followed by a gentle "What is it?"

"Emily," he called, "can I come in and talk a minute? I think I've figured something out."

"Of course, Tom. Just a moment."

He waited as she drew back the bolt and stepped aside to let him enter. Her hair lay gently on her shoulders, and she was wearing a dark blue dressing gown. She didn't appear to have just awakened, but Tom asked, "Did I wake you?"

"No," was the reply. "I couldn't sleep, so I was reading the Ninety-first Psalm and praying for Nathan and Mont. What's this you've figured out?" she asked eagerly. "Do you know something of the boys' whereabouts?"

"Maybe. Maybe . . . ," he said slowly as this new aspect of his dream entered his mind. "Listen to me. I'm sorry . . . can we sit down?"

"Come into the kitchen, Tom, and I'll make us each a cup of tea."

While he sat at the kitchen table, Emily stirred up the woodstove with a few pieces of oak, then put on the kettle. She sat down across from him and looked expectantly at him.

"Now, this may be nothing at all, so don't get your hopes up," Tom cautioned, "but the dream I had . . . I think it means something."

"Tell me from the beginning as much as you can remember, and don't try to explain it till you're done," she instructed.

His dream, which had seemed to last for hours at the time he had had it, took only moments to tell. He went slowly and carefully, trying to recall every event, every sight, and every feeling. "You see, it was the order of the two noises that bothered me that same night on the mountain, but I was too dazed to figure out what it meant. Later on, there was you and the boys to see to, and I guess I sort of blocked it out, just not wanting to think about it. But now I'm certain that what I heard was Jesse getting off a shot at whoever was pushing the rocks off the rim at him, and the shout just before the—" He stopped, unwilling to cause her more pain.

But Emily was all business now, the mother bear scenting the air for danger and preparing to defend her cubs. "Yes, I see. Whoever killed Jesse did so in order to prevent you two from either finding a route over or discovering some secret about Shadow Ridge, *without* causing further investigation. That must mean that you and Jesse were right about the stage robberies and Byrd Guidett being linked with a hidden way to cross. And perhaps it may mean that Nathan and Mont are being held there now!"

"At the very least," Tom pondered aloud, "there may be a clue to their whereabouts up there. And I aim to find it." He made as if to rise.

Emily stopped him. "Wait—there was more to the dream. Let's not run off without working it out while it's still fresh in your mind." The kettle was whistling on the stove, and Emily poured its contents into her blue china teapot.

"But it was all so confused and tangled," Tom protested. "How can it help us any?"

"Tell me the last part again," she urged. "About the chain."

"It was a silver chain that led down into a dark hole, and someone I couldn't see was trying to drag me backward into the path of the rockslide. It was wrapped around my legs. I remember especially that the links were around my cuffs, heavy silver links twisted around my cuffs, and—"

"What, Tom, what is it?" Emily asked.

"Cuffs and links, Emily—cuff links! I'm sure that's it! Now I know why Mullins didn't want anyone to go up Shadow Ridge or to get a posse to chase after Byrd."

"You're not making any sense. What cuff links? And do you mean Robert Mullins, the storekeeper? What about him?"

"Pour us some tea while I explain," Tom said confidently. "I even know how we can check to see if I'm right."

⋆ CHAPTER 18 ⋆

A solitary dog barked in alarm, and Tom froze in his tracks. He listened intently, every sense tuned for the banging door or creaking hinge that would indicate someone coming to investigate. Two anxious minutes passed with Tom pressed against the side of the hardware store; then the dog lapsed into silence, apparently satisfied that he had successfully repelled the intruder.

When another minute's silence went unbroken, Tom breathed a sigh and resumed creeping toward the store's rear door. He was struggling not only with the worry of being caught but also with how he could explain his actions. He doubted that anyone other than Emily would put as much credence in his dream as he did. Even in the midst of this exploit, which Tom felt driven to perform, perfectly reasonable objections kept asserting themselves. How could a man of such recognized standing in the community as Robert Mullins be a party to the crimes of murder and kidnapping? Could such a pompous but ingratiating manner conceal such sinister intentions? Tom's agony at uncovering the fate of his nephew and Mont drove him to believe the answer was yes. Not only was Robert Mullins a mass of flesh but a heap of duplicity as well.

And that, Tom reasoned, *is why I can't go to Pettibone or anyone else with this suspicion without something to back it up. Even if I could convince them to investigate, I might only succeed in giving Mullins enough warning to get away or cover his tracks some other way.*

So here he was, on a bitterly cold and thankfully dark night, preparing to break into Mullins' store. He knew what he was seeking, but even Tom wasn't sure why. He intended to retrieve the silver cuff link that had come from the body of the man slain by Byrd Guidett. For some reason Mullins had chosen to appropriate the cuff link and squelch any further reference to it. Tom's gut feeling told him the cuff link had some bearing on the whole mystery.

Tom wore his Colt Navy strapped to his side. He didn't expect to use it tonight, but he wouldn't have felt safe without it. Tom wasn't certain how to enter the store. He had chosen the rear because the front bordered the two main avenues of travel through the little town and made discovery much more likely.

Tom located the outline of the door and began to explore it with his hands. A quick investigation of the frame left Tom completely disgusted with himself for coming out on such a fool's errand without having found some pretext to check out this entrance first. His rapidly numbing fingers found that the rear door was completely set into the frame. It closed from the inside only and was apparently bolted from within, leaving neither bolt nor hinge on the outside. There was no lock to be broken, and the fit was so tight that there was little chance that a prying tool would work.

Now what? Tom wondered. *I've come this far; I'd best not go back without checking for some other way in.*

He circled the store cautiously, checking all the windows on the off chance that one had been left ajar. No such luck. He had almost reached the front of the building when he heard a noise from the road. No dog this time. Instead, it was a steady, measured footfall. Tom crouched down at the corner behind a scrawny lilac bush just off the porch that ran across the front. He hoped he would blend into the other dark shadows and not be noticed.

The footsteps turned off the gravel of the roadway and went unhesitatingly across the small yard with its two hitching rails. The unknown person stomped heavily up the wood steps to the porch and paused in front of the door. The jangling sound of a ring of keys came to Tom's ears, and he realized with a start that the bulky figure was Robert Mullins himself.

Tom's mind whirled at this complication. Should he wait until the shopkeeper had entered and then make his own getaway? Should he step out and boldly confront the man, hoping that the shock of his unexpected presence would surprise Mullins into revealing something? The hesitation caused by these two conflicting plans settled the issue for him, for as Mullins located the correct key and proceeded to unlock the door, he began to mumble aloud. Tom leaned forward to catch what was said.

"Should have thought of this before. Can't depend on that rattle-brain and his shifty-eyed sidekick . . . Think of some pretext to get into Baker's . . . delivering something . . . show him the recognition tokens. Ha! We can . . ." His words trailed off into inaudibility as he snapped the bolt back and threw open the door. He closed it behind him but did not latch it on the inside.

Casting aside most of his caution, Tom moved quickly onto the porch. He pushed the door open slightly, hoping to hear more of the monologue without alerting Mullins. Tom peered carefully into the store through a window beside the entrance.

At first he couldn't make out anything inside; then a spark of light flared as Mullins struck a match and lit an oil lamp on his counter. The hulking form fumbled with the key ring again before selecting another one with which to unlock his cash drawer. Suddenly, Mullins threw the ring of keys down on the counter. "Can't get too excited," he murmured. "Know they're in the safe where they belong. Can't be too careful. Oh, but we're close." He turned his massive body around with some difficulty in the narrow space behind the counter and made a wheezing sound as he bent over to reach his safe.

Silently praying that the hinges were well oiled, Tom eased the door open and slipped inside. He tiptoed almost up to the counter. From behind it a mixture of grunting noises and the soft click of the combination lock could be heard. On the wall an ugly shadow beast—half pig and half bear—played and stretched. A final click and the clank of the handle, and then Mullins gave a snort of satisfaction. He tossed something over his shoulder to the counter. No, it was *two* somethings—a pair of silver cuff links like the one bearing the initials *J. D.*!

Robert Mullins rose ponderously with the lamp in one hand and turned around to find himself looking into the cold, murderous gaze of Tom Dawson.

"Why, Mister Dawson!" sputtered Mullins. "Whatever are you doing here at this time of night?" Then, as if he realized that was not the proper tone to use, he added, "I'll thank you to leave my establishment immediately. If you have business to transact or something to discuss, come back tomorrow."

When Tom said nothing but continued staring into Mullins' startled and apprehensive eyes, the shopkeeper struggled to regain his composure. He put the lamp down on the counter. "I mean to say, why are you sneaking in here like this? Is something wrong? Is there an emergency?" His hands, like two fat spiders, began crawling across the countertop toward the cuff links.

At last Tom spoke. "Leave 'em right there, Mullins. I wouldn't want one of 'em to disappear before Colonel Mason had a chance to ask you how you came to be in possession of the twin to the cuff link found on a corpse!"

"Why, I can't think how it came to be here. I mean, I was looking for something else when—"

"It won't wash, Mullins. I heard what you were mumbling about recognition tokens. Let me take a guess. J. D. wouldn't stand for Jeff Davis, would it? Now, unless you want me to partly settle accounts with you about my brother before I turn you over to the army, you'd better tell me quick where the boys are."

A crafty smile played across Mullins' features. "Well, now, that is the problem, isn't it? If you want to see your nephew safe, I suggest that you let me go. You understand the character of the two men who are holding them, don't you? If I'm not able to call them off, let's just say I couldn't guarantee how long those boys would remain healthy."

"I'll healthy you, you—!" shouted Tom, lunging across the counter.

With a sweeping motion of his arm, Mullins knocked over the lamp, intending to plunge the room into darkness. Instead, it hit the floor with a crash and spread a pool of fire over the wood floor. Reaching under the counter, the shopkeeper yanked out a .44 caliber derringer.

Tom, who was sprawled across the counter, rolled to the side, but not before Mullins' shot took him on the side of the head. Tom fell heavily to the floor and lay still.

Mullins paused only long enough to sweep the cuff links into his fist before lumbering out the front door of the store. The stirring sounds of the community told him that the gunshot had not gone unnoticed. Cursing to himself and moving as rapidly as his bulk permitted, he made his way home to where his buggy was already hitched up and waiting.

On the way out of town, he noted grimly that the flames could be seen through the store windows, and as he rounded a curve shutting out the view, he heard the church bell begin to give the alarm.

"I hope he fries," he muttered as he drove off.

✵ ✵ ✵

Tom was dragged from the fire by the hotel proprietor, McKenna. Ignoring the frantic activity of men scurrying about trying to save the building, he noted that Tom was still alive. The wound, which had knocked him unconscious, had just grazed the side of his head. McKenna and Parson Swift carried Tom to the parson's home, as it was nearer than the hotel. The parson's wife held a cold compress to Tom's head, and soon the wound stopped bleeding.

Tom began to come around as Mrs. Swift bathed his face with cool water, and all at once he gave a jerk and cried out, "Mullins! He—!"

"Easy, Tom," urged the parson. "You've been shot, so lie still and rest."

Tom gathered his wits and then spoke again. "Did Mullins get away? Did someone catch him?"

"Do ye mean to say 'twas him as shot ye, lad?" inquired McKenna. "He hasna been seen by me this night. Have ye seen him, Parson?"

"No, but give the man a chance to tell us what he means, Mister McKenna."

"To be sure," agreed the Scotsman. "Just take yer time, lad, an' tell us what this is all aboot."

Tom opened his eyes, then grimaced in pain and shut them

again. Slowly, through gritted teeth he gasped, "Mullins . . . rebel spy or . . . something. He and Byrd. Got the boys. Killed my brother. Got to follow." As if even this effort was too taxing for his battered brain, Tom fell unconscious again.

Parson Swift looked at McKenna. "Go get Deputy Pettibone, would you please, Mister McKenna. I think he should hear this when Tom is able to speak."

"Aye, aye," agreed McKenna. "An' there'll be some others who'll take an interest in his tale as well, I'm thinkin'."

✤ ✤ ✤

Robert Mullins' mind was whirling faster than the buggy wheels were turning. His first thoughts were of escape only. If he stayed behind, there would be questions—too many questions. How did the fire start? How did Tom Dawson come to be there, shot in the head? Mullins wondered briefly if he could have convinced the town that Dawson was a burglar surprised in the act of rifling the store's safe. But no, no one would believe that.

What if Dawson lived? Mullins knew his bullet had struck Dawson, for the storekeeper had seen him fall heavily to the floor; but in his bolt for the door, Mullins hadn't even considered stopping to see if the man was dead. Cursing his panic, Mullins thought, *If the man is truly dead, then perhaps I could have sold the burglar idea. Well, no chance of that now. But what if Dawson lives and tells what happened?*

That thought made Mullins snap the reins on the back of his horse and push him to greater speed. What must be done now was a desperate gamble. He must go instantly to Baker's home. The papers must be there; they *must*!

Then he remembered the gold stored in the tunnel from the stage robberies in anticipation of the arms purchases. Right now, no one was pursuing him, but that fact might soon change. He might not be able to get back to Shadow Ridge to get the gold. Better to retrieve the gold first, then go and get the papers. He'd take Byrd from the cave as a guard, pick up Yancey at Baker's. Those two could be used to create a diversion if need be, or he could sacrifice them to fight his way clear. Even if he just delivered the gold to the Confederacy, he'd still be a hero, be recognized, be given his rightful place of honor. And, he reasoned, he needn't deliver all the gold. Some of it would compensate him for the loss of his store and his home in Greenville. Maybe there was a way to avoid paying Byrd and Yancey, too. He'd have to think about that.

And the two boys? Too much trouble to take along. Leave them tied up in the cave to starve? No, it would be better just to kill them now. The end result was the same anyway, but with no chance of their escaping or being found. But what if the papers weren't at Baker's? What if the Negro child wasn't telling all he knew? There was still the gold.

Yes, that was all of it. Leave no loose ends. Get the gold, dispose of the two witnesses, go to Baker's, if only briefly, then move on to . . . to where? San Francisco. Of course! He'd have no difficulty hiding in that booming town. Surely he could find someone to contact, even without the papers. But to live in luxury—ah, that had an attraction all its own.

Mullins had already reached the bend of the road marked by a big oak tree with a huge bare limb that protruded some fifteen feet above the ground. The hanging tree, it was called. Mullins pulled off the road onto a patch of rocky ground. He got out of the buggy and led the horse down a depression bordering Poso Creek and around some brush to a point out of sight of the road.

He retrieved a lantern from the buggy and lit it. Tying the horse to a fallen tree, Mullins clambered awkwardly over it and climbed a steep bank to where some elderberry bushes grew in front of an over-hanging rock. At one time a stream had flowed here, but its course had since shifted underground to join the Poso at a lower point, leaving this concealed tunnel entrance.

Some years ago Mullins had discovered this connection with the summit of Shadow Ridge and all the useful caves and passages in between. Actually, Byrd Guidett had located the upper opening on some occasion when he was fleeing from the law; but after a conversation with Tommy Fitzgerald, Mullins himself had explored the depths of the cave and come upon the lower exit exactly where

157

it was most needed. By leaving his horse at the top of Shadow Ridge, walking downward through the passage, and picking up a previously arranged fresh mount here near the road, a man could cut a full day's travel off riding around the circumference of the peak—the way the roads actually went.

Mullins had carefully cultivated the notion that the mountain was haunted, that it was dangerous, that it was impassable. So far these stories and the natural barrenness of the western slope, together with the difficulty of climbing the eastern approach, had kept the mountain's secrets intact. Once or twice it had been necessary for some unfortunately curious folk to get "lost" or have "accidents," but until Jesse Dawson, no one had tried to ignore the danger and live right beside old Shadow. Well, Jesse had been rewarded for his curiosity, all right; maybe now Tom Dawson had been taken care of, too.

Byrd Guidett threw his canteen down in disgust. *Cold water and cold beans! I'm sick of this waitin' around here. There's more blue-bellied Yankees hereabouts than fleas on a dog's back*—he paused to scratch vigorously—*or on me! An' for what? What if them papers ain't even in this here Baker's house? What if he don't know what I'm after? What if he tries to save his own skin by turnin' me in?*

Each round of Byrd's thoughts grew more and more angry. "An' even if I get them papers," he muttered, "Mullins'll jest take 'em without so much as a say. An' he'll be takin' the gold to spend on guns, which he'll try an' give to them crackers up in the hills. Huh! More'n likely they'll turn 'em on him! General Mullins! Governor Mullins! What a laugh! Now that gold! In the jobs we already pulled thar must be . . ." He squinted at the sky. "Thar must be close on a hundred thousand dollars! Man, I could live like a king in 'Frisco with that!"

The thought was more than he could stand. "What do I care who wins the war? I ain't seen 'em hang no medals on me, but if I stick around that fat fool Mullins, they'll be hangin' somethin' else!"

He jumped to his feet. "I'm for the gold," he declared to his horse, "an' right now!"

✷ CHAPTER 19 ✷

Tom shook his head and tried to clear it. He sat up, over the protests of the parson and McKenna, and put one hand to his now-bandaged skull. "Mullins. Did you catch him?"

"Na, lad, he's nae been seen, but the deputy is here now. Do ye feel able to tell him yer tale?"

Tom was able to repeat his story to Pettibone, giving more details about the cuff links. The deputy listened, his eyes wide with astonishment. As Tom recovered somewhat from the grazing wound, his explanation became clearer and all the pieces of the confusing puzzle fell into place.

"Then you believe Mullins masterminded the scheme to hold up the stages and use the gold for some plot?"

"Yes, but something got fouled up when Byrd killed that stranger. The only thing I can figure is that the dead man had something Mullins needed, so he had Byrd kidnap Mont to see if the child knew anything about it. He must think that whatever it is could be hidden in Colonel Baker's home, 'cause that's what I overheard him mumbling about tonight. He's bound to be desperate, because he must know that Baker's being guarded by the army."

Tom paused, and though he sat silently thinking, no one interrupted to voice an opinion. Finally, he began again. "That means that the boys, if they are still alive, are in terrible danger. Mullins must have decided that they are no longer needed. Anyway, we can't delay.

We've got to follow Mullins right away if the boys are to have any chance at all."

"But follow him where?" asked Pettibone. "We don't know which direction he went out of town or if he's goin' straight to Baker's or where his hideout is."

"Yes, we do! Don't you get it? Mullins kept you from searching Shadow Ridge for Guidett right after the killing at Granite. My brother was killed there when we went looking for a trail, and I don't believe any longer that it was an accident."

"But there is na trail on the Ridge; ye said so yerself," observed McKenna.

"That's right, but there is a cave *under* it! I saw one entrance the day my brother was killed, but I didn't know it for what it was, and afterward I forgot about it till my dream. It must go all the way through and connect up the Tailholt road with this side of the mountain."

"All right, Tom, you've got it ciphered out for sure," said Pettibone. "What'll we do?"

"Parson, you and McKenna should ride to Baker's and alert the soldiers. Have them hold Mullins if he shows up, and get them ready for an attack in case Guidett and some of his kind try to break in.

"Pettibone, take Red and some men and hurry over to Tailholt. When you get there, go up the slopes of Shadow. Even if we don't know exactly where that entrance is, they won't be expecting that bolt-hole to be watched, and you can block their escape."

"And what about the lower entrance, Tom—the one you say you saw on the Poso?" asked the parson.

"I'm counting on Mullins wanting to take his stolen gold with him. He must be going that way right now. I'm going after him."

Tom held up his hands to silence their protests. "There aren't enough of us to go around, and we've got to cover the other possibilities in case I'm wrong. But after all he's done to my family . . . just leave him to me; he's my meat."

❅ ❅ ❅

"Death come a-knockin' on dat gambler's door; said, 'O Gambler, are you ready to go?'" sang Mont.

"He said, 'No, no, no, no, no, 'cause I ain't got on my travelin' shoes,'" responded Nathan enthusiastically.

"Said, 'O Liar, are ya ready to go?'"

Even louder this time Nathan replied, "No, no, no, no, NO!"

"O Sinner, are ya ready to go?"

"No, no, no, no—AHHHH!"

The abrupt end to the song and the drawn-out scream from Nathan were caused by Yancey's sudden appearance in the entrance to the prison cave. His eyes were sunken and red-rimmed, which by contrast with his normally ashen skin color made his face appear skull-like. He had his boot knife in his hand, and he moved it across in front of his body in slow, downward stabbing arcs.

His words, when they could be understood at all, were slurred and crazy. "No. NO! It won't take me. No! Jest one small death will do."

"Mistuh Yancey, we din't hear you. We'll be quiet now. You—"

"Run, Mont!" yelled Nathan. "He's plumb crazy!"

As if to punctuate Nathan's words, Yancey turned one of his stabbing motions into an outward flip of his wrist. Had Nathan not jerked Mont aside at that instant, Yancey's knife would have been embedded in the black boy's chest. As it was, it bounced ringing off the rock wall.

"Come on, Mont!" Nathan yelled again, and the two dashed past Yancey toward the passage.

Yancey lunged at them as they went by, catching Nathan by the shirt collar.

Nathan twisted in his grasp, crying, "Lemme go! Lemme go!"

Holding the strangling Nathan up by the throat, Yancey turned the boy around so they were at eye level. Yancey reached behind his collar with his free hand to draw the other knife that hung there.

Before the man had completely drawn it from its sheath, Mont threw himself at Yancey's legs, and all three tumbled down together.

Yancey's cry rose to a screech. "I've got two for you. Two! Not me; I ain't ready. But here, come and take these!"

Mont scrambled onto the man's chest and flung himself on the arm holding the knife. "Let 'im go! Nathan! Nathan!"

Nathan broke free from Yancey's clutch and struck the outlaw in the face as hard as he could with his two hands doubled together. He and Mont jumped up and rushed into the other cavern.

"Which way'll we go?" cried Nathan.

"Grab de lamp," yelled Mont, "an' le's go down befo' he can get another light."

Snatching the lamp from the table, the boys jumped into the opening that led to the downward passage, just as Yancey picked himself up and came out the tunnel after them. He threw himself across the table at Nathan but missed him and sprawled across its top.

Down the boys plunged, on a steeply slanted narrow rock path. Here the floor was slick with moisture coming from the nearby underground stream. With no time to pick their way, the boys skidded around corners and slammed into rocks. From behind them they could hear a keening sound: "I'll find 'em for ya. Just you wait here a spell. I'll bring 'em back."

162

They came to a place where the tunnel branched. One fork led downward, and the other crossed the stream and went upward again. "What'll we do now?" asked Nathan. "He's still followin' us, like he can see in the dark!"

"No, dat ain't it," replied Mont. "He's jes' done dis trip enough so's he knows de way. But he can't foller de other path in de dark. Le's go up!"

The two plunged into the stream. It was icy and swifter than they expected. In an instant they were spun around. Mont collided with Nathan and both juggled frantically with the bobbling lamp. It fell against a boulder with a crash and was immediately extinguished.

Nathan leaped for the other bank and was rewarded with a handhold on the far side. Pulling himself out of the water, he turned and offered his hand to Mont. Mont climbed out on the bank, and they began crawling farther into the tunnel, judging their direction just by the upward feel. Behind them they could hear the water rushing down the narrow bed, but above that they could still make out Yancey's strange, crooning monologue: "It won't be long now. Oh no, 'most any minute we'll be a-knockin' on their door . . . knockin' on their door. Will they be ready? Le's go see; le's go see."

As the crying voice came closer, it was all the boys could do to lie still in the absolute darkness. They were afraid that Yancey would decide to cross the stream. Nathan and Mont hugged each other and trembled with fear and cold.

✳ ✳ ✳

Robert Mullins bustled up the tunnel. His thoughts were of gold and San Francisco, of opulent comfort, culture, and attentive service. Every few steps he paused to wheeze at the labor of the climb inside the mountain; then he resumed a panting pace, impatient now that his mind was made up to get his hands on the wealth stockpiled there.

He was sweating, partly with exertion and partly with the flush of anticipation. He'd decided that he could convince Byrd that it was time to transport the gold to buy arms; and after enlisting Byrd's help in loading the gold into Mullins' buggy, he'd make off with all of it.

With a smile he patted his huge belly at the top of his trousers. Abruptly his smile faded as the handle of the pistol he expected to feel wasn't there. He tried to remember what he had done with the derringer after shooting Tom. He could have sworn he'd thrust it into his waistband. Frantically he patted his vest and trouser pockets, then, with a relieved sigh, his outside coat pocket. There was the pistol. Mullins recalled that the thought of climbing over the rocks at the cave's mouth with a loaded pistol bound against his gut had made him uneasy, so he had transferred the small weapon to the deep pocket on the outside of his coat. He took it out to examine it in the lamplight and remembered that he had fired one of its two shots but hadn't reloaded it.

"Better safe than sorry," he muttered, and his pudgy fingers squirmed into a vest watch pocket until closing on another .44 cartridge. He broke open the breech and, discarding the spent casing, replaced it with the new one before returning the gun to his coat pocket.

The next part of his hike was Mullins' least favorite, for it involved his girth in a most unpleasant way. The passage he was in continued on past a crevice in the floor some hundred feet farther before coming to a dead end. The true route lay down through the

163

opening in the floor of the tunnel. A short drop would land him in another parallel passage, from which the journey up continued. A limestone ledge was only four feet below, but the process involved setting down the lantern, fitting himself into the opening, and groping with his feet for the ledge. There he could stand and retrieve the lamp before stepping down another three feet to the passage floor.

He put the lantern down close to the edge and eased himself into the opening. His small feet began pawing at the rock in search of the ledge as his weight transferred to his arms. The moment's effort made him puff, but his toes located the spot and he moved to grasp the lamp and continue down. But he couldn't move. He had grown so fat that, with the addition of the heavy coat and presence of the derringer pushing against his hip, he was unable to slide any farther down. Standing on his boot tips, he tried to raise himself back up to the space above, but his arms could not support his poundage and overcome the friction of the tight fit.

With his arms stuck above the hole and his legs straining sideways to maintain contact with the small ledge, he made a most effective cork in a bottle.

✸ ✸ ✸

"Where did ya go, little travelers? Come out and meet a friend," crooned Yancey. "Are ya ready to go?"

He scraped down the tunnel, past the side branch that the boys had chosen as a hiding place. Feeling his way along the limestone passage, he slowly waved his knife back and forth in front of him. Occasionally he would rub it against his shirtsleeve as if wiping it clean of blood.

He came to a place where the passage widened and then split into a maze of smaller channels woven among a thicket of limestone columns that extended to the roof. For some reason, Yancey decided that the boys were playing hide-and-seek with him in this room, so he began to creep softly around each corner, thrusting the knife ahead of him. He lowered his monologue to a whisper but continued chanting, "No, no, no, no, ain't ready to go, 'cause I ain't got on my travelin' shoes."

✻ ✻ ✻

Nathan and Mont were petrified. They had heard Yancey pass their escape route and could not bear the thought of his attempting to cross over. They feared that they could not cross the stream again without making so much noise that he would hear and return to catch them, so they decided to crawl farther into the side tunnel and hope for a way out.

Mont crawled in front, with Nathan coming along behind, one hand grasping Mont's ankle. They stayed down on all fours because in the total blackness they were afraid that they would fall over an unseen drop-off.

After crawling some distance, they felt rather than saw the passage widen around them. They had reached another good-sized room but had no way of guessing its extent, the height of the roof, or where it led.

"What if we're crawlin' straight for a dead end?" whispered Nathan.

"Does you want to go back?" returned Mont over his shoulder.

Nathan thought about the tunnel they had left behind with Yancey and his knife and shuddered. "No!" he whispered urgently. "Only, let's get on out of here." Then he added, "Please, God!"

To which Mont just as reverently whispered, "Amen!"

Mont put out his hand to move a bit farther and pulled back in horror. "Nathan, dey's a dead body here! Ah can feel his trousers, an' his leg is cold and stiff!"

Nathan jerked backward and wanted desperately to run, but a supreme effort made him hold still, deciding that a dead body was less of a threat than a live Yancey. "Are you sure?"

"Well, ah thinks I is. Here's his one leg an' here's another. My, dey do feel hard!" Gritting his teeth, Mont gingerly knocked his knuckles against the leg. "Whooee! It ain't a dead man; it's jes' a pile of sacks or somethin.'"

"Sacks?" breathed Nathan, curious in spite of the recent scare. "What would a heap of sacks be doin' here?" He crawled past Mont's side and reached out to touch the objects in front of them. "You're right. It's a whole mess of canvas bags. What do you suppose is in 'em?"

With these words he began to poke around the sacks, feeling the heavy oblong objects contained in them. After a moment's thought, he said excitedly, "Mont, it's the gold—the stolen gold! This here is the loot stolen from the stage holdups. I bet there's even a reward for findin' this!"

When Mont made no comment to share his friend's enthusiasm, Nathan asked, "What's the matter, Mont? Ain't this excitin'?"

"Nathan, it's *too* excitin'! Don'cha see? Dis here is de gang's loot! Dis ain't no secret tunnel; dey knows jes' where it is. An' sooner or later, dey's gonna think to look here!"

☆ CHAPTER 20 ☆

"Wal, wal, what have we got here? An ol' hog stuck in a gate? My, don't he squeal!"

"Byrd! I'm stuck in this cursed hole. Pull me up," Mullins demanded, "and be quick about it!"

"Now hold on a mite. I seen yer buggy a-settin' down to the bottom. You musta come here in the middle of the night. That ain't like you fat boys, what likes yer soft beds. Now, why d'ya s'pose a fine citizen like ol' Robert Mullins'd be out here this time of night?"

"Pull me out!" Mullins swore at Byrd but could move neither up nor down.

"Tut, tut! Such speech to be a-comin' from a churchgoin' feller." Byrd grinned, enjoying Mullins' predicament.

The storekeeper was strangely silent—not the response Byrd expected. Then Mullins asked, "Why are you coming from outside the cave? Where's Yancey? Why aren't you guarding those two brats? And who's watching Baker's house? Baker's . . . did you get the papers? Is that why you're here?"

"Naw," replied Byrd with a grin. "I'm here for the same reason as you, I reckon. I been wet, an' I been cold, but I ain't a-gonna be poor much longer."

Byrd could see Mullins shiver.

"You've got it wrong, Byrd," Mullins said in a soothing voice. "I was coming here to divide the gold with the three of us. Yes, that's what I came here for."

"Wal, the way I figgers, two shares is better'n three. An' one is even better yet. Ain't that the way you got it figgered?"

Before Mullins could utter a word of protest or plea, Byrd drew his Walker and shot Robert Mullins between the eyes.

Mullins' feet slipped from the ledge, and the weight of his body caused him to fall heavily through the opening.

"Ain't that somethin'?" remarked Byrd wonderingly. "He weren't really stuck any of the time."

"We are climbin' Jacob's ladder," crooned Yancey, "sol'jers of the cross." Around the maze of limestone byways he glided, stabbing his knife into corners and into side passageways before entering them himself.

"Climbin' Jacob's ladder, gonna climb them golden stairs. Golden stairs," he repeated. "Gonna climb right up to the sun. All kinds a light up on that golden stair. Gold. Up the ladder to the gold. My, my, my, what have we got here? Lights to light the night, right on up the golden ladder."

So saying, he produced a box of matches from his pants pocket, which his fever-ridden brain had not remembered till now.

Striking one, he turned to face the passage he had just descended and sang to himself, "Are ya ready to go? They said, 'No, no, no, no, no . . .'"

Tom halted Duncan beside Mullins' buggy and Byrd's horse. Not knowing exactly where to look along the banks of Poso Creek for the tunnel entrance he expected to find, Tom had ridden slowly along the road. His pace had been much quieter than Byrd's pounding ride, so it was easy to get off the road to watch without being spotted. Tom didn't know Byrd for who he was, but he reasoned that few people up to any good would be out in the middle of the night, and fewer still would have a reason to turn off at this spot.

He had allowed Duncan his head, and the canny horse, like a huge bloodhound, had followed Byrd's track as it wound down to the streambed. Tom had watched as Byrd lit a lantern and climbed up and into the entrance to the cave. What with Mullins having such a long head start, Tom had been convinced that to tackle the unknown rider would delay him further or in some way warn the fleeing storekeeper.

Now Tom tried to decide what to do next. He thought briefly of returning to town for help since his idea was correct and he had run Mullins to earth, but he was afraid they might leave before he could return. He also couldn't stand the thought of the boys being held captive one moment longer. Tom waited a couple of minutes; then taking a bull's-eye lantern from a saddlebag, he lit it and proceeded to enter the cave.

Inside the tunnel mouth, he heard a gunshot. Tom's heart sank. *Oh, God,* he prayed, *let the boys be all right! Don't let me come this close and not rescue them.*

He carried his lantern in his left hand and his Colt in his right. Even though his lantern might betray his presence, Tom hoped that anyone he might encounter would not be climbing around this secret place with his weapon at the ready, so he felt he would have the advantage.

169

Now his insides were twisting. He didn't know whether he should run ahead toward the sound of the shot or continue his cautious stalk. When no further shots were fired and no other sounds indicated another person's location, Tom continued moving quietly.

Up ahead, just around a bend of the tunnel, he saw a light. Tom dropped to a crouch. Setting his own lantern down behind him, he moved as far over to the other wall of the passage as possible, keeping close to the shadows and advancing with the Colt leading the way. Carefully he peered around a corner.

He saw Mullins' lantern sitting in the middle of the cavern floor. Tom wondered if it could be a trap. Reaching down with his left hand, he picked up a small chunk of quartz. Preparing himself to fight, he hurled the rock at the lamp. He missed, but the resulting clatter sounded as loud as an avalanche to his ears.

When nothing happened and no one appeared, Tom decided to chance going forward. He slowly approached the crevice, scanning all around as he did so.

After another glance around, Tom looked downward into the opening. There lay Robert Mullins, his jowls sagging limply. He seemed to have grown a third eye in his forehead. Tom guessed at what had transpired but wasted no more thought on Robert Mullins. Instead, he made a quick examination of the hole and spotted the ledge for stepping down. He swung his legs into the opening, aware that he was going to be completely helpless for a moment. With this thought, he skipped stepping to the ledge and allowed himself to drop through the hole in one motion, just missing Mullins' body as he did so.

Almost without thinking, he bent and scooped up the derringer that had fallen from Mullins' pocket and thrust it through his belt. Looking around quickly, Tom guessed that he would have already drawn a shot if there were a sentry, so he stepped back onto the ledge and retrieved the lamp from beside the hole. He then proceeded to advance up the passage as before.

✷ ✷ ✷

"Oh, Gambler, are ya ready to go? Go up Jacob's ladder?" With the help of the light, Yancey was moving rapidly back up the tunnel, striking matches as he went. He moved purposefully now, his knife carried blade upward in his fighting stance. No longer did he wave it around or stab it into corners. He clearly had a destination in mind, and he was heading there.

✷ ✷ ✷

The boys had climbed over the sacks of gold, reasoning that the best they could do now was try to get deeper into the side passage. They were still crawling, but now Nathan was leading.

Mont was praying aloud, "Oh, Jesus, he'p us. Jesus, he'p us get outta here."

✷ ✷ ✷

Byrd could hear some sounds ahead of him, but he couldn't quite make out the words. He drew his Walker. "What in blazes is goin' on here? Yancey? Yancey, is that you? Where are ya?"

✳ ✳ ✳

Yancey stopped lighting matches as he heard Byrd's yell. He had just reached the point at which the side tunnel branched off to the gold. Yancey lit one more match in order to get his bearings; then he stepped into the stream and crossed over. On the other side he stopped, his back pressed against the wall of the passage and waited. "Death come a-knockin' on that sinner's door," he muttered.

✳ ✳ ✳

Upward went Byrd. He noticed the trail of burned-out matches. "Those kids musta run off, an' Yancey's tryin' to find 'em. Why ain't he got a lantern, though?"

When Byrd reached the side tunnel, he raised his lantern high over his head to illuminate the far bank. Sure enough, he could barely make out the wet tracks where someone had crossed. "Yancey, c'mon back out here, an' we'll hunt 'em down together. C'mon, ya cussed snake, I ain't gettin' my feet wet less'n ya tell me what's up!"

There was no reply.

"You don't s'pose ol' Yancey got to hankerin' after that gold himself?" mused Byrd aloud. "You cain't trust nobody!" As he stepped into the stream, he saw a flash reflected from Yancey's knife as Yancey lunged from the shadows. Byrd's foot turned on a rock, his sideways sprawl saving him. Yancey's thrust was intended to catch Byrd in the stomach as he emerged from the crossing, but instead it caught only air.

Byrd's revolver leaped into his hand, and he fired. Byrd saw the first bullet strike Yancey, but in twisting around and firing, Byrd dropped his lantern into the water. He fired twice more in quick succession—once into the body he saw starting to topple and once more into the blackness of the floor where he believed Yancey to be.

All was still.

"Yancey," Byrd called softly, "I sure hope you is dead, but if ya ain't, you better talk nice an' sweet to me less'n my finger gets to jumpin' again."

There was no reply—not even a groan.

"I reckon I'm done with you," he concluded, pulling himself out of the water. Carefully he kicked Yancey's body, holding his Walker ready. He kicked again—harder this time. "Yup. I don't know what got inta ya, but I figgered it'd end thisaway anyhow, iff'n that's any comfort to ya."

Byrd rummaged through the corpse's pockets till he found the matches. "Jest a handful left? I guess ya won't be needin' 'em, ol' cuss, so I'll jest mosey along an' check on my gold."

※ ※ ※

The boys froze at the sounds coming from the tunnel behind them. They heard Byrd's yell echo down the passage: "We'll hunt 'em together." When the shots came, the boys didn't know what to make of it. They waited silently, hearts pounding like a blacksmith's hammers, to see what would happen next.

Back toward the sacks of gold they peered, straining to see something through the darkness. Presently they could see a flicker of light, and once they heard Byrd swear as he held a match too long and burned himself. They saw him illuminated in the scratching hiss of another match as he crouched over the gold, his face an evil mask of gloating delight, made hideous by the strange play of shadows around his beard.

Nathan gave an involuntary gasp and instantly clapped his hand over his mouth.

But Byrd had heard. He looked into the darkness where they lay and called, "Is you kids there? Come on out. I ain't gonna hurt ya. Yancey done went crazy, but I've fixed him, an' the ol' fat boy, too. Come on out now, I say."

When neither child moved or uttered another word, Byrd gave an exasperated sigh. "You'uns is determined to make this tough, ain't ya?" He shook out the match and lit another while counting to himself. "Le's see, one bullet for Mullins an' three for Yancey. Why, that leaves me jest enough, don't it?"

"Don't count on it," said a voice from behind him.

Dawson.

Byrd whirled, dropping the match and plunging the cave into darkness as he did so. He fired a shot in the direction from which the voice had come, then threw himself to the floor of the cavern and found shelter behind the gold. He heard a clatter and knew that his bullet had either hit its mark or spun Tom's gun out of his grasp.

"Whyn't ya shoot, Dawson?" Byrd called. "Could it be I've killed ya jest like we did yer brother? Like I'm fixin' to do with them two brats?" Byrd reached into his pocket and took out another match. Holding his cocked pistol across the canvas sacks, he struck the match on the cave's floor and held it aloft in his left hand.

Lying just a few feet away was Tom. Byrd noticed the shattered Colt Navy lying against the far wall and the bandages swathing Tom's head. "Why, Dawson," said Byrd, rising, "you was 'most dead already. But since I got this here bullet, I'll just use it on you, an' then I'll take care of yer brats. An' then—" he leered—"I aim to pay a little visit to that Emily lady."

At these words, Nathan rose behind Byrd, shouting, "No! no! You can't hurt my ma!"

"What the—?" was all Byrd got out of his mouth before Tom put a .44 slug from the storekeeper's derringer straight through his heart.

"Keep still, boys," called Tom. "Let's wait to see that this isn't a trick."

A moment later he called, "Say, where's that light coming from?" A faint silvery glow was coming from the far end of the tunnel. By it, Tom could see Nathan and Mont come out of their concealment and could make out Byrd's body slumped over the sacks of gold.

"Uncle, Uncle! Mistuh Tom!" came the glad cries as the boys ran to Tom.

After a moment of embracing, Tom observed, "That's got to be daylight, boys. Let's go see where it leads."

Around the next corner, the boys drew up against Tom in sudden alarm. Daylight was pouring into the cave through a hole in the roof, and lying at the bottom of a ramp of dirt leading up and out was the skull of Tommy Fitzgerald's gigantic grizzly.

Tom laughed as he hugged the two boys again. Putting his arms around the boys' shoulders, he climbed the incline to stand in the morning light. He stood looking down at the eastern slope of Shadow Ridge toward where the ranch and Emily and Jed were waiting. "Come on, boys. Let's go home!"

Cannons of the Comstock

Jesse Dawson was murdered in the
mountains of Shadow Ridge by rebel
sympathizers, leaving behind a
family and ranch in his brother Tom's
care. Now all Tom wants is a
peaceful life of growing potatoes
and breaking horses. But when
a secret Confederate society
begins to raise and equip an army
that would engulf California in the
Civil War and break the Union blockade
that strangles the South, Tom finds
himself the middleman in a bold
attempt to infiltrate and expose
the conspiracy. And the only link to
tracing the conspirators is Montgomery
James, a nine-year-old black child
and former slave.

Everything is Jake!

⁂ CHAPTER 1 ⁂

The clatter of hooves on the rust-colored cobblestones rang like musket fire down the lanes of Richmond, Virginia. As soon as one dispatch rider passed the bronze statue of George Washington, the staccato echo of another's approach could be heard in the distance.

Though they were official couriers charged with bearing military communiqués to the Confederate cabinet, the messengers could not help shouting their reports to the eager citizens who jammed the sidewalks. "The *Cumberland* has been rammed and is sinking!" cried one.

The crowds applauded and yelled their approval. "Hurrah for the *Virginia*! No Yankee blockage shall hold!"

Another rider cantered by.

"What news?" the mob demanded.

"Our iron-hulled alligator has blasted the *Congress* to kingdom come and is turning toward the *Minnesota*," the hoarse-voiced officer croaked.

Directly in front of Washington's statue, the rough, flushed face of Colonel James turned away from the excitement of the street to lock eyes with a small black child perched atop the eight-foot-high block of marble. "You, Mont! Look sharp," he demanded. "Don't forget why you're up there, or I'll whup your worthless hide clean off!"

The boy's vantage point on the statue's pedestal lifted him above the heads of the crowd, but he paid no attention to their enthusiasm.

The florid-cheeked colonel did not need to remind Mont of his assignment or the merciless temper behind the whip. The child was so intent that he did not even turn his head as yet another dispatch rider galloped past, bearing more news of the great naval battle taking place at Hampton Roads.

The sharp-eyed boy spotted the approaching carriage when it was still a full three blocks away. He could pick it out from the other traffic on the Richmond street because of its unmatched team of horses. The near horse was a gray, while the off horse was deep chestnut. In an era when respectable gentlemen prided themselves on the perfection of their teams, the object of Mont's search stood out like the wispy beard of President Jefferson Davis.

"He's a comin' yonder," called out Mont in a high treble.

"'Bout time," grunted Colonel James. "All right, shinny on down here right now."

Mont jumped down from his perch and took his position behind his master as the carriage came to a stop.

The young man who stepped from the carriage was clean shaven. He was not wearing a uniform as Mont had expected, but instead a brown suit coat with a dark brown velveteen collar. The knot of his cravat was crooked, and his movements seemed anxious and hurried. He clutched a scuffed leather portfolio against his chest with both hands and peered nervously up and down the street.

Colonel James made his customary approach. "I'm James," he announced with a squinted eye, "and your name is Hastings."

"Avery Hastings," agreed the newcomer. He extended his right hand, but James ignored it. Hastings awkwardly brushed it against the leather pouch. "How soon can you get me in to see him?" he asked abruptly.

"Depends," remarked James in a stone-cold voice. "President Davis is a very busy man." The two started to cross the street with Mont trailing along behind. "He don't have time to bother with every crackpot schemer that comes around." The distant patter of an approaching troop of cavalry could be heard from the far end of the avenue.

"Crackpot! Schemer!" Hastings bristled, stopping in his tracks and turning to face his accuser. "Colonel," he corrected in an intense whisper, "I'll have you know that it's in my power to deliver California and *all* its gold into the hands of the Confederacy!"

Colonel James remained unmoved and only returned a silent stare.

Hastings quickly yielded to the silence. "Where is my valise?"

"Boy!" James bellowed at Mont. "Fetch the man's bag and be quick about it." He gave Mont a shove that sent the child sprawling on the cobblestones. "Run!"

Mont jumped up and dashed back across the road in a flurry of eagerness to please. His dark eyes were serious, and he bit his lower lip as his skinny arms strained to wrest the heavy carpetbag from the carriage.

James and Hastings had turned away from the street to enter the office building but not before Mont caught an impatient glare that made him redouble his efforts. Raising himself on his tiptoes as he balanced on the carriage's running board, he mustered all his strength to hoist the case upward.

As this last effort freed the valise, Mont jumped backward into the middle of the boulevard without having paid any heed to the cavalry unit now bearing down on him less than fifty feet away. Mont suddenly felt the impending danger of the thunderous noise of hoofbeats.

Transfixed at the sight of twenty-five riders racing toward him, Mont saw a solid wave of angry-eyed bay war horses that stretched from curb to curb. The ringing of their hooves vibrated through him from the crown of his tightly curled hair to the worn-out soles of his cheap shoes.

The front rank reached him, seemingly a single beast with twenty-four flailing limbs and twelve blasting nostrils. No individual sounds could be distinguished. All Mont heard was a continuous roll of hoofbeats, shouts, and snorts. He could not even hear his own scream of terror as the foaming wave crested above him.

✳ ✳ ✳

Mont awoke with the cry stuck in his throat as the vivid sight of the Confederate cavalry troop replayed once more in his memory. Above the narrow bunk he shared with Nathan Dawson, gingham curtains at the window tossed on a swirl of frosty January air. Sheets and down comforters were damp with the sweat brought on by Mont's recurring nightmare. His heart still drummed in his ears like the echoing hoofbeats of the horses that had borne down on him that long-ago hot afternoon in Richmond. Was it only his heart he was hearing? Or was it something else?

A distant rumble of galloping horses seemed to float past the curtains. Mont covered his face with his hands to shut out the sound and the memory. But the drumming did not diminish. He sat up in bed and stared, trembling, toward the half-open door. If only he could escape the horror of the room—away from the sound . . . away from the dream that would not leave him alone. But his shaking legs refused to move, just as they had stood like wooden posts when the wall of horses had thundered toward him.

He squeezed his eyes tight and forced himself to remember how the brown-suited man had appeared out of nowhere and propelled him to safety.

A split second more and they would have perished. There had been no attempt to pull back on the stampeding horses. In that frantic moment, Mont had dropped the valise. The bag and its contents had been trampled into unrecognizable scraps of leather and tiny fluttering bits of ragged cloth before those churning hooves disappeared around the corner. Mont had stared in disbelief at the wreckage. It might have been his own body pieces on the street.

Mortified by Mont's stupidity, Colonel James had sworn to make the boy pay dearly for this public shame. He said it would have served Mont right if he had been trampled. The colonel had whipped the boy with a razor strop every day for several weeks after the incident. But Mont never dreamed about the sting of leather on his bare backside. He only relived the vision of those approaching horses.

Tonight he could not escape the nightmare. He was awake. At least he *thought* he was awake. This was California, not Richmond. His brutal master was long since dead. Mont now lived at the ranch of the widow Dawson with her two sons, Jed and Nathan. Eight-year-old Nathan was snoring soundly beside him. Why, then, could he still hear the sound that carried his mind back to that violent Richmond street?

Another gust of wind off the Sierras carried the rattle of iron shoes on ice-hardened dirt lanes. *Still dreaming?*

He reached out a finger in the darkness and poked Nathan as yet another shudder of fear coursed through his thin body.

"Huh?" Nathan responded sleepily. "Wha . . . Mont?"

"I hears h-hawses," Mont stuttered.

"You're dreamin' agin." Nathan moaned unhappily.

The ghostly drumming rose and fell. This was *no dream*!

Now Nathan heard it too and lay silently listening for a moment.

"Hear dat?" Mont whispered.

"Uh-huh." Nathan sat up beside Mont and scrambled to the window. Ducking beneath the curtain, he squinted out across the dark yard toward the barn.

Mont squeezed in beside him, greatly comforted that the hoof-beats were not merely in his mind and that his legs were working again.

The tiny orange flare of a match erupted behind the tack room of the barn, where Nathan's uncle, Tom Dawson, lived. Then the light became brighter as Tom lit the kerosene lamp.

"Uncle is up," Nathan said reassuringly. "Ain't no ghosts we're hearin', I guess."

From the lower bunk, Jed called out, "Go to sleep or I'm tellin' Ma. . . ."

Mont did not take his eyes from the backlit figure of Tom Dawson as the big, craggy man wrapped a blanket around his shoulders and stood beside the lamp to listen. Then he reached down to grasp his carbine and put it by the door. He quickly tugged on his trousers and boots.

The sound of approaching horses grew louder.

"Comin' this way," Nathan muttered.

By now the increasing noise of hoofbeats had stirred Jed to a wakeful apprehension. "What is it?" He pulled his comforter tight around him and climbed up to join Mont and Nathan at the window.

181

At the sight of his uncle emerging from the lean-to with rifle in hand, Jed added, "Call Ma!"

✳ ✳ ✳

A gray swirl of morning fog hung at streetlamp height above the intersection of Montgomery and California streets. The bustling activity of San Francisco's business district had not yet begun. A solitary pedestrian paused in the shadows in the middle of the block, beyond the reach of the lamplight. In unhurried fashion, he extracted a cigar from his waistcoat pocket and lit it. Ducking his head toward the match cupped in his hands, he took the opportunity to scan the sidewalks. Satisfied that no one was following him, he walked briskly toward an even deeper gathering of darkness and plunged into it.

One knock thumped on the alley doorway leading into the building of the Atlantic and European Express Company. After a pause, two knocks followed, then another pause and one more.

A gravelly voice from within demanded, "What is it?"

"An inquiry about shipping" was the short reply.

"Why so early?" The voice from the interior of the building sounded gruff and irritated.

"It is never too early for important business" was the precisely spoken response, every word distinct.

There was a rasping noise as a heavy bar was lifted inside, followed by the sound of two iron bolts being drawn.

"Come in slowly, friend," the whiskey-roughened voice instructed. "And don't do nothin' fancy."

The man with the cigar nudged the door open with his foot and slowly advanced into the spotlight of a bull's-eye lantern that shone directly into his face, blinding him. He carefully held both hands open in front of his expensively tailored coat. When he had moved to the center of the dingy room, he saw that the lantern hung from the banister of a dilapidated wooden staircase.

The door quickly closed behind him, and the bolts clanked back into place.

"Up the stairs," he was told.

Halfway up, it struck him that he had never seen the form, much less the face, of the doorkeeper. "Very impressive," he muttered to himself through teeth clenched around the smoldering cigar.

✳ ✳ ✳

Emily Dawson's room was below the loft where Mont and her sons were sleeping. But it was not the noise of the approaching horsemen that awakened her—she had roused before first light to stir the fire. The new day promised to be fair and clear skied, but the feeble light of the winter dawn would be a long time warming the air.

The rocky battlement known as Shadow Ridge curled down among the foothills of the Sierra Nevadas into as pretty an oak-trimmed valley as existing anywhere in the world. Three thousand feet above the level of the Pacific Ocean, which lay one hundred and fifty miles or so to the west, the Dawson ranch sat safely above the malarial fogs of the Great Central Valley but lower than the redwood-studded backbone of the Sierras. The high passes were shrouded with snow and would be uncrossable till spring, but in the watershed of the Poso, life went on.

Emily's husband, Jesse, had located well and had made a good life of farming potatoes and breaking horses. The Union army had proved a ready customer for both.

At first the War Between the States had been only a distant source of unhappy news, until a Confederate conspiracy reached California and engulfed the Dawson home. Jesse and his brother, Tom, had been close to uncovering the secrets of Shadow Ridge when Jesse was murdered.

Listening to the hoofbeats, Emily paused as she ran a brush through her honey blonde hair. Her fair complexion was smooth, but a deep sadness lingered in the depths of her blue eyes. Like Mont, she also noted when the approaching riders turned to cross the creek.

Drawing her dark blue dressing gown tightly around her, Emily looked for a shawl to throw over her shoulders. Best see that her brother-in-law, Tom, was awake. Shadow Ridge was still thick with Southern sympathizers.

As battles raged in the East, tempers flared higher here in the West. Why would riders come to the ranch at this hour unless they meant to settle some old score?

✳CHAPTER 2✳

As his apprehension mounted with the approaching riders, Tom Dawson levered a round into the fifteen-shot Henry rifle he carried. The cold of the brass receiver was enough to make his hand ache, but he took no notice. Five purposeful strides across the yard and he reached up to knock on the door of the house. "Em! Wake up, Emily. Riders coming!"

The door opened at the first knock, and Emily stood regarding him, a worried frown printed across her delicate features. "I heard them, too. What do you suppose it is?"

"More'n likely nothing fretful. But it's a sight too early and icy for this to be a social call. You and the boys stay inside with the door bolted till we see."

"Aren't you coming inside?" she asked, concerned.

"No, I'll be across the way there." He jerked his thumb over his shoulder toward the corral. "Get Jed to watch the creek side of the place in case someone sneaks up that way, and you—"

"I'll be right here beside the window," she vowed coolly, pulling a twelve-gauge double-barreled Thomas shotgun into view.

"Good girl," Tom said with a grin. "You just keep out of sight, and if need be—" he paused to nudge her shotgun's barrel—"let 'buck' do the talking for you."

Taking his position, Tom stood in the angle formed by the corral fence and the wall of the barn. From there he had a clear field of fire without shooting toward the house and a line of retreat into the barn if he needed one.

He went through the preparations for battle with a mechanical detachment, loading the Henry's tube magazine and checking the Colt Navy revolver. All the time his conscious mind was racing through a series of questions. Who could be coming? There were gangs of men calling themselves Southern sympathizers but who really were only thieves and murderers of the lowest sort. There had been raids by Confederate regulars into New Mexico and Arizona as well as the threat that they would rush into California.

Tom's last gun battle with one such outlaw came swiftly to mind. The ache in Tom's right hand was a constant reminder of that fight. Byrd Guidett was buried, unmarked and unmourned, in the pauper's corner of Oak Grove Cemetery. Robert Mullins, shopkeeper and ringleader, and Yancey, another outlaw, were also dead. But who knew the whereabouts of any other outlaws with whom they rode?

Tom crouched lower than the top rail and peered over the second whip-sawn two-by-twelve. Where he had placed himself gave him some advantage, but it wasn't perfect. Looking east as he was, the riders would be coming toward him out of the morning sun, which was just now climbing over the Greenhorn Mountains.

Sounds like five or six riders coming. Not good odds if they're hostile. 'Course, he reassured himself, *this isn't exactly a sneak attack either.*

The approaching riders turned the last corner off the road and onto the lane leading up to the Dawson ranch. The jingle of harness rings joined the rhythmically snorting breath of the horses. From the barn, Tom's own favorite mount, Duncan, bugled a warning.

They finally moved into his line of sight, a moving mass of dark-garbed men on muscled bays. Puffs of vapor from the horses' nostrils streamed back along the trail, as if tracing the passage of a steam locomotive. Brass buttons glinted on the men's caps and shoulders. Sunlight flashed on carbines slung over shoulders. Military men, for certain—but, against the morning's glare, what color coats did they wear? Blue or gray?

A tall, broad-shouldered figure rode at the head of the column of twos. He was flanked by a much shorter man dressed in lighter-colored clothing than the rest. The smaller man seemed to be haranguing the larger, who ignored him.

They clattered into the yard. The horses milled about and called out to those in the barn.

"Hello the house," called out the leader of the troop in a resonant bass voice. A reedy echo from the smaller man repeated the phrase. The two sat their horses nearest the door and were ringed by a semi-circle of four others dressed in the dark blue uniforms of the United States Cavalry.

Tom blew a sigh of relief and eased his grip on the carbine. He stepped on the bottom rail of the fence and casually swung the Henry across his arm. "Morning, Colonel. What brings you and Deputy Pettibone out here so early?"

✳ ✳ ✳

186

The worn stairs in the warehouse of the Atlantic and European Express Company swayed under the weight of the cigar-smoking man. He passed two landings with branching walkways leading into dusty storerooms; then the rickety treads made an abrupt turn and zigged back the other direction.

He knew he was being watched. He could almost feel the eyes peering at him from the dark shadows. The man smiled to himself because anyone trying to observe him would be able to track only the glowing tip of his cigar in the darkness-shrouded stairway.

A faint illumination suddenly appeared above him at last. The rectangular outline of a curtained doorway loomed above him, showing a rim of lantern light from the room beyond.

The man straightened his necktie and tile hat, then brushed a speck of ash from his coat lapel. Satisfied with his appearance, he pushed past the curtain and found himself in an anteroom confronting a pair of sliding oak doors. The solidly built doors were tightly shut, as if guarding the treasure room of some ancient king. *Or his tomb,* the man thought wryly.

He gave the same pattern of knocks as he had used to gain entrance to the building.

But this time a voice from within inquired through a tiny wrought-iron grille, "Who comes here?"

"A knight" was his reply.

"A knight of what allegiance?" the voice demanded.

"A knight of the Golden Circle."

"And where are you bound, Sir Knight?"

"From darkness to light, from oppression to freedom, and on to the glorious destruction of all tyrants."

"Enter, Brother Knight."

The room into which the new arrival ventured was grim and unappealing. The windowless walls were bare brick, and the air was thick and oppressively dust laden. He immediately felt as if he were choking.

A single lantern, reeking of rancid whale oil, sat on a circular table. Around the circle were nine seated men and a single empty chair. No greeting was given as he entered. Instead, the men sat in silence, waiting for the meeting to begin.

At the touch of an unseen doorkeeper, the oak panels slid shut behind him. Directly opposite the entry sat a man whose face was masked. He was sitting rigidly upright in a thronelike chair. Its scroll-carved back rose higher than the others, and the cigar smoker instinctively looked to its occupant for instruction.

But it was a man with a high forehead and a pointed beard seated on the left who spoke first. "Take your place, Brother Knight" was the order. An imperious wave sent the newcomer to the empty chair.

The bearded man continued, "The first meeting of the Knights of the Golden Circle for the year 1864 will come to order. The situation grows critical, and time is short, so we will dispense with formalities. Each of us has committed to finding and recruiting ten men of uncompromising convictions and unquestioning loyalty to the cause of the South. Each of those ten captains will be responsible for raising a company of soldiers under our command . . . twenty-five hundred men armed and ready to strike . . . within four months."

An outburst of noisy whispers erupted. Biding his time, the speaker grasped his beard thoughtfully, his head inclined toward a young, clean-shaven man seated on his left. The babble around the table concerned the time span named; no one thought that four months was adequate time to recruit and train such a number for their purpose.

Eventually the hurried consultations subsided, and the speaker resumed his remarks. "There are many good reasons why we must strike soon. Last November, before the victory of that fiend Grant at Chattanooga, we almost had the French and the British convinced to recognize the Confederacy. Gentlemen, we need California, and we need it *now!*"

He paused to allow his words to make their impact, then laid an approving palm on the back of the young man on his left. "We know how to obtain the necessary arms. Will you please tell us, Bro—ah, but, no. Where are my manners? We should hear first from our new acquaintance. Brother Franklin, late of Washington, D.C."

The man with the cigar crushed it out under his boot heel, stood, and looked at each man seated around the circle, then cleared his throat. He explained how he had been privy to certain war department planning sessions and could speak with authority on Grant's plans for the Union's spring campaigns.

"He will attack Atlanta, that's certain, and Mobile after the fall of Shreveport. It will cut the South in two. We desperately need your aid, brothers. You must prevent the flow of gold and silver from reaching the bloodstained hands of the baboon king, Abe the First. That's why I was dispatched here personally: to urge your immediate action and to carry back encouragement to our brave leaders by telling them of your progress."

As Franklin sat down, the leader in the mask nodded his appreciation of this message and spoke at last. "Atlanta and Mobile . . . truly terrifying and calamitous! It must be prevented at all costs. Exactly what our other source has indicated." His voice sounded muffled and sinister.

"What other source?" queried Franklin in consternation. "Only I was sent to bring you this secret and carry back your plans."

"Carry back our plans, eh? No doubt, no doubt . . . Seize him!"

The two men seated on either side grasped Franklin's arms and pressed them firmly against the tabletop. A third attacker swung around and dropped a loop of rope over his body, securing it to the chair.

"What is this?" Franklin sputtered. "This is an outrage!"

"Gentlemen," said the bearded man, "I give you not Franklin of the Golden Circle but Sterling of the Pinkertons!"

The man now identified as Sterling continued to squirm against the rope and protest his innocence. "I am Franklin."

"No," corrected the masked leader sternly. "We know that Franklin was killed. Obviously your masters did not know that we already had gotten word of his death."

Sterling's eyes grew wide with fear, and he tossed and struggled furiously. "Wait! You're mistaken!"

The bearded man slowly shook his head, his pointed whiskers describing a short arc like a swinging dagger blade. "Good-bye, Mister Sterling," he said, then lifted a concealed pistol from his lap and shot the helpless Sterling through the heart.

✣ ✣ ✣

The young, clean-shaven man jumped up in alarm. "Was that necessary? What if you were wrong? What if this was the real Franklin? How can you be so cold-blooded?"

"Sit down, Brother Hastings," commanded the leader. The burlap sack that served as his mask swelled and shrank ominously as he puffed with anger at the disapproval. "I shall overlook your rash comments this once—only because of your youth and inexperience. But let me warn you: *Never* be critical of a decision of mine ever again unless you wish to join the Yankee spy. Do you understand?"

Hastings turned ashen. In a stricken voice he muttered, "Of course, General. I forgot my place. Please pardon me." He sat down, tightly grasping his hands together in a vain attempt to stop them from shaking.

"By tomorrow, General, Sterling's body will be a crab's meal at the bottom of the bay," commented the bearded assassin. "And his hotel room is even right now having a mysterious and most destructive fire."

Smiles broke the lingering tension, and the Knights of the Golden Circle seemed genuinely pleased.

"Very good, Brother Perry," commented the masked leader.

Ignoring the body slumped across the loop of hemp and the growing dark red stain pooling beneath the chair, he continued, "Now, gentlemen, on to business. Prudence dictates that we conclude these proceedings quickly and reconvene tomorrow night at our alternate location. Remember, from now on, we must be constantly on guard against spies."

✴CHAPTER 3✴

The four troopers ranged around the dining table looked awkward and slightly ill at ease. Colonel Mason had ordered them to remain outside because of their trail-worn and mudsplattered condition, but Emily Dawson had overruled him and insisted they come in from the cold.

The cavalrymen were not used to seeing their colonel countermanded, certainly never successfully. They nervously handled the china cups Emily had distributed to them, as if enjoying their coffee would call down the officer's wrath. Could dropping a cup earn a man a firing squad?

But the officious and self-important Deputy Pettibone evidently felt no such reservations. The little man rattled his cup loudly on its saucer, sloshing the coffee over the sides, then helped himself to a refill and two more cookies from the tray.

Colonel Mason frowned at Deputy Pettibone, then continued his conversation with Tom. "As I was saying, we believe that the man known as Colonel James was linked to a secret California Confederate society that had a plan—"

"That's right," Pettibone broke in, his whiskers powdered with cookie crumbs. "James was supposed to deliver orders to the men who had been stealing the gold shipments, but he went and got hisself killed by Byrd Guidett sorta accidental-like over a card game 'cause Guidett didn't know who he was and—"

"Pettibone," snapped the colonel, "Dawson knows all that! He's the one who rescued the boy from Guidett after the shooting! Now keep your mouth shut and let me get to the point."

A crestfallen Deputy Pettibone plunged his drooping mustache into his coffee, while the wary troopers exchanged amused glances.

"We believe that the outlaw band here on Shadow Ridge was motivated by greed." Mason paused. "Nevertheless, we think the secret society is very real and still active."

"So what's the purpose of your early morning ride?" Tom wondered. "You didn't come all this way to talk about Guidett's gang. What help could I possibly be? I never saw Colonel James before his death."

"Not you," corrected the colonel. "We think that the child Mont may be able to tell us about others in the group whom James met."

"Colonel," said Emily, her eyes instantly flashing, "Mont is a nine-year-old who still has horrible nightmares from all he's been through. I'll not have him upset needlessly."

Now it was Mason's turn to fidget, picking idly at the crossed-saber insignia on the crown of his hat before replying. "Mrs. Dawson, I know the loss you have personally experienced, and I am truly sorry. But if the Union loses California, the course of the war will be prolonged at a cost of many thousands of additional lives. What's more to the point for your family is that unless we can stop this conspiracy before it takes root, California may become a battleground as bloody as Shiloh or Gettysburg. If this can be prevented, is it not worth the attempt?"

The round faces of two boys, one pale and one dusky brown, peeked over the rail of their sleeping loft. "Miss Emily, I kin answer questions," the dusky brown one called. "It cain't hurt me none."

"All right, Mont," Emily agreed with a sigh. "You boys come on down here."

Colonel Mason attempted to take Mont backward through his memory. "All right," he said kindly, "we already know that you stayed at the home of Thomas Baker down in the valley. While you were there, did you see anyone you had met before or hear any names mentioned?"

"No, suh, I surely didn't," declared Mont.

Trying a different approach, Mason asked, "Well then, how about before you got to the valley? Did you meet anyone in California that you had seen before in Missouri?"

Mont pondered this question with great intensity, frowning and wrinkling his forehead. Finally he shook his head. "No, suh, not so's I recollects."

The colonel tried once more. "Do you remember the names of any other places that you stopped in California?"

Mont gave a wide smile and nodded vigorously. "We was in 'Frisco! We stopped at a powerful fine hotel, too, and—" He stopped abruptly as a sudden thought galloped visibly across his face.

Mason looked at Tom and Emily and raised his eyebrows. "What is it, Mont? What did you remember?"

"Well, suh, does you care just about folks I seed in Califorry and Missouri?"

The colonel urged Mont to go ahead with whatever he could remember.

Pettibone took the opportunity to exhale loudly and cross his arms over his thin chest, declaring that all this was simply a waste of time.

"In 'Frisco I did see this man I seed befo', but not in Missouri."

"Where, then, Mont?" urged Emily gently.

"It was the same man what come to see Colonel James in Richmond."

"What?" burst out Colonel Mason. "Richmond, Virginia? Who was this man? What was the meeting about?"

"I don't rightly know, 'ceptin' . . ."

"Yes, go on."

"I heerd them say they was goin' to see Jeff Davis."

"Really!" exclaimed Mason, slapping his knee. "Now we're getting somewhere. Think, Mont, think. What was the man's name?"

Mont shook his head slowly. Even Pettibone sat motionless, waiting for Mont's answer. "I cain't recall no names, but I'd shor 'nuff know him agin to see him!"

Mason looked extremely pleased. "Mister Dawson, could you bring Mont to Fort Tejon in, say, two days' time? I'd like Mont to remember all he can, and then I have something to discuss with you. I also have a prisoner there I want Mont to take a look at."

Avery Hastings stood silently with Jasper Perry on Telegraph Hill, looking down toward the Vallejo Street Wharf and a picturesque scene. Moored at the right of their view was the river steamer *Yosemite*. The side-wheeler's paddle housings reached almost to the level of the wheelhouse, four decks above the waterline. A thin trickle of smoke from the twin stacks showed that the boilers were fired and being kept ready for departure upriver.

But the men's attention was actually directed at two vessels moored one dock closer to their vantage point. One of them was the Pacific mail ship *Arizona*, newly arrived from Panama with letters, parcels, and newspapers from "the states." The *Arizona* was a hybrid ship, carrying three masts for sail and a smokestack amidships as well.

The other occupant of the nearer wharf was the United States warship *Cyane*. She had also recently arrived from Panama after a voyage of fifty-one days.

"There is the hen and there the watchdog," said Perry, pointing first toward the mail ship and then at the man-of-war.

"What is the turn of speed of the *Arizona*?" inquired Hastings.

"Inconsequential compared to the *Cyane*. The warship is what we must be able to outrun, and then we'll have no difficulty overtaking our quarry."

"Have you a vessel in mind?"

"Come along and I'll show you," replied Perry as he turned and led the way to a waiting hack.

Montgomery Street was lined with pedestrians and cabs, and they all seemed to be flowing downhill toward the wharf at the end of Jackson Street. Avery raised his eyebrows in question at the seemingly single-minded crowd, but Perry only smiled knowingly and withheld his explanation until the Jackson docks came into view.

Moored there was a schooner bearing the name *Chapman*. It was being unloaded, the swinging cargo nets discharging piles of sacks labeled *beans* onto the dock that was bustling with activity.

"What is so special about this ship?" scoffed Hastings. "A little hundred-ton cargo ship entrusted with freighting beans? You must be joking."

Perry stroked his beard and studied the schooner without comment. A group of onlookers had gathered around the wharf, and there was a low hum of conversation.

"What is so special about the *Chapman*?" demanded Hastings again. "Why are all these people interested in her?"

"Thirty-eight days from Valparaiso" was Perry's quiet comment.

Hastings was examining the crowd and seemed not to have heard. "That man in the naval uniform is Bissell, commander of the *Cyane*. I believe the man he's speaking with is Ralston of the . . . thirty-eight days from where?"

"Valparaiso," repeated Perry smugly. "If memory serves, it's on the coast of South America."

"But that's—"

"Exactly," Perry interrupted, finally condescending to elaborate. "That is thirteen days faster than it took the *Cyane* to go half as far!"

Suddenly Hastings' former disdain was replaced with a curious enthusiasm. "And being schooner-rigged, she'll sail closer to the wind and be more maneuverable. She can also be handled by a smaller crew than the square-rigged ships require."

"And there is one more thing in the *Chapman*'s favor," Perry hinted.

"What more could there be? She already outsails one of the fastest warships. This sounds too good to be true."

Jasper Perry's smug look turned into a smirk. "She is for sale. The owners have asked for seventy-five hundred dollars, but I believe we can get her for less."

✳ ✳ ✳

The air was still and crystal clear as Tom and Mont rode across the toe of the Great Valley toward their meeting with Colonel Mason at Fort Tejon. The peaks they faced stood out in sharp relief, and the furrowed shoulders of the mountains were lightly dusted with powdery snow.

They rode up a treeless, mesquite-covered slope. A hundred miles of the Sierra Nevada Mountains sprawled out toward the east and equally as much of the coast range toward the west. Mont was riding Duncan, and Tom was riding on a young sorrel gelding.

With a delighted grin, Mont asked, "Ain't it real plain, Mister Tom?"

"Isn't what plain, Mont?"

"The smile on God's face when He sees what He done here?"

They stopped riding to gaze around them in silent admiration. Directly ahead of them was a great cleft in the mountains, which looked as if a giant ax had split the rocks to open a passage.

Tom considered the child's remark and smiled in agreement. Mont's insight had long since ceased to surprise Tom. *The depth of the small boy's understanding must also please the Creator,* Tom thought.

After a few reflective moments, the two urged their mounts forward again, the young red horse dancing sideways at times in his eagerness. Duncan tramped along steadily with the thickly muscled arch of his neck and shoulders leaning into the grade. Duncan had the appearance of a plodding draft animal, but his constantly flicking ears betrayed his alertness.

The wedge-shaped canyon looming ahead had been the subject of old Spanish legends. It was reputed to have been formed when a demon caballero burst out of his underground lair for a diabolical midnight ride.

Tom decided not to share this story with Mont or the fact that they had recently passed the place where, a few months earlier, Tom and a squad of soldiers had come upon a wrecked stagecoach and another of Byrd Guidett's murder victims. Young Mont was reveling in the grandeur of the scene; why disrupt it with unpleasant reminders of evil and human misery and destruction?

But for Tom himself, it was too late to push back the thoughts and feelings. Forcing its way into his mind was the additional memory that on the day of the stagecoach holdup, his brother, Jesse, had still been alive.

✶CHAPTER 4✶

The dusty brown adobe walls of Fort Tejon's barracks were barely visible through the screening branches of the leafless cottonwoods and willows along the creek. Once across the rocky ford, the grassy field of the parade ground began and fanned up the hill for three hundred yards.

Tom exchanged greetings with several soldiers he knew from his horse-trading activities.

"Hey, Dawson," yelled a stork-thin corporal with a prominent beak to match, "no horses this time?"

Mont received some curious looks. The sight of several whispered conversations told even a nine-year-old mind that his story was being shared with the new recruits.

A potbellied man with a bald head and ferocious side-whiskers taunted, "What now? Gone to sellin'—?" His question stopped abruptly with an exhaled gasp as the bony elbow of the corporal slammed into his gut.

"Dawson!" boomed the colonel from the wooden steps of his office. "Thank you for coming. Come in, come in." Turning to his left he said, "Corporal, have Flannery there see to Mister Dawson's horses."

The two men and the small boy climbed the wooden stairs to Mason's office.

"There are more secessionists in this country than the Easterners believe," Colonel Mason remarked to Tom and Mont. The colonel seated himself in a revolving chair next to his rolltop desk. He gestured out the faintly frosted window of his second-story office toward the stretch of valley spreading northward. "Perhaps as many as a third of California's population are from the South or, like yourself, from the border states."

"That doesn't make them secesh," corrected Tom. "Many, like myself, came West to get away from the war."

"True enough," agreed the colonel, "but the outspoken secessionists are not the real problem. The danger lies with those who are outwardly loyal but secretly traitors."

"What do you think this secret society can really accomplish? I keep hearing it claimed they can pull California out of the Union. How, exactly?"

The colonel shook his head. "That's what we need to find out. We know that as lone gunmen or in small bands they are capable of assassination and robbery, but whether they can actually organize an armed insurrection . . ."

Mont was sitting wide-eyed at being included in such a grown-up conversation.

Tom gestured toward the boy and asked Colonel Mason, "What do you expect to accomplish by having Mont look at your prisoner?"

"If Mont recognizes him and can tell us where he saw him before, we hope to trace the man's associations in order to get inside the ruling circle of the society. We have some isolated names of those we suspect, but the links between them are missing," replied the colonel.

"Has anything happened to make this more urgent than it was last fall?"

Mason looked at his hands, then up at his saber suspended by a tasseled cord over his desk. With embarrassment in his voice he replied, "Mr Dawson, I am a soldier, plain and simple. I never wanted to be anything else. But there is . . ." He spoke the next phrase with as much visible distaste as if he had just received a dose of cod-liver oil. "There is a *political* issue that cannot be ignored. There is a substantial and growing Northern peace movement. If this spring goes badly for the Union, then Mister Lincoln's reelection will fail. The new president may sue for peace, even at the cost of letting the seceding states depart."

Tom hunched over in his chair and rubbed his palms together beside a small cast-iron stove. "If that would stop the bloodshed, I'm not so sure it's a bad thing."

Mason stiffened visibly, but his voice was even and soft when he spoke. "I won't press you with emotional arguments about the sacrifice of those who have already died. But one fact cannot have escaped your notice: Do you want to see the continued existence of a system that would keep Mont here and millions of others as slaves?"

With the slightest motion of his hand, Tom beckoned toward the small boy who quietly listened to their conversation. Mont, who had been perched on the edge of the chair, jumped off and ran to stand at Tom's side.

"No," Tom said with finality. "No, I do not. Never again."

✳ ✳ ✳

The fort's jail was housed in a low-roofed adobe building across the frost-browned parade ground.

Mason stopped in front of a barred door and indicated it to Mont. "Take a good look." The colonel boosted the boy up to peer through the bars of the guardhouse.

A sullen-faced man with a tan complexion and dark brown hair sat on a rough wooden bench in leg-irons, even though the cell door was bolted securely.

Tom glanced in while Mont was studying the prisoner. "Shackles inside the cell?" he asked the colonel.

"You of all people know better than to underestimate the ruthlessness of the conspirators. This man killed two of my men before we captured him. Yesterday he clubbed the guard bringing his supper and almost escaped. I'm taking no chances. Seen enough, Mont?"

Mont nodded and Colonel Mason set him down. "Have you seen him anywhere before?"

"No, suh, I surely don't think so."

"Think hard," Mason urged. "The man's name is Wilson, or at least that's what he goes by part of the time. Does that help at all?"

Mont asked to be lifted once more, but he still shook his head after studying the prisoner a second time. "I never seed him befo'. I'se powerful sorry. They is one thing though. . . ."

"Yes, what is it?" asked Mason.

"Well," the boy began, then stopped, looking uncertainly at Tom. "That man in there, he put me in mind of Mistuh Tom."

A few moments later the trio was back in the colonel's office.

"Mont's sharp eyes confirmed what I had already noticed," observed Mason. "You bear a remarkable resemblance to our prisoner."

Tom studied the office warily. "So? What are you driving at?"

"It means, Mister Dawson, that if you are willing, you may be our method of gaining entrance to the secret society known as the Golden Circle."

"You want me to pretend to be this man Wilson?" asked Tom incredulously. "How do you expect me to carry it off? Isn't he known to the others in the group?"

"No, he isn't. He was imprisoned in the East for activities as a spy. When he escaped, we had word that he would sail for California to join a conspiracy group. Sure enough, we apprehended him when his vessel from Panama put in at Santa Barbara. But no one outside this command knows that, and all the Southern sympathizers have are Wilson's history and general description. That much we coaxed out of him.

"We believe you will be able to infiltrate the Southern sympathizers as well as give Mont an opportunity to keep an eye out for someone he recognizes."

✴ ✴ ✴

The thump of the iron against the ironing board sounded angry. Tom sat quietly at the kitchen table and waited for Emily to tell him in words what she was indicating every time she clanked the iron onto the hot stove and then tested the temperature of the second iron with the hiss of a drop of water.

"So you're leaving." Her tone was flat when she finally spoke. She set the crease on a flannel shirtsleeve and thumped the hot iron down hard against it.

Tom sipped his coffee and did not reply. Her words were not a question; they were an accusation. She knew that he was leaving her and Nate and Jed for a while. What else could he do?

"For how long?" she asked, not looking at him.

"I don't right know for sure, Emily, but—"

"What about the ranch? What about . . . what about Jed and Nate?"

Had she also been wondering what she would do without him?

"This is the best time of year . . . the only time, really, that I could go. Leave the ranch. Another month and there'll be calving to tend to."

"You'll be back in a month, then?" She looked up sharply.

He shrugged his uncertainty. What could he say? "If I'm not . . . well, I already talked to Pastor Swift. He'll lend a hand. And Deputy Pettibone, of course, if there should be any trouble."

"They know what the Union army has put you up to?"

"Not the details, of course. Not all. Pettibone says not, but Mason believes that what began here with Jesse's dyin' isn't over for us yet. Nobody's fooled about this, Emily. There's still plenty of men out there actively working to push California into the Confederacy." He was trying hard to justify leaving the ranch and the boys . . . and her.

Emily would have none of it. "And I suppose you're the only one who can put a stop to it?" She raised her chin in a mocking gesture. Occasionally, Tom had seen her look that way at Jesse when there had been a disagreement. Now she challenged him.

"There are hundreds of other men who could go," he replied softly. "But there's only one little Mont to go with them and point out just who a leader of the secesh movement is here in California. The boy *saw him,* Emily, in Richmond! He overheard it all because no one bothered to think that a slave child had the brains to remember their big talk." He leaned back in his chair and eyed her as she smoothed out the red material of his shirt with a slight touch of gentleness now. "And I don't aim to let anyone else take that poor boy on such a dangerous job. I've kinda grown fond of him, you see?"

She nodded. Her expression was one of misery and some shame that she had not seen it clearly without such a discussion. "You and your brother . . ." Her voice was laden with emotion. "Before Jesse was . . . before he left . . . we had the same kind of talk. A man has to do what is right. I know that. But *will* you come back?"

"Of course." He tried to sound light, even though his heart was heavy with the thought of leaving her. And the ranch, of course.

"Jesse *said* he would come back." Emily put her hand over her mouth and closed her eyes. Tears squeezed out from between the lids.

Tom knew what she was thinking. Jesse had not come back, and Tom alone had shared her pain and carried the family responsibilities.

Tom stood and put his hands gently on her shoulders. She did not look at him. Was she afraid, Tom wondered, of what her eyes might say to him? He kissed her lightly on the forehead—a brotherly kiss—but his voice was thick with emotion. "Emily. Emily. I could walk out the door this morning to mend a fence, and if it was my time, well then, I wouldn't come back. My life and yours are in the hands of the Lord. I learned that on a long, hard road."

He pulled her close against him and she laid her cheek easily against his chest. "So I'll tell you this . . . if it's what the Lord wants for me, I'll be back in time for the calving. And if it's what the Lord wants for *us*, you'll be here when I return."

✷CHAPTER 5✷

The buckboard rattled noisily down the snaking turns of the White River Canyon and past the mining town of Tailholt. In some years, crossing the log bridge over White River in January was hazardous because the storm-swollen creek raged through the narrow rocky arroyo. This year the passage was easy and the stream a modest trickle flowing quietly. Despite the early snows in the high country, not much had fallen since, nor had much rain come to the valley. It looked as if last year's drought would continue.

The climb out of the gorge wound around steep-sided buttes of decomposed granite. Dirty white boulders littered the landscape like the discarded toys of a giant's game of marbles.

To help pass the time, Tom told Mont stories from old Indian lore. "See that funnel-shaped rock? The one that looks like an Indian gathering basket? The Yokuts say that it was once an Indian girl who was turned to stone right on that very spot."

"How come?" Mont worried aloud.

"For looking back toward some evil her family was running from. You know, sort of like Lot's wife in the Bible."

"Jest granite, 'stead of salt," Mont observed.

Mont was still looking back at the upside-down cone of the boulder when the buckboard crested the rise out of the canyon. Spread out before them, yet still a thousand feet lower, lay the great fertile valley—only . . .

"Hey!" Mont exclaimed, spinning around on the spring seat. "Where'd the valley go? How'd all them clouds get down yonder?"

Tom chuckled, and Duncan's ears flicked back and stayed pointed at the humans as if he, too, were interested in the explanation.

"Tule fog," Tom said. "When it warms up on winter days with no wind, the next night that marshy land gives off a vapor. It goes on getting thicker and thicker till daybreak; then the sun goes to work burning it off. Sometimes it gets so thick it'll stay like that for weeks till some wind comes to blow it away."

"It look like big, dark water," commented Mont.

Tom agreed. The solid mass of dingy gray fog that stretched across the valley did indeed resemble a stormy sea lapping at the foothills of the Sierras. Here and there a taller knob of rock elevated itself through the mist like an island rising from the waves.

Wispy vines of fog drifted between the branches of the oaks, and soon the rest of the trees were obscured by the floating streamers of mist. A sudden dip in the road plunged the travelers into the dark sea of clammy vapor, and the cheerful yellow sun disappeared. Even the steady clip-clop of Duncan's hooves seemed muffled.

Tom felt Mont shiver. He could guess what the boy was thinking. In the dim obscurity, it was easier than ever to conjure up bears out of boulders and lurking Indians from fallen limbs. Tom was sure Mont was hoping that both bears and Indians would all stay frozen in place until they were past.

Tom also felt oppressed by the grayness. As the fog drew a curtain between them and the ones they loved, his thoughts drifted off into a melancholic study of the trip he and Mont were making and how long it would pull them away from home.

"Mother, come quick!" Nate's voice rang through the frosty air like the sound an ax makes biting into a cedar tree in the high country. Emily heard the edge of terror in his shout.

Fresh-baked loaves of bread just coming out of the oven spun off toward the corners of the kitchen, and the pan dropped unheeded on the floor. Emily grabbed the shotgun from the corner of the front room and raced out the door. What could it be? Her frantic mind imagined a hundred calamities: a rattlesnake? a mountain lion? the barn was on fire? Jed had hurt himself with the hatchet while chopping kindling?

Nate shouted again from inside the barn, still anxious but more controlled.

She was relieved to see Jed sprint around the side of the barn from the woodpile—one less possibility to fret about. Jed warned his mother to be wary in case a wild animal should burst out, but Emily paid no heed and ran headlong into the barn, calling for Nate.

In the same moment that the two charged in, Nate yelled again, "Mother!" He was inside the box stall of the young red horse. It lay prostrate on the straw, breathing in shuddering gasps. The fine sleek body was seized by a convulsion that started at its neck and rippled down through its whole frame. Every muscle became rigid and taut until it seemed that the flesh would tear apart the overstretched skin. Even the horse's lips curled back from his teeth in a horrid parody of a grin.

Just as suddenly, the grip of the seizure relaxed. The gelding was instantly gasping for breath as if he had been held underwater and almost drowned. He began to thrash his limbs in all directions, frantically pawing and snorting. He threw his head backward and forward, trying to escape the grasp of pain that had clutched his whole body. It was too great to be borne.

"Nathan!" Emily screamed. "Get out of there!"

Before Nate could make a move, he was bowled over by a fling of the sorrel's head. Thrown against the partition of the stall, he landed with a thud that left him dazed in the dirt.

"Get up!" his mother cried.

Jed vaulted the boards of the stall and scooped up his little brother like a sack of potatoes.

By the time Jed boosted Nate over the stall into his mother's waiting arms, he was able to speak again and pleaded, "Help him! Help him!"

"He's colicked," said Emily firmly. "I'll do what I can, but . . ." At the mute entreaty in Nate's eyes, she stopped and left the sentence unfinished. "Are you all right, Nate? able to help?"

Stifling a great shuddering sob, Nate controlled himself and pulled himself erect. "Yes, Mother. What can I do?"

"Run into the house and bring me the jug of molasses. Get an unopened crock of sausage out of the pantry. Pour the teakettle into the bucket and fill the bucket with cool water, then bring everything out to me. Quick as you can, now."

Before the final instructions had even left her mouth, the boy was out of the barn and dashing toward the house. She called after him, "Mind the kettle! Don't burn yourself." To Jed she said, "All right, we've got to try to get him up. Quickly now, before another seizure takes him."

Even as she spoke the horse became rigid once more. In the extremity of the convulsion, he ceased to breathe and his eyes took on a fixed, glassy stare. The color of his exposed gums turned a deadly white.

"We're losing him," Emily shouted, and just as unmindful of her own safety as she had been worried about Nate's, she rushed into the pen. She threw her weight on the sorrel's rib cage, forcing him to breathe.

After a few seconds that seemed like an eternity, the horse came out of the spasm. This time he was so weak that he could not even swing his head, let alone thrash his legs.

"Help me roll him upright," Emily said to Jed.

It took all their combined strength just to move the horse off his side and onto his stomach.

"Grab those feed sacks," she ordered, "and stuff them along here next to the wall. We have to keep him from getting down flat again."

By this time Nathan had returned with a double armload of the things Emily had requested. Tears were streaming down his cheeks, but he was all business when he set the water bucket down and lined up the molasses and the sausage crock for his mother's inspection. "Now what?" he asked manfully.

"Now pray," she instructed. Into the warm water she poured a half gallon of cottonseed oil that had been covering the sausages as a preservative. To this she added a pint of molasses. "Get the funnel with the longest spout you can find," she told Jed.

When Jed had returned, Emily had him pull the horse's tongue out the side of his mouth and hold it there. With his other hand he directed the spout of the funnel down the animal's throat. "Pray hard," Emily said again to both the boys. "If he seizes while we're pouring this down him, he'll strangle for sure."

"Wait!" demanded Nate. With his eyes screwed shut, he made a fervent request with moving but soundless lips. "All right," he said at last. "Do it now."

Emily poured the funnel full, then massaged the gelding's neck until swallowing motions appeared and the liquid in the funnel went down. She paused to look for signs of another convulsion, and when none emerged, she began to pour again. This process was repeated and repeated until every drop of two gallons of fluid had been drained into the animal.

"Now," Emily said, "let's see if we can get him up."

The warm mixture and all the human attention seemed to ease the horse's panic. He seemed to understand what was wanted even if he could not oblige.

"Rock him," she said, and the boys sprang to obey.

After several heaves and shoves and coaxing pulls on his mane, the red horse rose unsteadily to his feet.

Emily put the loop of a lead rope loosely around his neck and motioned for Jed to open the stall gate. Twenty paces down to the end of the barn, a short pivot. And twenty paces back.

"Keep him moving," she instructed Jed, who took over from her after ten turns around the barn. "We'll need to do this turnabout all day and through the night, till whatever bad he got into works its way out. I'll go heat more water so we can dose him again in a bit. Mind," she said, looking at Nate intently, "if he goes to take another fit, keep clear of him."

"Yes'm," agreed Nate. "We'll walk him good. Won't we, Jed?"

The two brothers started off on the first of hundreds of little circuits inside the barn.

✳ ✳ ✳

Emily looked out the window toward the barn for the tenth time in an hour. She watched the flickering lantern light shining through the half-open door until the shadows of boys and horse passed; then she returned to her sewing.

At least she tried to concentrate on the never-ending pile of mending. Even when not fretting about the boys, she was worrying about Tom and Mont. She wished that she had objected more to their going. She thought about how difficult life on the ranch was even when they were here. There were always problems with the stock, some machinery broken down, or something on the house, barn, or corrals that needed to be fixed. She sighed. Why compound all those things by going hundreds of miles away on business that properly belonged to the Union army?

The truth was, she and her little brood had grown very comfortable, despite the constant stresses of ranch life, and she hated to see that comfort disturbed. Having Tom around made her feel secure, almost like having her husband again.

She stopped and shook her head. That direction of thinking was no good at all. Best to not dwell on it.

Emily roused herself to look at the time: past midnight already. She decided to go out and check on the boys, even though their turn was not up for another hour.

At the stable she found a weary and leaden-eyed Jed tramping in smaller and smaller circles, leading a droopy-looking red horse. At first she could not see Nathan at all, then spotted him, curled up like a cat, asleep on the feed sacks.

"Jed, I'll take over now. You get your brother and go on in and get some sleep. I'll come for you when I need you."

"Huh?" was all the reply he could manage.

Shaking the slumbering Nate and putting his hand in Jed's, she led them to the door and pointed them toward the house. Then she resumed the circuits of the barn.

The air inside the barn was growing colder until it penetrated the coat Emily was wearing. She paused in her pacing to look around for something to throw over her shoulders. Her eyes lit on the empty feed sack Nathan had been curled up on, and she shook it out.

A scrap of paper fluttered free. Emily wondered if it had fallen out of Nate's jacket. She retrieved it and carried it till the next pass under the lantern gave her light enough to read.

In scrawled pencil marks the unsigned note read:

> *Dawson—*
> *This could happen to all yer stock.*
> *Keep cleer of are biznes.*

✶ CHAPTER 6 ✶

Visalia was the county seat of Tulare County in the Great Valley of California and was two days' travel down from Shadow Ridge. It stood on a plain noted by the old Spanish explorers for its grove of magnificent oaks. The confluence of the rivers draining the Sierras made the location a natural waypoint for hunters and prospectors as well as those who would sell to them and buy from them.

It was also home to a large population of people whose sympathies clearly lay with the Confederacy. The local newspaper, the *Equal Rights Expositor,* had an outspoken editor who saw every issue as an opportunity to brand the Union army as invaders, Lincoln as a tyrant, and Yankees as fools, generally. He was something of a local hero but had earned himself some enemies, too.

The paper's third issue of 1864 was especially strong. Half the columns were devoted to editorials exploring the brutality of Northern aggression. Garrison, the editor, took particular aim at the establishment of Camp Babbitt, near Visalia.

The ranchers and farmers in the valley had always been nervous about Indian raids sweeping in from the eastern reaches of the Sierras. When the regular army forces had been withdrawn from the valley to carry out patrol assignments in the deserts of the Southwest, the ranchers' concern increased even further. A volunteer force had been raised to fill in for the reassigned regulars. Camp Babbitt was the headquarters for a portion of the Second Cavalry, California Volunteers.

Lieutenant Colonel William Hardy commanded the detachment of horse soldiers at Babbitt. He and his patrol had just returned from two weeks in the high lonesome, chasing Indians who seemed little more substantial than the rapidly melting snowflakes.

Sparse snow had not meant sparse cold, however. Hardy and his troopers had gone to bed with icy winds howling through the passes and into their tent flaps. They had been treated to the experience of watching their breath solidify into ice crystals inside their tents. There had been no escaping the bone-chilling cold.

As if this were not bad luck enough, Hardy had received the additional indignity of coming down with the worst fever of his life. It was fortunate it came near the end of the ride. Now he was huddled in the eight-by-eight cabin that served him as both quarters and office. A shawl was drawn around his shoulders, and his feet soaked in a pan of steaming water to which half a bottle of turpentine had been added.

There was a timid knock at his door.

"What is it?" he croaked angrily.

The door opened a fraction and a wisp of fog drifted in, followed by a cautious Corporal Brant. "Sorry to disturb you, sir."

"Get on with it!" exploded the colonel. The last word was punctuated by a particularly violent sneeze.

"Yes, sir, sorry, sir. The Visalia telegrapher reports the line is down."

"Indeed? And since when is that army business? Tell him to attend to it himself. That's what he . . . he . . . *achoo!*" The corporal waited patiently until Hardy finished sneezing and concluded his sentence. ". . . what he gets paid for!"

"Yes, sir. But he found that the line had been cut. In twelve places."

"What!?" Hardy demanded, standing upright and almost tripping over the pan. He swore, sneezed again, and bit his tongue, which made him swear even louder. "Get Captain Warner. Tell him to take . . . what now, Corporal?"

Brant backed up a step before replying, which put his shoulders squarely against the cabin door. "Captain Warner is not in camp, sir. You sent him and Lieutenant Miller to Fort Tejon."

Hardy dismissed the rest of the explanation with an irritated gesture. "I remember. All right, sound assembly. Company A ready in fifteen minutes. That will be all, Corporal."

Brant fumbled with the door to make his exit. By the time he got it open, another monstrous sneeze and another violent burst of profanity propelled him out into the fog.

* * *

A handbill nailed to the trunk of a large oak caught Mont's attention. "What do it say?"

"Go on—you can make it out," Tom urged.

"'Tonight,'" the child read, "'Perfesser William Brewer will speech—'"

"Speak," Tom corrected.

"'Speak on the . . .' What did the rest say?" Mont asked since the buggy had by this time rolled past the announcement.

"It says that Brewer will speak on the drought in California. I've heard of Brewer. He's part of a group making a survey . . . you know, maps and such . . . of California's mountains."

"Kin we go?"

"I don't see why not. We're staying the night in Visalia, and we can find a place to camp close by the lecture hall."

* * *

Across the street from the newspaper office of the *Equal Rights Expositor* was the Odd Fellows Hall. The hall was a two-story affair with whitewashed board-and-bat siding. Downstairs it contained two small offices—one for a doctor and the other for an attorney. Only the physician's space was occupied for the time being; the lawyer had gotten himself killed in a stage holdup only a week earlier.

The lodge room upstairs was often used for community gatherings, town meetings, and the like, as well as serving as the temporary home of the Cumberland Presbyterian Church. The single large room that filled the second floor had a raised platform at the end opposite the door. The backless wooden benches could seat close to a hundred if closely packed, and half a hundred more could be accommodated with standing room.

There were nowhere near that number present for William Brewer's lecture. When Tom and Mont climbed the outside wooden stairs that led to a balcony outside the meeting hall, only thirty or so had come out on the foggy night to listen to the professor of agricultural chemistry.

The tall man with the stooped shoulders was already speaking. "And just how severe is the present drought? The year 1862 produced over twenty-four inches of rain in San Francisco, while in 1863 the same area received only three inches. What is worse, no rainstorm of any consequence has struck the southern half of the state since last January—twelve months ago."

Standing in the doorway listening was a short, skinny man with a disorderly ring of white hair around his otherwise bald knob of a head. In between nodding at what Brewer was saying, the small man cast an occasional look over his shoulder at the newspaper office. He gave no evidence of intending to step aside from blocking the entrance to the room but continued to brace himself between the doorposts like a miniature Samson in training for the destruction of the Odd Fellows temple.

213

Tom cleared his throat by way of asking for permission to pass, and the short figure did in fact whirl around at the sound. But instead of moving out of the way, he stretched out a bony finger toward the street and broke into a cackle of laughter that would have done credit to the black speckled hen at the Dawson farm.

Turning to see what the source of amusement was, they spotted a bedraggled troop of horsemen riding wearily into town. The men's heads drooped, and so did the heads of their mounts.

"Who are they?" Tom questioned cautiously.

The man stopped in the middle of his cackling and turned to stare at Tom. "Who are *you* is the question." Without waiting for an answer, he swung back to the scene below and said, "Them's farmers playin' at being soldiers," and went into another gale of raucous laughter.

"What's the matter, toy soldiers?" he shouted down at them.

"Can't find no Injuns to play with? Can't find no Rebs neither? Best you go back to your plows, boys, if you can still find them!" He laughed uproariously at his own jokes, and everyone at Brewer's lecture turned around to view the commotion.

A trooper muttered something, and another nodded tersely. A third made a little louder grumble and stopped his horse's shambling walk.

✳ ✳ ✳

Usually Colonel Hardy was a stickler for discipline and would not have tolerated speaking in ranks, but he was feeling too rotten to care. Besides, the little man's comments stung.

The self-appointed tormentor spoke again. "It's no wonder the blue dogs of the Baboon King are gettin' whipped. They can't any of 'em fight any better than you!"

214

Hardy's Company A from Camp Babbitt had covered thirty miles out and back. They had repaired a dozen places where the telegraph line had been cut. But when they came to a thirteenth break, they found that it was not repairable. It was not just cut; the line itself was nowhere in sight. For the space of four telegraph poles, the wire had been stripped completely and carried away.

Colonel Hardy had been alternately sneezing and coughing as the unit rode back into town. The vandals had left plenty of tracks to follow—tracks that ended beside Pronghorn Slough where the last telegraph pole perched next to a stagnant sheet of green, slimy ooze. But the slough ran for miles in both directions, giving the rebels plenty of maneuvering room to hide their trail.

Something in Hardy snapped. The fever and chills, the agonizing ride and the salty remarks rubbed into open wounds had pushed him over the edge. In a voice that sounded like a coffee grinder he ordered, "Seize that secesh and his treasonous paper!"

✳ ✳ ✳

Garrison, the infamous editor of the secesh newspaper, *Equal Rights Expositor,* was not to be deterred. He rushed down the stairs toward his business shouting, "Ned! Seth! Get the guns!"

Six troopers moved to carry out Hardy's order to seize the paper, and Corporal Brant went after Garrison. The banty rooster of a man lowered his shoulder and plunged straight into the surprised corporal, bowling him completely over. But two more soldiers had greater success, tackling Garrison and tying him up.

The two employees of the *Expositor* looked up from their printing duties to see half a dozen soldiers burst into the one-room building. Seth, the printer's devil, threw himself toward a cupboard beside the press and flung it open.

Ned rushed toward the counter across the front of the room, reaching it just as Trooper Stillwell vaulted over it. Ned's sweeping right fist caught Stillwell on the point of chin at the exact moment that the man's toes touched the floor. The impact lifted him so forcefully that it appeared he jumped backward onto the counter like a puppet suddenly jerked upward on its strings.

Brandishing a pistol, Seth spun from the cupboard, but a soldier on each side of him caught his arms at the same moment. There was a resounding roar as the Remington .44 exploded, but the shot went into the ceiling.

215

Ned turned from cold-cocking Stillwell to help his friend, but two more troopers jumped him from behind and wrestled him to the floor. The three men rolled over and over, crashing into the compositing bench. Slugs of type rattled and bounced, flying through the air like spent bullets.

Jerking free of his attackers, Ned grabbed the plate of text he had been completing. He swung it sideways into a soldier's face, smashing the man backward into a wall and leaving the word *tyranny* neatly incised across his cheekbone. An instant later, the butt of a carbine struck Ned behind the ear and he collapsed in a heap.

Two more cavalrymen ran into the *Expositor* office carrying a long coil of rope. As Tom and Mont watched from their balcony perch across the street, the end of the rope was soon brought back outside and made fast to Corporal Brant's saddle horn, while the bound Garrison screeched a protest.

At a nod from Hardy, Brant applied the spurs to his bay, which responded with a spurt forward. There was a thunderous crash, and

Garrison's printing press erupted through the wood of the counter and tore apart the doorway and one porch support before landing in the road.

Garrison raged and cursed, savaging all within sight and sound with a blistering string of foul oaths. The porch roof of the newspaper office tilted crazily, and an ominous screeching suggested that the entire building might collapse.

As Tom looked on with mounting horror, Brant returned, fashioning a noose in the rope he had retrieved. The corporal looked expectantly toward Hardy, who gave a grim nod. Then Brant tossed the coil over a nearby oak limb and tied it off so the loop dangled eight feet off the ground.

Another trooper brought his horse alongside Garrison, who was roughly boosted into the saddle. The spindly editor was led toward the waiting noose.

"No!" shouted Tom, almost involuntarily. "Don't!" To Mont he said, "Stay up here. Whatever happens, stay up here!"

Tom vaulted over the railing, landing catlike on his feet. He ran full force into the man holding the horse. The violence of the impact rolled the man completely over backward. The horse spooked and reared, tumbling Garrison off on the ground.

Grabbing the young rancher from behind, Brant roughly pinned Tom's arms to his sides.

The man Tom had knocked down rose and drew back his fist, aiming a blow at Tom's chin.

Tom twisted Brant sideways, and the hapless corporal caught the blow intended for Tom on his right ear. Howling in pain, Brant released his hold, and Tom added an elbow smash to Brant's face.

Snatching up his fallen rifle, the other soldier leveled a two-foot-long bayonet at Tom's throat.

Stopping perfectly still and without flinching, Tom yelled, "Colonel! Don't do this! Enough!"

Colonel Hardy turned his flushed face toward Tom. He squinted, as if his red-rimmed eyes had difficulty focusing on the man who stood before him. Hardy's breath was ragged, and a shiver worked its way down his spine and out to the ends of his fingers. He looked the part of a madman.

"Colonel," Tom repeated, "don't do this. Think what you are doing. Think of the women and children." He slowly gestured toward the crowd huddled on the balcony of the Lodge Hall, where all thought of Brewer's talk on the drought was forgotten.

Hardy turned his feverish gaze upward to take in the onlookers, then at the oak where the noose was dangling. Despite the chill, beads of sweat broke out on the colonel's forehead and ran into his eyes. He brought a gloved hand up to clear them. When he took it down again, new charity had replaced the glazed stare of a moment before. He looked at Tom and the group of soldiers preparing to lynch the editor, as if seeing them for the first time. "You there! You men, stop that! Hold that horse, Brant!"

There was grumbling from some of the cavalrymen, but most moved sheepishly to comply, as though glad that some force had stopped them short of the hanging.

"Brant," Hardy croaked at the corporal, "the others are to be released. Mister Garrison is under arrest. Bring him along."

With no word of acknowledgment to Tom or the others viewing the scene, Company A gathered and moved off toward Camp Babbitt.

Ned and Seth were left to nurse their wounds and collect ink bottles and overturned chairs.

Ned walked unsteadily outside, ducking to pass under the sagging porch roof. He rubbed a huge lump behind his ear and groaned. Stumbling toward Tom, he extended his hand. "Thanks, mister. I figured old Garrison for a goner an' maybe me an' Seth for after. If there's anything you ever need . . . what's your name, anyways?"

Tom looked down at a tug on his coat sleeve to find Mont trying to get his attention about something. . . . "It's Wilson," Tom said. "My name is Wilson."

"Are you just passing through, Mister Wilson?"

"We're on our way to 'Frisco. I've been told we'll find friends there who think like Garrison."

"'Frisco." Ned rubbed his head thoughtfully, as if making a careful assessment before saying any more. "Well, Mister Wilson, I can steer you to a mighty good place to stay. Look for the Tehama House Hotel. You'll find the company to your liking there. And before you leave, let me send a message with you. You just give it to the person at the desk. He'll take care of the rest."

CHAPTER 7

The threatening note fluttered in the hand of Deputy Pettibone. He squinted at the words and then looked at the weary sorrel gelding still being led slowly around the barn by Jed in the morning light. "You're mighty lucky you ain't callin' a crew to haul a dead horse out of that barn this mornin'. How'd you save him?" he asked Emily.

"I didn't think of poison. It looked like a bad case of colic, so first thing we did was pray; then we dosed him with cottonseed oil and . . . well, we've been walking him all night."

"And you all by yourself, too. A woman alone faced with such a thing." He clucked his tongue sympathetically. "That brother-in-law of yours done run off already, has he?"

"Not run off." Emily did not like the deputy's tone, even though there had been times through the ordeal when she herself had angry thoughts toward Tom. "He and Mont are gone on their business."

"Well, now." Deputy Pettibone suddenly seemed real interested. He looked at the note again. "Well, well. And you and these here boys saved the horse. What about the rest of your stock, Widow Dawson? Says right here . . ."

Emily put a hand to her aching forehead. How could she keep an eye on every animal on the ranch? How could she prevent anyone from carrying out a threat to poison the Dawson livestock? And whom could she trust? "Tom said you would help if we had any trouble."

"Don't know how even the Union army could stand guard against something like this." He folded the note and slipped it into his coat pocket. "Where's Tom headed?"

She paused before answering. Hadn't Tom told Pettibone where he was going? "San Francisco."

"Well then. Well, well, Widow Dawson. I'll tell you what I can do for you. I'm headed to Fort Tejon, then on to Los Angeles myself. I'll stop at the fort and inform the captain what's happened here. Tell 'im he oughta get word to that brother-in-law of yours. In the meantime, since the Union has borrowed your man, they oughta send a few blue bellies thisaway to help you out, I figger."

Emily nodded with relief. How grateful she was that Pettibone had stopped to check on her and the boys this morning. If Tom had not talked to the deputy, she felt it could be no accident that he had arrived just in the hour of her greatest desperation. "Will you stop and ask Parson Swift to come out before you leave, Deputy? I'm in need of his words of comfort after last night. I surely am."

"We must have a suitable captain," demanded Jasper Perry. "An experienced man, someone who knows these waters . . . a man with sand, who will stop at nothing."

Hastings looked crestfallen. "Is my appointment to mean nothing, then? My commission in the Confederate States Navy names me as captain."

Hastily hiding a mocking smile behind his hand, Perry said soothingly, "Avery, I mean no offense! You will have the command of the vessel, of course. But you agree to the wisdom of having a sailing master, do you not?"

Avery gave in to the soundness of this suggestion. "Do you have someone in mind?"

"By the stroke of good fortune, I do!" Perry explained that the man he intended to recruit for the conspiracy had once been an officer on the Pacific mail steamship *Oregon*. "He knows the routes of the mail ships and the thinking of their owners and officers. Come on—I think I know where to find him."

✴ ✴ ✴

Perry led Hastings toward a shabby waterfront saloon. The name
stenciled on the filthy smoked-glass window had been Devil May
Care, Perry said, but when one pane had been broken in a brawl, half
the sign was destroyed and never replaced. What remained in a quarter arc of dingy suggestiveness read Devil May.

Inside the dimly lit saloon were a handful of customers drinking
toasts to midmorning forgetfulness. As Avery stood in the doorway,
he saw a wrinkled crone leap back from rifling a rummy's pockets
as he lay sleeping across a table. When the hag saw that neither newcomer was the law, she brazenly returned to exploring the man's coat.

A nudge in Hastings' ribs startled him out of his disgusted stare.
"Keep one hand on your watch and the other on your wallet," Perry
hissed, but he was smiling as he said it. Jasper Perry did not seem out
of his element at all.

At a corner table that could barely be seen in the artificial gloom
sat a lone man with a squat body and a dark, leathery face. His broad
features included a nose that was little more than a shapeless lump of
red-veined gristle. Sagging jowls mirrored the corners of his down-
turned mouth.

The man was dressed in the dark blue denim of a sailor, so his
form faded into the black shadowy recess. His face and one bandaged
hand seemed to float above the greasy table like apparitions in a
spiritualist's show.

Perry approached the figure without hesitation, although
Hastings hung back a pace. "Captain Law?" Perry asked tentatively.

For a long moment there was no reply. Avery wondered if they
had made a mistake or if perhaps the man was deaf or in a drunken
stupor.

Perry was at the point of repeating himself when the sailor held
up his bandaged left hand. "I am not captain no more, they say. I
am a cripple and cannot command, they say. The infernal deep take
them all, I say! I have more to captain within these stumps than they
in their whole worthless carcasses!"

"How did it happen?" Avery burst out. He was instantly sorry that he had spoken, for Captain Law's upturned eyes engaged his in a murderous stare. The pale blue watery orbs bulged slightly from their sockets and reminded Hastings of the staring eyes of a drowned man he had once seen fished out of a river. *Dead lights,* he thought.

"Was a thieving kanaka, what done it. Caught him at the ship's stores. Would not take his medicine like a man. Fought me, he did. Me! His lawful captain!"

"You lost your fingers protecting ship's property and then the ungrateful owners discharged you?" said Perry.

"Claimed I need not have killed him, they did," continued Law. He leaned back from the table to display a sheath knife with a folding marlinespike in its handle. "Had a right tussle, too."

"Of course," blurted Avery. "He cut off your fingers in the fight— surely the owners can see that it was self-defense."

"Not so, neither," corrected Law. "'Twas not in the fight I lost 'em. When I went to put the noose around his scrawny neck to haul him to the maintop he bit one of 'em clean off, but the rest the doctor chopped. Gangrene from the stinkin' dog."

Perry looked at Hastings significantly, then said to Law, "Captain, we have a business proposition to discuss with you."

Avery Hastings hoped that he did not look as green as he felt.

The Market Street scene unrolling in front of Mont's view overwhelmed his nine years' worth of experience in a way he had never felt before. San Francisco was so amazing that despite this being his second visit, he was goggle-eyed. Three- and four- and even five-story buildings loomed all around, and hundreds of curious people walked or rode into his attention.

A covey of Chinamen in quilted cotton pajama suits shuffled by, chattering to one another in singsong cadence. Their pigtails and round cloth caps were bobbing in time. They appeared oblivious to Mont's stare.

From the other direction, three men in suits and bowler hats were riding two-wheeled contraptions with pedals on the front axles. Tom said that the machines were called velocipedes. Mont wanted to know if they were somehow related to the many-legged critters he had seen up in the mountains.

A horse-drawn streetcar made its appearance, announced by the plodding clop of hooves and the musical ringing of the bells for fares and crossings. Pursuing the streetcar were two nondescript mutts of indifferent breeding. The dogs were not actually running after the vehicle but kept a steady trot close behind. At the corner stop closest to where Tom and Mont were standing, an impressive figure in military garb stepped from the coach. In his epauletted uniform and plumed top hat, he plunged through the crowd directly toward them, followed closely by the two dogs.

Several passssersby tipped their hats to the portly, bearded man with the brass-headed cane and his canine attendants. Mont overheard him addressed as "Your Excellency," "Your Honor," "Your Highness," and even "Your Magnificence."

With single-minded purpose in his step, this high potentate, whoever he was, walked straight over to the two of them as if their meeting were prearranged. Stopping right in front of Tom, the man rapped the tip of his cane on the ground three times, as if calling a courtroom to attention.

"We note from your apparel that you are from the interior reaches of our domain," said the individual in the gold-braided dress coat. "We would inquire as to the state of our affairs in the hinterlands."

Mont wondered who the "we" was—he decided that it must mean the dogs who were now seated politely one pace behind.

If Mont was confused about the plural form of address, Tom seemed just as baffled by the questions. "Well, I—," he began, then stopped.

"Come, come, man, speak up. Is aught amiss with your home province? Is our attendance required to redress error and quell rebellion?"

Fortunately, Tom was spared further interrogation by the aid of a helpful newsboy who had been listening to the exchange with obvious amusement. "'Scuse me, Emperor, Your Highness. Jim Daly at your service. These here vis'ters don't speak any English. They are

223

just arrived from—" the boy pivoted quickly to slip Tom a broad wink—"Egypt."

"Splendid!" exclaimed the emperor, his ostrich plume waving with delight. "Welcome to our country! Quick, lad," he said to the newsboy, "proclaim us properly, Master Daly."

"Yes, sir, Your Majesty. This here is Emperor Norton the First of America."

"And?" prompted the emperor.

"Oh, I almost fergot. Protector of Mexico."

"Quite right. Well done. Well, we must be off. We are late for luncheon with the cabinet. Matters of state. Master Daly, direct the ambassador to come round and present his credentials when he has the proper formal attire, and render him every assistance." He snapped the ferrule of his cane alongside his hat in a kingly gesture.

"Bow," hissed Jim. "Bow, 'fore he gets mad."

Tom and Mont obediently bent their necks.

Emperor Norton smiled pleasantly and clicked his fingers. "Come, Bummer. Come, Lazarus. To luncheon." The emperor continued his stately progress down Market Street, accompanied by his bulldog and terrier comrades.

Tom, Mont, and the newsboy watched him until he paused before a sign that read Golden Nugget Saloon—Free Lunch. Emperor Norton pivoted with military precision and entered the saloon at the head of his happily wagging cabinet officers.

"Who was that?" burst out Tom with a suddenly exhaled breath and laugh.

Jim grinned. "Emperor Norton? He's just a poor crazy man what lost a fortune—and then lost his mind. Thinks he's royalty."

"Why isn't he locked up?"

The newsboy shot back, "He don't hurt nothin'. Everybody here is a little crazy . . . him a mite more'n most . . . but we like him that-away!"

"No offense, son," soothed Tom. "Thanks for explaining. Maybe you can help us with something else. We just left off our rig at the livery stable here, and now we need to get to the Tehama House."

"Tehama? Sure enough. Corner of California and Sansome." Jim proceeded to give directions, concluding with which stop to leave the streetcar. "You can see it from there."

"Much obliged," said Tom, reaching in his pocket.

"Naw," said the newsboy, looking down the street toward the Golden Nugget. "Wouldn't be right. It was a—what ya say, royal command."

"Then consider this a token presented by the ambassador of Egypt." Tom laughed and handed over a dime.

✳ ✳ ✳

"Leave off tellin' me how sure of success you be, and splice me the cable of your plan instead," demanded Captain Law.

The room on the third floor of the Tehama Hotel was occupied by Law, Perry, and Avery Hastings.

"Do you swear to be true to—," Hastings began.

"You can leave off unfurling any of your oaths, too," snorted Law. "I give you my word to say naught of your scheme. . . . That will have to serve, for I'll not promise more without the full chart of the voyage." His eyes flashed in defiance that clearly read: "You need me more than I need you."

Perry and Hastings withdrew to a corner of the room for a hasty consultation.

Law, meanwhile, wandered over to the window looking out on Sansome Street. He studied the forms of several passing women, squinting first one eye and then the other against the glare of the sun. His attention briefly touched on a tall, well-built man who walked up Sansome with a small black child at his side.

Hastings called Law back to the table. "All right, Captain, we will trust you with our entire plan, and then you can make up your mind."

Inclining his bulldog face in approval and carefully laying his injured left hand on the tabletop, Law prepared to listen.

"We intend to purchase the *Chapman* and outfit her with enough arms and men to seize a Pacific mail steamship," Avery explained.

"Hold fast there a minute," objected Law. "And what of the *Cyane*? You might stop one mail ship, but they'll have an escort after that. Your puny schooner may outrun 'em, but it can't outfight a warship."

Jasper Perry took over the narration, his brooding eyes growing more animated with his enthusiastic portrayal of the conspiracy. "We mean to use the steamer to transport men to seize the arsenal at Benecia and the warships at Mare Island. Next we'll sail down and capture or destroy the *Cyane* and occupy Fort Point."

"Lay off the point instead," remarked Law, shaking his head. "Where will this army come from?"

"We have trusted lieutenants who are even now recruiting loyal sons of the South from the goldfields between here and the Comstock. When the time comes, they'll be ready. But we must do our work as well to be able to furnish transport to the attack on Benecia and what follows."

Law considered the proposition. He stared hard at the stumps of his damaged hand, contemplating the fingers that were no longer there.

* * *

Uneasy around the sea captain, Hastings wished that they could hurry and conclude their business. He was glad he was leaving for the Comstock and would not have to deal with Law.

At last Law said, "And you want me to be master aboard *Chapman*; is that it? To command a pirate ship on a pirate's mission?"

"Privateer," Avery protested. "Duly authorized—"

"Bah!" Law snorted again, like the sound of a signal cannon firing. "Does a man's neck stretch any less if he be called 'privateer' when those that catches him decides to hang him? And you?" he added, sneering into Avery's face. "Mind you, it's all one to me. There's some as would say that pirate is a step up from the days when I was captain aboard a slaver on the New Orleans run. . . . All right, here stand my terms: *Chapman* is mine when the job is done. . . ." He paused to wave his bandaged hand under Avery's nose. "I want one thousand dollars, gold, afore we start. Do you have it?"

Hastings and Perry exchanged looks.

"No," Avery reported. "We only had enough for earnest money for the *Chapman*. We don't yet have the funds to complete the purchase or outfit her or pay you what you ask."

"And what will you do about it?"

"That is not your concern," retorted Perry. "We will have the additional amount soon. In fact, we want you to make out a list of equipment needed aboard the *Chapman*, and we will order it for delivery in two weeks. Our agent will have secured the money by then."

CHAPTER 8

With its green steep-gabled roof and white clapboard siding, Mount Carmel Presbyterian Church was a jewel among the surrounding buildings of Greenville in the valley below Shadow Ridge. The bell in its steeple had rung out to announce the election of Lincoln, and some months later, the beginning of the war between North and South. For a time, discussion of politics had been off-limits within its sanctuary. But the death of Emily Dawson's husband by the treachery of a member of the congregation had split the church. It had caused Emily herself to support the Northern cause with renewed dedication.

This morning several pews were empty as the congregation rose to sing the "Battle Hymn of the Republic." Even empty pews did not dim the fervor of those who sang and then prayed for the restoration of the Union. Those who supported the Southern cause met in a newly framed plainer building just across the street. Their voices bellowed the tune of "Onward, Christian Soldiers" in an attempt to drown out their Yankee neighbors. In Greenville, only the dusty road separated North and South, but the gulf between neighbors and one-time friends was as wide as an ocean.

Pastor Swift preached a mighty sermon from the thirty-seventh Psalm: "'Do not fret because of evil men. . . .'" He pounded the plain wooden pulpit, and his gray-streaked beard trembled with righteous indignation that had seceded from the union of his church.

"'For evil men will be cut off,'" he shouted, striking the pulpit again with energy that would have rivaled old John Knox himself. "'A little while, and the wicked will be no more!'" He waved his arm toward the Southern Baptist building. "'Though you look for them, they will not be found!'"

Nate grimaced at these words. Jed rubbed his cheek thoughtfully. Both boys had told their mother they would rather have their old school friends back in the pews with them instead of having swords pierce their hearts, as Pastor Swift said. The majority of their classmates cheered the victories of Jefferson Davis and openly cursed Lincoln's army. Would they ever be friends again?

Emily squeezed the hands of her sons when they leaned forward to whisper such thoughts to each other. Even a church, it seemed, was not the proper place to preach political peace and reconciliation.

"'The Lord loves the just and will not forsake His faithful ones,'" Pastor Swift preached on. "'They will be protected forever, but the offspring of the wicked will be cut off.'"

So much for the children of Southern sympathizers. Well, if the war didn't get over soon, a whole lot of offspring would be missing from school.

Nate and Jed did not want the whole Baptist building to disappear. But they did think it would be just fine, however, if the Lord would cut off the fellows who had poisoned the sorrel gelding and keep them from poisoning the rest of the stock. Such thoughts flew between them as Parson Swift delivered an ear-shattering message that certainly could be heard by the Baptists. The boys were relieved when the sermon finally ended and they sang the doxology.

Standing at the door to greet his parishioners, Parson Swift extended his gnarled hand to Emily as she passed by.

"I was expecting the whole of the Union army to be in church with you today, Sister Dawson. Have you left them back at the ranch, then?"

"They have not come yet," Emily answered quietly.

"Not come?" He seemed astounded by the news that Emily and the boys had remained alone at the ranch this past week without the protection Pettibone had promised to send. "How have you managed, woman?"

"We take turns through the night." She laid a hand on Jed's

shoulder. He stood a little taller. "We each keep a two-hour watch. Most of the stock has been brought in to the near corrals. We've hung lanterns on the fence posts and lit the barn as well."

The parson looked grieved at the news. "Sister Dawson! I do declare! You've managed the week without calling for assistance. Well, well, like the builders of the wall of Jerusalem, we must stand watch and pray! The days are evil. The nights a heap more so. Sister Dawson, you are most welcome to stay here at the parsonage until the soldiers arrive at your place." He placed his hand on Nate's shoulder. "Well, boy, would you like to move to town for a while?"

An instant of excitement passed over the faces of both boys; then Nate replied quietly, "No, sir. Tom told us we was the men on the place till he and Mont come home again. We ain't leavin'."

Pastor Swift looked surprised and then amused. "Well, now." He thumped Nate on the back. "A manly attitude, I'll say. And one your father would be right proud of. But your uncle had not foreseen what happened out your way with the horse and the threat to you. Otherwise he would have made arrangements for you to come to town and stay."

"We are managing fine," Emily said proudly. "Thank you for your concern, but you needn't worry yourself. I have not slept away from the ranch even one night since Jesse brought me here. And I will not be chased out of my home now. Besides, Deputy Pettibone was sure that the soldiers would be sent. Perhaps they've arrived while we've been at church."

✵ ✵ ✵

The muffled cry that reached Tom's ears from across Sansome was a high squeak abruptly cut off. Tom looked up and down the wood-planked street in order to find the source. No one was in sight in either direction on the still January night. The theater crowds had all dispersed, gone home before the thin sliver of moon hung its pale crescent overhead.

Tom had felt like a caged animal in the hotel room where Mont lay sleeping. After several uneventful days in San Francisco, what was supposed to happen next? It seemed as though even staying in a haven for Southern sympathizers like the Tehama House and the message he'd given to the desk clerk were no guarantee that Mont would ever chance across some conspirator whom he'd recognize. The people staying at the Tehama were more likely to sing the praises of Jeb Stuart and Bob Lee than Sherman or Grant, but so what? They were still only pursuing ordinary lives. There had been no knocks on the door, no one hanging around who looked sinister, and no one offering to buy military secrets. Perhaps the escaped spy named Wilson was not as hot a commodity as the army had thought.

So Tom had come outside to think. How long would they have to remain on this fruitless quest? Two weeks? Three? What if the "plot" turned out to be no more than the ravings of a few lunatics like the harmless Emperor Norton? The thought made Tom grin wryly to himself in the darkness.

A scuffling and another anguished protest froze the smile on his face. It sent Tom's hand to his side where the Colt, now on the bureau upstairs, would have hung. Slapping his palm against his leg in frustration, Tom charged across the street anyway, toward a blackened alley beside the American Theater.

Two dark-clad forms and one in lighter colors twisted and spun in the shadows. As Tom approached, the dimly seen figures resolved themselves into rough, drunken men and a panicked, desperate woman.

One man held the woman around the waist with one arm, while his other hand was clamped across her mouth. The second attacker, shorter than the first, tried to catch the woman's legs. The men struggled to carry her a few steps farther into the darkness of the alley.

Lunging and kicking, the woman partially freed herself, and the threesome spun and clattered again in a blur of rustling petticoats and coarse oaths.

Charging straight into the group, Tom tackled the smaller man in a headlong rush that drove both past a stage door and into a brick wall that stood across the middle of the passage. The man's head connected with the masonry with a satisfying crack, and Tom dropped him and whirled around.

The second assailant flung the woman aside. From beneath his dark blue coat he drew a knife with a blade that seemed to be a foot long. "You better go, mister. You hadn't ought to butt into Grove Kinnock's business unless you's fixin' to meet your Maker."

Tom circled warily, palms open. He kept his eyes on the knife hand of his opponent.

Tom feinted toward Kinnock, hoping to draw a rush that would give the woman an opportunity to flee.

But the knife wielder was too wary for that, and he stayed an arm's length from the woman, brandishing the tapering blade drunkenly toward Tom's face. "Cut you good, I aim to." Kinnock sneered.

Behind Tom, the smaller man groaned and stirred.

Now the struggle was reaching a critical stage. No doubt the second attacker also had a knife, and from the sounds, he would soon be awake enough to use it. Tom would be caught between the two, still without a means to free the woman.

His boot brushed over a hard, lumpy object—a loose cobblestone or broken chunk of brick. Tom stooped quickly to retrieve it—anything to even the odds.

Tom's fingers had just touched the stone when Kinnock attacked. Shouting "Grab him, Rafe!" to his still prostrate accomplice, he lunged toward Tom with a vicious swipe of the dirk.

The point of the blade caught the sleeve of Tom's denim jacket and slit it up to the elbow as he flung himself backward. A second slash of steel followed as a backhand arc at eye level passed within an inch of Tom's face.

Seizing the chance while Kinnock's guard was down, Tom swung the chunk of rock into the side of the man's head. Now it was Grove Kinnock's turn to jump awkwardly aside but not before the brick had grazed his temple, splitting the scalp and leaving blood dripping from his hair.

"Run!" Tom shouted at the woman, who was still in a tumbled heap of petticoats on the slimy stones. "Run!" he commanded urgently.

✷ ✷ ✷

With the blow, Kinnock's rage was up. For the moment, he forgot the woman. What he wanted was the chance to drive his blade into the foolish, interfering stranger's belly, leaving him to gasp out the ebbing of his life.

His alcoholic clumsiness burned away by his anger, Kinnock curled into a fighting crouch. He advanced with the lightly balanced tread of a man used to the rolling deck of a ship. "I'm gonna slit you from jib to mizzen," he hissed. "An' when I'm through, I'm gonna feed you to the fish piece by piece."

✳ ✳ ✳

Tom was silent, standing a pace out from the wall and throwing a quick glance toward Rafe, who was on his knees, struggling to stand. *Why doesn't the woman run? Is she hurt or knocked unconscious?*

The moment for pondering flashed by as Kinnock's stalking approach brought him within striking range. Though he was enraged, Kinnock appeared wary of the stone club Tom held aloft in his right hand. He had already suffered a stinging blow and now moved toward his prey cautiously.

Kinnock lunged with the point of his knife held straight ahead, like a sword thrust. As Tom jumped aside, the sailor turned the movement into a sickle's sweep, to catch Tom in the side.

Tom chopped downward with the improvised club. Using the stone like the primitive ax of an ancient tribesman, Tom snapped his elbow taut, speeding the impact of the jagged edge against Kinnock's forearm.

There was an audible crunch as Kinnock's arm shattered. A howl of pain and a clatter followed as the dirk fell from his fingers.

Bending swiftly to retrieve the knife, Tom caught an upraised knee on the point of his chin. Hundreds more stars than could actually be seen in 'Frisco's foggy skies exploded in front of his sight. He staggered back, shaking his head to clear his vision but only setting off more cascades of meteors. He could hear Kinnock cursing and scrabbling in the debris with his uninjured arm.

The sailor stood slowly, holding the knife again, his broken arm cradled against his chest. "I can stick you just as easy . . . with my . . . other hand," he panted. "Rafe, catch hold of this fella for me. I'm gonna gut him like a sea bass."

The smaller man was up now and staggering forward.

Tom still held the stone club, but there was little he could do with it against two. Kinnock blocked the exit and Rafe was closing in.

There was one chance. Rafe still looked unsteady on his feet, and Kinnock favored his uninjured arm. If Tom could maneuver himself behind Rafe, keep the smaller man between him and Kinnock's knife thrusts—

When Kinnock sprang again, Tom flung himself toward Rafe instead. The smaller man, taken by surprise, gave ground suddenly. The force of Kinnock's wild slash spun him around out of position.

Tom pressed his rush toward Rafe and had the man by the coat lapels. Swinging him around, Tom prepared to throw him into Kinnock when . . . Tom's feet slipped on the damp pavement, and he and Rafe tumbled down together. Over and over they rolled, thrashing in the alley. They fetched up against the brick wall.

Kinnock moved into position like a victorious spider, towering overhead. He held the long-bladed knife, point downward, like an ice pick. "Good. Hold him there, Rafe. I'm gonna poke his eyes out and *then* gut him!" The knife was drawn back to end the battle when—

The explosion of a pistol shot in the narrow confines of the brick canyon sounded like mortar fire. The thunderous roar deafened Tom to all but the reverberating beat of the echoes dying away.

Kinnock was flung back against the wall as if a giant windstorm had thrown him there. Like garments blown from a Telegraph Hill clothesline, he stood propped against the wall, motionless and still. An instant later, as a dying breeze releases its stolen prizes, he slumped into a heap.

"Grove? Grove!" shouted Rafe, kicking himself free of Tom. The depth of his concern for his friend evaporated, and he ran out of the alley and down California Street. The tromp of his footsteps on the plank roadway echoed hollowly. The diminishing sounds of his headlong retreat showed that he was still running after blocks and blocks.

The woman came to stand beside Tom.

"Did you do that?" he asked, gesturing toward the lifeless Kinnock.

"Yes," she said simply, "with this," and she handed Tom a two-shot derringer, still warm from the explosion of its first charge.

"Ma'am, I . . . ," he began.

She took his arm and pulled him toward the street. "Someone will have heard the shot, and the police will come to investigate. It will be much simpler for us to leave now. Please, I promise I'll explain. My hotel is just across the street."

✳ ✳ ✳

By the lobby light that spilled out on the street as the woman entered, Tom could see that she was startling beautiful. Dark ringlets of hair fell in disarray over the shoulders of the evening cloak she wore. She was tall and her disheveled clothes did not conceal her feminine figure silhouetted against the interior light.

Tom allowed her to enter first, alone, as she had requested. Shortly after, Tom also entered the Tehama House lobby. He wondered if all their caution was necessary. No one had come to investigate the gunshot, and the night clerk was dozing behind the counter.

Her room was 2-B, up one flight and immediately next to the stairs. The door opened quickly at Tom's quiet tap, and she pulled him into the room with a nervous glance down the empty corridor.

"Ma'am, I only came to see that you were all right," Tom said awkwardly. "I'll go on now—"

"Please wait," she insisted. "I want to thank you for coming to help me. It was a very brave thing you did."

Tom shuffled his feet and stared down at the roses woven into the carpet. He was trying to avoid looking at the expanse of creamy throat that appeared above the opening of her silk dressing gown. "It seems to me that I should be thanking you."

"Nonsense." She laughed. A slight tremor in her voice betrayed that she was not as entirely in control as she seemed. "Those brutes! I dropped my pistol in the struggle before you appeared. If you had not arrived when you did, they would have . . ."

Tom cleared his throat and again acted as if leaving as soon as possible would please him.

235

"Please sit." She seated herself on a mahogany divan whose nee-dlepoint cushions matched the carpet.

Tom obliged her by perching stiffly in a straight-backed chair near the door. The air seemed filled with an exotic aroma—the scent of a flower garden blooming in the dead of winter.

"My name is Belle Boyd," she said, pausing as if Tom should rec-ognize it immediately. When he made no comment, she continued. "I'm an actress. I stayed late in the theater tonight, studying lines for a new role. Since the theater is just across the street, I wasn't worried about coming out alone. But those two men! They were right outside the stage door and grabbed me when I stepped out!"

"Why didn't you want the police, ma'am? You could have described the second man. Perhaps they could have caught him."

"That's why I felt I had to explain. You know that those two men were sailors—*Yankee Navy sailors*," she spat, as if repeating especially harsh and distasteful swearwords. "My sympathies are well-known and clearly with the Confederacy—I would not have received justice. Not after having killed one of *them*. No, it's better this way."

✦ CHAPTER 9 ✦

The following morning Mont and Tom sat in the dining room of Tehama House having breakfast. Looking out the window toward the street, the two took in the porticoed veranda and wrought-iron scrollwork by which the builder conveyed an air of Southern gentility.

A lilting voice at their elbows made them turn abruptly. "This view always puts me in mind of Atlanta. Don't you think so, Mister Wilson?"

Both males jumped to their feet. "Ah, um, Miss Boyd . . . I'm sure the resemblance is exact if you say so," stammered Tom.

Her Cupid's bow of a mouth parted into a smile that included Mont. "What an adorable boy. What is his name, Mister Wilson?"

Mont took an instant dislike to the dark-haired woman, beautiful and friendly though she was. Miss Emily had never spoken *about* him as if he were not present. And besides, what right did this person have to be so familiar with Tom? Who was she anyway?

"This is Mont, Miss Boyd. Mont, make your manners to Miss Boyd," Tom directed.

Mont bowed stiffly from the waist and said in a too quiet, brittle-sounding voice, "Pleased to meet you, ma'am."

"Delightful!" Belle enthused. "So well trained. Have you had him long?"

At least this was a question Tom and Mont had rehearsed. "Oh yes," Tom replied, "and his family before him."

"How nice," Belle responded, but it was plain from her tone and the gaze she fixed on Tom that her interest in Mont had evaporated, if any had really ever existed. "May I join you?"

"Please," agreed Tom, signaling to a white-coated waiter passing by with a silver coffeepot.

When both adults were seated, Mont, who was still standing, said in a voice that was overloud this time, "Marse Wilson, shall I go up an' check on your laundry?"

*   *   *

Puzzled by the abrupt question and Mont's sudden need to depart, Tom agreed rather than asking in front of Belle for an explanation of this contrivance.

After Mont was gone and the waiter had poured two fresh cups of coffee, Belle launched into another lengthy thank-you for Tom's role in the events of the night before.

"It isn't necessary to thank me," said Tom, looking into the dark brown eyes that held his from across the table. "I could not have done anything else."

"But I am *so* grateful," purred Belle. "Besides, I sense a real kinship of spirit with you. You *are* the Wilson who rescued that dear little editor from those criminal soldiers?"

Tom acknowledged the event with a nod. "Nothing to brag about. I could not let the good man be lynched, even though he acted the part of a fool. There are more effective methods of dealing with Yankees than deriding them in public. But tell me, how do you know that story?"

Belle's chin tilted toward the dining-room ceiling as a peal of bell-like laughter bubbled from her throat. "Why, Mister Wilson," she said with mock sternness, "I'm surprised at you! A gentleman never asks a lady to reveal her sources!

"But since you are *that* Wilson, I don't mind telling you," she continued in a conspiratorial tone. She extended her gloved hand across the table toward Tom's coffee cup and wrapped her long, slender fingers around his sturdy, tanned fist. She pulled his hand toward her side of the table with a surprisingly strong grip, and Tom leaned in until their heads almost touched.

"There are still a few true sons of the South in this state," she murmured, "but not nearly enough that a gallant hero like yourself can go unnoticed or unremarked."

A whiff of the same exotic perfume Tom had noticed in Belle's room hit his senses. For an instant the clatter of crockery and the bustle of the waiters disappeared. It felt as if he and Belle were alone together. The two were eye to eye, only a breath apart.

The reverie was interrupted when a dark-suited man walked over to their table and stood alongside. Tom first noticed the pointed toes on the black leather shoes, then scanned upward to the pointed beard and the brooding eyes below the heavy, dark brows.

Unhurriedly, Belle leaned back in her chair and said in a completely conversational tone, "As I was saying, Mister Wilson, your actions have not gone unreported. The fact of the matter is that Mister Jasper Perry here would also like to congratulate you."

Tom stood and the two men shook hands. Perry had still not said anything. His eyes seemed to try to penetrate Tom's, and his expression was sharp, even harsh. He squeezed Tom's hand with a grip far stronger than courtesy suggested.

If that's how you want it, thought Tom, *I'll play along.* He returned the crush of the handshake, pound for pound.

He noted that Belle as watching the contest of strength with undisguised amusement.

The first indication that either man was faltering occurred when Perry unlocked his stare and glanced down at his hand. The tips of his fingers had turned white up to the second joints. A grunt escaped his tightly clenched jaws.

Tom immediately relaxed his grip and gestured with his free hand toward Mont's empty chair. "Please have a seat, Mister Perry."

"Sturdy handshake," Perry remarked gruffly. Then, as if remembering Belle's introduction, he continued in a friendlier tone, "It's fortunate that a man of your strength was around to come to my fiancée's assistance."

Tom's glance at Belle saw her momentarily flustered, but she recovered her composure quickly. A faint pink tinge lingered as evidence of her discomfort.

Perry draped his arm possessively across the back of Belle's chair. "The Yankee tyrant Lincoln, with his army of invaders, thinks that he can tread on the rights of sovereign states with impunity. Thankfully, courageous men like Garrison still stand up and spit in his eye! But the wheels of oppression are grinding harder and harder. Brave men are fighting and dying for want of assistance. We dare not stand idly by."

Tom's thoughts ran from how much like a prepared speech this sounded to how ironic it was for a cause that endorsed slavery to speak of being oppressed. "I have heard similar sentiments expressed before," commented Tom with an air of cautious approval.

"Stronger, Mister Wilson, stronger! You may speak your mind freely here—you're among friends! You were already vouched for, but your recent actions not only underline your character but place me personally in your debt. How may I improve your stay in San Francisco?"

Tom's look around the room paused briefly on nearby diners, judging whether the conversation had been overheard. His prolonged stare at a bald-headed man seated alone at a corner table caused both Perry and Belle to follow his gaze.

As if satisfied at last that he could proceed safely, Tom replied to Jasper Perry's offer. "I have been sent," he said with a note of mystery, "to offer myself to an extremely important effort to aid a glorious cause—at any cost." These words were part of a formula explained to Tom by Colonel Mason.

Perry's expression did not change. In an offhand way he said to Belle, "I'm sorry you have to leave, my dear. Thank you for your kind introduction." Perry stood and helped the actress up from her chair.

Belle looked nonplussed at the abrupt dismissal but offered no argument. "I'm sure I won't miss anything but boring man talk and speech making," she said with a flutter of her eyelashes. Then to Tom she said, "Don't believe *everything* he says, Mister Wilson. Mister Perry is prone to exaggeration." After this small act of defiance, Belle took her leave. It was clear from the way she bestowed smiles and hellos around the tables that Belle understood the power of her charms.

Both men followed her out of the room with their eyes. At last Perry spoke. "Your arrival could not be more fortunate. We need to move quickly and decisively."

"You are the leader of the castle, of course," observed Tom. "I knew it immediately."

Perry shook his head with a self-deprecating shrug. "No, not me. I am only a messenger—a foot soldier, if you will. But I'd like you to accompany me to meet our general."

"When?"

"Tonight."

✳ ✳ ✳

In a carriage with drawn shades, Tom was taken on a roundabout drive through San Francisco. When the ride was over, he was hustled into a warehouse.

"Greetings, Brother Wilson," said a breathy and muffled voice from someone in a thronelike chair with a mask over his face.

Tom took his seat in a circle of four men.

"As you see," Jasper Perry explained in rather unctuous tones, "we are small in number but not in courage. Many have abandoned our cause because of cowardice or personal greed, but those who remain are undoubted. You have shown yourself to be worthy of our trust."

Perry continued, "We need your help on an important matter. We want you to join forces with some brothers in Virginia City, Nevada Territory. Will you go?"

"What am I to do there?" Tom asked.

"That will be explained at the proper time," Perry responded. "All you must do for now is take a room at the Tahoe Hotel. You will be contacted there. Will you go?"

"Yes, of course," Tom answered, not really certain if he meant to go or not. "But I have business to take care of tomorrow. I can leave the next day."

"Very well," intoned the leader, concluding the discussion. "We appreciate your willingness, Brother Wilson. The others in Virginia City are expecting us to send assistance. When you get to the hotel and register, all you need to do is put this word—*Chapman*—after your name. You'll be contacted. Now, if you'll wait in the next room for just a minute. . . ."

✳ ✳ ✳

After Tom had left the room, the tone turned less formal. "Do Ingram and Hastings really need his help?" one man asked.

"Ingram has grit; he will stick. But Hastings is young and sometimes soft. He may need to be replaced," Perry said.

"But what do we really know about this man?"

"We have the description of what he looks like and the report of his escape. We know that he is brave and has shown himself able and willing to stand up to the Yankees. Besides, let me add that Miss Boyd will also be going to the Comstock shortly after. She will keep an eye on him as well. If need be, she can do more than charm him. . . ."

Perry smiled.

✳ ✳ ✳

The side-wheeler *Yosemite* was easing into the docks when Tom and Mont approached the wharf. The tall black smokestack towered over the paddle wheels and the walking beam amidships, dwarfing the pilothouse. But the flag of the United States waving bravely at the stern stood out plainly above the gleaming white ship.

"Isn't that a grand sight, Mont?" Tom asked.

"'Deed it is," agreed Mont. "Mighty proud!"

"You know," Tom went on, "if we go to the Comstock like Perry and the secesh want, that boat, or one like it, is how we'll travel upriver."

Mont's eyes grew as big as saucers. "You means we'd go 'cross the bay on it?"

The *Yosemite* seemed to sense his enthusiasm and responded by announcing its arrival with a great blast of its steam whistles.

"Not just across the bay but clear to Sacramento. From there the stage company runs to Virginia City, Nevada Territory." In an afterthought he added, "Of course, from Sacramento you could catch a stage back home, too. Yes, sir, just two days from where we're standing and we'd be home." He wished that indeed was the journey being planned, instead of one going farther away.

"Is we goin' to Virginia City for shore?"

"I don't know. I want to ask some advice from the two military men Colonel Mason mentioned to me. I'm afraid if I don't agree to go, then it will look suspicious to Perry and his group. But if I do go, I'm worried about taking you along. The Comstock is plenty rough at the best of times."

Mont started to protest that he'd be just fine, but Tom interrupted, "You know, if I had any good place to leave you, I'd have you stay here till I got back. I just don't know who with."

✹ ✹ ✹

Mont's mouth closed with a snap. He'd already decided that the sooner this subject got changed, the better.

They spotted the man Tom had come to see outside an office near the South Beach Ship Yard. Commander Fry was an imposing figure, as tall as Tom and nearly as muscular, despite his sixty years of age. He had a shock of white hair and impressive white burnsides. His uniform, all brass and braids, included a sword.

Mont thought the commander looked a lot like woodcuts he had seen of Andrew Jackson.

"Commander Fry?" Tom confirmed. "My name is Wilson. I believe Colonel Mason may have mentioned my name to you."

"Wilson, of course. Come in," Fry said tersely. Then to a man dressed in greasy coveralls who had been receiving rapid-fire instructions, he concluded, "I want them here tomorrow. Tomorrow, understand? Not one day later or by thunder I'll have a new foreman."

"Yes, sir, Admiral," said the worker in an Irish brogue. "Come sunup tomorrow, they'll be here. It'll be a grand sight, to be sure." The man pulled on his forelock and backed away.

Fry motioned Tom and Mont into a small office that contained only one chair and a desk overflowing with plans and blueprints. He did not seat himself, so all three stood in the tiny space. "Wilson," he said again, "heard from Mason. Think it's poppycock. This conspiracy. Anyway, no time to play games. Too busy already."

"Well, sir," said Tom, his rising indignation clear on his face, "Colonel Mason has reason to think there is truth to it, and I have already met—"

"Some secesh diehards? Rubbish," Fry said abruptly. "Good luck to you, Mister Wilson. What we're about here is more important than chasing fairies. Now if you'll excuse me." And he ushered them out and shut his door.

"Come on, Mont," Tom said, thrusting his hands into his pockets and walking with such long strides that Mont had to run to keep up. "Let's see if the army treats us any better. If nobody wants to give us the time of day, maybe we'll just go home."

✴ CHAPTER 10 ✴

The path leading down the hill toward Fort Point took Tom and Mont past the commander's house. They knocked, but no one answered.

The commander of Fort Point's garrison of two hundred men lived in a small frame house, freshly painted white and trimmed in forest green. It stood on a knoll above the brick fortress. From the yard beside the home, the soldiers on guard duty atop the walls of the fort could be seen patrolling their posts.

A northwest wind funneled past the Marin Headlands and made the flag waving over the casements snap on its halyard. It was a pleasant day for an outing to view the Golden Gate, the entrance to the greatest natural harbor in the world.

But if the scene from the knobby hill was inspiring and enjoyable, descending the wooden staircase to stand in the shadow of the three-story-high citadel brought back the reality of war. Soldiers were drilling on the cleared area in front of the fort's single entrance. They marched and countermarched under the critical eye of a red-bearded sergeant-major. He gave them the benefit of his opinion at every opportunity, expressed in a voice that resounded from the brick walls and rocky cliff side with such volume that Tom thought it must be heard in Sausalito across the bay.

Tom and Mont heard him question a soldier's intellect, morals, upbringing, and ancestry when the man had failed to execute "order arms" properly.

When the sergeant-major saw Tom and Mont approaching, he must have decided that another opportunity for a lesson had presented itself. He motioned to three soldiers and waved them forward. "Kirby, Seldon, Morris—you three are the guard detail. Kirby is acting corporal. Let me see you make a proper challenge and report."

"Halt! Who goes there?" demanded the one named Seldon, pointing a bayonet at Tom's midsection.

"Corporal 'the guard! Post number one!" shouted Morris.

"Escort the uh, the uh—" Kirby stumbled. He questioned Tom and Mont with a look. *Are you prisoners or visitors?*

The glare he received from Sergeant-Major Donovan would have melted one of the antique bronze cannons that flanked the entrance.

Under Donovan's withering stare, Kirby swallowed hard and reported, "Corporal 'the guard, Sergeant-Major. Post number one is escorting two unknown persons."

Donovan puffed out his whiskers like a surfacing sea lion and advanced past where Kirby stood quivering at attention. "Sergeant-Major Donovan," he announced to Tom. "What is your name and purpose?"

"My name is Wilson," said Tom, "and this is Mont. We are here to see Captain Tompkins."

"Regrettably, sir, Captain Tompkins is ill and in the hospital. Lieutenant Reynolds is in command."

"I see," said Tom with some consternation. "Would you please ask the lieutenant if he will see me? My business here was suggested by Colonel Mason of Fort Tejon."

"Of course. If you will wait here, please."

In a brief space of time, Donovan was back and offered to escort Tom and Mont to Reynolds' office himself. As they passed into the interior of the fort, the high walls shut out the sunlight. It felt like a prison cell.

Lieutenant Reynolds was a plump, soft-looking young man, about Tom's age. He had a receding chin and a prominent nose he looked down, as though sighting a cannon. He affected the dress uniform of the artillery, including a red sash and black ostrich-plumed hat.

After introductions, Tom proceeded to explain his real identity and his reason for being in San Francisco with Mont. "So you see," he summarized, "Colonel Mason believed that the plot was real enough to bear investigation and that Mont might recognize one of the principals."

"And has he?" Reynolds inquired, aiming his nose at Mont.

"No," Tom said, "but *I* may have stumbled on to something." He went on to describe Jasper Perry and the mysterious meeting that called for him to make a trip to Comstock.

When he had finished, Reynolds leaned back in his chair and laced his pudgy fingers together. "There may be some real importance to what you have uncovered, and I want you to know I take it seriously. But we must proceed slowly and carefully. It would not do to spook one bird and let the covey escape. Are you agreeable to going to Virginia City to see if you can discover the others in the plot?"

"Yes, except that I dislike dragging Mont all over the countryside. Besides, it could be dangerous for him. But I think the gang will be suspicious if I don't go."

247

"Acting reluctant at this point would certainly raise some questions," Reynolds agreed. "How about this: Mont can stay with me while you make a rapid trip there to see what you can discover, then return on some pretext, and we'll round up all of them you can identify."

"Leave Mont with you?" Tom said a little dubiously.

"Would you rather that we arrest this actress—what's her name, Boyd, for questioning? See what information we can get from her?"

"No, no," said Tom hastily. "You're right that we should know more first. We don't want to tip off the others."

"Splendid," said Reynolds. "You can leave Mont with me now and send his things back. Will you be leaving tonight?"

Tom looked over at Mont and thought he saw a tear forming in the corner of the boy's eye. "No, we have some important business tonight, Mont and I. Why don't you come and pick him up at our hotel, Tehama House, tomorrow at ten, if that's all right. I'll leave on the noon steamer."

"Excellent," answered Reynolds. "Now come and let me show you around the fort. Mont, you will see that it will be fun to stay here." To Tom he added, "And you will see how foolish it is to think of any

Confederate attempt to seize this position. By the way, I think it's best if you say nothing to anyone else about the plot. You can't tell who might be secesh in this town."

Their footsteps echoed hollowly as he led the way up dark staircases. They emerged on the highest level of the fort.

Walking over to a row of cannons, Reynolds patted one affectionately, as if it were a prize horse in a show ring. "Sixty-eight pounder," he said proudly. "Columbiad with a rifled barrel. This weapon can propel a shot two miles or more. The one hundred and twenty of these command more than a half circle on the entrance to the bay."

"What's this?" asked Mont, pointing at a brick and cast-iron contraption with a chimney.

"Furnace," observed Reynolds, "for heating shells red-hot."

"This is very impressive," commented Tom. "But what if the garrison were surprised and the guns seized? After all, these guns face the water."

"True enough," agreed Reynolds, "but we have field pieces and mortars to defend the landward side and two full companies of troops."

Tom and Mont prepared to take their leave then, after thanking Reynolds for showing them around. "Not at all, not at all," he concluded. "I'll see you both tomorrow."

He and Tom conversed quietly for a few more minutes; then Mont and the rancher from Shadow Ridge left the fort.

Halfway up the hill, the man and the boy turned to view the harbor channel one more time. A Pacific mail steamer was bustling into the gate, churning a streaming wake of white foam and a double trail of black smoke. She passed an outbound square-rigged sailing ship, and the two exchanged salutes—steam whistle screaming a reply to the sharp report of a swivel cannon.

Both ships dipped pennants by way of respect to the American flag flying over the fort. A thirty-two pounder roared a reply. It seemed also to be a reminder of how strong and solid the Union defenses of the bay really were.

Tom stood with his hand on Mont's shoulder, and both took in the panorama of the scene. "I can't understand how Perry and the others can be so confident," Tom said, half to himself. "Maybe they *are* crazy."

"I 'spect they see somethin' we doesn't see," Mont suggested.

✳ ✳ ✳

In the glow of the lantern light, Jed looked older than his eleven years. He perched on the hayloft with his father's old Greener shotgun across his lap. At Emily's footstep on the threshold of the barn, he challenged, "Who's that there?"

"Ma," she answered, struck by the manliness of his young voice. "I've brought you another blanket. Some milk and bread with butter and sugar." She stood at the bottom of the ladder as he peered over and then climbed down to retrieve the tin lunch bucket. "You let me know if you get too tired and I'll take the watch," she offered.

He replied with an indignant snort. "I ain't little no more like Nate. I can take his watch and yours as well if I need to. Nobody's gonna get past that barn door unless I give 'em permission."

She did not ask him if he was ever frightened. To do so would have been an insult. Nor did she admit that a dozen times throughout her own watch she had felt the chill of fear at the rustling sounds in the night. An owl hooting in the oak tree, the restless stirring of the horses in the corral at the side of the barn had tightened her grip on the stock of the gun and turned calm prayers into a torrent of frightened entreaties to the Almighty for protection.

No doubt Jed had felt the same. Little Nate had fled into the house and now could not stand his watch alone anymore. Jed simply slept beside him in the hay throughout Nate's watch. Numerous times Nate woke him with a shake and the frantic question, *"You hear that?"* After his watch, Nate would stumble into the house, and Jed would shake himself awake to sit alone for another two hours.

"You're doing fine, Son," Emily said with genuine admiration. "Just remember when you're tired, the Lord never sleeps nor slumbers. He is keeping watch over us in ways we cannot see."

Jed sipped his milk. "I just wish He'd send us some soldiers to help out. I mean, blue-coated soldiers that I could see." A wry smile crossed his lips. A smile so much like his father's.

"They're bound to come." She looked at the animals in the stalls and wondered if perhaps the Union soldiers did in fact consider guarding the Dawson ranch a trivial matter. Too unimportant to deal with. She did not express her doubt to Jed, however. "In the meantime, it's just us. And no doubt great armies of angels all around us. Enough for now or there would be others here as well."

He nodded and glanced up toward the loft. One hand on the ladder and then he froze. Emily heard it too. Far away in the darkness hoofbeats echoed on the rock-hard roadbed.

Jed shoved the bucket into his mother's arm and scrambled up the ladder to retrieve the shotgun. "Get to the house," he instructed her in manly tones. "They're still a ways off. Get the rifles and the revolver."

Emily ran to the house, wishing that there were soldiers of the blue-coated sort right now to help them! The hoofbeats came nearer, turning onto the lane that led to the ranch house. She took the Winchester from the gun rack and wrested the Colt revolver from its holster.

Asleep on the sofa, Nate stirred, groaned, and rolled over to settle into a deeper sleep.

It's good that he is unaware of my sense of fear, Emily thought. Then a renewed anger flooded her as she thought of Tom Dawson off chasing shadows when there was such a real and terrible threat right here at home! When were those soldiers coming? And when would Tom be back? She would give him a piece of her mind when he showed up!

She carried the kerosene lantern outside with her and put it on the tree stump beside the hitching rail. Then she stepped back in the shadows to wait as the riders came near. The Dawson family had rehearsed this plan several times.

"I'm here, Jed," she called loudly. "I've got the guns!" She hoped the riders would hear the threat in her voice and turn around. They did not.

"We got 'em covered, Ma," Jed called bravely. No doubt he, too, hoped to discourage whoever was coming.

It was then that a familiar voice rang out from the darkness of the lane. "Sister Dawson! Young Jed! Do not shoot! It is Parson Swift here! I've brought my sons along to stand watch with you tonight!"

CHAPTER 11

Mont watched the misty fingers of fog just beginning to relinquish their grip on the streetlamps. Today Mont would go to stay with the lieutenant at Fort Point, but right now he was waiting in the room at the Tehama Hotel.

Tom had left long before daylight. After checking steamer sailings from 'Frisco and stage connections from Sacramento to Virginia City, Tom had decided on the early departure. "I can save a whole day's wait in Sacramento this way," he explained to Mont. "Don't worry. I'll be back soon, and Lieutenant Reynolds will look after you."

The lieutenant had wanted Mont to stay at the fort last night, but Tom had insisted that he and Mont have dinner together and take in a show at the Melodeon Theater. Besides, Tom had suggested to Reynolds that Mont could point out secesh conspirators around the hotel. Reynolds had agreed. He would come in civilian clothes in the morning to pick up Mont. His army uniform would certainly frighten the rebels, and it could be disastrous if a Union officer were seen talking with Tom and Mont.

Even without the lieutenant's red sash and ostrich-plume hat, Mont spotted the officer coming up the street. Reynolds paused to strike a match on a lamppost and lit his cigar. He was wearing a plain, dark blue cape and cloth cap.

Mont was already dressed and bounced out of the room to the stairwell in anticipation of Reynolds' arrival. In the silence of the still early morning, Mont could hear the clump of heavy boots coming up the stairs. Ten steps to the landing and ten more to the second floor, Mont counted. The climbing tread stopped.

That's funny, Mont thought. *Guess he forgot we wuz on three.* He leaned over the railing to call down to Reynolds to come up one more flight.

Stretching out above the stairwell, Mont caught a glimpse of a dark blue back and shoulder one floor below. As he watched, a fist rose and fell on the door nearest the steps in two quick knocks, followed by two more. Evidently Reynolds knew someone else at the hotel. But who?

Then the door to the room was opened by Jasper Perry, with Miss Boyd standing next to him. Reynolds stepped hastily through, and the panel was quickly closed behind him.

Something is wrong, very wrong. Why was the Union army officer going to meet with the conspirators? It did not look like he was there to arrest them. Mont had to find out.

He tiptoed quietly down the steps, then looked all around to see if anyone was nearby before placing his ear close to the keyhole. The volume of voices coming from the room was loud enough that Mont did not have to strain to hear.

"What do you mean, he's not one of us!" shouted the voice of Jasper Perry.

"Calm down and lower your voice," demanded Reynolds. "There is no harm done. We'll take care of him the same way we did the other impostor."

"But he's already gone to the Comstock," murmured Belle.

Now it was Reynolds' turn to be surprised. "What? He wasn't due to leave till noon."

"I saw him off early this morning," said Belle, "on his way to the steamer."

"All right," said Reynolds, back in control. "Belle, you are leaving for the Comstock at once. I won't trust this message to the wire, what with Pinkerton men everywhere. You must see Ingram. Tell him to hire someone outside the circle, but do it quickly!"

"But, General, what about the brat?" Perry wanted to know.

"We'll hang on to him as a hostage till we know the job is done," Reynolds concluded.

"Ho there, you boy," boomed a voice down the hall behind Mont. "What are you sneakin' round that door for?"

The conversation in the room stopped abruptly, and running steps came toward the door.

Mont's flight took him down the stairs three steps at a time. At the bottom he did a neat swing around a wrought-iron banister and came off the last six steps airborne, flying feet-first.

His boots collided with the stomach of a well-dressed, portly gentleman. The collision produced an "oof," followed by a groan. The large man revolved slowly like a ship capsizing and sank down on the bottom step, holding his paunch.

Mont raced past the doorman.

✵ ✵ ✵

When Mont's pursuers reached the ground floor, they could not get by, since a large man's girth blocked the steps.

Reynolds made one polite, encouraging noise, asking the man to move. Perry tried to leap over the roadblock . . . unsuccessfully, as it turned out.

The large man had tried to oblige Reynolds by clearing the stairs, so he stood up just as Jasper Perry hurdled over. A kick behind the ear dropped the poor man to the floor again and sent Perry sprawling onto the marble tiles. He partly caught himself on his hands but not soon enough to keep his forehead from smacking the pavement. He got up looking dazed and wandered toward the desk clerk.

Running past the jumbled heap of bodies, Reynolds dashed out the front door. He spotted Mont a half block away, running north on Sansome.

At the same time, a policeman turned the corner of Sacramento Street, right in Mont's path.

Behind him, Reynolds yelled, "Stop him—he's a pickpocket!"

✳ ✳ ✳

The nine-year-old did not think of trying to explain his side of the story. All he saw was another pair of arms outstretched to grab him. Mont ducked his head one way and threw his body the other. The policeman's arms closed around empty air.

A bell began to clang behind him in furious alarm. Mont accelerated his pace, terrified at the size of the alarm that was being raised—all of San Francisco must be after him!

The clanging bell was getting closer. It seemed to be chasing him up the street. Everyone on the sidewalks had stopped to watch the pursuit. A pair of ladies in long-skirted dresses and high collars formed a barrier with their folded umbrellas. Mont jumped between them, barely clearing the spiked tips.

He caromed into a man wearing baggy trousers and holding a basket of oranges. The fruit the man had been displaying for sale spun up in the air and all over the sidewalk. A second later an orange flew past Mont's head, and a stream of angry foreign words like *cochito prieta* and *serpeinto* also pursued his flight.

Now the sounds of a whole cavalry troop chased Mont. His short legs were beginning to tire, but he forced himself to keep them churning, struggling to stay ahead of the army that must be pursuing.

A trio of boys a little older than Mont watched him run toward them. They made no move to step aside but kept staring back the way he had come as if they could not believe the strength of the chase either!

Mont lowered his head and plowed straight into them.

Cries of "Hey, watch out!" and "What'er you tryin' to do!" erupted.

Mont was showered with fists and boots, but he kicked free and made a dash to cross Clay Street. The terrible clanging alarm bell and the thundering hooves were right behind. Mont took off from the curb in a jump that would have landed him in the middle of the street—and was tackled from behind by all three boys yelling, "Look out! You're gonna get killed!" as the hook and ladder wagon of Engine Company Number Five rattled and rumbled around the corner.

The rear of the elongated vehicle careened around the turn,

brushing the lamppost that hung over the boys' heads. The iron-shod hooves of the coal black horses and the iron-rimmed wheels pounded past them only inches away.

"You better watch where you're runnin'!" yelled a towheaded boy in a cloth cap.

"Yeah," agreed another, "them firemen don't stop for nothin'!"

"What was you runnin' so hard for, anyway?" questioned the third, an olive-skinned street urchin with bare feet.

"I was . . ." Mont looked fearfully down the street. He spotted Reynolds, puffing and wheezing but still pursuing, two blocks behind. "I gotta go," he shouted, jumping up. "Thanks!" And off he went, sprinting around the corner on Clay, following the rapidly disappearing fire wagon with its load of men, ladders, and axes.

Setting his sights on a large brick and granite building ahead of him kept Mont from accidentally turning back toward his pursuers. He jogged left, then two rights, then left again. What he was in search of, he could not have said, except to be far enough ahead to have a chance to hide.

The opportunity just did not present itself. His landmark, when he passed it, turned out to be a bustling collection of businesses with offices of the Alta California newspaper and the Bank Exchange Saloon. The people there were all well-dressed men in business suits, top hats, and frock coats. Mont thought about asking one of them for help. Then he remembered that Jasper Perry was wearing a top hat and a frock coat, so he ran on, turning again toward the west.

When he reached Washington Street, two things changed: The most enormous hill yet reared up in front of him, and the nature of the pedestrians altered. As if by magic, the sidewalks were suddenly filled with hundreds of small pigtailed men dressed in dark blue tunics. Their shirttails hung below their waists, and the overlong sleeves concealed their hands.

An elderly Chinese man was coming slowly toward Mont. He wore the same flapping shirt and baggy trousers as the rest, but he had a black silk skullcap on his head. He was followed by two lean, angry-looking men who walked five steps behind. They were dressed completely in black, and their eyes were constantly moving from side to side as they scanned alleys, balconies, and doorways.

The rising slope of the approach to Nob Hill was too much for Mont's short, tired legs. His scamper slowed to a trot, then to a walk. He was even considering turning around and heading downhill when he spotted Reynolds, still chasing him. Mont tried to speed up again but found he could not. His legs felt like lead.

Reynolds was exhausted. His puffing and wheezing had made it impossible for him to call out for help to any of the passersby. He had tried to shout, "Stop, thief!" and wave his hat in the hopes that some citizen would tackle a supposed pickpocket, but the clanging of the fire wagon's passing had eclipsed his strangled yell. After that, he just had not had the breath.

When the lieutenant realized that Mont was leading him up Nob Hill, he knew it was over unless . . . bending down to a cross-draw holster that hung inside his cape, Reynolds drew an octagonal-barreled Colt and leaned against a lamppost to steady his aim.

The two bodyguards of the elderly Chinese man saw a man draw his gun. They had no idea why this man would want to kill their boss, but their job was to protect him no matter what.

From the deep pockets of their black tunics, both men drew short-barreled Allen pepperboxes and began firing. The range was long and the guns inaccurate even at a much closer distance, but their shots made Reynolds throw himself to the ground and hug the base of the post.

As soon as they had fired, the bodyguards dragged their employer into a shop that sold ginseng roots and disappeared with him through its back door.

Mont also managed to disappear at the sound of the first shot: He ducked into an alleyway so narrow that two men could not walk side by side.

There was a hole in the pavement of the alleyway. Ten running steps down the passage, the rungs of a wooden ladder protruded two feet above the surface.

Mont grasped the topmost rung and looked into the shadowy darkness below. Then making up his mind as he gathered his courage, Mont dropped quickly off the face of San Francisco and into the depths of Chinatown.

257

✴CHAPTER 12✴

The first thing Mont noticed when he descended into the man-made underground grotto was the incredible variety of smells. Not the dark or the dirt, although there were plenty of both. It was the strange, almost touchable swirl of aromas assaulting his nose that gave Mont the sense of having dropped into another world.

At first he couldn't quite identify the odors, but somehow they stirred up memories. Sharp but pleasant smells that brought to mind Emily's kitchen: tea. Steamy, starchy air full of reminders of iron kettles in slave quarters: boiling rice. Pepper, oranges, fish—dark smells, bright smells, clean smells, moldy smells, all jumbled in a stew of airborne concoction. Floating through the mix was a too-sweet, too-heavy aroma of decay . . . the odor of wilted flowers heaped on a grave.

Mont crept along the passageway toward a dimly flickering lantern. Beneath it, the corridor came to an intersection. Three underground roads led off in different directions.

The tunnel that went straight ahead had no features to distinguish it from the other two, but Mont chose it in order to find his way back to the ladder and the outside air. Another lantern in the distance provided a new goal as the tiny square of sunlight dwindled and finally disappeared.

A room opened beside the next lantern. It was a lower-ceilinged cavern packed with narrow, wooden bunks like the crews' quarters on ships. These bunks were only five feet long and were stacked five deep, with little more than one foot of space between them. At first Mont thought the room was empty, but his ears told him otherwise: Some of the bunks were occupied with gently snoring sleepers.

A soft padding sound like that a cat makes walking on a hardwood floor caused Mont to turn around quickly. He faced a pair of pajama-coated Chinese, whom he had not even heard till they were three feet behind him.

When they spotted Mont lurking in the doorway, both men burst into excited questions and accusations. Though Mont could understand no word of their talk, the meaning was plain: "What are you doing here? You don't belong here! Go away at once!"

Mont dashed off again, deeper into the darkness. Erupting from a lighted side passage ahead, a blast of steam shot into the corridor as if a dragon's lair shared the tunnel.

The chatter of voices slowed Mont's travel. He listened, trying to sort out the meaning of the repeated rubbing, thumping, and splashing noises. Slowly he went to the doorway and peered in. It was an underground laundry. Pigtailed workers stripped to the waist amid clouds of steam and vapors of soap, starch, and bluing were boiling copper cauldrons full of clothes, which they stirred with long wooden paddles. Near a staircase stood a thin man with sharp angles to his face. He was dressed all in black, and he kept apart from the workers' conversations.

The staircase looked promising. To be able to pop back out of this rabbit warren a different way than he entered seemed like a good plan. But would the Chinese notice him? Would they let him pass?

The question was answered as soon as Mont appeared inside the room. None of the workers saw him, but the man in black certainly did. Raising a yell that could not mean anything other than "Get him!" Mont again found himself pursued, this time by half a dozen Orientals. *How can everybody be in on trying to catch me?* he wondered. *Two hours ago, nobody was after me.*

Mont turned to flee the laundry but met with a greater problem. His desire to get out of the underground world was blocked by the approach of more shouting Chinese voices, so he had no choice but to plunge still deeper into the maze.

And maze it had become. At the next intersection Mont took
the path toward the right and almost immediately came to another
branching choice. This time the fork was not a straight line at all but
a sinuous curve. Several times it came to dead ends or blind corners
that required hasty backtracking. Twice he had to duck under a low
doorway, and twice more he had to jump and climb over a brick
partition. It was as if someone had built that passageway to be deliberately difficult to follow. The sounds of his pursuers dropped farther
and farther back and presently died away altogether.

Mont glimpsed a light ahead. He prayed that it would be a way
out, but still he approached it with caution.

The light came through a doorway blocked by a wrought-iron
grate. Mont could see a room beyond the grate, but he could not
tell if it was occupied. The boy stifled a cough as the sticky, sweet,
decayed flower aroma that pervaded the whole underground suddenly increased a hundred times.

Creeping up to the grate, Mont peered through. It was a dimly
lit room with walls painted dark red. Near the center of the room
burned a small coal fire on a short round stand.

Shifting behind the grate, Mont changed his angle to see as much
of the room as he could. Built against the wall opposite was a series
of bunks, much like the ones Mont had seen earlier, only these were
covered in black lacquer and had curtains that could be drawn across
the openings.

Mont jerked back into the shadows as a form appeared. A wiz-
ened man, whose sallow face sagged with the weight of his years,
padded noiselessly into the room. His pigtail was yellowed with age,
and his wispy yellow chin whiskers divided into two long strands that
hung down on his green silk brocade robe.

The figure bent over a clay jar that was emblazoned with inter-
twined red and gold dragons. From it he extracted a tiny quantity
of something on the tip of a long blackened fingernail. He rolled the
substance between forefinger and thumb, then inserted it deftly into
the small bowl of a short brass-bowled pipe from a rack near the fire.

A glowing splinter of wood grasped in one clawed hand and the
brass pipe clutched in the other, the ancient man shuffled toward

the curtained alcove. "Mista Sims," he called softly, "you likee mo' black smoke?"

From behind the curtain, a croaking groan emerged, followed by, "What . . . what time is it?"

The old man gave a low wheezing chuckle. "Is no time here, Mista Sims. In plenty black smoke is only dreams."

"Blast your eyes!" the croaking voice reviled. "What is the time?"

In a hurt tone, the withered stick of a man responded, "If you no wantee mo' pipe, I take away," and he turned half around from the bunk.

"Wait!" the man demanded. His hand tore open the curtain and grabbed the old man roughly by the shoulder. "Give me that pipe!"

"All light, Mista Sims. Takee pipe . . . here fire . . . good, good . . ."

The man named Sims seized the offered pipe and puffed it eagerly, then drew the pipe inside the bunk space and shut the curtain with a long contented sigh.

The old Chinaman returned to squat by the fire. As he rubbed his hands together over the coals, he appeared to recall some necessary errand. Slowly straightening to a crooked comma shape, he shuffled toward an exit at the far end of the room and disappeared.

Wincing at the creaking of the rusty iron hinges, Mont pushed on the lattice grate. A thin shriek of protest came from the little-used frame; then it swung open into the room. Mont breathed a sign of relief: He had been afraid it would be locked.

His head felt funny from the smoke that floated around the underground chamber. Mont listened carefully for any sounds of movement but heard nothing. Even the man in the bunk had fallen completely silent now. When a chunk of coal collapsed on the brazier into a pile of ash, Mont started nervously. He was ready to dash back into the tunnel, but he controlled the impulse, telling himself that the way out of this underground maze lay forward, not back.

At the far end of the room was a doorway partly concealed by a silk hanging. A stray breath of fresh air somehow found its way down into the den, stirring the thin cloth. *Hurry*, it seemed to urge, *get out quickly.*

Mont's headlong rush into the silk curtain made a pair of

streamers that flew from his shoulders as he raced through. Like a
Chinese kite trailing twin tails as it soars, Mont sailed up the incline
at top speed. And just as a kite's ascent is halted abruptly when it
reaches the end of the string, Mont's progress suddenly stopped as
a clawed fist seized him by the arm and demanded, "Where you go,
little black child?"

As Mont kicked and flailed his arms trying to free himself, a second ghastly set of fingernails closed around his neck. "You be still,"
the ancient Chinaman ordered, "or pletty soon I tear throat out!"
When Mont complied and stopped struggling, the old man observed,
"You no thinkee Wo Sing hear you breathe in tunnel? What you do
here?" He released just enough pressure from the nail points against
Mont's windpipe to allow a reply.

"Please, sir," Mont begged, "I was just running from some bad
men, and I come down here to hide. Can you help me?"

262

The wiry little man gathered both strands of wispy beard in the
claw he took off Mont's neck and stroked downward. "Helpee you?
Sure, sure. You come with Wo Sing."

The two walked quietly along another twisting passage with the
appearance of friendliness, but a threatening hand rested lightly on
Mont's shoulder all the time. Presently, they turned a corner to face
an alcove watched over by two black-suited guards.

Some discussion in Chinese passed back and forth before the
attendant was permitted to take Mont through the doorway. The
room beyond the door looked like the descriptions Mont had heard
of the throne rooms of kings. The walls were covered with red silk
hangings, embroidered with Chinese characters worked in gold. A
thick carpet lay underfoot, and overhead were round hanging lamps
made of pale green glass with brass fittings.

Against one wall sat a group of musicians, who seemed to be
tuning their instruments. When the discordant sounds continued
without pause, Mont decided that this was what passed for music
among the Chinese. A closer look revealed that Mont could not
recognize any of the instruments anyway—no wonder it sounded
strange to his ear!

Just as Mont was beginning to enjoy inspecting the alien surroundings, he was shoved hard from behind. "Is not time for gawking," said Wo Sing harshly. Mont was propelled toward a raised platform at the far end of the room.

On the platform sat a Chinese man of indeterminate age. He wore a long cream-colored robe, which Mont thought looked like a nightshirt, a dark blue vest trimmed in red, and a pair of round spectacles. He was smoking a long-stemmed ivory pipe, resting the bowl on his knee as he drew leisurely puffs.

Four men sat at a low table just below and to the side of the "throne." They had been eating and talking but stopped to watch Wo Sing bring Mont forward.

About halfway to the platform, Mont again received a shove from behind, this time throwing him to his knees.

Wo Sing got down beside him and hissed, "Knock head! Knock head! Do all same me." He proceeded to prostrate himself on the floor, while helping Mont by grabbing a handful of the little boy's tightly curled hair.

Wo Sing then crawled over to the edge of the platform, dragging Mont along with him. Every few feet, he paused to knock Mont's head against the carpet.

The man on the high seat gestured for Wo Sing to speak. A conversation took place in which Mont must have been central, because Wo Sing plucked the boy's sleeve several times and butted his head down to the floor twice more.

When the speaking was finished, Wo Sing again stretched himself on the floor and began crawling backward toward the door, leaving Mont behind.

"Hey!" Mont called, raising up and looking around. "Where you goin'? Do I get out of here now?"

Never pausing in his backward slither, Wo Sing merely shook his head and replied, "This great master of Sum Yop Tong, Fujing Toy. You belong him now."

Mont jumped up exclaiming, "Belong? I doesn't *belong* to nobody no more!"

From the shadows at the sides of the room, two more blackshirts rushed forward. They seized Mont and carried him suspended by the arms out of the room through a door behind the platform. Once in another dim passage, they opened a heavy oak door and threw him in.

✳ ✳ ✳

Reynolds had given up the pursuit and returned to the room at the hotel. "It doesn't matter. He can't harm us anyway. And if he turns up again, we'll—"

Captain Law burst into the room. His normally wary pale eyes were unusually animated as he waved his bandaged hand wildly. "It's the *Camanche*, I tell you! We've got to move now—now, or it's hopeless."

"Start again, man," Perry urged. "Slowly and from the beginning."

"Whiskey," Law demanded and Perry complied. After swallowing half a water glass full in one gulp, Law visibly took control of his nervousness and tried again to explain. "I was down on the docks, a-sizin' up wharf rats for crew, just as ye said. Outside the South Beach Boatyard, I sees a line of men a-waitin' at a guard shack . . . hundreds of men, maybe. I like to keep a weather eye on how blows the news, so I sharpen my course toward a likely knot of greasy-lookin' customers. 'Well, mates,' I sez, friendly-like, 'what's the scuttlebutt? Are you shippin' out for China or to go fight the Rebs?' An uncommon hairy one riz up on my port beam an' throws in with, 'We ain't no swabbies; we be mechanics.'"

264

"So what?" interrupted Reynolds in an exasperated tone. "The boat works has some rich man's yacht to float, no doubt. Probably ten or twelve underpaid jobs."

Law's eyes now snapped with anger as he shook his shock of white hair from side to side in denial. "Put a reef in your mouth and unfurl your ears. The hairy one sez they's hirin' close on *one hundred* men—*iron workers*!"

"Iron workers?" responded Perry incredulously. "What do they think . . . ?"

Law nodded vigorously, and the white stubble of his beard waved in agreement. "Now you catch my drift, *and* you can smell the storm on the breeze. Why *does* a shipyard need iron workers? And why hire such a mob all at once?"

"Because," Perry said soberly, sitting down abruptly on his bed, "they are finishing an ironclad—a monitor—right here in San Francisco Bay."

"Dead on! And in a terrible hurry, too. Word is the Navy Department wants this new Ericsson boat to protect the coastwise shipping against rebel attacks."

"No!" exclaimed Reynolds, horrified. "How can they know? Where is the traitor?" He shot a murderous glance at the sea captain as if he suspected Law of having personally given away their plans for piracy.

"Steady on," Law demanded, helping himself to another glassful of whiskey. "If they knew, they'd be a-hirin' police, not mechanics. This be a *pre*caution, I thinks, and a way to put fear into would-be rebels. How is the temper of *metal*, anyway?"

Reynolds considered what Law had said and began to regain his composure. "An ironclad here! Soon! This certainly changes things. We will have to move quicker than ever, *and* we will need to capture or destroy that ship, or all our plans will come to nothing. What did you say they call it?"

"*Camanche*," Law replied grimly.

Mont pounded on the cell door, but the dull thuds made by his small fists barely even echoed within the cell. Slowly his eyes adjusted to the darkness until the light from the corridor that outlined the crack around the oak barrier spread into a thin glow by which Mont could examine his prison.

His gaze froze when he discovered he was not alone. In the back corner of the tiny chamber stood a man. Or was he sitting? The figure's head almost touched the ceiling, but the bony projections drawn up in front of him had to be knees. *Impossible!*

"Who are you?" Mont breathed, backing up till his own head brushed the rough timbers of the door.

"Han" was the brief reply.

"Han," Mont repeated. "Is that your name? I is Mont, Mont James. Why is you in here?"

The gaunt-faced man responded slowly, "I ran from Fujing Toy."

"You mean you was trying to escape? Me, too," said Mont, eager for an ally in this strangely mysterious world.

Han stretched out his knees, and his legs extended half the length of the cell.

"Say," Mont marveled, "how tall is you?"

"Umm, seven feet," the man responded.

"Wow!" Mont exclaimed. "I never seed a Chinaman big as you. Fact is, I thought they was all short fellers. Is you Chinese?"

Han nodded wearily. "Mountain people in China. I brought here as slave for Tong lord Fujing Toy."

"You is big enough to wallop four of them blackshirts," Mont observed. "Next time you'll make it to freedom."

Shaking his head, Han replied, "They not feed me. . . . I too weak to fight boo how doys, blackshirts."

✻ CHAPTER 13 ✻

Each evening a different family from Mount Carmel Presbyterian Church arrived at the door of the Dawson ranch. While the men took turns sitting up throughout the night to guard the livestock against unseen threat, the women sewed and the children played upstairs in the loft until bedding down for the night.

What Colonel Mason and the Union army had not done to protect the Dawsons, the church family had managed nicely. Ranchers who could fervently belt out a hymn or recite a Scripture passage by heart now sat with scatterguns across their laps as they gazed down at dark shadows from the loft in the barn.

Pastor Swift preached that vengeance indeed belongs to the Lord, and the Lord would just as well use a shotgun as a bolt of lightning if any varmint tried to harm the widow Dawson and her young'uns or their stock!

Each morning, men chopped firewood while their women and children fixed breakfast in the Dawson kitchen. With the light of day, the watching ended. Except that Emily continued to watch the road for the return of Tom and Mont or for the coming of the blue-coated army that Deputy Pettibone had pledged to send.

✻ ✻ ✻

The next morning (at least Mont supposed it was morning), two small bowls of rice and a jug of water were thrust into the cell. A terse instruction delivered in Chinese was translated for Mont by Han. "We are wanted. We must be ready soon."

"Wanted for what?" Mont asked.

"Fujing Toy is master of Sum Yop Tong. Chinese warlord. When he meet other Tongs, he must impress them with his power and wealth."

"Meaning you and me go on display?"

"Yes," Han agreed. "If other Tong lords see plenty wealth, then maybe they settle fight with talk-talk." The giant took his bowl of rice. The cup disappeared within his massive hand. One swallow and the rice disappeared.

"Is that all they feeds you?" Mont asked.

"Fujing Toy keep me weak so I cannot escape."

Mont looked at his own bowl of rice, then at the huge man. "Whyn't you take this away from me?"

"No," Han replied, "we are brother prisoners. It not right."

Mont picked up Han's empty bowl. After a moment's thought, he scooped half of his rice into it and handed it to Han.

"Why you do?" the man asked.

"I'm smaller than half of you," Mont replied. "Reckon you need a lot more'n me."

At the far end of the reception hall, Mont could see Han standing stiffly at attention beside the door. Han's arms folded across his chest were at the height of the other men's heads, while his head was on a level with the lanterns hanging from the ceiling. He was dressed in finely embroidered silk to match the wall hangings, and he might have been mistaken for a carved pillar or oversized statue.

Mont's own place was beside Fujing Toy's throne. Mont was wearing a long coat that hung below his knees and a pair of pointed-toed slippers. Around his head a cloth was wound, and a long cane pole topped with a fan of peacock tail feathers was placed in his hand. He was instructed to wave the fan gently toward Fujing Toy but under no circumstances to move from his place unless told to do so.

An audience was in progress. Several Chinese merchants had

come to complain that boo-how-doys from rival Tongs had vandalized their businesses and injured their employees. Mont gathered this from watching the gestures and exclamations of the merchants and from seeing the bandaged clerks holding broken merchandise. That the subjects were impressed with the wealth of Fujing Toy's palace was also apparent from their expressions.

More than once the Tong lord had gestured toward Mont as part of the furniture and fixtures, but the merchants were even more impressed with Han. With his long face, high cheekbones exaggerated by the hollows beneath them, and his implacable features, Han looked to Mont like a Chinese angel of death.

More important from Mont's point of view was the fact that Han drew all the attention to the opposite end of the room. The little boy was then able to pick up pieces of dried fish from a serving cart and fill his pockets. Later Mont saved one small piece for himself and gave the rest to Han.

✳ ✳ ✳

Tom's first glimpses of Virginia City were not inspiring, to say the least. After the awesome scenery of the High Sierras and the majesty of Lake Tahoe, the descent to Carson and the barren hills of the Washoe Valley reminded Tom of the Hebrews turning back to the desert after glimpsing the Promised Land.

Clouds of acrid dust churned up from the wheels of the Pioneer Line coach as if a perpetual sandstorm accompanied the stage. The fine gray powder settled on everything. *In everything,* Tom thought as he futilely tried to clean out his grit-caked eyes and ears.

Glancing at the other passengers with their sour expressions and comical appearances, Tom imagined ruefully how silly he must look. Shirts became a uniform shade of dun, as did beards, hats, hair, boots, coats, and trousers. The only exceptions made matters worse: where weary travelers wiped their faces, a lighter shade of grayish pink contrasted with the surrounding darkness till everyone resembled either piebald horses or war-painted Indians.

The coach rattled onto C Street past brick buildings, timbered sheds, and canvas awnings. The principal decorations seemed to be handbills. Silently acknowledging the barrenness of the surroundings, the advertisements covered every available wall, post, and boulder. Each strove to outdo the others with bright colors, flamboyant claims, and lurid drawings. "Buy Dr. Fry's Liver Tonic," shouted one. It posed a consumptive, bald man with a sunken chest next to a robust fellow with a full head of hair. Another ordered, "Look Here! Square Meals at the Howling Wilderness Saloon!"

Mounds of pale dirt and dark ore were piled around every curve and beside each level stretch of road. The dumps from the mines formed conical heaps like the frenzied work of giant, demented ants.

Over the entire scene hung a pall of white steam compounded with black smoke and mixed liberally with noise. An incessant battering from the hundreds of stamps in the mills crushed quartz rock into rubble, and rubble into gravel, and gravel into sand, with a pounding as if the mountain's heart beat just beneath the surface.

The stagecoach pulled up in front of the Pioneer Stage Company office. Near at hand was a bar called the Fancy Free and a billiard parlor of doubtful reputation known as the Boys' Retreat. Nearby were the Tahoe Hotel and the much-advertised Howling Wilderness Saloon.

The storm of dirt that accompanied the travelers roiled up and over the coach, and for a time Virginia City disappeared behind a curtain of dust. All nine passengers inside the coach gave way to fits of coughing. Eyes streaming tears, Tom stumbled out of the stage, vaguely wondering if the six passengers riding on top had fared better or worse than he.

When the air cleared to the point of being breathable, the buildings of C Street reappeared. Tom retrieved his carpetbag and crossed the busy road toward the Tahoe Hotel. The ground was formed of a curious pavement mixture known as "mining-camp macadam"—dirt, broken boards, cast-off boots, battered tin cups, and ragged playing cards all stuck together with tobacco juice.

"Tom! Tom Dawson!" The familiar, friendly-sounding voice with the funny drawling whine at the end of the words floated over the passing rumble of an eight-ox team hauling a high-sided ore wagon.

Oh no! thought Tom. *Someone who knows me has spotted me. This is sure to give me away.* He scanned the streets, sidewalks, and store-fronts but could not locate the source of the greeting.

The voice called out again, "Hey, Tom, up here!"

Behind him and on the balcony of the Pioneer Stage Company office was Sam Clemens. Sam and Tom had known each other in Missouri, and both had left about the same time with similar desires to get away from that war-torn area. Sam was . . . a writer and some-thing in politics. Tom had gotten a letter. He could not remember exactly what, only that Sam's brother, Orion, had been an official of the territory and had planned to get Sam a post.

"Hey, Sam." Tom waved. "Good to see you!"

"Stay right there," Clemens ordered. "I'm coming down."

In a few seconds the skinny young man with the wavy dark brown hair and the drooping mustache appeared in the street beside Tom. His black frock coat, plaid vest, and baggy trousers spoke of money and quality but were wrinkled and creased.

Sam always did have a rumpled look, Tom thought.

Sam grasped Tom's hand and pumped it vigorously in genuine pleasure at the reunion. "It is so good to see you. Now things can get lively again around here."

As he spoke, a pair of brawling miners crashed through the doors of the Fancy Free Saloon and wound up wrestling in the dust twenty feet from where the two friends stood.

No one in Virginia City, least of all Sam Clemens, paid any atten-tion. "Where you staying? International Hotel, of course," he both asked and answered.

"No," corrected Tom. "The Tahoe."

"That dump?" questioned Clemens. "No, no. It'll burn down most any day. Why, the way the wind blows right through its walls, the management has taken to advertising 'scenic views' from the mountains of sand that pile up in the corners!"

"Come with me, Sam," suggested Tom. "I promise I'll explain if you'll just wait till we're in the room and don't question anything you hear me say."

Clemens narrowed his bushy brows, and his eyes twinkled with mischievous delight. "I love mysteries. We haven't had a mystery in

271

Virginia since some unknown scoundrel substituted a woodcut of a skunk for the profile of the publisher on the masthead of—"

Tom never got to hear the conclusion of that story, because right then a runaway horse and buckboard came plunging and careening down C Street directly toward the two men. The snorting and bucking chestnut draft animal was racing as if his life depended on getting away from the wagon chasing him.

Tom grabbed Sam and threw both of them aside and to the ground, rolling under the belly of a parked ore wagon. There was a terrific crash as the runaway horse pivoted away at the last second, spilling the buckboard broadside into the ore wagon. The buckboard's rear axle broke with the force of the impact, sending a spinning wheel flying under the ore wagon. It narrowly missed Tom's head, bounced off the boardwalk, and rebounded to land on top of the two friends.

Clemens opened one eye and peered around cautiously. "I think it's done," he said in a shaky voice. As they crawled out from under the ore wagon and dusted themselves off, he regained his sense of humor and added, "Greetings from the Comstock! That's what I call a real Washoe welcome—almost crushed and decapitated at the same time—show me another town that can arrange that!"

The buckboard's owner, a short Irishman with flame red hair, came running over. "For the love of . . . What could of did it? I had me rig's brake set."

"Ah," demanded Clemens sternly, "but did you have the horse's brake set as well?"

✳ ✳ ✳

Nighttime at the Tahoe Hotel. The shabby furniture and the thin, bare walls and floor contrasted hugely with the remembered beauty of the hotel's namesake. Tom prepared for bed by hanging his clothes over the foot of the cobbled-together bed frame and his hat on the nail that protruded from the door. He placed the Colt Navy near at hand on the wobbly table that served as nightstand, desk, and makeshift dresser and blew out the oil lamp.

When he lay down on the straw-stuffed mattress, more grayish dust puffed upward. As tired as he was, Tom did not expect to get to sleep soon. Even if the hurdy-gurdy music from downstairs had not come up in full volume through the floor, the hammered piano tunes from the saloon next door or the jangling banjo from the dance hall across the street would have served to keep him conscious.

Taking stock of his situation, Tom was not impressed with his prospects of accomplishing anything useful on the Comstock. As he had explained to Sam that afternoon, he did not know who was to contact him, did not know what he would be asked to do, and in any case, did not have Mont with him to identify a supposed conspirator as part of any real threat.

Clemens had agreed. "There's fifteen—maybe twenty thousand folks living on the lead between Virginia, Gold Hill, and Silver City—more if you include every canyon round about. Every one of them is crazy all right—but about speculating in silver, not about the war."

Ownership of the Comstock mines was by the *foot,* measured along the lead. Stock in the Ophir mine was being sold at over two thousand dollars per foot; that of the Gould and Curry at just under four thousand. These proven producers were mining such rich ore that any rock assayed at less than fifty dollars of silver per ton was discarded as being not worth the trouble.

But according to Sam, the speculation was wildly inflated and dangerously fraudulent. "No more than twenty out of hundreds of mines have ever paid expenses, let alone showed a profit, but that doesn't stop the speculators, no sir. Let a man turn one shovelful of dirt and pretty soon he's printed fancy stock certificates and listed on the 'Frisco Change as a 'promising prospect.' Next he buys new clothes, a fancy rig, and dinners for his friends and pays for it all with *feet*! And *everybody* accepts it!"

The fantasy outstripped the reality, but even so, Sam reported that the mines were producing and shipping close to a *ton* of bullion a *day.* That information would be attractive to anyone outside the law, whether rebel operative or common thief.

The loud music from downstairs took on a frantic tone as the accompanying din of loud voices swelled to include the smashing of furniture and the shattering of glass. That a brawl was breaking out was neither a surprise to Tom nor did it interest him.

He got out of bed and stood at the window in his nightshirt. His mind was far from the Comstock mines, the rebels, and the war. He stared out his south-facing window and cast his thoughts across the intervening three hundred or so miles between Virginia City and Greenville . . . and Emily.

He missed her—missed having her to talk to, missed her gentle, forthright counsel. Too bland, that thought—he missed her warm smile and the way she lit up a room. He thought about her honey blonde hair and the way she looked dressed in blue calico. The vagrant image of Belle Boyd entered his mind—saucy curls, white throat, and exotic perfume. Tom shook his head as if to banish the distraction. He wanted to think about Emily and nothing else.

Trying to return to thoughts of Emily was not possible, even when the ghost of Belle had vanished into the dusty Comstock air. A volley of gunshots broke out downstairs as the ruckus escalated one more notch. A musical crash came as a hurdy-gurdy player dived for cover. Booted feet running toward the exits added to the impression of a stampede or a cavalry charge. More shots were fired, and there was more smashing glass as someone jumped through a window.

Tom was still facing the street when three loud raps spun him around. He could not see, but he could smell a new cloud of dust floating about the room. Edging around the wall to the nightstand, Tom relit the oil lamp.

The blanket that covered the straw-filled mattress had three new holes in it that Tom did not recall. Grasping the corner of the bed frame and giving a downward yank that flipped it toward him, Tom pulled it over on its side. Sure enough, in the planks of the wooden floor, grouped directly beneath the center of where the bed had stood, were three bullet holes. A hand's breadth would have covered the spread.

✳ CHAPTER 14 ✳

"Han," Mont said after they were locked in for the night, "you could be the greatest warrior Fujing has. Why don't you join his boo-how-doys for real? Then they'd feed you real good and not keep you in this cage."

The giant looked distressed that Mont would suggest such a thing. "Oh no. They are bad men who kill with guns and hatchets. If I join, then this is what I will have to do also . . . and for what? So Fujing Toy can rule over three more streets of frightened shopkeepers? It is better this way."

"But if you was free, couldn't you defend them shopkeepers? Help 'em out?"

Han seemed thoughtful. "Back in my mountain home, this is what a man once said to me. He told me that God wanted me to use my great size to help others. When I asked him which god wanted this, he named one I did not know—Christos."

Clapping in surprise and delight, Mont exclaimed, "He meant Jesus Christ. Han, that man was a Christian."

The giant agreed. "So I found out later. But I was taken away as a slave and heard him speak no more. Perhaps you can tell me about Him, the one called strong and gentle?"

"'Deed I can," said Mont. "'Deed I can!"

And so he did.

✳ ✳ ✳

The small amount of sleep Tom caught the rest of that night came while sitting cross-legged on the floor and leaning back in a corner of the room. Just before dawn there was a furtive tap at the door; then the lockless knob turned, and the panel was pushed inward.

Tom made no sound. He slowly elevated the muzzle of the Colt until a .36-caliber slug was ready to greet an unwanted visitor. The door continued to swing open, but no one came in. From the shadows of the hallway, Tom heard a muttered exclamation and then the whispered comment, "Something's wrong. He's not in there!"

Two vaguely seen forms advanced into the room. When both were clearly inside the doorway and their dark shapes plainly outlined against the paler walls, Tom cocked the Navy. The double ratchet and locking click had an air of authority in the tiny room. Both figures stopped dead still, one with a foot upraised in midstep.

At last a nervous voice spoke. "Mister, whoever you are . . . we are not armed."

"*I am*," commented Tom, "and if you don't want further proof, you'd better walk to the far end of the room and lean your palms up against the wall."

The two men complied.

Rising from the floor at last, Tom struck a match against the thumbnail of his left hand and touched it to the lamp's wick. Eyes and gun barrel never left their target.

By the warm glow of the oil lamp, Tom could see that the men were well dressed. Both were shorter than he, one with wavy light brown hair, the other with slicked-back dark hair. "Turn around slow," he ordered, "and keep your hands out where I can see them."

"Are you Wilson?" asked the dark-haired one when he had turned.

Tom offered no confirmation and only waited to see what would follow.

The lighter-haired man, younger than the other, slowly lowered his hands. "If you are Wilson, then there is no need for that gun. I am Hastings and this is Ingram. The word is *Chapman*."

"Why so nervous, Wilson?" asked the one referred to as Ingram. "Are you always this cautious, or have you been followed?"

"I generally get like this when somebody tries to plug me when I'm sleeping." Tom gestured with the gun barrel toward the overturned bed. "See for yourselves."

Hastings looked at the splintered trio of bullet holes and gave a low whistle. "Who is trying to kill you?"

"I thought you fellas might be able to answer that question," Tom replied. "Where were the two of you last night?"

"Listen, Wilson," said Ingram, "if that's really your name. Accidental shootings are five for a quarter around this town. Sure, you got cause to be upset, but coming up through the floor like that . . . if someone had meant to kill you, he did a mighty poor job of it."

Tom frowned at the thought that maybe it had been a mindless act by some drunk after all. He lowered the hammer of the Colt to the half-cock safety.

Ingram continued in a less belligerent tone. "Besides, if Hastings or me *had* fired those shots, would we come around here this morning? 'Howdy do, Mister Innkeeper. Find any fresh corpses this morning? Mind if we lay claim to one?'"

"Why *are* you here before sunup?" Tom asked.

Ingram refused to answer any questions. He said Tom had to prove his identity as a member of the conspiracy. After being satisfied that Tom had been sent by Jasper Perry, he explained the early morning visit. "We don't think we should be seen in public together. Hastings and I even came here by different routes. Too much depends on pulling this off for us to take a tumble now."

"What is the delay?" Tom asked. "Perry seemed to think you'd have the money by now."

Ingram looked angry as Hastings answered in a chagrined tone. "It's the boom . . . bonanza . . . flush times. Call it what you will, the Comstock is *too* successful. All the men we thought we could count on are either mining or speculating. All those traitorous souls who pledged an oath to our Glorious Cause have renounced their vows for the sake of silver. But to arm the *Chapman* and seize a steamer, we must act soon."

Tom turned the bed back upright and gestured for his visitors to be seated. Finally he was getting close to the plan. He kept the Colt in his folded arms while he remained standing with his back to the corner. "So what's to be done? We three are not enough to take an express wagon by force."

"Working on it," said Ingram gruffly. "We'll have help when the time comes. We've got one superintendent who may still honor his oath."

"And what do you want me to do?" Tom inquired.

"We need better information on shipments. Any way you could get close to a mine official or an assayer? Someone who might hear news of a useful nature?"

Tom appeared to be thinking for a time before he answered, even though his mind had jumped immediately to what he thought was a perfect strategy. "Well," he said slowly, "I do know a reporter for the *Enterprise*."

✳ ✳ ✳

Sam was agreeable to participating in the ruse. "Sure, I can pretend to take you in, show you around, that sort of thing. But these fellas aren't too bright, else they'd know that nobody *ever* tells a reporter the truth!"

Tom grinned. "I didn't know you had made such a name for yourself, *Mark Twain*," he quipped, leaning heavily on the writer's pseudonym.

"A passing fancy," said Sam, airily waving an unlit Eureka cigar. "There's no fame and glory in writing satire. But what about your safety? And mine, I might add. What if these characters are danger-ous, even if they aren't smart? Why not turn them in now?"

"I thought of that," Tom replied, "but there's still a bigger group out there, including this mine official, whoever he is. I don't want to alarm the rest if we can identify them all."

"All right, let's start poking around today, and day after tomor-row I'll take you down in a mine. I always get a good reception. Royal treatment. Just the fact that a reporter is looking raises the price of the 'feet' by a hundred dollars or so.

"By the way," he went on, picking up his flat-crowned, rolled-brim hat, "I wouldn't worry too much about the shots from below. Friend of mine was sitting on his bed taking off his boots. He was just straightening up when a celebratory bullet came up through the floor, right between his feet. Carried away an eyebrow and a lock of his hair."

"What did he do?" asked Tom.

"Same as you're fixing to do . . . changed hotels."

✳ ✳ ✳

Mont was awakened by the noise of Han exercising. Uncurling himself from the single blanket and the pile of straw on which he lay, Mont opened one eye and looked around.

In a corner of the room was Han. His legs were braced against the floor, and the upper half of his body strained against the brick wall as if he were trying to push it over. *Like Samson,* Mont thought.

Mont waited until the exercise was complete, then asked in a low voice, "Han, why didn't you try to escape again before you lost your strength?"

Regarding Mont as if deciding whether to tell him or not, Han at last said, "If Han escape once more, Fujing say boo-how-doy put out my eyes."

"But you can't live like this," Mont said angrily. "They can't keep you between starvin' and blind."

"Ah, my little friend, but they can," Han said.

"'Pears to me," Mont concluded, "what we really need is a permanent escape."

✳ ✳ ✳

The next day was Sunday, but from the window of the International Hotel where Tom now had a room, the tramp of men toward the seven o'clock shift changes looked like any other morning. Four dollars a day was the going wage for a hard-rock mine. A man could take Sunday off if he elected to, but, of course, he went unpaid.

Giving up one-seventh of your income was more than most would do. Living on the Comstock was not cheap. With two-dollar rooms and fifty-cent meals, four dollars did not stretch very far—not far enough to cover a whole day lost.

Tom turned around at a knock on his door, laying his hand on the Colt. He relaxed when he heard Sam's cheery greeting.

Clemens entered the room. "Watching the parade of honest miners?"

A steady stream of denim-clad men flowed past. Almost to a man, each was bearded, hatted, and booted. Then Tom noticed one figure that stood out. He wore denim and boots, but his white hair was uncovered and the face clean shaven. What was more, the man seemed too frail and stoop shouldered to be a miner.

"Who's that?" Tom asked, pointing.

"That's my good friend the Reverend Bollin on his way to conduct services," Sam replied. "Looks like a broken-down prospector from the days of '49, doesn't he? But he's a lot tougher than he looks. Been here since the beginning practically."

"Where does he preach?"

Sam's eyes twinkled as he said, "Right in the teeth of Satan . . . a little district called Devil's Gate. Has a regular church there, too. When he holds forth with one of his two-fisted, sin-killing, devil-chasing sermons, the monte dealers head for the city limits. He gets up early to catch the men coming off shift, and he'll preach three times today."

"Is he as old as he looks?"

"Older, maybe. His son David is running a mission church in Hawaii that the father founded back in the twenties."

"Can I meet him? He sounds like someone who knows what's happening around here."

"Sure," agreed Sam, obviously surprised at the sudden interest in the preacher. "I'll fix it for tonight."

✵ ✵ ✵

Just as Tom and the good reverend had settled down in the parson's cottage for a cup of coffee, there was the sound of running feet and urgent pounding on the door.

Pastor Bollin opened it to find a raggedly dressed boy of ten or eleven years bent over on the front step, trying to catch his breath. "What is it, son? What's wrong?"

The boy fluttered a hand across his chest to signal his inability to talk.

The pastor called for Tom to bring a glass of water while he patted the child's heaving back.

Presently, the spasmodic shuddering of the boy's shoulders eased, and the single-knotted suspender holding up his overalls stopped bunching up and down. "Come . . . quick. Miss Eva . . . hurt bad . . . Miss Sally sent me."

"I'll just be a moment. Let me get my coat." The pastor emerged with a coat and a Bible. To Tom he said, "I'm sorry. We can have our visit another time."

"No apology needed, Pastor. Mind if I come with you? Maybe I can be of help."

The preacher sized up Tom's six-foot-plus frame and remarked, "Maybe you can at that. Miss Eva lives below D Street. It can be a very rough area."

The hike from the pastor's home on the hillside above A Street went straight down the incredibly steep slope to which Virginia City clung.

On the way, the small messenger gasped out his story. "Miss Eva has a steady caller name of Stone. He a powerful mean secesh. Tonight he catch her with a Yankee feller. The men, they go to tusslin' and Miss Eva, she try to stop 'em."

"Yes, boy, and what happened?"

The boy gulped as if even retelling the next part frightened him. "Miss Eva, she got stabbed! The Yankee, he run off. Miss Sally hear the screamin' and try to help, but Stone won't even let her in. He drunk and he says Miss Eva got what's comin' to her. Miss Sally send me for you."

The row of shabby clapboard one-room houses that formed the Maiden Lane of Virginia City soon came into sight. In front of one stood a woman screaming at a man who fended her off by waving a bowie knife in her face. His other hand held a large pistol.

"All right, son," said the pastor, "I understand now. You run along home."

Tom drew his Colt and checked the loads.

Pastor Bollin laid a cautionary hand on his arm. "Let's see what we can do without more bloodshed first. Stone is a genuine killer who will shoot us both and no doubt some other innocent bystanders if we crowd him."

Tom replaced the weapon in its holster and dropped a few paces behind the preacher.

Bollin went directly up to the hysterical woman, whom Tom guessed must be Sally, and steered her back from the doorway.

"Keep her away," slurred Stone. "Else I'll give her some of what the other tramp got! Serve her right, taking up with Yankees."

"Help her, Preacher," sobbed the woman. "She's dying in there. . . . I heard her scream! Won't somebody *do* something?"

Pastor Bollin passed the woman to Tom, asking him to stay by her; then he confronted Stone from two arms' lengths away. "Lijah, it's not like you to pick on women. Let me see to Miss Eva. Quickly, man!"

"No!" thundered the cutthroat. "I ain't never put no woman in my private cemetery a'fore this, but this'n deserves it! Ain't no business for a Bible-thumper, any road."

"You aren't thinking straight, Stone," argued Pastor Bollin. "This town won't stand for it. For your own good, then, let me help her."

As if adding her agreement, an anguished groan came from the wounded woman inside the house.

It was more than Sally could stand. She squirmed in Tom's grasp on her shoulders, twisting to reach the Colt Navy. "I won't let her die!" she yelled, grabbing the pistol and wrestling with Tom.

Stone saw the struggle and raised his own pistol.

Before he could aim, the preacher had stepped inside his guard and knocked the gun hand aside. Stone's pistol discharged into the ground with an explosion that caused the growing crowd of curious onlookers to dive for cover.

Stone bellowed like an angry bull and aimed a knife thrust at the preacher's chest.

Pastor Bollin parried the jab with his large black leather-bound Bible. The sharp tooth of the bowie penetrated cover and pages but was caught and swept aside. Bollin followed this move with an overhand right that arced down on Stone's eye with a crunch that drove him to his knees. Without even waiting for any further outcome, the preacher jumped past the outlaw and crashed open the door.

Stone started to rise. His pistol was aimed at the preacher's back, and he was thumbing back the hammer when Tom leaped on him from behind. The gun flew from his grasp and slid into the house. It came to rest beside Pastor Bollin, where he knelt next to a woman lying on the floor in a pool of blood.

Tom and Lijah Stone rolled over and over on the muddy slope of Virginia City. Tom was the stronger of the two, but he held off the knife with difficulty since the outlaw outweighed him by forty pounds.

A savage chop downward thrust the bowie into the hillside, just missing Tom's left ear. As he concentrated on keeping the knife hand tied up, Stone unleashed a roundhouse left that hit Tom over the other ear.

Tom threw his weight into pulling around on Stone's captive right arm. As they rolled over again, Tom thrust his forearm up across Stone's throat as hard as he could. The larger man's eyes bulged, and the knife flipped from his fingers as they clawed at the earth. Tom threw the forearm yet again; this time his elbow smashed into the side of Stone's head. The big man sagged, gasping for air.

Tom retrieved the bowie and thrust it into his own belt, then entered the cabin. Pastor Bollin was tearing a bedsheet into bandages and using them to bind Eva's wounds.

At his side was a softly crying Sally who kept repeating, "Will she live? Will she live?"

Completing his work before he responded, the preacher at last replied, "You must pray now. We have done all that can be done till the doc arrives. The knife wounds on her face and arms aren't deep. The worst one, the one in her chest, turned on a rib and is not as bad as I feared. But she has lost a lot of blood and won't be out of danger for some time."

Tom picked up Pastor Bollin's Bible. A jagged tear penetrated over halfway through but stopped with the tip resting on Psalm 91. "His faithfulness will be your shield," the verse read.

✦CHAPTER 15✦

Tom was pulling a pair of canvas overalls on over his Levi's and flannel shirt. The borrowed work outfit was discolored with brown dirt and streaked with the traces of black and yellow ores. It was sweat stained, and the shoulders were spotted with drops of candle wax.

He paused before adding the floppy felt hat with the dented crown that completed the mining costume. "If I'd come to Virginia City dressed like this," he said, laughing at Sam, who was similarly fitted out, "you'd never have recognized me."

Sam nodded. "That's because you stood out like the thirty-five-foot flag waving on top of Sun Mountain. Now you look like one of the boys."

He took his turn to laugh at Tom's grimace before he continued, "You know, the boys figger you for real brave, standing up to Lijah Stone like that."

"Oh?" Tom replied blandly. "You can't call it bravery if there isn't any choice. I'd say the real courage was shown by Pastor Bollin."

"No dispute there, but I hear tell that you had your hand in it, too. The boys think you should have killed Stone while you had the chance. How soon does your stage leave?"

"You know I'm not through here yet," Tom responded. "Do 'the boys' figger me to run away?"

Sam looked genuinely concerned for his friend. "You don't understand," he said seriously. "Lijah Stone chews railroad spikes for amusement, but that's not how he got those notches on his pistol grips. You shamed him, and he'll be on the shoot for you till he cleans his reputation."

"Why isn't Stone arrested for attempted murder? Isn't there any law and order in this town?"

"'Course there is, or at least there's plenty of law—every third rock's got a lawyer under it. But order—now, that's altogether different. Judge Turner swore out a warrant for Stone's arrest, but he can't get anybody to serve it!"

Tom snorted with disgust. "That's enough about the quaint customs in Washoe. Let's go look at a mine."

The two friends fell in with a file of miners walking toward the shafts of the Gould and Curry Mine.

"There are three ways into the diggings," Sam instructed. "We can walk in through a long tunnel in the side of the hill, we can climb down a thousand feet of ladders, or we can ride the lift. What'll you have?"

"Seems to me the lift would be the easiest," Tom observed. "Let's go that route."

"Everybody says that," replied Sam with a grin. "Just remember, I *did* give you a choice."

The hoist operator greeted Sam like an old friend. When Tom was introduced, the man respectfully removed his hat and shook his hand with reverence. Tom was puzzled until the man glanced around, then announced, "It's about time someone stood up to Stone. Nice to have you visit us. When you're ready to come up, give me three rings, then three more."

The lift platform was only four feet square and made of oak planks, reminding Tom of the door to the hayloft back home. The lift was suspended from the four corners and the center by ropes that met in an iron ring hanging from a cable ten feet over their heads.

Both men stepped onto the platform and reached for the center rope. "You may want to use both hands," Sam advised when Tom grasped it with only one.

"Why?" Tom started to ask, "How fast does this thing—?"

Suddenly the tiny section of wooden floor dropped toward the center of the earth!

"How . . . does . . . it . . . stop?" shouted Tom as the square patch of daylight dwindled overhead and the lift shot into the mountain's heart.

"Clutches," the reply was bellowed back. "If the operator doesn't misjudge or the cables snap!"

"What happens then?" Tom's words whirled up the shaft.

Tom thought he heard the words *an inquest,* and just then the platform slowed and the stretching and contracting cables bounced the lift to a halt.

✻ ✻ ✻

At the top of the shaft, the lift operator hummed contentedly to himself. He was pleased to have shaken the hand of the man who bested Lijah Stone in a fight. "Do you remember sweet Betsy from Pike?" he sang in an off-key tenor.

From behind a pile of cable spools stepped a man whose battered face bore the marks of a recent battle. The butt of the Colt in his hand had a string of notches filed into it. He walked almost casually up to the lift operator and stuck the barrel of the Colt in the man's ear.

"What the . . . ?" the operator stammered, then stopped abruptly.

The hoarse, rasping voice of Lijah Stone demanded, "Was you sayin' you were glad someone stood up to me, Clay? How was that again?"

The operator stuttered, "Mister Stone . . . I didn't mean . . . that is, you . . ."

The gun's muzzle twisted into Clay's ear. "Now suppose you just shut your mouth and listen so's I don't have to clean your ears with this here .44. You know, I always wanted to learn how to run a hoist, and you're gonna show me."

✻ ✻ ✻

Pushing aside two swinging half doors, Sam and Tom stepped into a rock-walled chamber that opened to a tunnel in front of them. Miners, all dressed exactly as Tom, passed them. Some were carrying picks or shovels, and a few transported heavy-looking wooden crates marked Danger—Explosives.

But the first thing that caught Tom's eye was the timbering. Huge square posts, eighteen inches thick, supported a framework of similar shoring all across the ceiling. By the flickering oil lamps hanging at intervals along the tunnel, Tom could see the cells made of beams marching into the far distance.

"Deidesheimer square sets," Sam explained in response to Tom's look. "The hard-headed Dutchman wouldn't believe it when people said you couldn't mine this deep without cave-ins. Said he got his inspiration from looking at honeycombs. Whole forests of trees have been replanted down here."

✳ ✳ ✳

"So this here lever runs the cage up and down; is that it?" questioned Lijah Stone.

Clay, the lift operator, nodded slowly, grimacing at the feel of the gun barrel in his ear and the harsh grating of Stone's voice.

"And this little red knob speeds the whole shebang up or slows it down?"

Again, a single nervous nod.

"My, my." Stone chuckled hoarsely. "Ain't we learnin' fast?" He removed the muzzle of the Colt from Clay's ear and negligently waved it around the little room that contained the hoist controls. "And when someone wants brought up or down, that here bell rings?" he asked, pointing with the Colt.

"Yes, sir, Mister Stone, it surely does."

"And the signals tells you what direction and how far, even who it is doin' the ringin'?"

"Yes, sir," Clay agreed, trying to sound obliging. "It's kinda like a private telegraph, don'cha see and . . ." He stopped abruptly, afraid that he'd been too agreeable.

"So when the scribbler and his tinhorn friend want to get all the way back up here, it'll ring three times and then three more, and won't nobody else ring that ring. Well, well."

✳ ✳ ✳

Tom and Sam walked down one of the seemingly endless corridors.

"Try not to think about the thousand feet of solid rock that these tiny tree stumps are holding over your head," Sam said with malicious glee. "Actually, the biggest problem down here is water, not rock. You get . . . well, here, see for yourself."

At intervals along the gallery, drifts opened on either side, and in these men were working. As the vein of silver ore slanted downward into the great mountain, the antlike efforts of humans followed. The ringing of picks and the clatter of shovels echoed noisily out of the right-hand chamber.

As Tom and Sam stopped to look, a yellow-bearded man with enormous shoulders pushed an ore car up out of the blackness along a narrow set of rails. "Step aside, please, gents," he said as he muscled past with a quarter ton of bluish black rock.

Tom pressed himself back against the tunnel wall to avoid being run over by the cart; only the thickness of the timber sets gave room to stand.

"Say, friend," Sam called to the miner, "are they pumping on this level?"

The miner shook his head, waving the candle mounted in the reflector on his hat. "Down one more."

✻ ✻ ✻

The rattle of tin lunch pails and the stomping of boots alerted Stone to the approach of a group of men. He moved back behind the stack of cable spools. "Now, Clay," he advised the lift operator, "you just do your job nice and easy-like. I like you; this here Colt ain't so sure . . . and it has a nasty habit of blowin' big holes in things it don't like."

The group of miners tramped onto the lift platform and waved at Clay. "Goin' down to three," one of them hollered.

As Clay moved the lever and pulled the red knob, the great spool unwound and lowered the men into the shaft. If Clay acted any differently than usual, the miners never seemed to notice.

✻ ✻ ✻

In the next chamber on the left, the ore had already been removed. All that remained in its place was a dark hole from which a ladder protruded. A rhythmic chugging noise came up from the hole. "How far down is it to the next level?" Tom asked.

Sam shrugged. "Hard to say. That little black hole may be twenty feet deep or may be eighty. Two days ago a miner slipped and fell in one like it. Dropped over a hundred feet. His funeral is today."

Tom was extra cautious in the placement of his feet on the rungs and his grip on the ladder as they descended. When they reached the bottom, they discovered a steam engine was the source of the chugging sound. It was struggling to operate a pump to drain a sulphury-smelling pool of steaming water.

The two men stood for a while in the stench and the noise but exited to a quieter drift before speaking. "There you see the real difficulty facing the Comstock," Sam pointed out. "Sometimes just the swing of a pick will bust through a place and water will come pouring in faster than it can be pumped out."

"And hot, smelly water at that," Tom observed.

Sam nodded. "Scalding sometimes. More than one miner has died from burns. After the cave-in that hit the Ophir mine, one entire gallery flooded in the space of two hours."

"I thought you said the square-set timbering prevented cave-ins."

The light from the candle flickered on the merriment in Sam's eyes and his teasing grin. "I did not say *eliminated*."

❋ ❋ ❋

"What would happen if you was drunk on the job?" asked Stone. "Couldn't you drop some folks clean to the bottom and squash 'em like eggs?"

"No," maintained Clay stoutly. "This rig has got a governor and a . . ." The sound of what he was about to say rattled through his head, mimicking the chatter of his teeth.

"A what?" Stone demanded.

"A dead-man set," Clay finished with a gulp. "It keeps the hoist from runnin' too fast or past the bottom gallery or from flyin' out of the shaft comin' up."

"Hmm," Stone pondered out loud. "Then the only thing can go wrong real bad-like is if that cable or them ropes should bust."

✳ ✳ ✳

"So what is the answer to the problem with the flooding?" Tom asked as he and Sam returned to the hoist.

Sam shook his head. Little drops of candle wax ran off the sides of the candleholder and dripped from the brim of the felt hat onto the shoulders of his coveralls. "I don't know for certain. A man named Sutro claims he can tunnel clear up from the valley and hit the two-thousand-foot level here; drain the whole mountain."

"Do you think it'll work?"

"Some experts say it will. Others say it'll cost too much. It's eight miles down the outlet from here. That's millions of dollars spent before one pound of ore much below where we're standing ever gets mined. Well, what do you think? Have you seen enough?"

At Tom's nod, Sam flicked the switch of the telegraph three times, a short pause, then three more.

✳ ✳ ✳

Stone's face lit up with a broad smile that showed his missing front teeth when he heard the signal bell. He held his breath and, when it rang three more times, said exultantly to Clay, "Go on, Clay. Send it to 'em. Don't be makin' 'em wait, now."

The lift dropped away empty into the blackness. Stone watched the great spool of cable unwind and lower downward till it slowed and finally stopped.

Over Clay's shoulder he asked, "How do you know when they're ready to come up?"

Without Clay needing to reply, the signal bell gave one long continuous peal.

"That's just fine," Stone remarked casually. Without warning he slammed the gun barrel into the side of Clay's head, and as the operator slumped to the floor, Stone yanked back on the lever.

✳ ✳ ✳

"The boys say the Comstock is the richest silver lode in the world," Sam commented as the lift started up the shaft.

"What exactly does that mean?" Tom asked.

The hoist pulled even with another gallery, then continued upward between barren rock walls. The momentary glimpse of miners' candles looked like fireflies darting about in the cavern's gloom.

"It means that Virginia City and the other mining towns of the Comstock will ship somewhere between twenty and thirty *million* dollars of bullion *this year*."

The hoist was accelerating now, speeding upward past three galleries in quick succession. A brief swirl of cooler air blew on the two men as the mouth of each tunnel yawned and closed.

"That makes this territory a real prize for . . . say, are we stopping?"

The platform slowed and halted with a jerking, bouncing motion and hung suspended. "Maybe somebody else is ready to . . . no, that can't be; we're between galleries."

It was true: The flickering glow cast by the candle stubs burning in their hat-top holders showed four rough walls of granite with streaks of shiny quartz but no opening.

"Confound that Clay," spouted Sam. "What's he playing at, anyway?"

At that moment, the platform started upward again with a bump. Sam just had time to remark, "About time," when the cage stopped, then dropped suddenly. Beneath the candle's feeble light, Tom could see Sam's bushy eyebrows knit together in consternation.

"I bet that scoundrel Higbie is behind this," he said. "I wonder how much he paid Clay to give us a rough ride."

This descent did not end with a gently rocking bump. Instead, the cable stretched downward with a complaining creak. The lift rebounded sharply, as if someone had shifted from downward to upward without slowing the machinery.

Up charged the platform, gaining speed. Just as abruptly the hoist paused once more. The oak floor continued on a few feet by its own momentum, floating up the shaft before falling freely.

Before it could hit bottom, the winch was unwinding again, speeding the descending lift downward. Overhead, the ropes securing the platform to the iron ring began to sing with an ominous twang, and the platform yo-yoed up and down.

"Sam!" Tom called sharply as the hoist topped out another rapid ascent and again fell freely before hitting the end of the restraining cable. "Sam, this is no joke! Someone's trying to bust the platform loose!"

"What'll we do?" shouted Sam over the creaking, grinding sounds.

"Get ready to jump for the next tunnel mouth as we pass."

The next upward swoosh and downward plunge extinguished both candles. Now in pitch blackness, suspended hundreds of feet above a crushing impact, neither man could even see the other, much less the momentary shadow that meant a lead to safety. Far overhead, a tiny scrap of daylight winked mockingly.

"Now what?" Sam yelled.

"We'll have to jump one at a time. On the next drop, I'll drag my boot along the shaft," ordered Tom. "When I yell, jump!"

When the next stomach-wrenching swoop occurred, the hobnails of Tom's boot sole cast tiny sparks as the heads grated on the wall. Feeling the gap, Tom hollered.

With a fragment of a cry, Sam disappeared! One second he was on the platform and the next he flung himself outward through space. Tom was alone on the lift.

The platform hit the bottom of its fall. With the twangs of bow-strings and the sharp cracks of pistol shots, two of the suspending ropes parted. The lift tipped toward the unsupported edge and began to drag along the rock walls, canted at a crazy angle.

Tom clung desperately to the center support. His feet dangled over a gaping crack that would either drop him to oblivion or catch him and crush him against the granite shaft.

Like a giant hand trying to shake off an obstinate drip of water, the platform rose and fell, almost jerking Tom's grip loose from the cord. His boots drummed a running clatter on the oak planks as he struggled to push back upward.

The lift rose and halted, then dropped again, slapping at Tom as if the platform were a threatening palm trying to swat him like a fly.

He heard a shout from the blackness. "Tom! Up here!" Sam's voice, just above his head.

Only one second to decide, an instant to make a choice which might be no choice at all but a farewell.

Tom jumped for the unseen lip of the tunnel mouth, pushed off hard with his feet. One boot tangled in the center rope and spun him half around. His leap was not clean, and only one hand caught the ledge of the passage. The other hand scrabbled for purchase, only to scrape bare rock.

His right arm and shoulder screamed with the pain of his weight hanging from his clawed hand. He heard the motion of the lift reverse and knew it would knock loose his fragile handhold, dropping him into the pit.

A dangling rope brushed his face—one of the broken support cables dragged over his shoulder. Another fraction of an instant to decide, then his wildly flailing left hand grabbed the rope. His body instantly jerked upward.

The handhold gone, Tom swung wildly, blindly, toward the tunnel mouth. He left the rush of the lift at his feet when something wrapped around his knees, pulling him toward the darkness.

"I've got you," Sam yelled, and they tumbled down together onto the rocky floor of the mine tunnel.

✶CHAPTER 16✶

T he place Ingram selected was near the top of a grade on the climb out of the Tahoe Basin. Cedars and tall ponderosa pines surrounded the looping roadway so only glimpses of sky could be seen through the overhanging trees.

Snow had collected to a depth of eight feet all along this stretch of highway. Avery had heard the Pioneer Stage Company driver talk about the years before the drought when the snow had reached twenty- or thirty-foot depths along the same route. He could scarcely credit such a story, believed it to be a whopper until Ingram confirmed it as fact.

In years like those, the stage and express companies suspended their operations for the duration of the first big storm. Then they brought out special coaches built on sled runners that were able to glide over the icy surface. But this year and last, it had not been necessary. Several teams of mules drawing iron-bladed buck scrapers were kept in constant employment keeping the roadway clear.

The coaches operated in an eight-foot-deep canyon of hard-packed snow, but their wheels stayed in well-worn ruts, and commerce over the Sierras continued unchecked. The cleared passageway was barely wide enough for two teams to pass each other, and heaven help the teamster who swung too wide on a blind curve.

Two hundred yards below the summit, the road made a sharp turn to the left coming out of a canyon. Next, a sharp switchback to the right for fifty yards elevated the coach almost to the peak, when another abrupt turn to the left reversed the direction of the travel once more. Given the steepness of the grade and the icy conditions, drivers favored breaking into a gallop as soon as they came out of the canyon. They were trying to keep the momentum up all the way to the peak.

The highway plunged down again immediately after reaching the summit. There was no more than a five-hundred-foot-long level spot at the top of the ridge.

The most logical place for a holdup was just after the third switchback when the horses were laboring on the steepest stretch. Their energy would be spent on the galloping climb, and the coach would be starting to slow.

✹ ✹ ✹

The straining bodies of the six-up team rippled with the demands of the load and the mountain. The salty acrid odor of their own effort drifted back to the driver on the wagon box.

Floyd was a careful driver—careful of his teams, if not always so cautious with the comfort of the passengers. He knew better than to push the horses till they sweated, and he kept the pace one notch less than enough to lather them, knowing that the 35-degree air of the eight-thousand-foot pass would kill a sweaty horse the same as a man.

Passengers with their complaints about the ride and the temperature in the coach had always rubbed Floyd the wrong way. After all, he was completely out in the open the entire time, right? What business did a puny, thin-skinned fare payer have voicing anything other than gratitude?

Floyd was thankful that he no longer had to cope with the foibles of passengers. Since leaving the Pioneer Stage Company to take on the Wells Fargo express wagons, Floyd was much happier. He was still driving a six-in-hand over the same magnificent alpine scenery, but now there were no whining passengers to bother him.

Glancing over his shoulder at the shotgun-toting guard in the wagon bed, Floyd wondered if he had any complaints. The difference was, guards were employees, and Floyd was their boss as long as the wheels rolled—he could tell them to stow it. Not that this one made any complaints or any small talk either. He was huddled down inside a fleece-lined jacket as if trying to disappear completely.

Ordinarily there were two guards on the box, but one had not appeared at departure time. "Drunk, more'n likely," Floyd had remarked to the station agent.

The two outriders were within call, but the one ahead appeared and vanished with each curve of the road. Floyd had not seen the one behind since they began the ascent of the Truckee.

The heavy iron ice shoes rang with every step up the grade, but the enforced slow pace made it a dismal sound, like the tolling of church bells for a funeral. Floyd noted the slack in the middle line of the three thick leather straps moving through the fingers of his left hand. He gave it a quick flip and called to the nearside bay of the swing team, "Get up there, Candy. Quit yer loafin'."

Jerry, the guard in the box, stirred and stretched his legs. "It's almighty cold today, Floyd."

Letting rip a string of profanity, Floyd promised to make things real hot, real quick if he had any more complaints. The nerve! All the guard had to do to earn his pay was sit tight and hold on to a twelve gauge. How would he like it if he had to sense every change of gait, every curve of the road, every different surface, and—

A shout from ahead brought Floyd out of his indignant reverie. He jerked his hand up and called to the guard, "Look sharp. May be trouble."

From around the bend of the road ahead came Clive, the point rider. His hat was tied down over his ears with a bandanna or otherwise it would have flown off. He waved his arm and shouted, skidding his chestnut gelding to a stop beside the wagon. "Floyd, there's been an accident up ahead!"

"Bad one?"

"Powerful bad! Wagon turned over, two men down, blood all over!"

"Could you help any of 'em?"

Clive looked startled. "I come straight back here to tell you. I didn't think—"

"You sure enough didn't! Now get outta the way!" Shaking the lines with a sudden snap, Floyd yelled to the leader, "Get up, Abel! Rattle your hocks, Ben!"

The express lurched into motion. "Fire a shot, Jerry," Floyd ordered the guard in the wagon bed. This was the signal for the drag rider to come up pronto. "And keep low. If this is some sort of trick, you be ready to go to blastin'."

The scene on top of the rise was a grisly one indeed. A Murphy wagon was upside down off the side of the road. One man was pinned beneath it. Only his floppy black hat was visible. Another body lay flung like a rag doll on the snow on the other side of the road. Dark crimson blood streaked his face and clothes and was splashed on the snowbanks all around.

Floyd stopped the express wagon as soon as the accident was in view. He gestured curtly to the guard. "Don't just sit there gawkin'! Get on up and see if you can help!"

Floyd regretted the missing guard. Talking aloud to himself he said, "You be watchin' the back trail and the woods either side. Yup, that's the ticket."

Clive stepped off his horse, tying it to the wreck, and the box guard, Jerry, joined him beside the overturned wagon. Clive whistled a sharp note and shook his head. "There ain't nothin' to do for this one, Jerry. The box pert near cut him in two—musta throwed him off, then rolled acrost him."

✳ ✳ ✳

Fingering the shotgun nervously and glancing around at the snow-covered trees, Jerry stayed far back. He was young and scared—Jerry was the Virginia City Station agent's nephew, and he owed his job to that relationship. Right at the moment, he was wishing he had stayed in Ohio, but his ma had sent him west to save him from the war, and here he was.

Clive crossed the icy expanse of roadway toward the blood-spattered second body.

Jerking his attention away from the flattened figure, Jerry ran after the point rider. In his haste to catch up, Jerry failed to account for his slick-soled boots and the skating-rink quality of the highway. Three running strides and he lost his balance, giving three awkwardly bouncing hops to try to regain it, and then sprawled backward, with both feet flying up in the air. It cost him his pride and a sharp rap on the head, but it saved his life—at least for the moment.

✳ ✳ ✳

Clive was bending over to examine the corpse when the body on the ground grinned through its mask of chicken blood and raised a sawed-off double barrel from beneath a fold of oilcloth duster.

The load of a double shot at a distance of three feet almost cut Clive in half. Echoes of the shotgun's explosion bounced from rocky ledge to snow-covered meadow and down the mountain slope, till the continuous roll sounded like thunder in the high peaks and clumps of snow fell from the trees.

✳ ✳ ✳

Floyd saw the blast that killed Clive and whipped up his team. He drove with one hand, his calloused right fist closing around the double-barreled scattergun he carried beside him and thumbing back the hammers. "Keep down," he yelled to Jerry.

The advice was unnecessary because the young guard had also seen Clive's death. Jerry crouched below the margin of snowbank that bordered the road. A second barrel of buckshot tore into the frozen crystals right in front of him, pelting him with icy fragments. He touched off a blast of his own shotgun without ever lifting his head from where he had it buried in the crook of his arm.

✳ ✳ ✳

The man under the faked wreck was having trouble struggling free. The setup was almost too realistic, and for a moment he really was pinned. He fired two more shots at the driver, but the depression of the roadbed, coupled with his own prone position, made the bullets pass harmlessly overhead.

✳ ✳ ✳

The hooves of the six-up team clattered and skidded on the frozen lane. The express wagon lurched forward with Floyd standing upright on the driver's platform, holding his shotgun pressed tightly against his side. He fired a round at the robber who had just succeeded in crawling from beneath the wagon. The boom of the twelve gauge was like the climax of a conjuring trick: The bushwhacker dived headfirst back under the overturned wagon and disappeared.

Clive's horse reared against the reins by which it was tied to the tongue of the Murphy wagon. The second time the animal reared, plunging and kicking, the leather leads snapped and the horse bolted across the road.

In a move that would have done credit to an Oglala buffalo hunter, Jerry sprang up and grabbed the horse's neck. Using the animal's momentum to his own advantage, Jerry swung aboard the saddle. He discovered, to his amazement, that he still had the shotgun in his hands.

But the magic could not continue. Floyd could not reload as quickly as Clive's murderer could fling aside the sawed-off weapon and produce a Colt.

Three shots in quick succession hit Floyd high in the chest and toppled him from the wagon seat. He stood up tall as if to urge the team for one last burst of speed, then pitched headlong off the side.

The sudden yank to the left as Floyd fell, followed by the slack in the line, confused the six-up team. The leaders jerked the others off the road into deep snow. They continued to pull a short distance, floundering, then stopped.

Jerry had seen Floyd shot off his perch—knew he was dead. Two shots from the Colt whipped past him, but he was already far enough away to spoil the aim. He never slackened his pace away from the scene . . . just rode as fast as he could for help.

Ingram wiped the chicken blood from his face on the sleeve of his duster and hurried over to the overturned wagon. "Get on out," he called sarcastically to Avery, who was still hiding under the wreck. "Fat lot of help you turned out to be. Whyn't you shoot?"

Trembling all over like an aspen leaf in a high wind, Avery crawled out of his hiding place. "So bloody."

"Yeah, so what? Now shake yourself and lead that express wagon over to the trees where we got our rig. Hurry, you worthless lump! We ain't got forever!"

Avery did as instructed, but he kept repeating over and over, "So bloody, so bloody."

⁕CHAPTER 17⁕

Maguire's opera house had been playing to packed houses ever since it opened in Virginia City some months earlier. Anticipation was running high for the coming attraction *Mazeppa*. Lurid handbills depicted scantily clad actress Adah Isaacs Menken bound to the back of a fiercely snorting runaway stallion. It caught the boys' attention. Each one imagined himself as her rescuer, a modern-day knight-errant, dispatching villains with a six-gun instead of a sword.

The boys liked drinking and gambling as recreations, but they liked variety, too. A pretty actress and an opening night provided just the different kind of excitement they craved. Even though Belle Boyd did not have the reputation or the promotion of "the Menken," her soft-spoken, helpless femininity inspired the boys to chivalrous thoughts. This was especially true since the advertised production was *Fortune's Handmaid*, a riches-to-rags-to-riches story with despicable, thieving relations and a much-abused, pure-hearted heroine.

Maguire's was filled to capacity. From the orchestra pit to the billiard tables in the foyer, it was crowded with mine superintendents wearing diamond stickpins and miners wearing their only clean shirts.

Lijah Stone was holding court in one of the red-velvet-lined boxes in the second tier of private rooms. Without giving specifics, he was bragging about having evened a score. Stone was secure in the belief that even when the double murder came to light and people began to speculate, old Clay would be too terrified to ever act as a witness against him. The proof of the accuracy of his belief was the fact that while the town had already heard of the wreck of the Gould and Curry lift on the previous day, it was being referred to as an accident. Stone figured that the bodies had not yet been found and that Clay was keeping quiet.

The opening notes from the orchestra hurried the late arrivals into their seats and urged the last-minute drinkers to leave the ivory-inlaid mahogany bar. Lijah Stone and his cronies settled back in the gilt chairs as the houselights reflected in the crystal chandeliers began to dim.

A spotlight aimed from the catwalk overhead was directed toward the center of the still-closed curtain. It illuminated a beautiful painted backdrop of sparkling Lake Tahoe surrounded by an evergreen forest.

There was only a moment to admire the painting; then the curtain was raised. The opening scene showed the interior of a mansion's great hall and a beautiful woman caring for an invalid father.

There was a disturbance at the front of the theater as a latecomer made his way down the aisle. He probably would not have attracted Lijah's attention except for the fact that he came all the way down front. The front row of seats was reserved for the drama critics and other reporters of the *Enterprise* and the *Union* and the *Gold Hill News*. This tardy playgoer walked into the ranks of newspapermen and singled one out for a greeting. That man stood and started up the aisle in a hurry. His characteristic shuffle was gone, but there was no mistaking his face.

Stone leaned over the railing and started. It could not be, but it was! Somehow Sam Clemens had escaped from the mine shaft. And if *he* had, then perhaps . . . Stone half rose from his chair to find himself staring into the barrel of Tom Dawson's Navy .36.

"Stone," Tom said softly, "some folks want to talk to you about a little mining accident." He gestured over his shoulder toward three grim-faced Gould and Curry security guards.

"Why me?" blustered Stone. Heads in the audience swiveled to look up at the box. Stone saw the bandaged head and fiercely cold eyes of Clay, the hoist operator.

"Attacking a woman one day and a mining operation the next," said Tom, shaking his head. "Seems to me you managed to get everybody in the Comstock down on you this time."

Stone started to protest, then noticed his former friends melting away and disappearing through the curtained exit behind the guards. "Here now," he said, extending his hands in front of him. "I'll come peaceable."

Everyone was so eager to see that Stone kept his hands empty and in plain sight that no one paid any attention to his feet. With the toe of one boot underneath the velvet-cushioned chair, Stone smacked it sharply upward, flipping the chair into Tom's face.

Tom fought to knock the chair aside without accidentally firing his Colt, for fear of hitting a bystander.

Stone had no such compunction. As soon as the furniture was airborne, he went for his gun.

The first shot hit an oaken chair leg, which deflected it just enough to make the bullet miss hitting Tom in the chest and smash a brass lamp instead.

The guards scattered, and several women in the audience screamed.

Firing again, Stone jumped toward the painted wooden railing that marked the front edge of the theater box. This second shot was not aimed at all and crashed harmlessly into the ceiling, but it made half the theatergoers hug the legs of their chairs, while the other half drew weapons of their own.

The drop to the opera-house floor was fifteen feet, but Stone vaulted the rail without a moment's thought. He smashed, boots first, into a recently vacated chair, splintering it into a myriad of pieces and sending another wave of screams through the audience.

Onstage, the invalid father experienced a remarkable healing, jumped up from his sickbed, and ran with his daughter into the wings.

As they were rushing out of the spotlight, producer Maguire ran into it. With both arms raised, he pleaded for calm. "Please, please! No more shooting! Settle your differences somewhere else!"

Stone came up from the floor with the seat of the broken chair tangled around one leg but with his pistol in his hand. He knocked aside a fiddle player, then hoisted himself onto the stage.

"Give it up!" Tom yelled over the hubbub of shouts and cries. "You can't get away."

The only reply Stone made was to fire another awkwardly off-balance shot toward Tom. This third slug clipped a crystal chandelier and sent it plummeting toward the crowd, who clawed all over one another to escape its crushing impact. For an instant, everyone's attention was distracted, and Stone ran offstage into the wings, where Belle had taken refuge.

"Not that way," she hissed, as Stone made for the stage door. "Up to the catwalk and out on the roof."

✵ ✵ ✵

The audience on the floor of the theater could not see where Stone had gone. They guessed that he would exit by the stage door, so a large crowd of men brandishing guns surged out the rear of the auditorium along with the guards who had been with Tom.

From Tom's position in the box, he could see Stone pause halfway up the ladder to thrust his pistol into his waistband. Glancing toward the catwalk, Tom spotted Stone's goal: large windows set into the ceiling above the narrow iron ledge that provided ventilation for the hot lights. If Stone reached them, he could escape onto the roof of the opera house and, in the darkness of the surrounding shops, make good his escape.

"He's headed for the catwalk," Tom shouted. "After him! He's trying for the roof!"

But no one heard him amid all the other noise and confusion, and Tom's warning went unheeded.

The unarmed spotlight operator saw Stone coming up the ladder and ran for his life. The man pushed open one of the large windows and took himself out of harm's way.

There was one chance for Tom to head off Lijah Stone. Along the corridor of the second-story boxes were French doors that opened out onto a balcony. Tom threw open the closest one and jumped through to stand on the overhang. A drainpipe provided a means of ascent to the roof and the row of rooftop windows through which Stone would be coming.

Tom pulled himself onto the roof not an instant too soon. The dark mass of a man's body appeared, framed in the open window, as Stone stood on the iron railing of the catwalk. "Hold it right there, Stone," Tom demanded.

In response, Lijah Stone drew his pistol at the same moment that this boot heel slipped on the slick iron rail of the catwalk. His hand flew up and the pistol struck the window and was knocked from his grasp. It spun away from him and dropped to the theater floor.

"Come on out, Stone," Tom instructed, gesturing with his Navy.

"Come in and get me," Stone retorted, then jumped from the railing back down to the catwalk's iron grate. He turned to run back toward the ladder.

Diving in the window right after him, Tom landed on Stone's back and knocked him down on the narrow hanging ledge. The two men grappled on the walkway, each struggling for control of Tom's pistol. Tom tried to turn the muzzle toward Stone to call a halt to the battle, but Stone smashed Tom's hand down again and again on the sharp metal lip of the catwalk's floor.

Feeling his grip weakening as his hand numbed, Tom pounded Stone in the kidneys with his left. In return he caught a head butt that opened a gash above his left eye. Fearing that Stone might get the pistol, Tom deliberately let it fly from his hand and off the catwalk the next time his wrist was pounded on the metal.

Stone gave an angry, frustrated bellow. He locked his hands together and brought them down hard toward Tom's face.

Tom jerked aside, and the blow thudded into the iron grate.

Sitting upright to give himself more force, Stone tried again to land a pile driver on Tom's head. It was a blow intended to crush his opponent's skull like an eggshell.

Using the force of Lijah Stone's downward swing to aid him, Tom kicked up hard in an attempt to roll Stone over his head.

Stone tried to keep from being thrown off by stopping the swing of his arms and flattening out his body as Tom pushed him over. Instead of rolling off Tom onto the catwalk, Lijah Stone sailed through the opening between the narrow iron rails and plummeted forty feet to the opera-house floor.

✳ ✳ ✳

There were a few people who remained in the auditorium. They heard the noise overhead and watched the fight on the catwalk, dodging the falling pistols. A collective intake of breath went up when Stone jackknifed through the bars. After he landed with a dull thud in one of the aisles, there was a momentary silence, followed by a clamor of exclamations and questions.

✳ ✳ ✳

His face streaming blood, Tom held a bandanna pressed over the wound for a moment before tying it around his head. He walked unsteadily to the ladder and slowly descended it. Partway down he had to stop and squeeze his eyes shut till a wave of dizziness passed.

A few moments later, Tom stood over the crumpled form of Lijah Stone. He was not dead but nearly so. "Get a doctor," Tom called to the people who stood milling around. "Get a doctor!" he said again with exasperation.

"No . . . time. Get preacher, 'stead. Quick!" Lijah Stone bit off the words in a spasm of agony. "Get Bollin . . . nobody else!"

Tom looked to see that someone was going to get the pastor, then sat down and stared at the wreck of a man. A wasted life, now in terror of his soul's unreadiness.

One of Stone's eyes took in Tom's presence. The other already seemed fixed and vacant. "Want to tell you, Dawson—"

Tom started. Stone had used Tom's real name. His identity was known!

"They are on to you . . . hired me to kill you . . ."

Tom nodded. "Then you're the one who fired through the floor of the hotel and caused the wagon accident?"

Stone's face contorted in a mixture of agony and confusion. "No," he said with difficulty. "Don't know what you mean. . . . They came to me after our fight. . . ."

"Who?" Tom asked. "Who came to you?"

"Don't know names." Stone's head lolled to one side when he tried to shake it; then it would not straighten up again. "Get . . . get preacher!"

"All right, Stone, lie quiet. I'm sure he's on the way."

"Good." Stone's word came with a long, drawn-out sigh, and his body arched again in a spasm of pain. "Dawson! Girl . . . the actress . . . she's one of 'em."

"I know," said Tom quietly.

Pastor Bollin was hustled through the doors of the opera house. He came and knelt beside Stone.

The killer's eye flickered on Bollin's features, and one corner of his mouth twitched in a smile. "Knew you'd . . . come. Best man I . . . ever saw. Don't mind losing . . . to better men." Stone's breath was shallow, and a pink froth appeared on his lips. "Help me, Preacher. . . . I'm so scared."

Tom stood and, moving all the curious onlookers before him with the force of an expression that accepted no argument, cleared the great hall. At the last he looked over his shoulder to see Pastor Bollin bent to speak in Lijah Stone's ear and the dying man's attempt to nod.

✳ ✳ ✳

Sam met Tom on the steps outside Maguire's. "You all right?" he asked, looking with concern at the clotted blood drying on Tom's face and the gory bandanna.

"Stone's dead," Tom said. "He tried to escape and fell from the catwalk. Where'd you go, anyway?"

"Message came right before things heated up at the opera house. Bullion shipment was robbed tween here and Tahoe. Only one guard escaped alive."

"That's it, then," concluded Tom. "I'm sure of it. They put Stone up to finishing me off while they went after the silver. How much did they get?"

"Twenty or thirty thousand. Oh, and there's more. Soon as the word came in, a reporter tried to meet the mine superintendent, a man named Baldwin. Seems he lit a shuck out of here earlier today. What do you make of that?"

"Same as you. He must have had a hand in the robbery. Posse out after him?"

"And the army," Sam amended. "Some reporter for the *Enterprise* tipped off the soldiers that this was a secesh plot." Sam looked very pleased with himself.

"Well, round up some more men," Tom instructed.

"What for? Who's left to arrest?"

"Belle Boyd."

"The actress?" Sam asked with surprise. "What's she got to do with this?"

"She's in it up to her pretty neck," said Tom grimly. "But on my word, she's about to get helpful."

✴ CHAPTER 18 ✴

Reynolds, Perry, Hastings, Ingram, and Law gathered aboard the *Chapman.*

The recently stolen silver shipment had already been exchanged for weapons through a Mexican arms dealer who asked no questions.

"'Five cases of powder,'" Perry read from a list. "'One hundred fifty revolvers, thirty rifles, one hundred fifty pounds of bullets, two hundred cannon shells, and—'" he paused impressively—"'two brass twelve pounders, brought aboard in crates labeled Machinery.'"

"Well done," complimented Reynolds, "and again to you, Ingram and Hastings."

"I still want to know when the thousand-man army will show up," growled Law.

"Hold your tongue," snapped Perry. "Just let us seize one Pacific mail steamer and the take won't be thirty thousand dollars; it'll be three hundred thousand or even three million. Men will flock to our recruiting."

"Maybe," said Law without enthusiasm. "One passage at a time, I says. Where's my next payment?"

Reynolds handed it over grudgingly. "See that you earn that."

"Aye," agreed Law. "Reckon I will day after tomorrow."

"Are you certain, Ingram, that Dawson is disposed of?" Perry asked.

"Nothing easier," said Ingram. "Stone told us that the spy and a newspaper snoop were both at the bottom of a thousand-foot shaft."

✳ ✳ ✳

Tom shook hands with Sam and prepared to board the Pioneer Stage Company for what he hoped would be the fastest possible trip back to 'Frisco. He had set one foot on the coach when Belle Boyd was led out of the Express Line office in handcuffs. "Just a minute," he called to the driver, and he moved in front of the procession leading Belle to jail.

"You can only have a minute, Mister Dawson," said the Express Line guard in charge. "We've lost two good men and thirty thousand in bullion. This little she-devil don't even try to act innocent. She's been spoutin' venom about Abe Lincoln and everybody else since we caught her. The big bosses want her locked up pronto an' us to hit the trail after Superintendent Baldwin."

"I won't tell you anything, Mister Wilson or Dawson—whatever your name is," Belle spat at Tom.

"Belle," Tom said reasonably, "the game is up. You're already an accessory in two murders. Tell me what you know before your gang gets you involved in more."

Belled smiled a malicious smile. "Here's all I'll tell you: You won't see that little black brat ever again!"

311

✳ ✳ ✳

The audience chamber was especially tense. Two ranks of boo-how-doys stood attentively in front of Fujing Toy's throne. Each carried a hatchet at shoulder arms and appeared ready to use it.

The reason for the special precaution was the arrival of an emissary of the most powerful rival Tong, the Sue Yops. It was not impossible to think that this ambassador might have orders to assassinate Fujing. The show of force was to impress on the visitor how immediate and horrible would be the vengeance if any such attack were attempted.

The emissary announced that he had come bearing a gift from the Sue Yop leader to Fujing Toy. Before he approached any closer, two blackshirts stepped forward, and at his permission, the ambassador allowed himself to be searched. He was in formal attire, wrapped in yards of silk that rustled continuously. The ambassador advanced on his knees with the parcel, also wrapped in rustling silk, and placed it at Fujing's feet.

A snap of the fingers summoned Mont.

He placed his peacock fan in a brass holder and crept forward on his stomach as he had been taught.

Loops of bright yellow ribbon tied up the lid of the box. Mont carefully untied the bands, then looked to see if Fujing wished him to open the present further. A frown of the impassive face told him that Mont should only pass the box up to the Tong lord's lap.

Mont was still kneeling at Fujing's feet when with a final rattle and rustle of the silk wrapping, the Sum Yop master thrust his hand into the box. A terrible scream erupted from his mouth, and he flung himself backward and the box away. The rattlesnake that had been coiled inside the gift had attached itself to Fujing's forearm by its fangs.

The ambassador-assassin grabbed the fallen box and from inside the thickly padded interior drew a pistol.

Fujing was still screaming and shaking his arm frantically, trying to dislodge the snake. Its fangs had pierced the brocade of his sleeve as well as his flesh, and it continued to hang there.

Two of the blackshirts went down in quick succession to shots from the emissary's pistol; then there was a crash against the entry door and armed men burst in. These were also dressed in black, but they wore yellow armbands and carried two-pronged pitchforks instead of hatchets.

Fujing had finally succeeded in shaking the snake loose. It fell across Mont's back, where he cowered at the foot of the throne. The rattlesnake slithered onto the floor of the platform and quickly retreated under the throne, where it coiled and struck out at the air.

Reacting swiftly to the invading Sue Yops, Han picked up a solid oak table that was almost eight feet long. He turned it into a combination shield and battering ram, carrying the front rank of the enemy soldiers back through the door.

Suddenly he stopped and flung down the piece of furniture. Ripping a leg the size of a fence post off the table, he set out across the throne room, scattering startled musicians, fearful guests, and confused bodyguards in all directions.

When a blackshirt sized him up as a traitor and took a swing with a hatchet, Han parried the chop with the improvised quarterstaff. He then spun the end around so that it caught the man under the chin and lifted him completely off the floor with its impact.

The assassin had killed two more of Fujing's men before their hatchets had silenced him, and now several waves of yellow armbands flooded through the doorway. Every boo-how-doy was engaged in fighting for his life, and no one had any time to regard Han, except when he grabbed two opposing bodyguards and smashed both their heads together before leaping over them.

The dread master of the Sum Yop Tong had fallen off his throne. He had fainted, and his unconscious form lay on top of Mont.

Picking up his recent owner as if he were a fragment of lint to be brushed away, Han flicked Fujing against the wall. Then gathering up Mont by a handful of robe, Han made a hasty exit through the passage behind the throne.

"You all right?" he asked Mont when he had ceased swinging the boy like a dinner pail and raised him head high.

"Yes." Mont coughed. "Just a little shook up is all. Does you know your way out of here?"

The giant man shook his head.

Mont thought for a moment. "Can you get us back to the main corridor?"

"Yes," Han replied. "This I do."

"All right, then," Mont concluded. "I'll show us the way out."

✳ ✳ ✳

"Oh no," worried Mont as he and Han stood in front of the iron gate that covered the passageway behind the opium den. "It's locked!"

Han rattled the grille with one hand. "So it is."

The fleeing pair had traveled fast, but the news of the great battle raging between the rival Tongs seemed to have traveled even faster.

All the usual traffic in the underground tunnels had suddenly disappeared. The normal commerce of the common Chinese folk would resume as soon as it was safe, and it mattered little to them which master won.

Han and Mont had needed to hide only once on their flight to the iron gate. But as soon as the group of yellow armbands raced by, the two continued their escape and now stood before the locked gate.

"So it is," Han said again, giving the gate another shake. He set Mont down a few paces behind him and off to the side. "Wait," he said simply.

Curling his fingers around the latticework, Han bent his back like an ox leaning into a heavy load. There was a moment of immobility, and then a rending sound as chunks of bricks and mortar fell from the gate's anchor bolts. The entire gate and its frame pulled free of the wall, and Han threw it aside with a crash.

When they at last emerged into the alley off Washington, it was late at night.

"Good thing," Mont observed, looking down at his own fanciful robes and up at the imposing height of his friend. "We two is gonna stand out like . . . like I don't know what!"

"Where we go now, little friend?"

"Well, now we . . . that is I . . ." Mont paused and considered. "I don't rightly know. We can't go back to the hotel 'count a dem bad fellers might still be there, an' I don't know if Tom is back."

"If we seek your home?" Han asked.

"Greenville? It's a powerful far piece from here. I think de best thing to do is to put some miles tween us and 'Frisco. How 'bout we cross the bay by steamer and figger the rest out tomorrow?"

Han agreed and the two were soon slipping through alleys on their way to the wharfs. They had just turned the last corner before the waterfront when they heard several men approaching.

By much folding of knees and tucking in of elbows, it was just barely possible for Han to conceal himself behind a packing crate.

Mont peeped around to examine the passersby who stood together in a little huddled cluster beneath a streetlamp. "It's them!"

he exclaimed in a stifled whisper. "The pointy bearded one and the army man! And with 'em is . . . the one I saw in Richmond!"

"It a blessing, then, that we see first," Han said. "Come, we slip back quickly."

"No, wait," Mont insisted. "I gots to see where they go. This is what I come all this way for."

The men walked toward a small sailing ship docked at the wharf. They descended belowdecks on the schooner, leaving a hatch cover half open, from which a lantern light glowed.

"Come on," urged Mont. "Let's get closer. I gotta hear what they says."

Without waiting for Han's approval, Mont darted across the intervening space and sneaked onto the deck.

Han followed and plucked at Mont's sleeve with huge but gentle fingers, wanting the boy to come away.

Instead, Mont put a warning finger to his lips and bent his ear to the hatch cover.

"Is everything on board?" a voice asked.

"Loaded and stowed," answered another. "The twelve pounders can be rigged out in five minutes."

"When do the recruits get here?"

"First light. Then we can get under way. Where are Ingram and Law?"

"Coming," a younger voice replied. "Should be here any minute now."

Mont shot a worried look at Han, and they started to creep back toward the gangplank. The clump of heavy footsteps along the dock sent them scurrying aft. Han had to lie down flat on the deck to fit behind the boom and furled sail of the mizzenmast.

Reynolds greeted Ingram on the deck. "All the officers are here except Law. I'm going back before I'm missed. Get under way as soon as you can after the crew arrives."

✦ CHAPTER 19 ✦

Waking with a start, Tom had a moment's difficulty in placing his whereabouts. Dimmed lanterns casting a glow over tufted velvet cushions and a steady drumming served as reminders that he was in the forward passenger salon of the steamer *Yosemite*. Thirty-six hours of churning stage and steamer travel had given him plenty of time to ponder questions but produced few answers.

Had Belle been telling the truth about Mont? Were the secesh holding him as a hostage, or had something worse happened to his little friend? Tom not only did not know the answer, he could not figure out how to easily determine it. As far as the gang knew, Tom reasoned, only two people in San Francisco knew that Wilson was really Dawson: the gruff, unhelpful Commander Fry and the obliging Lieutenant Reynolds.

Suddenly, Tom realized one of the two had to be a traitor. Either would be in a position to assist the Confederacy in a scheme that involved piracy and seizing of forts and arsenals. Perhaps both men were conspiring against the Union? How was he to tell? If Reynolds was a traitor, then Tom had delivered Mont right into the gang's hands. Then again, maybe Mont was really safe at Fort Point—but now he must find out without revealing himself or risking Mont's life.

One other troubling question remained: What about the other attempts on Tom's life? Was there an unknown member of the conspiracy who had been stalking Tom? But how could the others not already know?

Tom went outside to stand alone on the fog-shrouded foredeck. He listened to the mournful fog whistles and hoped that the chill-swirling air would clear his head.

✳ ✳ ✳

Mont and Han stayed concealed behind the sail, hoping for a chance to somehow get off the *Chapman.* Each time they made a move toward the gangplank, another small group of men would arrive out of the darkness and send them scuttling back to their hiding place.

Toward dawn, Mont had actually fallen asleep in a fold of the furled sails while Han kept watch. A sharp poke in the boy's ribs with a twice-normal-length finger woke him. "What is it?" he asked sleepily.

"Shh," Han cautioned. "Men talk louder now."

It was true. The quiet rocking of the ship and the gentle lapping of the waves against the side were disturbed by arguing voices. "He's not coming, I tell you! He's sold us out!" worried one.

"Then let's sail right now," said another.

"We can't none of us navigate. We'll sink for sure!"

"Do you want to rot in a federal prison instead?"

The clamor rose even louder, with some voices calling to cast off at once, while others argued that the enterprise should be abandoned altogether.

From the steps of the companionway, a somewhat shrill voice climbed above the rest. "Nobody is going anywhere! This Colt and I will see to that. We'll stay here, quiet, till full light. If Law hasn't shown by then, we'll sail without him. You all know too much to leave now! Is that clear?"

Mont and Han did not stay to hear the response. Fearful that the crew were coming up on deck, they slipped down a small aft hatch that led into the evil-smelling darkness of the ship's bilge.

There they waited and prayed.

✳ ✳ ✳

Yosemite's forward flagstaff carried the sky blue triangular pennant of the California Steam Navigation Company. Tom glanced at it, then back to the gray water streaming past the broad prow of the ship. He shivered slightly in the chill and wished he'd put on his jacket before coming on deck. *How much longer?* he wondered. *Can't this thing go any faster?*

Tom put his hand up to lean against the flagstaff when a furtive tread behind him made him turn. As he did, a gun barrel slammed into the side of his head, and a boot in his back tried to shove him into the bay.

Spinning half around on the pole, Tom crouched on the deck and found himself staring into the business end of a Remington .44. Raising his eyes from the gun, he took in a form bundled in a thick blanket coat with the collar turned up. Next he saw an enormous mustache and behind it the cold, intent face of Michael Pettibone. "Pettibone! So, it was you all along!"

"Keep your voice down, Tom," the deputy ordered. "I didn't aim to shoot you, but if you yell I won't have a choice."

"But you were going to toss me in the bay. Why, Mike?"

Pettibone shrugged. "The Golden Circle paid me to keep quiet about some holdups; that's all. And everything was quiet, too, till you decided to stir things up again. I kept hoping I could scare you into giving up and going home. But it's too late for that now and—"

"And now you've got to kill me; is that it?"

"'Fraid so, Tom," Pettibone agreed, gesturing with the pistol for Tom to stand.

Tom studied the distance to the deputy, knowing that he'd have to spring into the blast of the gun.

Pettibone's finger tightened on the trigger.

That's it, Tom thought. *He's waiting for the next time the fog whistle blows.*

Tom sprang, and at that exact second the whistle sounded. Not the hooting noise of the fog signal, but the long, drawn-out scream of the collision alarm. *Yosemite* swung sharply to starboard and heeled over with the momentum of the turn. Tom's lunge connected with the pistol just as it fired, the bullet striking the deck between his feet.

A shuddering crash made the steamer tremble all over like a wet dog shaking himself dry. The unexpected impact threw Tom and the deputy spinning toward the rail and over it into the icy waters below.

Striking the surface flung the two men apart. Pettibone floundered in the heavy coat he wore, struggling frantically, before slipping beneath the waves.

The current carried Tom alongside of the steamer. He fought to keep his head above water, gasping for air, unable to call out for help and alarmed at the numbness already overtaking his arms and legs.

A round tower loomed out of the fog, like a giant floating tin can. *I must be dying,* Tom thought. *I'm seeing things.*

His hands struck hard metal and scrabbled at a deck that looked like an iron-plated raft. The next instant, strong arms were lifting him out of the water. Two bearded sailors snapped to attention as an office strode over and demanded, "What's the damage? This fog and *Camanche*'s profile so low in the water, too. I . . . Dawson, is that you?"

Through chattering teeth, Tom assured Commander Fry that it was indeed. "But what is this?" he asked as he was wrapped in a blanket and helped below.

"This," Fry announced proudly, "is our new ironclad, *Camanche*. She's steaming away right enough. Glancing blow only. She struck us. Good thing it wasn't the other way round. Our ram would have ripped her belly out."

"Commander," Tom said urgently, "the secesh plotters have seized a bullion shipment and are arming a ship—perhaps have already done so. What's more, I think Lieutenant Reynolds at Fort Point may be one of them."

"Old news, that," commented Fry. "Reynolds was arrested last night. Seems Captain Tompkins wasn't ill; he was poisoned but lived. What's this about a ship?"

"The *Chapman*, sir. The plot is to outfit her as a privateer."

"*Chapman*, eh? I know where she's berthed. We'll steam over there now and take a look."

"One more thing," said Tom, looking back at the departing bulk of the *Yosemite* and the receding line of the foaming water where Pettibone sank. "Has anyone seen the black child Mont James?"

✷ CHAPTER 20 ✷

Hey, Han," Mont whispered, "what are all those noises?" The *Chapman's* hold had been as quiet as a tomb. Now running feet could be heard along with shouted commands and a creaking, sighing commentary from the ship herself.

"Very bad," observed Han, holding Mont close. "Ship making sail—leaving dock."

"Come on, then," Mont exclaimed, struggling free. "We've got to get off!"

Mont started up the ladder when an arm as long as he was tall reached out a hand to grasp his ankle and draw him back.

"I will go first." Han picked Mont up and set him on a cold coil of rusty anchor chain.

✸ ✸ ✸

"There's the *Chapman* now," said Fry, pointing, "and she's already under way. Helmsman, steer to cross her bow."

Camanche turned to intercept the schooner, whose sails were hoisted and filling with the rising morning breeze.

At a distance of three hundred yards, there was a flash from *Chapman*, a splash nearby *Camanche,* and then the report of a cannon.

"Shelling us, by thunder," commented Fry. "Foolish move. No doubt of their intentions right now."

"Why don't we fire back?" asked Tom.

"Can't," answered the officer, indicating the empty gun carriages inside the revolving turret over their heads, where *Camanche*'s cannons would go. "She's not armed yet. This was only supposed to be a sea trial, not a combat patrol."

Another flash aboard *Chapman*, and a shell smashed into the ironclad's deck. There was a loud clanging and some exclamations of alarm from belowdecks, but no damage done.

"More speed," Fry ordered. "If she gets the wind of us, she can outrun us."

Camanche's vibrations increased as more steam pressure was applied to turn the propeller, but the *Chapman* was still pulling away.

"She's making to round Alcatraz on this leg, then turn downwind for the run down the channel," Fry observed.

"We can't let them get away," Tom said anxiously. "Can't we stop her?"

"Not without a miracle," Fry replied. "She's got her speed up now. There's no way we can catch her."

✳ ✳ ✳

The hatch cover slid back noiselessly. *Chapman*'s deck stretched forward of the small opening, with the men on deck grouped around the twelve-pound cannons or tensely holding rifles. They were arguing and pointing.

Han climbed the ladder. The closest sailor was the helmsman, who was alternately looking up at the sails, out toward the approaching *Camanche*, and ahead to the dim outline of the rock of Alcatraz.

For Han, the distance to the helm station was only two strides. There was not even a startled exclamation from the sailor when two fists the size of melons struck him on both sides of his head at once. The man fell in a crumpled heap, and Han peered anxiously around for a small boat in which he and Mont could escape.

✳ ✳ ✳

The helm, untended, spun lazily off course. The sails flapped, and *Chapman* began to lose speed. The men on deck did not seem to notice as they clumsily loaded and fired the cannon, with Jasper Perry maintaining order at the point of a gun.

※ ※ ※

"We're gaining," Tom observed.

"Yes," agreed Commander Fry as bullets began to rattle and ricochet off *Camanche*'s iron hide. "We're inside small arms range now. Helmsman, I'll have that ship rammed, if you please." To a knot of sailors gathered below, he said, "Mister O'Toole, have the men prepared to board that vessel and seize it."

※ ※ ※

"Helmsman!" shouted Perry, finally noticing *Chapman*'s decreasing speed and wandering course. "You at the wheel, where are you steering? Who is that?" he yelled, catching sight of Han's looming figure.

"Rush him, whoever he is!" shouted Ingram. "Shoot him down."

Han seized a fire ax and in one swing chopped the main sheet in two, dropping the sail and spoiling the aim of the confused mass of men up forward. He then severed the line that restrained the boom of the mizzenmast. With a huge shove, he swept the boom up the length of the schooner, catching the knot of men who were advancing on him, carrying eight men over the side, and crushing the others against the rail and into one another.

※ ※ ※

"Brace yourself," Fry called below. "Prepare to ram!"

Camanche's broad iron wedge plunged into the *Chapman* amidships. With a splintering roar as if a thousand trees were felled at once, *Camanche*'s ram ripped into the schooner, tumbling the secesh sailors about the deck like marbles.

"Stand to the gun!" Perry roared as men began raising their hands in surrender.

"Stand and fight!" yelled Ingram as he leveled his pistol at Tom and the sailors swarming out of *Camanche*'s hold.

From the rear deck of the *Chapman*, a hundred pounds of chain came whirling through the air like a runaway saw blade. It struck

Perry and Ingram as they stood beside the cannon and wrapped completely around them both, binding them together in an iron embrace. There was just time for each to vent a horrified scream directly into the other's face before the weight of the chain carried them over the side and out of sight into the depths of San Francisco Bay. All the others threw down their weapons and begged to surrender.

Tom vaulted over from the deck of the ironclad to the steeply listing *Chapman*. Out of the fearful, clamoring men on board, he selected Avery Hastings and demanded, "Where is Mont James? Where is the black child? Talk quick or I'll throw you in after your friends."

"I swear I don't know," pleaded Avery. "Don't kill me, and call off your Chinese giant. He's a madman!" He looked nervously at the giant, who loomed overhead with a menace.

"My giant?" asked Tom.

"Hey!" said a small voice from the stern hatch. "I wants out of here!"

The giant leaned over the opening and reached his arm in like a cargo crane lowering his hook. Out of the hold and into the brightening sunshine rode a laughing and smiling Mont James.

* * *

The front room at the Dawson home was buzzing with eager questions for Mont and Tom from Emily, Nathan, Jed, and Colonel Mason.

"You mean that Pettibone poisoned our horse and then came back here the next day?" Emily shuddered.

"Yes," Tom agreed, "but only because he didn't know that Mont and I had already left. He was trying to frighten us out of going."

"It certainly frightened *us,*" Emily said.

"Twice more in Virginia City he tried again, each time a little more murderously," Tom added, without going into detail. "The funny thing is, none of the *Chapman* conspirators knew him to give away his guilty secrets, so he was really running from shadows."

Emily nodded. "The wicked flee when no one is pursuing."

"Sometimes the innocent do a heap of fleeing, too, right, Mont?"

The boy bobbed his head vigorously.

"Was you really in a Chinese opium den?" asked Jed. "I seen pictures of them in the *Police Gazette.*"

"Saw them," Emily corrected, "and I'll not have you reading that trashy magazine. The very idea!"

"No'm," Jed said, hastily redirecting the conversation. "What about this Hand feller, Mont? Is he really seven feet tall?"

"Han," corrected Mont, "an' he look ten feet tall to me!"

"What happened to him, Tom?" Emily asked.

"With his share of the reward money for helping to recover the silver shipment, he could afford to go home to China and live like a king," Tom explained. "But he bought eighteen others out of slavery and hired 'em on to run a laundry! What I still wonder is what panicked the gang into sailing so abruptly."

"Seems I get to answer one," said Colonel Mason, laughing. "They thought that their hired captain turned traitor, but Law never sold them out after all. He was discovered two days later in his hotel room, stinking drunk."

Emily asked, "And what about the army traitor?"

"He will probably hang, ma'am," said Mason.

"I see," said Emily. "And the man Mont saw way back in Richmond; that one glimpse that started this whole chase? He seems very young and more misguided than evil. What will happen to him?"

Tom and Colonel Mason exchanged grins, and then Tom answered, "Seems that the *Chapman* was piloted correctly after all, and that brief voyage took Hastings exactly where he belonged. He will be staying for quite some time as a guest of the Union army . . . at the military prison on Alcatraz."

"And will you be staying for quite some time with us, Tom?" asked Emily with a sudden change of tone that stopped Dawson's revelry in its tracks.

The silence that followed had Tom searching for an answer. "It's good to be . . . home, Emily." His tone matched hers, and their eyes met. Neither looked away.

"It wasn't quite home without you," Emily spoke through shining eyes.

Both of them knew what was *really* being said. Convinced that Jed would figure it out if they kept this conversation going, Tom said quickly, "Sounds like we've got a lot to talk about, Em—*later*!"

Riders of the Silver Rim

A tragic accident sends blacksmith
Joshua Roberts west to find peace.
What he finds is raw trouble.
He's nearly burned to death
in the desert, then is brought back
to life by a mysterious stranger.
Plunged into life in a lawless silver
mining town in the Sierras, Joshua
faces his greatest threat yet—
greedy, unscrupulous enemies
who will stop at nothing . . . even
hurting those he has come to love.

To the memory of Jesse Dodson Wattenbarger,
Potsy . . .
accomplished blacksmith,
skillful stage driver,
and master storyteller . . .

✶ PROLOGUE ✶

He was not sure when he abandoned the blanket roll. He probably parted company with it sometime after discarding his coat and before losing the empty water bottle. He had continued to carry the bottle long after its contents were gone, hoping against hope that he would soon locate a spring. Later on, the loss did not seem to matter.

Even with a derby on his head, the sunlight beating down on him became a physical weight on his neck and shoulders. His back and legs ached from supporting the burden. His head felt swollen to the point of bursting, while his body seemed shrunken, aged, and frail.

The sun reflected off the sand into his face, hitting him mercilessly on both cheeks as wave upon wave of heat rolled over him. It was like walking into an oven. His features were baked like overdone bread, his eyes had swelled to blurred slits, and his lips were cracked and blackened. His enlarged tongue had the texture of an old, dried-up stick.

He no longer perspired. His body had no more moisture to contribute to the Mojave afternoon. What sweat had dried and darkened into salty rings on his flannel shirt now gritted and chafed against his parched skin. But he did not notice anymore.

How he continued to move forward he could not have said. The trail stretched clearly in the heat-swirled distance, but he saw only the space of his next three steps. A nagging voice in the back of his mind told him that to stop moving was to die. For a time he argued with the voice, favoring a rest, a short break, a chance to sit down. Now the effort of disputing it seemed greater than the plodding on. He resolved to walk until he found water—or until night fell and he could no longer keep to the path.

One step became two, then three, then another and another. There was no feeling in his tormented feet. Perhaps their ache blended with the rest of his misery. Despite his constant motion, he might as well have been simply marking time. The mountains ahead came no closer, and the hills he had descended to reach the desert plain had receded to merge with a brown horizon. The salt pan that he had been crossing for what seemed like weeks now appeared bowl shaped, curving upward all around him.

Maybe the desert really *was* beginning to curve upward. Or maybe he was losing the strength to step over the grains of sand in his way. In either case, his constant tread became a lurching shuffle, his body bent forward from the waist. As if he were walking into a gale-force wind, the heat would not let him fall. He leaned into it, embraced it, as if to straighten up would push him over backward.

He continued staggering forward until something besides the heat worked its way into his thoughts. The sound had been there for a long while without his notice, and when he did notice it, he ignored it. Finally something demanded that he seek the source of the whispering, sighing noise. He peered about him, moving his head cautiously from side to side, as if he feared it would topple from his body. Nothing around for miles seemed to have the capacity for sound, yet the sighing had moved in closer. It had become a rustling.

He blinked, then stopped stock-still. The dull realization dawned that he *hadn't* blinked—a shadow had passed over his path. He forced himself to lean back, painfully straightening his neck, willing his chin from his chest, sending hammer blows of pain into his back.

His face sought the sky, and through the slits of his tortured eyelids, he saw it momentarily darken, then brighten again. He had the fleeting thought that he was grateful for even an instant's respite from the intense rays of the sun.

Then he saw it: A buzzard flew in lazy circles over his head. Higher still, two of its feathered companions soared, banked, and spiraled. The wings of the nearest bird made the slightest whisper as it passed directly overhead. Otherwise the three were silent.

The man bared his teeth, even though the grimace made his lips split and crack more. He raised a clenched fist over his head. A guttural croak escaped him, more from his chest than from his burning throat.

He swayed, moving in an arc counter to the circling birds. His chin, once stuck to his chest, now seemed impossible to lower. He saw rather than felt his arm fall heavily to his side. He attempted to turn his head, surprised at the involuntary action, but his whole body twisted instead, and he fell awkwardly on his side into the sand.

✳ ✳ ✳

A shadow crossed his face, then returned to hover directly above, and something rustled close by. He struggled, attempting to flail his arms to ward off the vultures.

My eyes, he thought, *they're after my eyes!* His convulsive heave produced only a shudder of his frame. *Roll over,* he pleaded with himself.

Then the stirring came again, a soft fluttering. When it stopped, a voice spoke out of the shadow. "You poor man! Just lie still. Here's some water."

Water! Like rain the words splashed on his soul: *Water! Saved!* A delicious coolness soothed his lips. He pursed them in a sucking motion. The moisture trickled down his throat, shocking his senses, as if he had swallowed ice.

Tiny sip followed tiny sip. Some of the cool liquid spilled over onto his eyelids, and a hand as gentle as a feather's touch soothed his ravaged cheeks. He jerked his head, trying to shout not to waste a single drop.

The voice came again. "Don't worry. There's plenty."

Another splash on his lips and then another on his eyes. His body began to wake up, as if missing parts were getting reattached.

"More," he managed to groan, "more."

"Yes, of course, there is more. But slowly, slowly." The voice sounded like distant chimes.

This time he felt the touch of the bottle on his lips. Panic struck him. He must have the water bottle! His arms responded to his brain, flinging awkwardly together over his chest. His clawing fingers found a sleeve, an arm, then lost it. There was a startled half cry, and the shadow over his face retreated. The water bottle dropped onto his chest, sprinkling his face even as he grasped it eagerly and upended its contents into his mouth. His eyelids parted momentarily, and he saw the most delicate features framed in a ghostly shimmering light.

Half the contents of the bottle crashed into his stomach at once and hit his racked and twisted insides as if he had swallowed a rock. The rock became a bomb that exploded in his brain, and consciousness fled away, leaving his punished body in peace.

⁕ CHAPTER 1 ⁕

From the high vantage point of a rock-strewn bluff, the old Mojave Indian chief watched the struggle of the tall white man in the strange hat against the sun and the vultures.

The old chief could see what the white man could not: The town of Garson was only a short walk from where he had fallen. He knew the miners of the Silver Rim also could look up into the sky and see the black dots of the turkey buzzards as they swooped and circled overhead. Perhaps they would come to the sunlight from their dark hole in the ground and think a wild horse had fallen to die in the desert. Later they would hear that one of their own had fallen. They would wag their heads in wonder that anyone had tried to cross the desert of the Mojave without water, without a horse, and in head-gear that wouldn't keep the sun off a prairie dog.

For a long time the Indian watched as the body of the fool was slung across the back of the mule. Perhaps the man was dead. He would be taken to Garson and buried, then. If he was still alive, it would not be long before he died. *These white men do not belong in our land,* the chief reasoned. *The spirits take revenge beneath the sun.*

As the mule was led away, the old chief turned his eyes back toward Garson and then to the west, where his own village nestled between the cliffs of Wild Rose Canyon.

Once his people had been fierce and proud. They had contested dominion of the western lands with the Navajo and the Apache. The coming of the white man with their repeating rifles had broken them. Now the soldiers thought so little of them that the Indians were left to fade away in the desert.

The chief knew his white neighbors would not even consider their little camp a village. A migratory band, his tribe traveled from the Sierra peaks, where they gathered pinyons for grinding into flour, to these desert canyons, where they obtained maguey for making pulque, a venomous, fermented brew that whites would not drink. Wild Rose Canyon was more a favorite campground than a permanent settlement.

Chief Pitahaya sighed. *I am only half a ruler now,* he thought with sorrow.

They had a miserable existence, their old glory gone. The whites despised them, and they were an easy prey to white diseases and vices. Some Indians would even barter their squaws for whiskey, which they much preferred to pulque.

Chief Pitahaya argued, threatened, and railed against the growing depravity of his people but without the authority to force compliance. The white man's Indian agents offered no assistance, and the army said it was no business of theirs. There was no law in the desert.

The chief watched the dust stirred by the little mule while he thought what must be done. He closed his eyes and considered the frailty of these white intruders. "What we need," he whispered to the spirits, "is a good war. What pride we had in the days of my youth when a call to punish the Membreno horse-eaters would be answered by two hundred strong warriors! Even when the whites came to our sands, we made them go everywhere in companies of fifty for safety. And many were the fifty who never reached their stone lodges."

Now look at us! the old chief mourned. *Faugh! We are too feeble to fight a determined gang of lizards. Nothing seems to stir us enough to shake off this sleep-with-open-eyes. Perhaps I was wrong when the white soldiers grew so powerful that I counseled Sihuarro to give up war. Perhaps I should have told him, "It is a good day to die."*

❊ ❊ ❊

Joshua Roberts sat bolt upright. His heart was pounding so hard that with each beat it threatened to burst out of his chest.

"Easy there, young fella," ordered a gruff voice. "You'd best lie still a mite longer."

"Longer? How long . . . ? Where? Who?" Joshua was trembling all over like an aspen in the breezes of the Sierra passes.

"For a fella pretty much cooked, you're plumb full of questions, ain't cha?" The voice was amused. "Lie down 'fore you shake the bed apart."

Joshua obliged. It wasn't difficult to see the wisdom of the advice, especially since he had to squeeze his eyes shut to make the room stop spinning. When he opened them again, he found himself staring at a patched canvas roof strung over a frame of mismatched wooden slats.

He was lying on a cot in someone's tent, but he could not remember how he had gotten here. He touched his face gingerly and noticed that the skin felt thick and leathery. The swelling around his eyes had gone down, and his tongue seemed to be in working order again.

A round, bearded face leaned into his view. Bright blue eyes peered out from lines and crevices that mirrored the desert landscape. The old man appeared to have been carved from the desert floor and brought to life. Curly gray hair escaped from a crushed and shapeless felt hat and blended into a curly gray beard clipped short around his jaw. He was dressed peculiarly in red flannel long johns, stained with sweat, and caked with a layer of dust from his hat to his toes.

Joshua was trembling with cold. How had he come to be in a place so cold when the last thing in his memory was the searing heat?

"Who are you?" he managed to ask. "And where am I?"

The old man spread another blanket over him. "More questions, eh? Why don't cha save them questions for later an' concentrate on breathin' first?" The dusty face split into an enormous grin. The leathery skin folded into a thousand fine lines, as if life here had eroded away his youth.

Joshua touched his own face. Did he look like the man? "Please," he whispered with a shudder, "how long have I been here?"

"Well, for three days you been out of your skull, boy. Ravin' on 'bout this an' that—now an' then you'd haul off an' yell, 'My eyes! They're after my eyes!'"

Joshua nodded grimly as waves of the horrid memory flooded

through him. "It was the vultures. I thought they were going to pluck my eyes out."

The old man shook his head. "It like to clabber my blood the way you was goin' on. Plumb loco."

"There *were* vultures. And then the lady—" He stopped abruptly and struggled to sit up. "Where is she?"

The old man stepped back warily. "Are you fixin' to rave some more, boy? There ain't nobody here but you an' me."

Joshua let his head fall back. "I'm sure of it. There *was* a woman, a beautiful woman, just after I pitched over in the sand. Thought I was a goner, but she gave me a drink. I'd like to thank her."

"There ain't nobody here besides us two, unless you count Jenny out yonder." He jerked a thumb toward the open tent flap. "She's a gal all right, but she ain't no lady."

Joshua carefully propped himself up on his elbow. Through the flap he could see a little mule with her head drooping and her eyes half closed in the early morning light. "But I saw a lady—I even touched her arm." The vision in his mind was strong.

The old man shrugged and reached for a pair of mud-caked trousers that probably could have stood alone. "When I found you, I thought you was dead. Propped against a rock like you couldn't go no further an' had given up. Ain't no fine lady gonna be out here, boy."

Joshua lay still, struggling to reconstruct how he had gotten here . . . wherever *here* was. He hadn't the strength to ask more questions, and the old man set about his morning chores without offering further explanation.

Presently his host returned with a tin plate. "Sorry it ain't more, boy. I ain't much of a hand at cookin', an' I ain't had time since comin' across you to get no Mexican strawberries on the fire." He thrust the plate into Joshua's hands. Two rock-hard, oversized lumps of dough that Joshua recognized as yeast powder biscuits sat in a puddle of bacon grease.

Joshua dipped a biscuit in the fat and took a tentative bite. He was surprised to discover how good it tasted. Between mouthfuls and sips from a canteen, he listened as the old man launched into an account of himself and the last few days.

"My folks hung the name of John Springer on me. But where I'm known in these parts, folks call me Pickax. Pick for short. This is my digs for now. 'Course, I might be forty mile away after breakfast, if I've a mind." Pick waved a stubby arm toward a lumpy sandstone rise visible across the dry wash. "You was just over that ridge yonder. Town of Garson is up that way a piece. Fact is, I was comin' back from there with my grub when I seen you. You didn't weigh no more'n a sack of potatoes, you was so dried up. I slung you over Jenny an' brung you here."

Josh's eyes narrowed, and his expression turned grim. "You meet anyone coming from Garson? I mean, did you see a man dressed in dark clothes? Dark hat? Swarthy skin?"

"Is this another dream, boy? Ain't nobody crazy 'nough t' be out in the heat of the day 'cept you an' me. An' I can't figure why you was out there without water."

"I *had* water. I may be a tenderfoot—" Joshua shrugged ruefully at the accuracy of this statement—"but even I knew not to start out without water. I met up with a man in Mojave who said he knew the way to the mines, and we traveled together. He said he knew a shortcut, so we turned off the road. Slept out that night. Next morning, he was gone—with both water bottles and every cent I had in the world."

Pick made a noise low in his throat like a dog walking stiff-legged toward a fight. "An' then what happened, boy?"

"I figured I could follow his tracks. Figured he would head for more water. I finally struck the road I was following when you found me, but I never saw the man again."

Pick's face grew dark as Josh told him the story, and his outrage exploded. "He ain't nothin' but a murderer! Ought to be strung up pronto for doin' you that way. D'ya think you'd know him again?"

"Anywhere."

"Know his name?"

"Called himself Gates."

Pickax nodded solemnly. Then after a few minutes of pondering the tale, he studied Josh curiously. "Well, you know *my* name, an' I know *his* name. But you ain't give me *your* name, boy!"

Joshua extended his hand with some effort. "My folks gave me the name Joshua Roberts. And that's what I go by. My friends call me Josh."

✳ ✳ ✳

After two more days in the care of the old prospector, Joshua was able to move about again, but slowly.

On his walk across the desert, Joshua's feet had burned and blistered inside his boots. Pickax had cut away the leather and soaked his raw flesh in a bucket of precious water. In this way, Pickax explained, Joshua absorbed two quarts of fluid while still unconscious.

As he regained his strength on biscuits, bacon, and the beans that Pickax called Mexican strawberries, Joshua had time to ponder the strange vision of the woman who had given him a drink. And during the long, cold nights, he considered the thief named Gates, who had left him to die.

Pickax said that the robber must have taken one look at Joshua's size and strength and known he couldn't take him any other way than by stealth. "You got the hands of a blacksmith, boy," the old man had commented.

When Josh confirmed that blacksmithing had indeed been his trade, Pickax grinned and shrugged as if he'd known all along.

This last matter troubled Joshua. What might he have said about his past when he'd been out of his head? Did the old man know about the dead teamster back in Springfield? Had he pieced that part of the puzzle together?

"Men ain't got a past when they come out here," Pickax told Josh one night as he blew out the lantern. "Your life. My life. It ain't between nobody but you an' the Almighty. There's no laws out here, boy. An' nobody needs to know your business."

And so the terrible accident that had driven Joshua from his home and led him to this desolate land remained unspoken. The colors of his old life had been abandoned to bleach away in the sun of the Mojave. Yes, he was still Joshua Roberts, but when he looked into the cracked mirror in Pick's tent, he could find only hints of the man he'd been in Illinois.

Perhaps he had finally run far enough to escape his memories. Maybe this place was close enough to hell that just *being here* was his atonement! With its freezing nights and searing days, the desert offered a man no comfort, no real peace.

There was no past here, Pick had said. Only now and the future.

Joshua Roberts had three things he wanted to do: Work again, find the woman who had given him water, and find the man named Gates, who hadn't bothered to waste a bullet on him but who'd left him most certainly to die in the desert sun.

⁂CHAPTER 2⁂

Joshua's still-tender feet were sheathed in an old pair of the prospector's boots—mercifully, a size too large. He had not shaved in two weeks, and what precious water remained did not allow for washing his clothes. He wanted a bath more than anything, and although Pickax did not himself approve of baths, he informed Josh that such luxuries were indeed available in Garson.

On this morning, without warning, Pickax announced, "Goin' to Garson. Grub an' water. Grab your hat if you're comin' along," he said, eyeing the derby a tad dubiously.

Joshua pulled on his hat and lent a feeble hand loading the empty water barrels onto Jenny's back. It was fourteen long miles to Garson. Fourteen miles to water. Joshua suddenly realized what a sacrifice the old man had made to share water and food with a half-dead stranger. And Joshua didn't have a penny to repay him.

"I'd like to find work and pay back what I owe you," Josh said as they led the mule away from camp in the predawn light.

Pick glanced back at his ragged tent. "It don't matter none. I enjoy the company. You talk better'n ol' Jenny here. I'll put in a good word for you with Mister Morris at the Silver Rim Mine. Maybe you can grubstake me someday."

As they trudged over the desolate countryside, Joshua could not help imagining that he would find Gates in Garson and recover what had been stolen from him. Then he would be able to repay Pickax, buy himself some clothes, and have a bath. Pick told him that he should buy a gun and learn to use it. Joshua had never felt the need to carry a sidearm before.

Back in Springfield, few men had dared to challenge the strength in his six-foot-three frame. He had used his size to wrestle down horses protesting a shoeing. But out in the West, Pick insisted, it was prudent to carry a gun.

"There ain't never been a sheriff in Garson," Pick explained. "It ain't likely one would live too long, anyway."

He then proceeded to spend the hours of their journey telling Joshua the history of the little town. After all, he had been here looking for the Lost Gunsight Mine long before Garson was anything but a couple of tents and a well. It was hardly more than that now, according to Pick.

Still an hour's walk away, the little town became visible in the distance. It was a ramshackle collection of wooden and canvas buildings shimmering in the heat. Some of the structures were more permanent than others but none very substantial. Pickax claimed you could throw a Chinaman through any of the walls, and the truth of this had been demonstrated more than once.

For all its flimsy construction, Garson performed the necessary functions to be called a town. About half the population consisted of hard-rock miners. The other half were there to sell their wares to the miners—or was it to prey on them? Shopkeepers, saloonkeepers, bankers, cardsharps, cooks, seamstresses, and ladies of easy virtue made up the citizenry that was not mining.

Garson had a chance to become a town twenty years earlier than it did, Pick explained, owing to an unusual circumstance. A French prospector named DuBois had passed through the area hoping to locate gold. He had arrived in California too late for the rush of '49 and ended up wandering through the Panamint and Argus mountains, hoping to make his pile. When he discovered that his rifle sight was broken, an Indian guide from the local band of Mojaves offered to repair it. Reasoning that if the firearm was never returned it was useless anyway, the prospector agreed. To his surprise, it was returned in perfect working order with a new bead of pure silver!

When pressed to reveal the source of the silver, the Indian became frightened and fled. DuBois searched the canyons unsuccessfully until his water ran low and forced him to a more hospitable area. He never returned—partly because of the harsh landscape but probably more because the lure of gold was so much stronger than silver.

Pick recalled that over the years the legend of the Lost Gunsight Mine was told, retold, and embellished or scoffed at. Occasionally it was searched for but never successfully.

Then the gold began to play out. The placer mine's heyday was done in California, and mining began to be run by the big-money moguls who could afford the equipment for underground operations. It seemed that lone prospectors had lost the chance to strike it rich—lost it, that is, until the wealth of the Comstock lode was trumpeted around the camps. Then "Silver!" became the cry.

The fact that fabulous wealth could be found in parched, arid lands like those of Virginia City, Nevada, miles from running water, gave the tales of the Lost Gunsight new credibility. When Pick prospected in the area, he found silver-bearing ore even if he didn't find lumps of silver sticking out of the walls of an ancient Indian tunnel.

Just as important, the returning prospectors found water! Drilling a test hole, they were startled to find a water table at only twenty feet. Without ever coming to the surface, an underground stream was gurgling its way to the salt flats of the desert floor.

Overnight a tent city sprang up, and soon after came a parade of merchants to see to the miners' needs. How the town came to be called Garson, Pick did not know for certain, but it's likely that it was an attempt to call it Garçon, in honor of the Frenchman DuBois. By 1875 it didn't matter what anyone called it; fifteen hundred souls called it home.

Even if their clothing was the same, the miners were distinguishable from the merchants by the speed of their activities. The miners were either in a hurry to spend their money, lose it at the card tables, or drink it up. The clerks, bartenders, and the town's undertaker were much more deliberate and methodical in their approach to life. Maybe the difference was in their knowing that wealth would come to them in someone else's pockets.

Garson's main street required no name because it was the only street in town. Josh noted that most of the buildings were grouped along either side of the wagon road that served as highway. The other structures comprising the town were set amid the creosote bushes just as their builders saw fit, without regard to straight lines or intersections. The businesses along the road had more semblance of permanence only by leaning together in what appeared to be mutual intoxication. The Red Dog Saloon leaned against the Tulare Hotel, which leaned against Jacobson's Hardware Store, which leaned against (and was leaned on by) Fancy Dan's Saloon and Faro Parlor.

Across the rocky street the scene was repeated, with the Kentucky Gentleman Saloon and the Chinaman's Chance providing rather alcoholic bookends to an office building housing a lawyer, a doctor, a dentist, and the Golden Bear Mining Company.

The livery stable and corral stood alone at the bottom of the dusty slope upon which the town was spread. At the top, dead center, was not a church or school but Freeman's Mortuary. Pickax explained that the saloons flanking the business district were the pillars of society, and Freeman's commanding position at the head of the town showed how well the results of society's practices were provided for in Garson—or words to that effect.

Around these businesses in random disorder stood the tents and cabins of the population. The most elaborate of these consisted of two twelve-by-twelve rooms separated by a roofed open space or dog run. At the other extreme were canvas awnings covering cots and bearing grandiose names like Sovereign of the Sierras Hotel.

But Garson was definitely growing, and more importantly, families were starting to put down roots, and a few children could be seen running through the streets.

* * *

Into this scene Pick led Jenny and Joshua. After turning Jenny into a corral, Pick and Josh unloaded the wooden water casks and filled them from the well that stood outside, then rolled them into the barn to keep them cooler.

The essential job done, Pick turned and remarked, "What say

we go see who all's in town t'day, boy? Maybe we can find you some work, like you been wantin'."

Joshua nodded, and the two walked up the slope through town. Pick pointed out the various establishments, passing judgment on the quality of their liquor and food and greeting several other miners pleasantly with his ready grin.

Joshua's city clothes and derby hat caused some second glances, but the costumes to be seen in Garson were so varied Josh soon gathered that his very presence with Pick caused as much curiosity as his dress. Josh returned their looks, searching each face for the man called Gates, but to no avail.

Pick guided him past all the businesses on the main road and turned aside into the mesquite just before Freeman's. The brush had been cleared off a space just big enough for a canvas tent to be erected.

"This here's the No Name Saloon, Josh. Pard o'mine by the name of Jersey Smith owns it. He came here as a miner but couldn't take the heat. So he brung in a case of Who-Hit-John an' set up this here tent. Somebody asked what the place was called, an' he allowed as how it weren't fancy enough to have no name. Well, sir, that hit the fella's funny bone, so it kinda stuck." He gestured broadly and waved Joshua through. "Welcome t' Garson an' the No Name."

Four tables, all of different ancestry, and fifteen assorted chairs completed the furnishings—except for a wooden counter along one wall. There were no windows, let alone mirrors or paintings. In fact, everything, including the patrons, seemed to be a uniform shade of dust. Everything, that is, except the proprietor.

"Great Caesar's ghost!" erupted a voice from behind the counter. "Pickax, what's the meaning of this? Is it true you've found the old Gunsight after all? You're here to celebrate and share your wealth with your old friend and bosom companion?"

"Naw, Jersey, put a cork in it. If I tumbled onto that treasure vein, I sure wouldn't tell you—leastwise, not till it was registered proper an' guarded."

At Jersey Smith's hurt expression Pick hurried to add, "Not that you'd jump it, understand. But you sure as shootin' couldn't keep a secret, an' I don't want ever'body from the Trinity to Sonora knowin' my business."

"Ah, but I'd only wish to rejoice with you, my friend. To help you celebrate your good fortune."

Jersey Smith eyed Joshua briefly, while Joshua returned the gaze at an equally tall but thin man. Jersey's shock of white hair was combed straight back, and his white beard was small and pointed. His green eyes moved constantly. Joshua assessed him as a man of quick wit to match his glib tongue.

Jersey broke the silence first. "And who might this strapping fellow be? Don't tell me, Pickax, you've finally parted with your hoarded wealth and hired an assistant to do your work while you supervise."

"Now, Jersey, this here is Joshua Roberts, late of Illinois. He an' me run onto each other out by my place, an' I brung him in t' look for work. He ain't no actor fella like yourself, nor a broken-down old rock hopper like me. He's skilled in the smithin' trade."

343

Josh was glad that Pickax had glossed over the circumstances of their meeting, and he did not offer to elaborate. Instead he stuck out his hand and grasped that of the bartender. "I'm pleased to meet you."

"The pleasure is mine, I assure you," responded the carefully modulated baritone. "Men as good as Pick are difficult to discover. If he vouches for you, then your credentials are impeccable. What's your pleasure, gentlemen? The first is on the house in honor of a new acquaintance."

Before either Pick or Josh could reply, a slurred growl interrupted. From a table back in the shadows, a fleshy figure dressed in denim and flannel and packing a Colt Peacemaker stood and swayed slightly, then advanced to stand before Jersey Smith.

Of medium height, he wore his coal black hair greased down to a bullet-shaped skull. Three days of black stubble grew on his face, and from the half-open shirtfront, a tangled thicket of coarse black hair bristled.

At the sight of this intoxicated, menacing figure, Josh thought instantly how much like a bull he appeared. From his beefy arms to his thick neck and powerfully compact build, the man seemed a perfect image of an Angus in human form.

"What do you mean, on the house?" he slurred out. "What're you playin' up to this ol' dusty lump o' broken-down trash for? Las' time I asked you, you wouldn't even allow me the price o' one stinkin' bottle. Me! Mike Drackett hisself! Now set 'em up, you pasty-faced ape. You kin have the pleasure of buyin' a real man a drink!"

"Mister Drackett," replied Jersey quietly, "I've told you before that I don't extend credit, and if you don't care for my house rules, you may take your business elsewhere. As for my guests, I'll give them a drink if I choose to, and I'll thank—"

Jersey got no further with his little speech because Drackett shouted, "Shut your gob! I'll just help myself" and lunged across the countertop. Smith tried to dart out of the way, but Drackett's powerful right hand grasped the proprietor's shirt and dragged the thin man back over the bar in one jerk. "Where's the key to your good stuff, beanpole? I ain't gonna drink no more rotgut, neither. I just bet that key's 'round your neck. Lemme see." Suspending Jersey on his toes with his right, Drackett made as if to grasp the bartender's neck with his left.

But before he could do so, Drackett's left wrist was caught in a grip like a steel manacle and a second later bent up behind his back.

Dropping the white-haired man to the earthen floor, Drackett swung around but found himself confronting no one. Joshua had danced around behind him, all the while wrenching upward on Drackett's wrist.

"Hey, what the—? Come here, you, an' fight." Drackett attempted to reach Josh with his right but stopped abruptly with a howl of pain.

"You're breakin' my fingers," he shouted as Josh coolly bent Drackett's fingers backward. "Stop! I didn't mean nothin'. I was just havin' some fun."

"Your fun, as you call it, is not to my liking nor to Mister Smith's. Apologize to him."

"Apologize? To that fancy—stop! All right, I'm sorry! Sorry, you hear? Lemme go now!"

"Just you hold on t' him another minute, Josh, whilst I relieve him o' this here piece." Pick slipped over and drew Drackett's Colt from the holster he wore tied low on the left and stepped back. "Right, now I reckon he's harmless enough. Let 'im go."

Joshua released Drackett's arm, and the brawny man whirled around as if to resume the fight but stopped at the sight of Pickax casually waving the .45 back and forth. Drackett abruptly changed to rubbing his injured left hand and wrist, but it was plain he was controlling himself with difficulty.

"As I was saying, Mister Drackett, in my establishment, I'll buy drinks for whomever I choose. And as for you, you need not bother coming in here again. Henceforth even your *cash* is no good here." Jersey regained some of his ruffled dignity.

Drackett looked angrily back and forth between his Peacemaker in the hands of Pickax and the haughty Jersey Smith. In transit his gaze stopped and moved upward to lock eyes with Joshua.

"Who're you, anyway?" he asked sullenly.

"Name's Roberts. Joshua Roberts. Now don't you think you'd better do as Mister Smith says and take your business somewhere else?"

Drackett turned his head slightly toward the side and gave a jerk of his chin.

Without a sound, two men rose from the corner table where Drackett had been sitting and followed him out through the tent flap.

Pickax moved to the entrance and watched as they made their way down the slope and back into town. "By gum," he chortled, returning to stand by Josh, "ain't nobody *never* put a stopper to Mike Drackett afore and without a gun or even an ax handle!"

"I'm genuinely grateful, Mister Roberts," Jersey added. "That ruffian and his kind are all too ready to cause destruction and are not usually to be dissuaded."

"No matter," said Josh modestly. "Besides, he was all liquored up and didn't know what he was doing."

"Don't you believe it," offered Pick. "They's a rough string of hombres that's been hangin' 'bout lately, an' Drackett's as bad as they come. You'd both best watch your backsides. Drackett'll not like bein' showed up. He's one who'd dry-gulch a fella. Now hold on t' this Colt—after all, you won it fair an' square."

"No, thanks, Pick. It wouldn't do me any good. I never learned how to use one. Why don't you keep it or give it to Jersey here?"

"Don't they have no learnin' where you come from, boy? Ain't you never heard of self-defense?"

"Joshua, let me offer you a gift and some advice," put in Jersey Smith.

"What's that, Mister Smith?"

Reaching under the bar, he pulled out a sawed-off shotgun. "Ever use one of these?" he asked in a whisper.

Joshua and Pick moved in closer.

"Not on a man," Josh answered. "I've hunted pheasant and grouse some."

"Well then, take it with my compliments. If you want to swap the Colt, that'll be all right, too, but I'll make you a gift of the greener in any case." Jersey carefully removed the shells and reversed the stock to hand it to Josh.

"That's real nice of you, but I don't think I could drop the hammer on a man. Maybe you'd better just keep it and the pistol, too."

"No, my boy. When you think of this in the future, remember I offered not only a present but some advice as well. Here it is: A well-prepared man doesn't have to fight as often as one who is not prepared. Just the fact that you go about armed may convince some ruffian to avoid tangling with you. It's amazing how persuasive these two barrels can be, especially if one is looking into them. Remember, the evildoers we're speaking of have no qualms about shooting an unarmed man just to rob him, let alone one who they feel has shamed them. Please accept this weapon and practice with it. Then perhaps you'll have no need of it."

Joshua reflected an instant, then nodded. "All right, then, what you say makes sense. I'll take it—the greener, you say—and thank you."

"Good. Now promise me you'll practice until you are proficient and—" Jersey raised his voice so that all the customers looking on this scene could plainly hear—"no one will bother you unless they want to be chased out of town by a load of buckshot. You'll have to control that violent temper of yours, or it and these hair-triggers will get someone killed."

Dropping his voice, Jersey added with a conspiratorial wink, "Dramatic effect. It won't take long for word to get around. Before nightfall, you and this shotgun will be the terror of the county."

CHAPTER 3

Pick escorted Joshua over to the offices of the Golden Bear Mining Company, owners of the Silver Rim Mine. The Golden Bear was the largest mining company operating in Garson, which didn't say much for the others. Despite its proud and rich-sounding name, the Golden Bear was struggling, Pickax told Josh. The quality of silver ore recovered from the mine was tolerable, but since Garson had no stamp mill, the ore had to be shipped to Turbanville, a hundred miles away, to be processed.

Pick explained that the costs of shipping and processing and the increasingly difficult task of removing ore from deeper and deeper in the mountain kept the Silver Rim on the edge of closing. At the time of Joshua's arrival, the mine was producing two thousand dollars per week in silver bricks. A third of its profit went to pay for the shipping and processing. Since the miners were paid twenty-five dollars per week, this left very little earnings for its superintendent, Mister Morris, to report.

Morris, Pick told Joshua, was an interesting man. In a rough country of shaggy, unkempt men, Morris was clean shaven and kept his hair neatly trimmed—"a real gentleman" was Pick's assessment. He had experienced all the ups and downs of mining life, having struck it rich in '49, only to be swindled out of his claim by the collusion of a trusted partner and the claims recorder. Never one to give himself over to bitterness, Morris had struck out again into the canyons of the mother lode.

Pick said he'd heard that Morris had again located a rich gold claim, and this time he saw to it that his work was duly registered to his name. He remained partnerless. Later on he had sold out to the Golden Bear Mining Company in exchange for cash, Golden Bear stock, and a seat on the board of directors.

Morris had thought himself settled into a life of ease when the mining company dividend payments began to drop off. Upon investigating, he had discovered that none of the other board members had any actual mining experience. Assessments for mine improvements were eating up the profits.

Morris, according to Pick, demanded the chance to improve the situation, so he was dispatched to oversee the Silver Rim Mine. He had succeeded in reducing expenses, and he still believed in the value of the mine, but it appeared that for once his luck had failed him. He hadn't yet made enough difference in production for the mine to turn the corner to prosperity.

Pick and Josh waited respectfully for Morris to finish giving instructions to one of his foremen.

"Now, Dub, I want you to see to it that the new face on the third gallery is cleared tonight. I want that drift to make twenty feet this week, so as to intercept the vein coming off of two."

"Yessir, Mister Morris. Is that new shipment of timbers here yet?"

"No." Morris frowned. "But it will be by tomorrow if I have to go get it myself. Now go on with you." The foreman departed.

As Morris looked up, a pleasant smile replaced his frown. "Well, Pickax, come in. Come in. What brings you to my office? Don't tell me you've finally decided to take me up on my offer of a position!"

"No, sir, Mister Morris. I thank you right kindly for settin' such store by me, but the truth is, I got this here young man t' see you 'bout it."

Morris rose and stuck out his hand. "Pleased to meet you, young man. What did you say your name was?"

"My name's Joshua Roberts, Mister Morris. I'm a smith by trade. I just came here from Illinois, and I'm anxious for work."

"Smithing, eh?" Morris stopped and appeared to be sizing up

Josh much as one would choose a draft animal. "Are you a drinking man, son?"

"No, sir. I'm not—," began Josh.

Pick interrupted by snorting. "I'll say he ain't! Why, he even turned down a drink after the offer of it 'most got him killed. He disarmed Mike Drackett slick as you please an' still didn't take no drink t' celebrate!"

"What's this? Are you a brawler, then, young man?"

Josh opened his mouth to reply, but Pick again saved him the trouble of answering. "A brawler? He ain't no brawler. He's a genuine iron-corded set o' human manacles!" Pick proceeded to recount the events in the No Name Saloon with great gusto, while Morris nodded, raised his eyebrows, and smiled occasionally.

When Pick finally subsided, Morris turned to Joshua. "If you are half as good as Pickax here claims, you can have an immediate position with me as a security guard. I'll pay you twenty-five dollars a week."

"No, thank you, Mister Morris. I'll tell you what I tried to tell Pick and Mister Smith. I'm no hand with a gun, and fighting's not my line. They seem to think I should practice with this old scattergun, but I wouldn't care to be a guard. Don't you need a smith, sir?"

Morris shook his head as if disappointed but replied, "As it turns out, we do. Even though I've known him a long time, I had to discharge our blacksmith just yesterday for being drunk at work. He has ruined four hundred dollars' worth of drills by his inattention. You can have the job, but I'm afraid the pay is only twenty dollars a week. Are you certain you wouldn't consider the guard's position?"

"No, thank you anyway, Mister Morris. That blacksmith spot suits me right down to the ground. What time do I start?"

"Come tomorrow at seven. I'll have Dub Taylor, the general foreman who just left here, line you out."

✶ ✶ ✶

Josh found lodgings in the modest but clean Tulare Hotel. Its proprietor, Mrs. Flynn, as Irish as her name, took an immediate liking to the young man and saw to it that his cot in the dormitory-like room he shared with seven other men had a clean Navajo blanket rather than the old army-issue wool blankets that served the others.

"Ten dollars a week an' two square meals a day goes with it. Leavin's can be taken for your work meal. No drinkin' nor fancy gals in my place, an' I'll have no smokin' or chewin' in the sleepin' room, if you please. Smokin' an' chewin' is permitted in the parlor, except on Sundays."

Josh replied to each of these pronouncements with a respectful "yes'm" and "no'm."

"Breakfast is at six an' supper is at four. Look sharp, or you'll get naught. Unless," she said, softening a little, "you come to be workin' graveyard, then I'll be savin' you some biscuits for when you come off shift." She paused, as if remembering something. "But no—the smith works morning tower except at need. If I want some repairs done, likely you can work out some costs, if you've a mind."

"Yes, ma'am."

"An' one more thing," she said, her flattened *o* betraying her County Cork origins. "I run a quiet house, so's men can get their sleep. My dear departed Clancy, God rest his soul, was a miner, an' he swore by good food an' good rest."

✳ ✳ ✳

Joshua lay awake in the dark room of the Tulare Hotel and listened to the night sounds of Garson as a cool breeze passed through the open window.

He hoped that the good food promised by Mrs. Flynn was better than the good rest she held in such high esteem! The hoots and whistles of Josh's seven snoring roommates kept sleep far from him.

A dance-hall melody emanated from Fancy Dan's Saloon. Then, of all things, hymn singing began to rise and fall in a strange counterpoint to the honky-tonk music.

"*Shall we gath-er at the Riv-er. . . .*"

"*Thar's a yel-low rose of Tex-as! I'm go-in there to seeeee . . .*"

Joshua had not seen one church among all the saloons and gambling houses in Garson. Yet he was certain he heard church music—women's voices!

"Yes! We'll gather at the Riv-er. . . ."

"No-body else could love her, not half as much as meeeee . . ."

Joshua sat up, careful not to bump the little miner from Cornwall who slept beside him.

The little man stirred. "Seems the Crusaders are at it again."

Josh was glad someone else was awake. "The music—," he began.

"Aye, they'll stop soon enough. There's a group of 'em. They've taken the pledge."

"The *pledge*? You mean there's a Women's Christian Temperance Union in Garson?"

"Aye," replied the weary voice. "They'd close down every saloon and bawdy house in town if they had their way. Every night a differ-ent shift of 'em sings until Fancy Dan's closes down. His place is the only saloon with a piano." He yawned. "You'll get used to it."

Joshua was smiling at the image: members of the temperance union singing hymns in the dark outside the town's biggest saloon. He was himself a man of temperance where whiskey was concerned, although he had never made an attempt to awaken the conscience of a drinking man. And as for religion, well, when he'd left Illinois and struck out for the West, he'd left all of his background behind.

"Are there miners singing with them?" he asked, hearing a male voice in harmony.

"Some. And she's *even* managed to save the souls of a few of the Calico Queens!"

"*She?* She who?"

Now the Cornishman chuckled. "You haven't met her, I see. Do your utmost *not* to meet her, Mister Roberts." He rolled over. "Aye. She's tough as iron! Spotted me right away for the sinner I am." The voice became sleepy and faded into a soft snore.

Now the music shifted to "The Battle Hymn of the Republic" as Joshua envisioned the town battle-ax leading the chorus. He would do his utmost to avoid her—*whoever* she was! Like Pick commented, his past was his business. Between him and God, he'd said. And frankly, Joshua wasn't sure that God wanted anything to do with him now . . . not after what he'd done.

But Pickax had not warned him about the battle-ax. No doubt

such goings-on were one reason the old prospector chose to live fourteen miles out of town!

Joshua finally fell asleep, an amused smile on his lips, as the members of the Garson Women's Christian Temperance Union continued their musical showdown late into the night.

✳ ✳ ✳

Fancy Dan's Saloon and Faro Parlor was operated by Fancy Dan McGinty. So called because of his flashy manner of dress, it was an image he not only enjoyed but fostered.

McGinty was a little over middle height and stockily built. Despite his last name, his olive skin and wavy black hair owed more to his mother's Mediterranean forebears than to his Irish father.

Early in his life, McGinty had discovered that living by his wits was preferable to using his muscles, and it was easier to part others from their hard-earned money than to earn his own.

He lived by two mottos: "You can never have too much wealth or power" and "No one should be allowed to stand in your way of increasing either."

McGinty had amassed a significant amount of capital by fleecing the miners of Virginia City, Nevada, with a crooked faro game. When he heard of the silver strike in Garson, he decided the time was ripe to invest on the ground floor of a new opportunity. This decision to relocate was motivated in part by a disgruntled group of miners who had threatened to stretch McGinty's neck. He concluded that a change of method as well as venue was required.

Since arriving in Garson, McGinty had risen in both wealth and popular opinion. His saloon, if modest by the standards of a more civilized part of the world, was opulent for Garson: a real wooden building, plank floors kept swept, and a genuine mahogany bar polished to a dull sheen. Behind the bar were signs advising miners to enjoy the free lunch and admonishing them to write home. Paper and ink were supplied gratis.

McGinty's employees were the best. He tolerated no obvious cheating, relying instead on paid shills who encouraged both immoderate drinking and excessive betting. He also maintained a group of strong-arm types who not only kept order but saw to it that the house got its proper share of the profits. No one working for Dan McGinty went independent and stayed healthy in Garson.

But for all his success, McGinty was not content. He was steadily increasing his fortune, but what was there to spend it on five hundred miles from nowhere? He dreamed of returning to his hometown of San Francisco in regal style—building a mansion on fashionable Russian Hill and mingling with the Hopkins and the Crockers. This dream could not be realized, however, without his becoming *really* rich, even fabulously wealthy. He calculated that owning a top-producing silver mine would do it.

Fate certainly seemed to be smiling on Dan McGinty. In his clandestine recruiting efforts among the miners, he had not hired all of them away to become shills, cardsharps, and bouncers. Some he conveniently left in place as informants and for other purposes as the need arose.

None of these confederates was more valuable to him than Beldad, the graveyard-shift foreman at the Silver Rim. A small, bitter man with a much-inflated opinion of himself, Beldad believed that he should have been made the general foreman of the Rim, and when he was passed over for this position, he made his displeasure known around Garson.

A few dollars and the promise of elevation to his rightful place had more than won Beldad to McGinty's side. Beldad was angry at the whole world. Mine Superintendent Morris became his convenient target, and he eagerly encouraged griping among the miners. McGinty's grand strategy called for the work in the Silver Rim to be slowed to a virtual standstill in every way possible. Fancy Dan reasoned that when Morris was shown to be a failure and the Rim near insolvency, the rest of the board of directors of the Golden Bear Mining Company would be pleased to unload the whole boondoggle for a very modest price.

All had been going according to plan until Beldad brought some unexpected news to Fancy Dan. Tonight Beldad did not enter the front of Fancy Dan's Saloon to drink and gamble with the rest because two dozen Temperance members were singing on the sidewalk outside the saloon. Instead he climbed the back stairs leading to the second floor.

Two raps in quick succession, followed by two more, and the door was opened by McGinty himself. "What is it, Beldad? I've got Dr. Racine, Freeman, and the new Wells Fargo agent coming over in about twenty minutes for a little card party. Make it quick."

"Boss, you won't be thinking about cards when you hear what I've got to tell. It's bigger 'n anything."

"All right, spill it. What's this great news that can't keep?"

"You know that new gallery we're opening in the mine on level five?"

"Yes, what of it?"

"After we shot the south face last night, I was the first one back in there. Boss, we've hit it—I mean, really hit it! There's a silver vein there as wide as this room and so rich it almost glows!"

"Are you certain? Morris was positive the best chance was on three—you told me so yourself!"

"I know, I know, but Morris is wrong. Five is smack-spraddle of the sweetest ledge you ever saw, perfectly cased in clay and running down into the mountain. Morris could stay on three the rest of his life and never lay eyes on this."

"Have you tested a sample yet? I mean, you're not getting the 'fever,' are you?"

"Boss, listen. This ledge—blue cables, more like! I chipped out a piece for the fire assay—and mind you, I was in a panic to get out before the men came in to see what was keeping me, so I didn't pick and choose. Boss, that bit assayed out at two thousand dollars per ton!"

"Two thousand per ton! Are you positive?"

"Absolutely certain."

McGinty grabbed the smaller man's shoulders and held him, frowning in deep thought. When at last he spoke he looked squarely into Beldad's eyes. "Not a word of this to anybody, or I swear I'll give you to the vultures piece by piece myself."

"No, no. Not a word."

"Also, this changes things. We've got to work faster. We can't take a chance on Morris discovering the ledge. If he does, Golden Bear'll never sell out, and he'd have all the financing to develop a mill right here. We've got to speed our plans up. Do what you can to delay any further work on five while I figure out what's to be done. We've got to keep Morris so busy with everything else that he won't even have time to think about mining. Nothing must interfere now. Nothing!"

Beldad exited McGinty's office by way of the back stair. He could still hear the strains of "In the Cross of Christ I Glory" competing with the raucous version of "Sweet Betsy from Pike."

A short looping walk in the darkness brought him back onto the road at an angle that suggested he was coming directly from his cabin. He was still early for the change of shift, and he saw no one on the way to the Silver Rim.

Beldad acknowledged the hoist operator with a curt "Going down to three." As the wooden floor of the lift began to drop down into the blackness of the shaft, he flicked the butt of a cigarette into a mound of sand. He watched overhead as the gallows frame, which supported the great block through which the cables ran, was briefly silhouetted against the stars. As the lift dropped farther, it disappeared from his view.

Stepping off when the platform halted on the third level of the mine, Beldad glanced around. As he expected, no one was yet approaching the lift to return to the surface. He had arrived unseen.

He could hear the clang of the double jack and drill and the singsong cadence of the miner's picks working the face of the ore on level three.

The rumble of an approaching ore car was just becoming audible as Beldad turned sharply to his right. Near the lift was an unused winze—a vertical shaft that connected different levels of the mine by ladder.

Elsewhere, the winzes were in use, but this one was so near the hoist that it seldom had traffic. Beldad was able to descend by its wooden rungs all the way down to the deepest part of the Silver Rim.

Pausing at the opening of a connected passage, Beldad listened for any human noise to accompany the clank of the pump. When he judged the way to be clear, he stepped out into a chamber where a fit-fully flickering lantern marked the location of the pump laboring to remove water from level five.

Nearby, on wooden skids, sat a replacement pump, ready in the event that the first failed in some way.

Glancing around once more, Beldad took a wrench from one pocket of his long coat. He quickly removed the cover from the pump. Then, from another pocket, he retrieved a sack of iron filings. He poured these into the mechanism and replaced the cover.

By the time Beldad repeated this process on the spare pump, the first was already making strained, complaining noises.

CHAPTER 4

At 6:30 the next morning, Josh was waiting outside the foreman's shack near the entrance to shaft number one of the Silver Rim Mine. The foreman, Dub Taylor, was just exiting from an ore car that he had ridden to the top of the shaft. He was addressing a short, stocky, bald-headed man who had come up with him.

"How do you explain that pump breaking down so fast, Win?"

"It was no breakdown, sir. It was wrongly installed, I'm thinkin'."

"Wrongly installed? But how can that be?"

"Well, sir, I canna rightly say."

"All right, then, I'll have a word with Beldad, and I'll see that Parker hears about it. He'll have to stop the work on three until we get gallery five cleared; otherwise we'll lose it."

He turned to see Joshua waiting, then pulled a Rockford dollar watch from his pocket and examined the time. "Come early your first day, eh? I like that. Mister Morris sent word to expect you, Roberts. I'm Dub Taylor."

"Pleased to meet you, Mister Taylor. It sounds like you're having some trouble."

"That we are, indeed. What do you know about mining, son?"

At Josh's shrug Taylor went on. "Well, no reason why you should, blacksmithing being a lot the same for farming or mining, I guess. Anyway, these mines are deep—" he waved his hand toward shaft number one—"and the deeper we go, the more we have to fight to stay ahead of the water. Mister Morris thinks the vein we're following on three is fixing to widen out into something worthwhile. But now I've got to jerk my crews off of three till we get five pumped dry and the damage repaired."

Taylor shook his head, then smiled briefly at Joshua. "Anyway, it's no concern of yours. Come on with me to the smithy."

Taylor led Josh up the hill a short distance behind the foreman's shack. Josh identified the smithy by the heaps of iron lying around and the glimpse of a forge through the half-open door.

Dub nudged a pile of drill bits with his foot, then said in a disgusted tone, "I don't know how much Mister Morris may have told you about the man you're replacing."

"Well, he said he was drunk at work," Josh replied quietly.

"Drunk at work is right! And not the first time, either. But this time it wasn't a bolt cut too short or a shoe not fit properly. It was hundreds of dollars of drill bits just brought in to have the edges put back on them. Now look at them. Every one bent out of true and absolutely useless!"

Josh nodded and leaned over to study the obviously curved metal spikes. "I can fix these."

"If you can, it'll be a miracle. We need those bits sharpened to replace the ones we're using now; otherwise it brings everything to a stop to re-edge the one set. If we sent for more, it'd take two weeks for them to get here, and it's an expense we can't afford right now."

"Just let me get to it," Josh said.

Dub shrugged doubtfully but shook his hand and turned to go. "No harm in trying. If you need anything, see Parker," he called over his shoulder. "He's the day-shift foreman. I'll send him over to meet you."

Josh inspected the smithy with a critical eye. The slag had not been cleaned from the forge any time recently, and the floor appeared never to have been swept. Since straightening the drill bits would require a precisely controlled fire, Josh decided to attend to the forge first. He cleared it out completely, then restacked it in a careful pyramid shape of coke built over charcoal and kindling.

A shot of coal oil, and the forge was blazing cheerfully. While Josh waited for the blaze to subside before working the bellows, he located a broom and swept out the place. Next he rounded up a variety of hammers and tongs and cleared a workbench of debris. As he was filling the tempering keg, a tall, red-haired man walked up.

"I'm Parker," he announced. "Best luck with those bits, Roberts. I hear there's a peck of trouble on five, so I've got to go. I'll see you at the end of the shift." With no more conversation than that, he was gone.

Joshua worked steadily all morning. His pace was unhurried as he gave attention to each bit in turn, judging with his practiced eye when each was the exact shade of cherry red to be re-formed. His hammer made a rhythmic sound as it bounced from steel rod to anvil in a precise cadence.

As he completed the straightening of each bit, he returned it to the forge and heated the cutting tip to the white heat required to form the edge for splitting the silver ledge a hundred feet below where he stood.

The morning was heating up after the cool of the desert night. As each rod was finished, Joshua allowed himself a moment to stand in the shade of the doorway and catch a hint of breeze. From where he stood he could gaze across the valley floor west of the mining camp. Sometimes it would be obscured by dust devils and made hazy by waves of heat. At other times it cleared for a second or two—long enough for him to see the bright white reflection of an ancient, dry lake bed.

Most often his eyes did not linger on the desert floor but would be drawn upward to the gray mass of the Sierras beyond. Though they were far enough away to be indistinct, an occasional peak thrust up into the morning light radiated a glistening shine off its snow-covered summit. In his mind's eye, Joshua could see an eagle turning lazy circles over those peaks, gazing down at majestic pines and redwoods reaching heavenward from rocky slopes.

Josh shook his head and sighed, then returned to his forge. By noon he had completely reshaped and sharpened all the drill bits and turned his attention to other projects he found lying about in obvious neglect. He repaired several buckets and welded the broken stem of a windlass handle. He was debating whether to repair a broken wagon spring or straighten a pick head when a shadow fell across the workbench. Someone was standing in the doorway behind him.

Shading his eyes against the gleam of the westering sun, Josh walked toward the door to see what was wanted. A blast of whiskey-laden breath almost knocked him back a pace.

"What you doin' theah?" demanded a slurred and angry voice.

"I'm the blacksmith," replied Joshua. "What can I do for you?"

"The devil you say! I'm the blacksmith heah—Big John Daniels. Now get outta my way," the man demanded, roughly shouldering his way in.

Josh had moved to the side as Daniels entered. Now that Josh could see the man better, he saw that Daniels was as black as night. He was also enormous—six feet six, three hundred pounds. The man's shiny, bald head seemed his only part not able to grow with complete success.

"Daniels, Mister Morris told me you were let go. I'm the new smith here," said Josh simply.

"Says who?" Daniels sneered. "You gonna put me out, you little pip-squeak? Ain't nobody fired Big John. I'll go when I've a mind to an' not sooner. Now you better skedaddle, or I'll crack yo' head like an egg!"

"Listen here, Daniels, you've not been doing your job around here, and being drunk like you are now almost cost this—"

Joshua never finished the sentence, for with a roar that was probably heard in Mojave, Daniels grabbed a hammer from the workbench and charged at Josh.

Josh ducked under the blow and a good thing too, because the descending hammer and the force behind it knocked a hole completely through the west wall of the smithy.

Josh put the forge between himself and Big John as the giant lumbered around in a clumsy circle. "Stand still an' fight, you little rat," Daniels bellowed, "or I might just wreck this place so's *nobody* works here." At this he seized an iron bar and, with a roundhouse sweep, took out the bellows chain, dropping it crashing to the floor.

"That's enough!" shouted Joshua, and he leaped to catch the bar at the end of its swing, pinning it against the ground.

Big John struggled for a few seconds, attempting to free the bar from Josh's grasp. He was obviously startled at Josh's strength and perhaps even more surprised that Josh stood up to him.

When his fuddled brain finally understood that he could not wrestle the bar away from Josh, he dropped the hold he had on it with his right hand and drew his fist back for a swing aimed at the back of Josh's head.

This was exactly what Josh had expected, and he was ready for it. Even before the blow began, Josh gave a sudden shove on the bar directly toward Daniels.

The move caught Daniels off guard. Pulling on the bar with his left hand, he was not prepared to stop its plunge into his midsection. His breath exploded with a convulsive burst, and he began panting in short gasps.

Despite his heaving, he put his head down and charged Josh. The reach of his arms and the force of his rush propelled Joshua back into the opposite wall. With a crash and a clatter that sounded as if the mountains were falling, tongs and hammers and blanks of iron for horseshoes flew from their shelves.

Big John's eyes lit up with unholy glee, and he raised both fists over his head, ready to smash them down on Joshua.

Josh threw a hard right that caught Daniels on the jaw and rocked his head back. A left drove into the big man's rib cage just above his massive stomach, and Daniels staggered.

He lunged forward again, as if intending to catch Josh's neck in the crook of his arm. But Josh flung both arms up, threw off Big John's grasp with an upward motion, and in the same move grabbed the giant's head behind both ears.

Josh threw himself back violently, at the same time yanking Daniels' head downward with all his might and raising his right knee to meet it.

A sickening crunch resulted, like the noise of a rotten tree when it falls. Daniels' nose and mouth burst like a watermelon dropped from a wagon bed, and he slumped to the floor.

Josh backed up, breathing heavily, and took stock of his injuries.

His shoulders and the back of his head felt like they were on fire from being jammed against the wall, but otherwise he was unhurt.

He picked up a ball-peen hammer and moved cautiously over toward Daniels. As he approached, Daniels moaned and stirred slightly, and Josh raised the hammer. Then a hissing bubbling escaped the fallen giant as he exhaled a lengthy sigh from his ruined mouth and nose. Josh shuddered at the thought of further violence and threw the hammer to the floor.

A noise at the doorway made him glance in that direction. There stood not only Parker, the day foreman, but Mister Morris and a crowd of miners.

"Are you all right, Roberts?" asked Morris.

"Man, it looks like an earthquake hit here," commented Parker. "How did you keep from being slaughtered?"

"Got lucky, I guess."

"Lucky, nothing!" said Parker. "Nobody has ever bested Big John in a fight, drunk or sober. Half the miners off shift came running to tell me Big John was coming with blood in his eye to wreck the place. The other half are laying odds on how many pieces you'd be found in!"

"Not *all* the others—several came to warn *me* that Daniels was on his way up here," commented Morris. "I came as fast as I could to see if we could subdue him, but here you've done it all by yourself!"

"Maybe God Almighty is just looking out for me," Josh said. He was uncomfortable with the obvious respect on the faces peering at him.

"That may be, my boy; that may be, but you were brave enough to stay and look out for mining-company property when a lesser— and more sensible man, perhaps—would have run away. I want you to reconsider working as a guard for me. I'll make it thirty dollars a week."

"No, thank you, Mister Morris. As I said before, I'm a smith, not a guard or a lawman."

"Well, now," began Parker, "what are we to do with Daniels there? I mean, we don't want him to be loose when he wakes up."

Morris stared at the hulk on the floor. "Say, that's right. We could . . . maybe in the . . . perhaps the basement of . . ." He stopped in consternation. "Where is there a place strong enough to hold him? We don't have a jail in this town, and if we weighted him down with enough iron to hold him, we couldn't move him ourselves. Besides, he'd tear down any place we confined him, weighted down or not.

"All right, Parker," he continued, "detail off some men to guard him." He stopped as Parker and the others who were crowded into the doorway began backing up. "Well, what is it? Are you all afraid of him? Come, come, where's your courage? Can't you put some guns on him? He wouldn't charge a hail of bullets, surely."

"It ain't just that, Mister Morris," Parker said. "Sooner or later he'll have to be let go, and he'll remember every mother's son who guarded him. Big John ain't much on thinking, but ain't nobody can hold a candle to him for getting some of his own back!"

Morris looked around the circle. "Do all of you feel that way?"

A vigorous nodding was his reply.

Morris turned to Josh, who was gazing speculatively around the smithy. "And what about you, Roberts? Do you have any ideas?"

"Have you got a length of ore-car track to spare?" Josh asked.

Morris glanced at Parker, who replied, "Sure, we've got a whole stack the other side of shaft number three. So what?"

Josh addressed Morris again. "And that level space that's cleared down there—" he motioned toward a vacant patch of ground behind the foreman's shack, out of sight of the road from the mine to town—"the one with the pit in the middle. Is that to be used for anything?"

"No," Morris answered. "It was an exploration shaft, only five or six feet deep. The clearing is to be the site of a new mine office, just as soon as we bring in the big vein, right, men?"

A chorus of halfhearted affirmatives responded, but Morris ignored the lack of enthusiasm. "What have you got in mind, son?"

"I think I'd better show you. Mister Parker, how long is one of those rails?"

"Twenty feet."

"That will work just fine. Could you get some men to bring a rail to that cleared space?"

Parker looked puzzled and glanced at Morris for approval. When

Morris nodded, Parker addressed the group of miners. "Jones, take nine men with you and bring back that rail, double-quick now. All right, Roberts, what next?"

Josh selected a piece of metal rod about four feet in length and handed it to Parker. "Have someone bolt this through the tie flange of that T-rail."

The men glanced at each other dubiously.

"All right," he went on, "help me drag him down to the clearing."

There was a general movement backward, which Morris attempted to stop with threats of firing.

But Josh was even more convincing. "You don't want him to be loose when he comes to, do you?"

There was a rush forward, and soon ten men were dragging Daniels down the short slope to where the rail rested with the cross-bar already bolted in place.

When the pit had been filled in with rocks and leveled under Josh's direction, the rail was standing upright in the center. Josh was about to ask the men to drag Daniels' still-unconscious bulk to the rail. But the miners had already guessed his intent, and in a flash Big John was seated on the ground with his legs straddling the rail and his battered face leaning up against it.

It took no time to fashion manacles and leg-irons from chains, hammering the bolts so that the chains could not be released without being cut free.

When the last stroke was completed, Josh stood and addressed Morris. "There's your jail, Mister Morris. Even Daniels can't pull that rail free of two tons of rock, and he can't climb fourteen feet of rail trailing those chains, either."

"Brilliant, my boy, brilliant!" Morris spouted jubilantly.

Parker spoke up. "There's just one thing, Mister Morris."

"What's that?" said Morris, who was beaming in satisfaction.

"Well, sir, I expect you'll be sending for the deputy sheriff to take charge of Big John, and seeing as how it'll take three or four days to get him here, who's to care for Daniels meantime?"

"I thought you or your—"

"No, sir, I don't think so. I mean, we didn't sign on as no guards, and anyway, we got some mining to do. Ain't that right, men?"

This time the chorus of assent was loud and enthusiastic. Clearly no one wanted to be remembered by Big John as having been the cause of his confinement.

Joshua sighed and shook his head ruefully. "I guess it's up to me, Mister Morris. After all, it was my idea, and here he is, right in my front yard, so to speak. I'll see to him."

A relieved murmur went through the crowd.

Morris grasped Josh's hand eagerly. "Well done, my boy, well done! Now listen, you men, this is the kind of spirit that will make this mine prosper and all our livelihoods will be secured. Roberts, I'm upping your pay as blacksmith to the thirty-dollar-a-week figure anyway. And—" he groped in his pocket and displayed a gold double eagle—"here's a twenty-dollar bonus!"

✳ ✳ ✳

Later that evening, Josh went back to the mine property with a jug of water and a plate of beans. He told no one what his plans were and spoke to no one as he went. Over his shoulder he carried a Navajo blanket.

The sun was setting as he stopped by the foreman's shack. No one was inside, but he borrowed a lantern anyway, and when he had it burning cheerfully he stepped outside and went around the back.

Big John was still leaning against the T-rail, but a stirring let Josh know he was awake.

Josh stepped to the edge of the filled-in pit. "I've brought you some supper and a blanket."

Through bruised and swollen lips, a garbled voice replied, "What makes you think I want anythin' from you? All I want right now is ta git my hands 'round yo' neck an' pop yo' head off yo' body like a cork outta a bottle."

"I figured you'd be feeling that way about now," Joshua replied evenly. "But even so, I said I'd be responsible for seeing to you, so here's food and bedding. What you do with them is up to you."

He set the plate, bottle, and blanket down within reach of Daniels but on the opposite side of the rail. Joshua then backed up slowly, taking the lantern with him. Once out of the small circle that made up Big John's cell, he turned to go.

"Hey!" shouted Daniels after him. "Ain'tcha gonna leave that lantern here?"

"What for?" asked Josh. "You aren't going to be walking anywhere, and you said you didn't want anything from me, remember? Anyhow, it's company property, and I've got to return it."

"How long you gonna leave me like this? I mean, how about turnin' me loose?" Daniels whined.

"No, I can't do that. You put yourself in this fix, and I can't get you out of it. As to how long—well, I think they've sent for some judge or other."

"A judge? That could take almost a week! Say, don't cha know they's rattlesnakes and scorpions out here at night? What'm I s'posed to do about those?"

"Well, now, I'll tell you. If it was me, I'd wrap up good and tight in that blanket, and I'd lay real still all night and roll over real carefully come morning."

"*What?* Why, you—I'll break ev'ry bone in yo' sorry carcass. I'll string yo' intestines up like sausages an' use yo' guts for garters. I'll—"

But Big John was shouting imprecations at empty space. Josh had taken the lantern and departed.

✴CHAPTER 5✴

The next morning Josh carried a plateful of biscuits and sorghum and a jug of buttermilk with him to work.

He found Dub in the foreman's shack. Dub eyed the food and shook his head with a wry smile. "I don't envy you, even if I am sorry I missed seeing what happened yesterday. How'd you get stuck feeding that wild bull? Didn't anybody tell you he never forgets and never forgives?"

Josh grinned. "Back home my daddy taught me to break horses by keeping them tied short and giving them fodder and drink by my own hand. That method never failed to bring around the most cantankerous, rough stock you ever saw, so I thought maybe it'd work on the same kind of human stock."

"You'll pardon me if I don't go with you to watch," said Dub. "I don't even want to be associated with you in Big John's mind. Just leave me an address of your next of kin so I can deliver your remains."

Josh stepped around the building, unsure of the reception he'd receive but not wanting to voice any of his own doubts.

Big John was standing upright, the blanket around his massive shoulders barely reaching around him against the morning chill. The plate from the night before was clean, the empty bottle on top of it.

"Good morning," greeted Josh. "I won't ask if you slept well, but I don't see any dead rattlesnakes laying around, so you must not have had to wrestle any of them. Are you hungry?"

Big John started to snarl a reply, but a long look from Josh seemed to get his attention. In a less belligerent tone he said, "Man, I can eat six times a day and still be hungry. Can I have the plate of biscuits, or are you fixin' to torment me?"

"No, no, I was just testing to see what kind of mood you were in. Here you go." Josh stepped directly up to Daniels and extended the breakfast.

Big John looked down at the food, then at Josh standing less than three feet away, then at his shackled hands. He shrugged and reached for the plate.

"You're welcome," said Josh meaningfully.

"Right—yeah, thanks," Big John mumbled.

"Nothing to it," said Josh. "I came early today so I could rig a little tarp for you before I go to smithing. I figure today's gonna be a scorcher."

❊ ❊ ❊

369

"I can't understand how that second pump could have broken down so quickly." Morris was speaking to the men assembled in his office.

Dub Taylor squirmed uneasily in his chair and looked around at the others to see if anyone else would offer an opinion. When none did, he cleared his throat roughly and began. "It sanded up real bad, I guess, and when it froze up, nobody caught it in time. The shaft is bent all to thunder. Even Josh Roberts says he can't straighten it to where it'll run true."

"How did it happen that no one was watching more closely?"

Again there was some shuffling of feet and spitting of tobacco juice into spittoons before Taylor continued. "Near as we can figure, it happened on the change of shift. Beldad's crew was coming off, and Parker's hadn't moved in yet. Beldad here thought I was sending someone down to watch it, and I thought he had detailed off somebody to stay with it."

Taylor looked miserable, Beldad defiant, and Parker and the other foreman, Sexton, concerned.

"Well, this really tears it. I don't have to tell you men how far off the pace we are now. The only thing to do is abandon five for the time being. It'll probably take two weeks to replace that pump. We'll press ahead on three and hope we get a break soon."

Parker finally spoke up. "Are you gonna keep us at full crews, Mister Morris? And if so, what'll you want the boys to be doing?"

Morris looked unhappy and stared at his desk blotter before replying. "There's no way we can absorb the expense of keeping a full roster now. Only a few at a time can work on three. The others will be laid off."

There was a low murmur at this news, but no one spoke.

"Emphasize to the men that the situation is only temporary and will be corrected as soon as five is workable again or as soon as we make the breakthrough on three."

Sexton, the evening tower foreman, said, "How'll we pick who goes and who stays? Can I keep my best men?"

Morris' reply was firm. "No. I feel an obligation to this town and those who are raising families here. We'll keep the married men and let the singles go. A man without dependents can move more easily to another job—or town, for that matter. I don't want to impose that on wives and children if I can help it—"

"The men won't like that, Mister Morris," Beldad interrupted. "It isn't fair unless it's by experience or time to the Rim. We're liable to have more trouble."

"Trouble? What sort of trouble?"

"Well, I can't say exactly, but we don't need any kind of problem with the men right now, do we?"

"I'm sorry, Mister Beldad, but my mind's made up. I *will* support families first. We'll just have to bring the rest back as soon as we can."

✳ ✳ ✳

Four nails dangled from Joshua's lips as he hefted the rear hoof of Pick's little pack mule.

"'Bout done?" Pick asked as he leaned against the doorjamb of the blacksmith shop and gazed down at the forlorn figure of Big John.

"Hmm-mm. You in a hurry to get somewhere?" Josh muttered through the nails.

"Yup." Pick scratched his beard thoughtfully. "I aim t' be on the

other side of the Sierras when you get around t' unchainin' Big John."
He grinned broadly, showing his nearly toothless gums, and turned
to pat the mule on her rump. "Ain't that right, darlin'? We saved this
here fool so's he could catch hisself a grizzly an' get hisself killed
proper!"

Joshua tapped in another nail and crimped the sharp point,
bending it down on the outside of the hoof wall. Every nail entered
the hoof at the proper angle—deep enough to hold the shoe securely
but not deep enough to nick the tender quick. It was a good job.
Joshua picked up the rasp and carefully filed the rough edges of the
hoof until the iron shoe blended perfectly with it. He deliberately
ignored Pick's gibe.

The old prospector leaned against his mule and tried again. "I
ain't but halfway jokin', boy. I reckon the minute you turn Big John
loose an' turn your back, he's gonna get hisself another gallon of ol'
tangle-leg an' drop an anvil on your head when you ain't lookin'."

"Then he'll find himself hugging another iron rail when he
comes to, won't he?" Joshua let go of the mule's stout leg and
straightened slowly.

"He can be a mean'un."

"When he's drunk."

"When he's sober, too." Pick narrowed his eyes in warning. "I
reckon he's sittin' down there right now, listenin' t' you clangin'
around here in his territory, an' he's figgerin' just what it'll take to
make you git!"

Josh retrieved his tools and shrugged as the mule stretched her
neck and bared her teeth, braying loudly.

"That's right, darlin'!" Pick nodded. "You tell 'im! He's a fool if
he—"

The mule's bray was answered by a whinny of a horse from the
road below the shop.

Pick peered out of the building and in an instant forgot what he
wanted to say. "What in tarnation!" he exclaimed, stalking out of the
building and raising his hand to shield his eyes against the sun.

Josh wiped his hands on his farrier chaps and followed.

Behind them the mule brayed again and was answered by a dappled

371

gray mare pulling a buggy. An ancient Chinaman, complete with pigtail and black silk cap, was driving the buggy. In the seat behind him sat a young, dark-haired woman in her early twenties. Even from this distance, Joshua could see that she was lovely. *Elegant* was a better word. She wore a blue dress and carried a parasol to shield her fair skin against the sun. She sat slightly forward in her seat, and her head was tilted upward, as if searching the sky for something. Her eyes were hidden by round, smoked glasses. To Joshua she was the very picture of the fancy ladies who rode in their carriages through the city park back home. The Chinaman driver and the bleak surroundings of the Silver Rim did not do her justice.

"Who is she?" he asked as the muttering of Pick broke into a full-scale tirade.

"Why, that good-for-nothin' . . . that old laundry-totin' prune! I told him not t' bring her up here! Her pa is gonna hang him up by that pigtail of his!"

Josh laughed involuntarily at the image spun by Pick. It would be easy enough to hoist the tiny Chinese driver by his long gray braid. The man was not more than five feet tall and probably weighed less than a hundred pounds.

As the horse trotted smartly up the road, Josh took Pick by the arm and held him back. "Well, who are they, for goodness' sake?"

"The one drivin' the rig—the little shriveled-up one with the droopy whiskers and the funny silk shirt—his name is Ling Duc Chow. Lean Duck, we call him around here. He's Chinnee. . . ."

"I guessed that much." Joshua's eyes were riveted on the young woman.

"Says he's the oldest human on earth! An' by gum, he just 'bout makes a feller believe it! He looks at you with them black eyes an' slaps your hand like you was a kid when all you was doin' was tryin' t' taste one of his biscuits! Why, he told Mister Morris I was stealin'!" Pick looked like a rooster scratching the ground before a fight. "An' now look at him, bringin' Miss Callie right up here when I told Mister Morris that she ought not come!"

"Pick!" Josh spun him around in frustration. "You're not making sense!"

"Oh yes I am! He might have been cookin' for Mister Morris a hunnert years longer than I been prospectin', but this time he's gone too far!"

"Pick!"

"Bringin' Miss Callie here to feed the grizzly bear! She told me she was gonna bring supper, an' I told her—"

"Who is she?"

"Are you blind, boy?" Pick gestured angrily as the buggy pulled to a stop near Big John's makeshift prison. "That is Miss Callie Morris!"

"The wife of Mister—"

"*Miss!* Are you deaf? His *daughter*. Head of the Temperance Union, Lord help us all! She's got no business comin' here. It ain't no act of mercy, neither. Pure foolishness! That Lean Duck oughta be . . ." Pick's words degenerated into an unintelligible mumble as the Chinaman tied off the reins and hurried to take the outstretched hand of the young woman. Her chin was still slightly upward, and she seemed to grope for the little man's hand.

"It ain't proper, I told her!" Pick continued. "It ain't right for a blind girl to be feedin' a black man like that!"

Blind!

Ling Duc Chow helped the lady from the buggy. She was slender and well proportioned and several inches taller than he. As the driver retrieved a large basket from the buggy, she waited with her hand poised expectantly. She smiled as her guide took her arm and led her over the uneven ground toward the iron rail.

Ignoring the prating of Pickax, Joshua found himself moving swiftly down the hill toward the rail and Big John. Pickax scurried indignantly after him. Two dozen miners, just off their shift, gathered a few feet beyond the perimeter of the tarp and out of sight of Big John. Their laughter floated up.

"Miss Callie!" called a dirty-faced miner. "What do you want to waste all that good food on Big John Daniels for?"

"'Specially since he seems to want to bust up your daddy's black-smith shop so bad?" said another voice.

She laughed upward at the sky. "Is that Mister Crawford there?"

"Uh . . ."

Josh noticed that the man slunk back into the crowd, as if he'd rather not be identified in front of Big John.

"Well, if you remember your Bible," Miss Callie continued, "you'll recall that we are told by our Lord to feed the hungry!" She raised her voice a bit over the laughter of the spectators. "Are you hungry, Mister Daniels?"

More laughter.

Big John Daniels squirmed at the rail. A hulk that enormous was in need of vast amounts of food. Certainly a few biscuits were not enough. He lowered his chin. "Yes, ma'am. Very hungry."

A young miner scowled. "Why don't you throw us some of that, 'stead of wastin' it on a drunken black man?"

Someone nudged him when the young woman stopped in her tracks and snapped her head in the direction of the comment. "God has seen to it that you are all black to me," she replied, anger in her voice.

Ling Duc Chow looked first at her, then at the men, and finally at Big John.

The laughter stopped abruptly. Seconds ticked past.

"Now go home to your own suppers," Callie Morris said.

Joshua watched the standoff with admiration. Here was a display of the iron-toughness the Cornish miner had warned Joshua about.

One by one the men backed up a step, tipped their hats to the sightless daughter of their boss, and left. Only Joshua and Pick silently remained at a distance. Joshua kept his fingers securely clamped around the old prospector's forearm, warning him not to interfere.

Big John sat with his back to Joshua and Pick. Callie and Ling Chow faced him. The withered little Chinaman studied Joshua, but he did not mention their presence to the young woman who now took one step closer to the iron rail.

"Are they gone?" she asked quietly.

Ling Chow met Joshua's gaze again. "Yes. They are gone."

"Good," she answered. "We aren't here for a show. Where is it?" She extended her hand, and Ling Chow guided it to the rail. She touched it gingerly and winced. "Horrible. Horrible to be put on display like this."

Joshua recoiled. What else could he have done with Big John?

"But you deserve it, Mister Daniels," Callie continued.

"Yes'm."

"You have brought yourself to this shame."

"Yes'm."

"You were a free man, and you brought yourself back into slavery to the bottle. That's worse than being chained to this post."

"Yes'm."

"Whiskey. Who-Hit-John, they call it. Now look at you, John Daniels! Somebody hit you. Somebody bigger than you . . ."

Josh smiled slightly. Actually, Big John was a lot bigger than he.

"And I'll tell you who it was that hit you," Callie finished. "It was the *Lord*! Brought you right here in the dust. They call your whiskey old tangle-legs. Look at you. Your legs all tangled around this iron rail. And you deserve everything you got because you gave up your freedom. Gave up a fine job. You did not drink like this when you shod the horses of General Grant. And now look at you!" She raised her chin. "I don't have to see you. I can *smell* you—smell the stale whiskey. You should be ashamed!"

The shiny bald head of the prisoner lowered. "That I am, Miss Callie." His small voice sounded genuinely penitent.

Pickax jerked his head back in unbelief at the words. He stared in wonder at the bald dome and scowled when Ling Chow shrugged at him.

"I was told not to come to visit you—you, who cared well for my father's horses for so many years—but I had to see for myself. Yes, I said *see*. My soul can see quite clearly, you know, Mister Daniels. And the Lord has told us to visit those who are in prison. He is not speaking always of walls and bars or iron rails in the ground. Sin is the prison you have chosen for yourself." The words were direct, but her tone was compassionate.

The big man sagged in misery against the rail. "Yes, Miss Callie. Lord help me!"

"Ling Chow will feed you now," she said in a matter-of-fact voice.

Then she turned to the Chinese cook. "Big John has some praying to do, Ling Chow. I shall wait in the buggy while you pray with him. Some things are not for a lady to meddle in." She turned slightly. "Read the Scriptures with him, man-to-man, when he has eaten."

Big John was weeping in earnest now. Ling Chow escorted Callie back to the buggy and helped her in. With that, the pint-sized Chinaman retrieved a small wooden stool from the buggy and placed it beside the shackled giant. He removed a well-worn Bible from the food basket, handed a plate to Big John, and filled it with food. Before he could take his first bite, Ling Chow placed a restraining hand on his arm. "Thankee God for food," he suggested, and Big John meekly bowed his head. "All good things come from Your hand. We thankee You."

With that Ling Chow opened the Bible to the sixth chapter of the book of Romans and began to read.

Big John continued to nod and clank his shackles as he cried, "Amen! Yes, Lord!" between bites.

Joshua and Pickax exchanged wondering looks as they retreated back to the safety of the blacksmith shop to watch the strange spectacle out of earshot. They were even more amazed to see Big John stop eating and bury his face in his hands.

✾ ✾ ✾

Pickax's amazement mellowed into a philosophical amusement after a few minutes' observation. "Yep, my ol' ma used t' say that when a feller wakes up feelin' halfways between 'Oh, Lord' an' 'My God,' he knows he overdid it!"

"Looks to me like Miss Morris and the Chinaman have moved Big John closer to 'Oh, Lord,'" Joshua commented dryly. He was in awe of the transformation . . . but couldn't help but wonder how long it would last.

"Yeah. That pigtailed Temperance man learned the Good Book from them Boston missionaries in the Sandwich Islands. He come as a coolie workin' the sugarcane fields." Pick spit a stream of tobacco into a ground-squirrel hole and wiped his mouth on his sleeve. "Then he come to 'Frisco on a sailin' packet in '48. Worked on the railroad as a cook for the coolie crews. Did more preachin' than cookin'. Don't ask him about it. He'll tell you more'n you want to know!"

Joshua was not as interested in Ling Chow as he was in the young woman who waited quietly beneath her parasol in the buggy. He let his gaze shift to her and linger there. Beautiful. Strong-willed. "What's a woman like her doing in Garson?" he asked Pick.

"Her pa's here. An' she says one place looks the same as another to her. Since her ma passed on, she figgers her pa needs her, this bein' his last chance at makin' the Silver Rim pay off."

Joshua did not take his eyes off the slender figure. She shifted the parasol, leaving her face in shadow while the sun glinted on her thick black hair. "But she's blind. How can she be of help to Mister Morris?"

"She can't play poker or checkers; that's true enough. But she's smarter'n ten men put together. She ain't always been blind, neither. Some quack doctor put a poultice on her eyes when she was a young'un. She remembers colors an' critters an' just 'bout everything, I reckon. In a way, she sees a whole lot better'n folks with two good eyes. She was one of them Christian Temperance workers in Boston an' a teacher at a blind school." Pick nodded with authority. "Yep. Readin' little bumps on paper with her fingers. She showed me—like readin' a map in the dark, I figger. 'Course I can't read a-tall, an' you know I got the eyes of a brush wolf . . . spot silver from ten miles off!"

Joshua viewed the girl in the buggy with a mixture of curiosity and respect. He turned back to his work with a half smile and the comment, "Strong woman." Retrieving a cherry red metal bar from the fire, he placed it on the anvil for shaping beneath his hammer. He could not help but wonder about the fires and the hammer that had shaped the life of Callie Morris.

✳ ✳ ✳

Beldad addressed the group of miners assembled in the Chinaman's Chance Saloon. "It's not right, I tell you. It's not fair. Some of us been busting our hump longer'n anyone else for the Silver Rim, and now His Highness, King Morris, up and decides to play favorites."

"Yeah," a voice responded. "You tell 'em, Beldad."

"He can't run us off."

"We'll show him he can't work the Rim without us!"

"It won't even come to that. He ain't man enough to look us in the face and tell us we ain't wanted!"

Jan Svenson, a burly Swede who normally preferred to listen rather than talk, now spoke up. "Yust a minute, Mister Beldad. How can you be shoor Mister Morris goin' to lay anybody off?"

"Haven't you been listenin', Swede? I'm a foreman. I tell you, I was there when Morris said so. He said, 'We'll send the single fellows packing—there aren't any of them worth a plugged nickel, and they're drunk all the time besides.'"

"What? That no-good polecat!" someone burst out.

"And what about you, Mister Beldad?" Svenson interjected. "If you are such an important fella, you must not be worried about your job. Why are you tellin' us all this?"

"Because I'm on your side, man. I aim to see everybody treated fair and square," responded Beldad.

"What'll we do, Beldad? What's the plan?"

Jan Svenson stood, and his massive size called for respect even if his opinions didn't. "I say you are all about to give Mister Morris a good reason to let you all go. He's been fair and straight with us all along. If I had a family here to care for, I'd be glad he gave that some weight. Besides, as long as I've got these," he declared, raising two fists the size of hams, "I can find work. After all, I was looking for a job when I found this one. Don't cross Morris, men. He's played fair with us."

Beldad glared down at the Swede, but it was a short angle even from where Beldad stood on the tabletop. Svenson looked directly back into his eyes without wavering.

Finally Beldad spoke. "Swede, there ain't no more pleasure in your company than in a wet dog's. Why don't you go on and shine old Morris' boots?"

Svenson scowled at Beldad before spinning on his heel and exiting the saloon.

As he went, Beldad caught the eye of Mike Drackett, who had been standing in the shadows at the back of the meeting. As he did so, he gave Drackett the smallest of nods, and Drackett left right after Svenson.

✻ ✻ ✻

Joshua worked silently while Pick watched out the door of the smithy and muttered to himself. After a time he exclaimed, "Well, sure as my name is Pickax, you're in for somethin' now!"

Joshua continued to shape glowing metal into a horseshoe without reply. He had learned that sooner or later Pickax would explain himself.

"My pa always said you could tell what a mule was thinkin' by watchin' the way his ears pointed. Now, I'll tell you—Miss Callie's got them little ears of hers pointed right up here where you're bangin' an' clangin'! I bet my last nugget she's fixin' to come up here with that Lean Duck."

The thought of meeting Callie Morris pleased Joshua. Here might be opportunity to at least satisfy some of his curiosity. He imagined that she might have a word of congratulations for him since he was the only man in town who had been able to stop the rampage of Big John.

"I told you, boy. Here they come! Right up the path like they was out for a Sunday promenade in 'Frisco. It'll give me a chance t' give Lean Duck a piece of my mind. Bringin' Miss Callie out here t' feed that grizzly—" Pick stopped. "She ain't lookin' none too pleased, neither. I seen that stubborn look on her face afore, an' I know—"

The brash courage of Pickax faded away the closer the two came.

Joshua laughed. "My daddy said, 'What you can't duck, welcome.' You afraid of a lady?" he asked, poking yet another iron in the fire and pumping the big bellows a few times.

But Pick didn't reply.

Joshua was smiling when Callie Morris entered the shop with Ling Chow. His smile, like the bravado of Pickax, soon disappeared.

"Your name is Joshua Roberts, I am told?" she said, her pretty features set with indignation.

Joshua cleared his throat. Her face turned toward him as if she were staring at him. "Yes, ma'am," he answered with respect. "And your name—"

"Callie Morris. And this is Ling Chow." She paused. "And I can tell Pickax is in the room as well. What are you doing here?"

Pickax shuffled forward, now completely docile. "Why, Miss Callie, I was just here gettin' shoes for Jenny." He glared at Ling Chow. "Me and Josh saw that you brung supper to that ornery grizzly down there, an' I was just sayin' I'll bet your pa wouldn't like you mixin' with that no-good—"

Callie raised her hand to silence his protest. "You know Big John has been a faithful employee of my father's for many years." Her tone invited no argument. "He's been trussed up like some sort of animal."

"Hold on just a minute, Miss Morris—," Josh began to argue.

But before he could continue, she inclined her head. "No, *you* hold on. Perhaps Big John Daniels fell into bad ways, but he is not a steer to be bound hand and foot for branding."

"But, Miss Callie!" Pick protested. "You ain't never seen such a mean drunk!"

"He is sober now," she said. "He needs to be released."

"I can't do that." Joshua narrowed his eyes. "Not until I'm sure—"

"I will speak to my father," Callie replied evenly, as if the matter was already settled. "In the meantime, please put up a tent for Big John."

"I did put up a tarp," Josh defended.

"Over his head." She raised her chin slightly, and her voice trembled. "But what about his—his personal, private needs? No human should be put up to public ridicule."

"Ain't nobody laughin' at Big John to his face," Pick said quickly. "Only a fool would laugh at him out loud."

She was adamant. "He needs privacy. Even in jail, there is some privacy. It doesn't matter what he has done."

Joshua now regretted his curiosity. He looked at the stack of cold iron shoes and then at Callie Morris. She was indeed strong. Strong-minded. Strong-willed. Too strong, to his way of thinking. "Ma'am, he has not been sober for weeks. You know that as well as I know it, and I am a newcomer here. I have done only what I needed to do in order to restrain him."

Her face softened a bit. "Well, that may be so. But he does need a tent. Provide him with a chamber pot and water with which to wash.

In private. Away from the eyes of the miners, Mister Roberts. That is only common decency."

She was right. Josh hadn't thought of it. He did not like being ordered around by a woman, but she spoke the truth. He stared at her, considering how strange it was that a woman who could not see was so aware of what it meant for Big John to be totally without privacy.

"Yes, Miss Morris," Josh replied. "Common decency."

"Thank you," she said abruptly, turning to reach for Ling Chow's arm. "We are agreed. Ling Chow and I will be back with breakfast for him in the morning. I hope this matter will be taken care of before then." Her tone indicated that Josh probably wouldn't want to be around if she found anything different than that.

Josh and Pickax exchanged looks as Callie Morris and Ling Chow drove away from the blacksmith shop.

"Well, Pick," Josh said dryly, "I purely admire the way you gave them a piece of your mind."

381

✳CHAPTER 6✳

Joshua awoke early. For a moment he was not certain what had interrupted his peaceful sleep. He lay on his cot, glancing out the window toward where the faintest of predawn gray was beginning to brighten the eastern sky. He looked around the packed room; none of the miners was awake. Listening to the chorus of snores, snorts, and wheezes, Josh couldn't imagine that any outside sound had penetrated even these thin walls.

Then he heard it again: the call of a horse, answered by another, and the clattering of hooves on the rocky slope leading upward toward Garson from the desert below. Josh swung his legs over the cot and sat up, drawing on his Levi's and thrusting his stockinged feet into his boots.

Joshua clumped downstairs. On the way he heard the banging of pans in the kitchen, indicating that Mrs. Flynn was getting the day in order, but he saw no one.

Out to the board sidewalk he went, leaned over a rail, and looked down the slope. Now he could hear human voices mixed in with the horse whinnies. One said, "Get up there." And another called, "Whoop, whoop." A couple of sharp whistles and the smack of a coiled rope against a leather-covered thigh accompanied the voices.

Presently the first of the herd of horses came into view. They were scruffy, wild-looking creatures, with flaring nostrils and tangled manes and tails.

A rider galloped alongside the herd to unlatch and open the corral gate. He did this all from the back of his horse, a beautiful glossy-coated bay. At a slight urging from the reins, the horse backed up to block the road.

The rider then removed his hat and stood in his stirrups to wave the leading horses into the pen. As he did so, Josh got a good look at this tall man who rode with such assurance. He was flamboyantly dressed in a bright yellow shirt with a red bandanna knotted at his throat. But the most amazing aspect was the man himself: he was black. To his recollection, Joshua had never seen any other black cowboys.

The herd of wild horses needed little urging. When they came within sight of the corral, they turned quickly into the gate, as if they could smell the watering trough.

A second cowboy had come up along the left side of the herd. He was white, similar in size to the first rider and equal in horsemanship as well as age. Both men looked to be in their early twenties.

Josh counted fifteen horses as they paced into the corral. The first horseman moved his bay back to the gate and shut it quickly behind the last mustang.

The drag rider was older than the other two and had a slightly shorter and stockier build. His sun-browned face broke into an easy grin as he slapped the back of first one cowboy and then the other in mutual congratulations.

Josh strolled down toward the pen, curious about the obviously friendly group. As he approached, the three were dismounting and preparing to lead their horses into the livery stable.

"Howdy." The older rider spoke to Josh as he passed by into the barn. The other two touched their hat brims and nodded politely but said nothing.

Josh could overhear the instructions the old man gave the liveryman regarding the care and feeding of the saddle horses and the rough stock. "Grain these three up good. We had planned to be here last night but ran out of daylight up the trail apiece, so we turned 'em into a box canyon and came in this morning."

The three riders strode back out into the brightening morning light. Garson was beginning to come to life, and the sounds of the awakening town filled the air.

"Wonder where's a good place to put on *our* feed bag, Pa."

"I don't know, Nate, but perhaps this gentleman can tell us," the older man said as he approached Joshua.

"Yes, sir," replied Josh politely. "I think you'd find the food at my hotel, the Tulare, to your liking. Mrs. Flynn's cooking isn't fancy, but she doesn't stint on the portions."

"Sounds just like what we need, eh, boys?"

"You bet," the younger white man responded.

The black cowboy replied, "Sounds good to me, Pa," to Josh's surprise.

"Lead the way, young man," said the man to Josh. "And perhaps you'll join us and give us some information about this town."

The introductions that followed Josh's agreement revealed that the older man was Tom Dawson, a rancher from Greenville on the other side of the Sierras. "Up in God's country," Dawson said, "where the land grows grass and trees instead of rocks and cactus."

Tom gestured to the younger white man and indicated him to be his nephew Nathan. He referred to the other cowboy as his son, Mont James. Mrs. Flynn was pleased to have three more paying customers for breakfast, and when Tom indicated that they were interested in a room as well, she was even more generous in ladling out gravy for their biscuits.

"What brings you to Garson, Mister Dawson?" inquired Josh.

"We've been rounding up wild stock out of the desert and breaking them for the army," Tom replied. "But the army's interests of late have moved quite far from California, what with the Sioux troubles and all, so our market's dried up some. Anyway, Mont here had an idea. Tell him, Mont."

The cowboy finished swallowing a mouthful of biscuit and washed it down with a swig of coffee before answering. "I thought maybe we could find some takers in these mining towns who were in need of desert-bred stock. Plus, I figured if we rounded them up and did the breaking here, instead of driving them home and back again, it'd save some expense and wear and tear on us."

"Anyway," broke in the one named Nathan, "we thought we'd make this a trial run and see how it turns out. Would you be interested in purchasing a fine broke horse, Mister Roberts?"

"I don't think I can afford one just yet. And I should tell you that I'm probably not the one to ask for information about Garson. You see, I'm pretty new here myself."

"You didn't steer us wrong about food," said Tom. "Why don't you just fill us in on what you do know?"

Josh described the town's situation as best he could, including the troubles besetting the Silver Rim and Mr. Morris' efforts to make it pay. "I don't know that you'll find many buyers among the mine workers. They don't have anywhere to go and not much money to spend. But the storekeepers and merchants might be interested."

"I guess we'll sound them out directly," concluded Tom. "Anyway, we plan to put up here for a month or so while we're putting some school on these cayuses."

* * *

Chief Pitahaya regarded the two young Mojave Indians before him. *Sotol and Turtleback have shown some courage,* he thought. *Perhaps their smoldering hatred of the whites can be fanned into flame.*

"Sotol," Pitahaya said to the taller and brighter of the two, "have you had any word of Yellow Plume since she ran away with the white man?"

Through gritted teeth Sotol replied, "As you know, Pitahaya, her brother here and I tracked them to the white village of Darwin. But the whites there laughed at our demand that she be returned."

"Indeed," Turtleback added. "They called us *dirty Injuns* and drove us out of their village with rocks."

Pitahaya eyed them both. "How is it that you let such insults stand, my brothers?"

Sotol and Turtleback exchanged looks. Sotol replied, "They have guns with which to give their taunts force, Pitahaya. Pistols and long guns which shoot many times, while we have none."

"So," mused Pitahaya thoughtfully, "you do not lack courage, only guns. Is that so?"

At the nods of the two younger men, he continued, "Here is what should be done. In the white village of Garson they sell the guns which shoot many times—" Pitahaya raised his hand to cut off the protest he saw coming. "What we must seek are the whites who newly come to this land and who would not be sought after should they lose their way in our desert. Do you understand?"

Sotol and Turtleback grunted in reply. They agreed to take turns watching Garson, exchanging places from Wild Rose Canyon by night.

✳ ✳ ✳

"Good day, Mister Jacobson," called Callie to the proprietor as she left the hardware store.

"Yah. Und tank you, Miss Morris," replied the portly little shopkeeper.

Callie felt the stares of two men she had heard enter the store after her. *They must be new in town.*

"Und what can I do mit you, gentlemen?" Jacobson asked.

Their full reply was cut off by the closing door but not before Callie heard, "Do you have ammunition for Winchester . . . ?"

"Come along, Ling Chow. Don't dawdle," chided Callie Morris over her shoulder.

"No, missie, I come plenty fast," puffed the little Chinaman over the basket he carried piled high with groceries.

Callie strode briskly along the boardwalk in front of Jacobson's Hardware Store. Her familiarity with the limited business district of Garson enabled her to walk with all the assurance of a sighted person.

She paused when her hand encountered the gap in the rail indicating the front of Fancy Dan's Saloon. Here she turned and prepared to cross the road to her carriage, which was tied up in front of her father's office.

Callie listened carefully for a moment, preferring to judge for herself if the street was clear for crossing rather than calling on Ling Chow's assistance.

While she waited, a carefully modulated voice spoke from behind her, "Good day to you, Miss Morris. May I offer you my arm in crossing the street?"

Recognizing Dan McGinty's voice, she replied, "No, thank you, Mister McGinty. I can manage just fine."

"But I insist," he said, stepping up beside her and overpowering her with a wave of bay rum. He gently but firmly placed her left hand on his right arm and prepared to step out across the street.

"May I say how lovely you look this morning, Miss Morris? You certainly add a note of classic beauty to our humble surroundings."

"You are a flatterer, Mister McGinty, and a rather forward one at that," Callie responded tartly, lifting her hand from his forearm.

"If I cannot be of service, then I certainly don't wish to impose," said McGinty, with a quick fan of breeze that indicated a sweeping bow. Then he was gone with a light step and a creak of new leather boots.

Callie paused, her cheeks burning. *I like his flattery a bit,* she admitted to herself. *But he is not a man I can trust,* she thought as she walked determinedly to her carriage.

"And you are certain, Sotol, that these two white men know no one in the white village on the rocky slopes?"

"No one, Pitahaya. I was outside the Place of Iron Tools when I saw them leave and heard them ask directions of the prospector known as Pickax.

"The man pointed them toward the north and told them of water to be found at such and such a place. Then they told that they were from the land of the Utes and were newly come to this place."

"We think," said Turtleback, "that the meaning is clear: They are so newly come as to need directions to water. When they obtained food, they left again quickly without being much regarded."

Pitahaya nodded slowly. "And what have they of use to us?"

Sotol glanced at Turtleback before replying. "That is truly the best part, Pitahaya. Each carries a shining Colt six-shooter and a Yellow Belly. We saw them load boxes of bullets for these on their two fine, strong horses."

"You have done well, Sotol, and you also, Turtleback. Now let us plan what is to be done. Will they camp near Three Kill Spring tomorrow night?"

"Yes, Pitahaya. We believe we can meet up with them in the canyon that lies before Three Kill Spring."

✦ CHAPTER 7 ✦

"Hey, somebody better come here quick!"

"What's the matter? What is it?"

"I dunno. Is somebody snakebit?"

"Could be. I just heard the hollerin'."

There was a flurry of activity around the first dry wash north of Garson. Someone had spotted something at the bottom of the little canyon and gone down to investigate. Immediately afterward came a series of yells until a stream of miners had scrambled down the rocky slope, around the jutting overhang of rock, and into the bottom of the draw.

"It's Jan Svenson!"

"Sure enough is. Is he hurt?"

"I'll say so. He's dead!"

"Dead? What happened to him?"

"Don't be thick! Look up there at that drop and then where he's layin'. He musta got drunk and walked off that cliff in the night and broke his fool neck."

"Powerful shame. I liked ol' Swede—he was a good'n. And I never knew him to be much on drinkin'. But he'd have to be drunk to end up down here."

✦ ✦ ✦

The lead horse, a tall, long-necked bay, pricked his ears forward again. His rider took no notice and neither did his partner, riding a few paces behind and leading a pack animal.

But the second rider's horse, a smaller and better-proportioned, apron-faced sorrel, did catch some of the other horse's agitation. Neither horse stopped, shied, or snorted an alarm, however, and the riders were too inexperienced to catch the subtle signs.

The canyon through which they were riding was narrow and winding, the sandstone walls rising thirty to forty feet on either side. Yucca and creosote bushes grew on the plateaus, but the canyon walls and floor were almost without vegetation. A blue-bellied lizard skittered out from between the lead horse's feet and disappeared into a crack in a low ledge.

The two men knew where they were headed but not how long it would take them. Their destination was Three Kill Spring, where they had been told they would find water.

Both men suffered from the worst malady that could befall a desert traveler—overconfidence. Even though both men realized that they were new to the desert and its ways, neither was smart enough to feel the least apprehensive or even cautious.

The two young men, Easterners out for an adventure, had come west intending to prospect for silver and gold in the Comstock Lode. When they reached the Great Salt Lake, they met up with a returning party of discouraged prospectors. They were told all that was left was hard work for poor pay.

The two were considering going straight on to San Francisco before returning east by ship when they heard some interesting news. Silver had been located in the Panamint Range and the Argus Range of eastern California. They began to hear names like Death Valley, Lone Pine, and Darwin.

By train they got as far as Carson City, Nevada, then turned south and took the stage for Independence, California. At Independence they parted with some of their stake and proceeded to outfit themselves.

They bought horses, packs, mess kits, boots, picks, shovels, flour, and coffee. Most exciting of all to their spirit of adventure were their firearms—brand-new, six-shot Colt revolvers and lever-action Winchester rifles nicknamed Yellow Bellies because their brass receivers gleamed golden yellow in the light.

Their choice of weapons happened to be good. Both pistol and rifle fired the same .44-caliber ammunition, making it unnecessary to carry two different loads. Unfortunately, neither knew how to hit anything that wasn't stationary, and neither had ever had occasion to fire a shot in self-defense.

The man on the lead horse turned in his saddle to inspect his companion's progress. "That pack saddle is slipping again, William."

William also turned around and regarded the mound of gear loaded on the last animal. The canvas-covered bundle of supplies was leaning precariously to the left. In their travels so far, the supplies had never been carried for more than two hours without a stop to read-just and tighten the ropes.

Their concern about the pack was caused by an experience they'd had early after leaving Independence. After a lengthy spell of inatten-tion, the gear had slipped completely under the pack horse, and the lead rope had come loose. Two miles later they finally caught up with the horse, but it took another half day to recover all their belongings, strewn over a thousand acres of sagebrush, granite boulders, and ground-squirrel holes. They never did find the package of chewing tobacco, but neither of them chewed, so it wasn't much loss. They had only bought the tobacco on the advice of the storekeeper, who told them that all salty prospectors chewed.

"You're right, Lawrence. I suppose we'd better stop and fix it right now." William pulled his red horse to a stop.

He struggled with the girth that secured the pack frame. When he first tried to right the load by yanking on the offside, it refused to budge. He loosened the cinch that secured the pack frame, but it began to slip before he got around the animal again. He returned to stop its slide and succeeded in pushing it back upright, but the ineptly tied load had shifted under the canvas, so it continued to lean.

Frustrated, William looked up at his partner who, still mounted, was staring intently at the canyon. In an exasperated tone William said, "Aren't you going to help me, Lawrence?"

Lawrence gestured for silence without turning around, and as his angry partner moved beside him, he said in a hoarse whisper, "Did you see him?"

"See him? Him who?"

"An Indian, I think. I didn't see anyone when we were riding or when we stopped, except just out of the corner of my eye. I thought I saw someone stand up, and as I turned to face him, he disappeared."

"You're imagining things. Or perhaps it was a mirage."

"Why would a mirage suddenly appear and then disappear?"

"Who can explain what a trick of refracted light may do? Come on. Give me a hand with this pack animal, or we'll never make the spring by nightfall."

Lawrence stood up in his stirrups and surveyed the trail ahead before shaking his head and stepping down from the animal.

Together the men spent twenty minutes untying, rearranging, and resecuring their belongings. The load looked no more secure than before, but at least it perched mostly upright. Both men remounted the horses and prepared to continue forward.

"Don't you think we should at least have our weapons handy?" asked Lawrence.

"I can't think that we'll be needing them, but if it will make you feel better, all right."

Both men drew their shiny new Winchesters from leather rifle boots and chambered rounds of ammunition. Following instructions, they carefully let the hammers down to the half-cock safety positions. They were sure they were ready for any trouble.

They topped a ridge of sand in the canyon's throat, a formation that would have been an island in time of flood. Before them the canyon opened out wider on either side, and the steep walls leveled out at the bottom.

"You see, Lawrence?" insisted William. "There's nothing in sight for miles. Besides, if Indians were lying in wait for us, why wouldn't they have attacked us back in the narrow part of the canyon?"

"I suppose you're right," replied Lawrence, attempting to urge the bay down the sandbank. But the horse was suddenly uncooperative. He shifted his weight from one foot to the other and swung his head from side to side, as if being asked to make a dangerous leap. His rider didn't help matters by pulling reins counter to each movement of the horse's neck until both came to a confused stop.

"What's the matter now?" called William.

"It's nothing; he's just being fractious. Come on, fellow. Come on," replied Lawrence, and he administered a kick to his mount's rib cage with both heels. The bay jerked forward, blundering between two sand piles on the short slope.

Instantly the heaps of sand erupted. A Mojave Indian jumped up to grab the startled lead horse's bridle, while on the other side, another Mojave jumped to his feet and seized the .44 rifle.

A more seasoned man would have instantly given up his hold on the rifle and drawn the Colt at his side, but such experience was not available to Lawrence, and he struggled to retain the Winchester. With the horse being pulled one way and the struggle for the Yellow Belly taking place on the other, rider and horse parted company and Lawrence was thrown to the ground. He had only an instant to experience the pain of an arm broken underneath him in his fall, for the successful Mojave spun the captured rifle in a flashing arc that brought it smashing down on Lawrence's head. After that he felt nothing at all. . . .

Sotol let the bay prance around in a circle as he held on to the bridle and watched the end of the tug-of-war for the rifle. Then he turned to see what had happened to the other white man.

Turtleback and a fourth Mojave had also been disguised as mounds of earth forming a line just below the rim of sand. Their simple strategy had been to arrange themselves so that the second white man had to descend the slope between two Indians. Turtleback and his companion had also jumped up when Sotol struck, but they had run immediately toward the pack horse.

The second white man's reactions were no quicker than the first man's, but he'd had an instant longer to think. As the other two Indians ran toward him, he threw down the lead rope of the pack animal and raised the Winchester to his shoulder. His first shot took Turtleback in the cheek, shattering his face and taking off a considerable part of the back of his skull as it exited.

His second shot missed the other Mojave entirely, but in that same second the Indian threw a razor-sharp hatchet that hit the white man just below the knee and neatly sliced down his shinbone. He cried out and almost dropped the rifle, but his horse showed greater presence of mind. The sorrel spun around to bolt back into the canyon.

The white man reeled in the saddle and almost fell. He held both reins and rifle in his right hand and clutched his bloody leg with his left. He bent low over the horse's neck.

His eyes were squinted shut against the pain when the remaining two Mojaves, who had remained hidden to cut off such an escape, jumped up to block his path. Their sudden appearance made the already panicked pack animal rear and swing broadside to the onrushing sorrel. In the collision the white man went flying over both horses, the spinning rifle sparkling golden in the sunlight.

One of the Mojaves caught the Winchester in midair and waved it in triumph. The other rushed to stand over the white man and to slit his throat, only to discover that the man's neck had snapped. He was already dead.

✳ ✳ ✳

Tom Dawson had asked Josh to see to the shoeing needs of their three mounts, so Josh was working beside the corral after his smithing duties at the mine were done for the day.

The three cowboys were finishing their own day's efforts, sacking some horses who were still pulling back against lead ropes, putting weighted saddles on others, and tying still others up to stand with bits in their mouths.

Josh had already completed the shoeing of Tom's mount, a horse named Duncan, and was fitting a second shoe to Mont's. After clenching the nails and ringing them off, he allowed the hoof to slip to the ground and straightened up with a creak of backbones.

"Hey, Josh," called Nate Dawson, "which of these plug-uglies do you like best?"

Josh let his eyes rove over the herd standing in varying degrees of submission. All were lean and scraggly in appearance, but one caught his attention. The animal Josh admired was taller than the rest, a buckskin with a dark mane and tail and four black stockings. He stood with his head held high and his body turned along the length of the rail to which he was snubbed. He appeared to be watching the proceedings in the corral with an intelligent and interested eye.

Josh waved toward him and replied, "That buck there."

Mont looked over from the roan he was sacking and commented, "You got a good eye, Josh. I figure he ran off from somebody. He's mostly broke already. Not like this flea bag." He indicated the roan that had begun plunging and straining at the lead rope even *before* Mont had waved the saddle blanket.

"Well, I'll be hog-tied and hornswoggled!" Mont exclaimed.

Josh followed the line of the man's outstretched arm past the buckskin, beyond the corral to the mesquite-covered hillside beyond.

Down the trail slanting away from Garson rode Pickax on Jenny. Behind him, at the end of a lead rope, was a stylish gray mare, and seated on that mare was a very erect young woman wearing smoked-lens glasses.

"That is Miss Callie Morris," Josh explained, "the daughter of mine superintendent Morris. I didn't know she could ride, and I'll bet her daddy doesn't know she's doing it, either."

All four men stopped to observe the progress of the two riders across the field. Apparently Pickax was calling out instructions over his shoulder, for he kept turning in his saddle, first one way and then the other, to watch Callie's ride.

And then it happened. As he was turned to watch her, a rattlesnake must have buzzed across the path in front of them. Jenny was a desert-wise creature who didn't buck or bolt, but her sidestep and twist off the trail was enough to tumble the backward-facing Pick into the dirt.

The gray was neither desert-bred nor very bright. At the first nervous activity by Jenny and Pick's clumsy sprawl right in front of her, the mare reared and bolted off across the hillside.

By sheer grit and determination, Callie kept her seat, but whether this was good fortune or bad remained to be seen. The mare, sensing the inability of the rider to gain control, plunged headlong through the mesquite and creosote, occasionally leaping over clumps of brush. And, of course, with every stride the horse was in danger of dropping a leg into a ground-squirrel hole or coming to grief on the uneven ground.

Josh took in the unfolding disaster at a glance. Without a second thought he threw himself at Duncan's lead rope. With a yank on the quick release that spun the startled horse around, he vaulted onto Duncan's back.

Dear God, help Miss Callie! came unbidden to his frantic mind as he felt the cow pony gather his haunches under him and spring away from the rail. He desperately hoped that the horse would respond to leg pressure, for he had only the free end of a lead rope in one hand and a handful of mane in the other.

Josh immediately discovered just how well trained Duncan was. Tom Dawson's jug-headed horse was nothing special to look at, but he was smart and quick to pick up what was needed in the situation.

Almost as if he knew without being told what Josh wanted, Duncan galloped after the bolting mare. His great muscled neck stretched out front. His ears were pricked forward, and it was obvious that he was enjoying the chase.

The same could not be said of Josh. The blood was pounding through his heart like the hammer on his anvil. His breath caught in his throat with each leap and pivot of the gray mare, wondering when he would see Callie falling off the mare's back to be broken against the rocky slope. The thought that this uncontrolled, desperate flight was happening to a blind girl filled him with dread.

He urged Duncan to even greater speed. For what seemed like an agonizingly long time, the gap between the racing horses remained the same, until at last Duncan's greater muscle and length of stride began to tell.

As Josh and Duncan began to overtake the mare, Josh shouted ahead to Callie, "Hold on, Miss Morris. I'll get her stopped for you."

Over her shoulder, blown to him on the wind of the rushing horses, he heard, "I—have—no—intention—of—letting—go!"

Gradually Duncan drew up alongside the racing mare. Lathered with exertion and fear, the gray rolled a wild eye sideways at Duncan before spurting away again. A quarter of a mile ahead, Josh could see the line of mesquite shrub beginning to dip into a boulder-strewn ravine.

Josh leaned far out over the horse's right shoulder, holding with great difficulty to both lead rope and mane clutched in his left hand.

He had to trust completely in the sureness of Duncan's pace and in the horse's sense of what was at stake. He urged Duncan on to the limit.

His fingertips stretched out toward the bridle of the mare. Another inch closer, and Josh glanced over at the blind girl. Though she had not screamed, her clenched fists on the reins and her face, completely drained of color, spoke of her fear.

Now his fingers touched the bridle, grasped the cheek strap, and pulled the mare alongside Duncan as Josh straightened himself upright. Still apprehensive that the mare would pitch Callie off, he did not try to bring her to an abrupt stop. Instead he turned Duncan and the gray in a wide circle around to the left, back toward Garson. "It's all right, Miss Morris. I've got her now. Just another moment," he assured her as calmly as he could.

Slowly slackening Duncan's speed, Josh brought the mare under control. At last Josh turned them through the deepest sand he could find, and the gray gave up the race and shuddered to a stop.

Josh slid off Duncan wrong-sided, afraid to release his grip on the bridle. When he stood alongside the mare, he shoved his left shoulder up under the gray's chin. Only then did he reach up to assist Callie Morris down from the sidesaddle on which she had perched for two terrifying miles.

"Here, Miss Morris, let me help you down. It's Josh. Josh Roberts. I've got you."

"Thank you," she gasped. "Oh, thank you. I'm quite all right, Mister Roberts—" Then she collapsed into his arms with her face buried against his chest as the two horses snorted off steam and pawed the sand.

Josh couldn't help but notice that she smelled like wildflowers.

❋ ❋ ❋

"You there! Yes, you, Indian. Come here." McGinty gestured emphatically toward Sotol, who had been squatting unobtrusively around the corner of Fancy Dan's Saloon out of view of the street.

Sotol looked up, then away, staring out at the mesquite as if he hadn't heard a word.

McGinty walked over to the Mojave and stood, eyes squinted, regarding him. "I know you speak English; I saw you look up when I first called you."

Sotol grudgingly agreed, "I speak."

"Yes, and you understand even more than you speak, curse you. Now get up. I need you to carry a message to your chief."

Sotol returned McGinty's stare.

Peering into those hard, dark eyes, McGinty almost changed his mind and turned to walk back into his saloon. He swung back, trying to give as much smoldering hatred to his gaze as the Indian was giving him, but found himself averting his eyes.

Angrily he reached in his vest and withdrew a .44 shell from his watch pocket. He threw it down at the Indian's feet. "Go show that to your chief. Tell him I want to talk to him about it. Tell him I'll be at the old shack by Poison Well tomorrow night at moonrise."

397

Sotol looked at the shell lying on the ground but gave no indication of agreement, not even a grunt.

McGinty was inwardly relieved at the break in eye contact, so he didn't press the issue. He turned around and went to the outside staircase leading to his office.

As he reached the corner of the building he glanced over his shoulder. Sotol and the cartridge were gone. Though the plain around had no brush taller than three feet for miles in all directions, the Mojave had disappeared as completely as if he'd never been there at all.

✦ CHAPTER 8 ✦

Joshua soaped up again as Pick dumped yet another bucket of steaming water over his head.

"Somehow it just don't seem right usin' precious water for washin' all over." Pick shook his head. He kicked the small tin bathtub where Josh sat folded up like an accordion. "An' what's gonna happen to this water after you get out of it? Why, it ain't good for nuthin'. Can't cook in it. Can't drink it." He sniffed thoughtfully. "S'pose a feller could water his mule with it, 'cept the soap would make it sick."

"Well, now, Pickax," Josh said as he scrubbed his neck, "we might be able to stretch the use of this water. You can take a bath after me."

"No, thanks. It ain't natural, a man gettin' wet all over. Don't know why you want to do it. Miss Callie ain't gonna see if you've got clean ears or dirty."

"No, but she has a fine-honed sense of smell. She recognized you by odor the other day in the blacksmith shop."

Pick aimed at the spittoon and let fly with a bullet of tobacco. "And I wouldn't think of deprivin' the lady o' that clue, neither. Why, she's gonna think Joshua Roberts skedaddled an' sent a well-oiled Mississippi gambler over to eat supper in his place. She ain't gonna know you all sweet-smellin' like lye soap an' lavender water! You better sleep in the livery stable tonight when you're done, or one o' these drunk miners is likely to mistake you for one of them Calico Queens!"

With that, Joshua dipped the tin cup into the water and drenched the old prospector.

"Take your own gol durn bath!" Pickax roared. "Now I'm gonna smell like a wet dog!"

"That's some improvement, anyway," Joshua howled as Pickax hurled the bucket at him and stomped out of the small room.

✳ ✳ ✳

The truth was, Joshua had no explanation as to why he now stood in front of the washstand mirror and worked to straighten the part in his hair. Pick was right. Callie Morris couldn't see him, so why had he taken a week's earnings and spent an hour at the general store picking out a new shirt and trousers and a celluloid collar? Why had he stood scowling down at the too-short sleeves of the only Sunday-go-to-meetin' coat in the place? Why had he washed his socks and dusted off his derby hat like some city slicker greenhorn from St. Louis?

Indeed, it was a mystery even to him. But when she had collapsed into his arms, when she had leaned against him, showing she was made of much softer stuff than he had thought, he had forgotten that she could not see him. As he had lifted her onto Duncan and escorted her back, he'd had the fleeting thought that in the future she should not meet him on the street and recognize him by the same method she had identified old Pick!

She was truly a beautiful woman—as fine and mysterious and strong, yes, but also soft and sweet as any woman he had ever seen. That kind of beauty deserved to be in the company of a man with a straight part and a clean shirt. After all, she hadn't invited a mule to supper, so Joshua reasoned he ought not smell like one!

Garson had no flowers for Joshua to bring to her, so after he had bought his new duds, he spent his last two bits on a bottle of lilac water. He hadn't forgotten that her skin smelled like a flower garden. He would bring her the scent as a token of the flowers he did not have.

✳ ✳ ✳

Joshua had not counted on Pickax's ability to provide an instant crowd of grimy spectators. As he emerged from the boardinghouse, a chorus of hoots and yelps and hurrahs greeted him.

A group of two dozen laughing miners swelled to four dozen as

399

he strode, red-faced, down the street. The No Name Saloon emptied out when customers mistook the cheering, jeering uproar for a brawl.

"Ain't never seen a blacksmith so clean!"

"Kin you *smell* him? Hey, Josh! You fall into a barrel of eau de toilette or somethin'?"

"He's either died or he's gettin' hitched!"

"What's the difference?"

"He smells too nice to be dead!"

"Naw! That's the new embalming fluid!"

"It shore beats ice!"

"So does a warmhearted woman!"

At that, Joshua stopped in the center of the street and turned around to face the audience. The last comment had pushed the fun too far. After all, Miss Callie Morris was for sure not one of the girls in the town bordello.

The men nudged each other playfully as they saw Joshua's obvious irritation. He clenched and unclenched his fists and stared down the rowdies.

The laughter died to a nervous twittering.

"Who said that?" Joshua's voice was low and menacing.

Silence fell over the crowd. The men gulped and stepped back, their smiles apologetic. They had gone too far. After all, this was the man who had beat John Daniels.

Pickax shrugged. "We didn't mean nothin' by it, Josh. The fellers wasn't talkin' about Miss Callie disrespectful. They was just meanin' that women in general was better than ice."

Josh considered his words. He scowled deep and mean at a young fella who seemed to have developed the shakes. "You think women are better than ice, do you? *Well, I say . . .* that just depends on how hot the desert is!"

With that the group once again roared with laughter. Grimy hands reached out to clap Joshua on the back as he yelled above the boisterous tumult, *"Now quit following me before I take you on one at a time!"*

Content, the group turned back to the saloons of Garson, leaving Joshua to walk the last quarter mile to the Morris house in peace.

✵ ✵ ✵

Josh had hoped that the invitation to dine at the Morris home had been Callie's idea. Now as she sat silently across the table from him, Josh was certain that the invitation had been Mr. Morris' plan.

The small, tissue-wrapped bottle of perfume seemed to mock him from his pocket. *What were you thinking of, Josh Roberts? Even if she could see your face, she wouldn't look twice at you. You're a black-smith, not a gentleman.* The new collar seemed suddenly too tight. The starch in his shirt made the fabric rustle when he reached out for the bowl of mashed potatoes. He wondered if word had gotten back to Callie that he had bought himself new duds for the occasion. He wondered if she could sense his embarrassment.

Ling Chow placed a heaping platter of fried chicken in front of Callie as Mr. Morris laid the purpose of this meeting on the table. "I'd like to appoint you town constable, Joshua. Marshal of Garson, if you prefer that title," he announced as though it was already accomplished.

401

Joshua ducked his head slightly, and after letting the words sink in, he chuckled carefully. "I prefer blacksmith. Just . . . blacksmith, Mister Morris."

Now it was Morris' turn to chuckle, and he glanced at Callie, who did not respond. "You were right, Daughter." He turned back to Josh. "She told me you wouldn't want the job."

"She was right. I . . . I thank you, Mister Morris, for the honor—if it is an honor. But I've no desire to get near anything hotter than my forge."

Morris stuck out his lower lip and glanced first at Callie then back at Joshua as he considered the refusal. "You're a good man, Joshua. Good with your fists and good with this." Morris tapped his forehead lightly. "Any fool can pack a sidearm. I could hire two dozen gunslingers tomorrow and pin badges on them, but they'd still just be trash behind tin stars. No. The Silver Rim . . . Garson . . . we're in need of a man who can think on his feet. You're our man."

"I've had little choice in any of the circumstances. It's not that I—"

"Nonsense!" Morris interrupted his protest. "If you had not done what you did, Callie would be dead. Tom Dawson said as much, and I believe him to be a man who speaks the truth."

Joshua shrugged. He had lost his appetite. The thought of keeping the peace in a town like Garson was the last assignment he wanted. "Anyone would have—"

"And then there is the matter of Big John." Morris cleared his throat authoritatively. "Not easy for you to say that anyone would have stopped *him*. But you found another way. I've been out in the West long enough to know that plenty of men have used the law as an excuse for killing. You had plenty of reason to pull the trigger and put Big John permanently into a hole in the ground. No one would have blamed you."

Callie still did not react to her father even though Josh was quite certain she would have had plenty to say if Big John Daniels had been killed.

402

"I might have killed him," Josh admitted, "if I had thought of it." He looked quickly at Callie, trying to judge her expression.

Mr. Morris raised his hand to silence Joshua. "Tom Dawson tells me you were admiring that big lanky buckskin they're breaking down there." Was Morris changing the subject?

"He seemed the best of the remuda." Joshua nodded, relieved that the conversation had taken a different turn.

"He's yours, then."

"But—"

"It would not be proper for the constable of Garson to go around on foot."

"But, Mister Morris—"

"You'll need a saddle. Pick out something down at the livery stable and send the bill to me. Tom Dawson and those boys of his will finish breaking the buck and then choose a second horse from the herd. You might need a spare."

Joshua glared at the oblivious mine owner. Now he could see where Callie Morris had acquired her obstinate nature. He waited until he was certain that Mr. Morris had finished speaking. "I am just a blacksmith, Mister Morris. Every day of my life since I was a boy, I've wrestled with horses and mules and pounded hot iron. It's no miracle that I could wrestle down John Daniels, no great shakes that I could pound him into submission. He is smaller than a horse and less ornery than a mule. There is nothing unusual in what I have done." He paused, then said as firmly as he could, "I am no lawman."

Callie now smiled softly. She turned her face slightly away from him and said almost coyly, "Come now, Mister Roberts. Some men have the law written in their hearts. My father has taken you for one of those."

Morris nodded. "That makes you lawman enough for me."

"Steel," Callie said in a voice that touched on admiration, "tempered with the gentleness of mercy." Her face shone in the soft glow of the candles in their silver candlesticks. Joshua saw his own reflection in the smoked glass of her spectacles. He felt trapped, unable to refuse her words or the tone of her voice. "My father is right, Mister Roberts. You are quite ideal for the position."

"Except that I don't *want* it," Joshua replied incredulously.

Morris looked toward his daughter as if appealing for help. Although she could not see her father's face, she seemed to understand his feelings instinctively.

She smiled as if coaxing a reluctant child. "Joshua," she said, using his given name for the first time, "often we are called on to do things we do not wish to do. But we do them because there is simply no one else." She laid her hand palm up on the table. Instinctively, he responded to her gesture and placed his fingers against hers. It was as if their eyes had met.

"But there must be someone else," he said lamely.

"No," she replied, "there is no one else. You're the man for the job."

✳ ✳ ✳

McGinty paced around inside the tumbledown shack, absently kicking a broken chair leg.

Mike Drackett, who was leaning against the doorframe, grinned at his boss's discomfort and remarked, "If you'd set down a spell, you wouldn't be raisin' so much dust."

"Shut up!" said McGinty abruptly. "They aren't coming after all. Look there—" He gestured toward the almost-full moon that had risen over the starkly outlined cinder cone to the east. "We've been here since an hour before moonrise, and now it's an hour past. Let's get out of here; maybe this was a dumb idea all along."

Drackett was surprised to hear Fancy Dan admit to having second thoughts. *'Course it's not like I wasn't havin' no jitters myself,* he thought, then said, "You was gonna give them Mojaves rifles to stick up the stage; is that right?"

"Certainly. Only *we'd* tell them which ones to attack so as to cause Morris the most grief over lost payroll and people."

A sigh, softer than a breath of air, sifted into the cabin. Outside, the shadows of the cat's claw bushes reached gnarled talons toward the cabin, retreating reluctantly before the rising moon. A nightjar twittered softly.

Drackett blinked, then rubbed his eyes. *Was that shadow that large a moment ago?* he wondered, a stab of fear quickening his pulse. Almost of itself, his left hand eased his Starr revolver a little higher in his holster.

From behind him a voice with the age and gentle power of a shifting sand dune spoke. "You will remove your fingers very carefully from the pistol."

Drackett and McGinty both had the good sense to freeze where they were. Drackett's hand slipped up across his stomach. Making no sudden movements, they turned slowly around to see Pitahaya standing in the deepest shadow of the room. *How did he get there?* Drackett wondered briefly. But his attention was more intently focused on the muzzle of the rifle Pitahaya held.

"Why have you called me to this meeting? I know you to be a seller of the water-that-burns-with-fire, but my people have no money with which to buy. And what means the little-death-carrier you sent which is now in the fire stick pointed at your belly? I have done speaking."

McGinty explained to the chief his plan to help the Mojaves know which coaches would be carrying the payroll shipments. With that much money, he explained, Pitahaya's people could buy rifles, whiskey—anything they wanted.

"And when the pony soldiers come against us, what then?"

"It won't last that long. Two or three times at the most, and your people can go to your mountain camps with enough money for supplies to stay a year. By then this will be forgotten."

"And why do you make war on your own people?"

"Because others have what should belong to me and I want it," McGinty said cautiously.

"Bah! You are no man of honor, Mig-In-Tee. But we will fight this fight, and we will go to the mountains to live better than we do now. I want fifty of the golden-sided rifle-that-shoots-many-times and twice ten hands of bullets for each."

"Fifty rifles and a hundred rounds of ammunition each?" exploded McGinty. "I don't want to make war on the whole state; I just want you to knock over a couple of stages!"

At the angry tone in Fancy Dan's voice, Drackett's hand crept back down toward the butt of the revolver. His fingertips had barely touched the wood of the grip when he felt the prick of a steel knife point on his neck and a chill of fear down his spine.

405

"I know, Mig-In-Tee, that you wish us to be blamed for doing evil for you. You say the army will not come before we have gone. This may be true, but still we will be ready to fight them or we will not walk the war trail with you."

"All right, fifty rifles and the ammunition," McGinty agreed. "But it will take some time; I can only give you ten rifles now."

Pitahaya grunted a reply, which Drackett assumed was assent.

McGinty continued. "Also, you must only attack those whom we say. I know about the two prospectors you killed. That's where you got the Winchester you're holding."

Pitahaya shrugged as if the matter was of complete indifference to him. "It may be so. Who can say? The desert claimed them for its own; that is all. They were not wise in its ways."

"If we're agreed, then tell your friend there to take the knife out of Mike's neck," commanded McGinty.

The pressure of the knifepoint was withdrawn, and Drackett, who had been holding his breath, sighed with relief.

"Now about those first ten rifles . . . ," McGinty continued.

But Pitahaya had already gone as soundlessly as he had come.

✳ ✳ ✳

Nearly everything had been settled by the time Ling Chow cleared away the dishes and poured coffee into the fine china cups. They were not made to fit the finger of a blacksmith. They were made for the delicate hand of a woman.

The observation gave Josh determination to speak out. There was something that had troubled him ever since Callie's mare bolted with her on its back. Josh knew more than a little about horses, and he was certain that the flashy gray was not made for the young woman who sat across from him now.

He cleared his throat. "That's a fine-looking mare you've got, Miss Callie. . . ." His voice trailed off. After all, the choice of a mount was a very personal thing, like the choice of a friend.

"She was a gift. I brought her with me," Callie said abruptly, without a smile. Did she guess where he was leading?

"A fine animal for a bridle path in a park, no doubt." Josh glanced at Mr. Morris, who encouraged him with a nod.

"Yes. I spent many afternoons on her, with a friend at my side. I can ride as well as a woman with sight. What happened last Tuesday was just a fluke, Mister Roberts. It might have happened to anyone."

Josh plunged ahead. "It *would* have happened to anyone on that horse."

"There is nothing wrong with the horse. She was frightened by that snake, and—"

"And she almost got you killed," Josh interrupted.

"It could have happened to anyone," Callie insisted, but her voice quavered slightly.

"Not with the right mount," he said firmly. "I know a little about horses. That mare is too high-strung for this part of the country." He was careful not to add that the horse was too high-strung for Callie Morris.

"I am used to her," Callie argued with lifted chin.

"She'll get you killed," he repeated, determined to see the discussion through by the hint of helplessness in her voice. She did argue, but certainly she understood that he was telling her the truth.

"But I love riding; it is the only real freedom . . ." She faltered.

"Look, I watched those Dawson boys break a whole string down there." Excitement edged his voice. "They've got one little bay mare—a pretty thing, she is. Black mane and tail, black stockings and good feet. And she's the kind of horse that just *wants* to please. Miss Callie, I trimmed her feet, and she was just the sweetest thing—practically turned around and said thanks! I said to myself, 'Now, this is a horse a man could ride from here to Mexico and never feel it!' And she's careful. Watches where she's going. Mont James rode her all over these hills, and her ears were perked and listening to every word he said. And I told him, 'There's a horse for Miss Callie.'"

She sat silently as he paused and waited. A slight smile curved her lips. "Then . . . you aren't saying I should never ride again?"

"No, Miss Callie. You've just got the wrong animal for the territory. But there is a right one for you. . . ."

Now she inclined her head toward her father, who had chosen not to enter into the discussion with his strong-willed daughter. "Papa, could you arrange . . . I mean, if I am going to be riding again in the desert, perhaps Shadow is *not* suitable. If Mister Roberts says there is a horse which will be better . . ."

407

Josh pretended to convince Mr. Morris, who looked relieved. "She's a three-year-old. Mont James says he'd be happy to put a bit more time on her and then give your daughter a hand until they're acquainted. No two horses are ever broke alike, but I never saw a horse so willing."

"Well then—" Morris eyed Callie—"it's rare to find a filly so well-tempered. I'd be a fool to pass her by."

A smile of genuine relief filled Callie's face. "May we go now and see her? I could use a little walk after Ling's dinner."

"Now? After dark?" Josh was surprised by her eagerness and pleased he had pursued the offer.

"The dark does not hinder me, Mister Roberts . . . *Joshua*. I can lead if you like." She laughed lightly, at ease with her handicap. "And please call me Callie."

And so Callie Morris took Joshua's arm and strolled slowly toward the corral, where the new horses milled around. Josh liked the warmth of her small hand on his arm, and so he did not tell her that the sky was lit up with stars that illuminated the world from one horizon to the other. Instead he let her guide him.

"This is going to be a real town someday," she said quietly. "Thank you, Joshua, for agreeing to be the constable. My father really needs your help with this. I wasn't just trying to sweet-talk you into doing something you didn't want to do."

He quipped, "Just so long as I don't have to do it forever!"

"You see that knoll over there?" Callie pointed, and indeed there was a knoll to her right. "I told Papa that as soon as the mine pays off we are going to have a church there. You can't have a town without a church."

He chuckled. "In this town we'd better have a jail built first. You can't have a town without the law."

"No. First the church, so that the jail will more likely be empty." In the distance the low nicker of a horse was heard. Callie stopped and turned to face Joshua. "Thank you for what you did in there." Her voice was full of gratitude. "Pick had taken me riding before, but we didn't want to worry my father, so we kept it a secret. Even the time we found you dying in the desert . . ." Her face flushed. "I didn't know who you were then, of course."

Joshua's mouth fell open. "So it was *you*!"

"After what happened this week, my father told me I would not be allowed to ride her again," Callie continued. "He said the incident occurred because I am blind, and—well, I almost believed it myself. Anyway, thank you for—" She did not finish.

Josh placed his hand over hers lying lightly on his arm. "I reckon you can do almost anything better than any other woman I know." Could she tell he was smiling at her? Did she know he wanted to kiss her?

She raised her face slightly as if to look at him, and he leaned toward her, smelling the fresh scent of lilacs. She smiled gently and lifted her chin toward him. He kissed her tenderly, and after a long moment she squeezed his arm.

"We'd best get back to the house now, Joshua," she said quietly. "But thank you—thank you for everything."

✦ CHAPTER 9 ✦

Big John," said Josh to Daniels, still chained to the post of his improvised jail, "aren't you about ready to get loose from there?"

"You got that right! I been here a month, seems like, an' I keep thinkin' 'bout them creepy crawlers, so's at night I don't sleep much."

"You know, they told me they were gonna send for a judge or deputy for your case. But now I hear tell they've got some kind of inquest going into the death of two prospectors found over by Three Kill Spring. Nobody seems to know what to do about you, much less care, but I personally don't like the idea of leaving you tied up. Now if I cut you loose, are you gonna take out after my hide again?"

"Ah, *naw,* Josh! Shucks, you been right good to me. Feedin' me an' fixin' this here tent an' all. I figger as off my head as I was, I coulda wound up shot an' throwed to the coyotes. I only gets mean like that when I mix it up with the tangle-leg. Then I wants to mix it up with ever'body."

"Yeah, I figured that out. You ought to stay away from that rattle-snake juice."

"I try to, Josh. I really do. But when I'm a-workin' the forge, an' he comes by an' says, 'Come on, Big John, come an' wet your whistle,' why I just natur'ly did what he said. An' he kep' sayin', 'Drink up; plenty more where that come from.' By then I'se too far gone t' see straight, much less stop."

"You keep referring to 'he,' Big John. Who is 'he?' Who gave you the whiskey?"

"I thought you know'd, Josh. It was Beldad, the night foreman."

＊ ＊ ＊

Before they'd reached a final agreement, Josh had given Morris two conditions for accepting the job of constable. The first was that Big John Daniels be reinstated as blacksmith. Morris agreed only after Josh assured him he would take full responsibility. The second was that Josh be given a week with Pickax to learn the ways of the desert.

As the two approached Pick's camp, the old man made a wide sweep with his arm in a gesture of welcome. "All right, boy, if you've a mind t' study the desert, just remember that she don't take foolin' with. You gotta go with her, not agin her."

With no more preamble than this remark, the lessons had begun. Pick started by asking if Josh knew why the camp was located in this spot and why the tent flap opened in the direction it did.

The miner nodded when Josh explained correctly that the campsite was shaded from the afternoon heat by the shadow of the overhanging bluff, and the tent opening was such that it kept the prevailing wind from filling the tent with sand.

They reached the tent and unsaddled their mounts. Josh gathered some dry mesquite branches, then collected some of the fleshy bulbs of prickly pears, as he had been instructed. "What do you want these for?" he asked curiously as the miner got a fire going.

"Lots of good in a cactus, boy. Look here." Pickax proceeded to singe the barbs off the plant before tossing it to the ground. Jenny eagerly began to nibble the cactus shoots before they were completely cooled. Then Josh's horse followed suit.

"Desert-bred critters can usually forage for themselves," commented Pick, "but sometimes we help 'em out a mite."

＊ ＊ ＊

The next few days passed quickly with Pick proving an apt instructor and Josh an eager pupil. He learned which trees indicated the presence of moisture beneath the sand and how to keep himself and his horse fed.

Pick told Josh to gather mesquite beans, which could be eaten, and pointed out the value of lizards for roasted meat. Josh also learned of a good poultice for snakebite—chewing tobacco.

"You gotta watch out for them little sidewinders an' Mojave greens," warned Pick. "They hide in the sand with just their eyeballs out. An' they don't give no warnin' before they take out after you, neither."

✵ ✵ ✵

The one topic Pick laid the most stress on was the need for preparation and planning. "I seen people come to grief out here who shoulda knowed better. Like they was countin' on findin' water at a certain tank, an' it was dry. They shoulda planned for that! They shoulda kept back enough water to get them by to the next spring."

"But what if that hole was dry, too, Pick? What then? How can you plan for that?"

"Why, in that case they better be planned up on how they's gonna meet their Maker, 'cause they shore 'nuff'll be seein' Him pronto. The trick, though, is doin' your plannin' so you don't see Him too soon! I seen men crazy fer water drinkin' sand, an' I seen men drink horse blood so's they could make one more sunset.

"Just remember, a man with a mount an' water is home safe. A man with only his horse or only his water can tough it through. But a man with neither horse nor water is a *dead man!*"

Whenever Pick saw that he was dishing out information faster than Josh could take it in, he'd call a halt to their classroom time. Then they'd retreat up the draw behind Pick's camp for a little shotgun practice. Josh had not carried the greener around town, but in his new job as constable, he agreed with Morris and Pickax that he should carry a weapon.

"No, boy, no, ya gotta clamp that scattergun tight against your side, less'n you want to be missin' some teeth when she goes off!"

Josh quickly concluded that there weren't many fine points to blasting away with a sawed-off shotgun. The idea seemed to be to point the greener in the general direction of the target and keep a good hold on it so it wouldn't leap out of your hands when fired.

"This here rig is a whole sight better'n them old cap-fired models. Why, a man can load an' fire these little paper cartridges faster'n you can holler, 'I quit!'"

Pick walked over to Josh's target area. "Looky here at this heap of prickly pear you just blasted. Throwed pieces out in all directions an' ain't any of them pieces too big, neither!" He laughed and shook his head. "Remember, son, a six-gun'll give you a scratch, but buckshot means buryin'."

✴ CHAPTER 10 ✴

Josh took to his new duties with sincere interest, if not enthusiasm. He practiced the frontier proverb "You play the hand you're dealt." Only he would have said, "You shoe the horse they bring you."

The merchants and townspeople were, for the most part, supportive of his appointment. They saw the establishment of a full-time peacekeeping position as one more step toward civilization, respectability—even permanence.

Jacobson, the hardware store owner, was especially agreeable. "Yah, dis a great day for Garson. We haf ben mitout a lawman long enuff, und de riffraff is gettin' too big mit der britches, yah?"

"*For* their britches, Mister Jacobson," Josh corrected. "But I hope you don't expect the town to change overnight just because I'm around. As long as there's drinking and miners mixed together, there's always a match to the dynamite, I think."

"Yah, but you are de strong breath to blow out dis metch. You und dat cannon you have der." He gestured toward the shotgun that Josh carried muzzle downward by a sling around his right shoulder.

Josh reached over with his left hand and grasped the greener around its stock. "You're right about that. Even folks who'd argue with me don't care to get into a dispute with this."

Their conversation was interrupted by gunfire. A man Josh recognized as an employee at the Red Dog Saloon burst out of the swinging doors and ran up to him. "Hey, ain't cha the new constable?"

"That's me. What's the trouble?"

"You better come with me pronto. There's this Texican shootin' up the place!"

Josh moved cautiously toward the saloon while Mr. Jacobson dashed inside his store and bolted the door.

"Whoopee! Ah'm the original, double tough, quick as a rattler, death dealer! Whoopee!" With the second yell came another gunshot that shattered the Red Dog's front window and made curious citizens across the street run for cover.

Josh had unslung the shotgun and held it at ready as he crouched beside the building, but his mind was racing, looking for some way to avoid a shoot-out.

"Barkeep! Barkeep, I say! I don't like the looks of that lady's pit'cher up thar. She's lookin' at me funny. Turn her face to the wall, barkeep, and be quick about it."

Josh peered cautiously around the corner through the broken window and saw the drunken man holding a six-gun on the trembling bartender as the latter tried to reach a painting hanging over the bar. When he still could not reach it after climbing up on the shelves of liquor, the Texan said, "Let's see y'all jump for it." He fired another round, just barely missing the bartender's foot.

The bartender fell sideways in a crash of bottles, smashing three shelves down to the floor.

Josh knew it was only a matter of time before someone started shooting in earnest. Hanging the shotgun back over his shoulder, he stood up and called loudly into the saloon, "Where you at, you old cuss? Hey, don't be bustin' up all them bottles; save some for me!"

The Texan whirled around and stood swaying slightly as if pondering this interruption.

Josh gave him no time to respond. "Where you been keepin' yourself? Why, I ain't seen you since Waco. How ya been?"

The cowboy's eyes squeezed shut, then opened slowly and focused on Josh with difficulty. A gambler was hiding under a table by Josh's feet as he stepped over the windowsill and into the saloon. He called out, "Shoot him. Shoot him quick!" He was silenced by Josh's sudden kick into his midsection.

Josh continued to address the drunk in a loud voice. "Still usin' that same ol' Colt, ain't you? A fine piece. Is your eye as good as it was when y'all shot twelve bull's-eyes runnin' at that turkey shoot on the Brazos?"

The Texan considered this question by looking down at the Colt in his hand, then back at Josh. He nodded slowly, then yelled, "Wanna see? Prop up one of 'em tinhorn gamblers. I'll shoot out his gold fillin's!"

"Naw, old hoss, now that ain't no contest. See if you can shoot the flies offa the top of that wall there." Josh waved toward the side wall of the saloon, away from the street and the rest of the town.

The Texan squinted and remarked with confidence, "Ah'll take the one on the left first!" He fired another shot that hit high on the wall.

"You nailed him. Can you catch his friend there, too?"

Without further comment, the cowboy fired again and with evident satisfaction yelled, "Whoopee! I kin lick my weight in wildcats, an' shoot faster'n greased lightning, I—"

Josh added quickly, "Hey, hoss, that little one up there's gettin' away."

"No, he ain't!" shouted the Texan, and *click* went the hammer on an empty chamber.

"Grab him, boys," ordered Josh, and the cowering drinkers and gamblers wasted no time in subduing the cowboy.

"Don't hurt him," cautioned Josh. "Tie him up and bring me his rig. Take him upstairs and let him sleep it off; then let's see about cleaning up this mess."

✳ ✳ ✳

"What about that Roberts fellow?" McGinty asked Beldad.

Mike Drackett leaned forward in his chair and grinned. "Lemme take care of him, Boss. I been itchin' for the chance."

McGinty spun his office chair around to face Drackett. "No, you ignorant lunk, do you want to really unite this town against us? I don't mean *eliminate* him. I'm talking about *recruiting* him."

Drackett snorted, "Him? He's Morris' right-hand man after savin' that blind gal. What's more, I hear tell he's sweet on her. I can take him, Boss. I know I can. Lemme just solve this problem once and for all!"

McGinty wasn't so quick to reply this time. "Not now, not yet. Not while he's riding so high and has those friends in town. The Dawsons are no folks we want to cross. We'll give Beldad a chance to sound Roberts out and wait for those cowboys to get out of town. All right, Beldad?"

"Sure, Mister McGinty, anything you say. But Mike here is right. Roberts can't be bought, I'm thinkin'."

"Everyone has his price," murmured Fancy Dan softly. "We just have to find out what his might be."

✳ ✳ ✳

At twilight Josh was leaning against the wall outside Jacobson's Hardware, watching the progress of traffic up and down the road. Despite rumblings from the workingmen of Garson about the upcoming lay-off, no violence had broken out, and the town seemed calm.

Beldad approached Josh from across the street. "Hello, Roberts."

"Beautiful evening, Mister Beldad. Are you headed to work?"

"Directly, directly. Time enough for a drink first. Thought I'd ask you to join me."

"No, thank you, Mister Beldad. I believe I'll just stay here and enjoy the evening."

416

Despite this refusal, Beldad gave no indication of intending to move on. Instead he moved closer to Josh and dropped his voice. "You know, there's something I've been meaning to speak to you about, having to do with the welfare of this town and the mine and all."

"Yes, Mister Beldad. What might that be?"

"The men are not going to stand for this unfair treatment by Morris. You can see they'll be able to prevent any work from being done at all if Morris doesn't change his mind. Anyway, it's important for us to know where you stand."

"I'm curious about who *us* might be, Mister Beldad, but then you haven't been exactly keeping your sentiments quiet. Even though you're a foreman, you belong to the so-called Working Men of Garson, don't you?"

"There is no shame in being connected with a group who are standing up for their rights and demanding fair treatment."

"No, that's correct as you have described it. But what I see of these who style themselves Working Men is a group of loudmouthed bullies. Your group, Mister Beldad, seems to contain a high percentage of men who were already discharged for drunkenness or loafing or being general troublemakers. I'll bet the actual number of single miners who wholeheartedly support you is very small indeed."

"And you, Roberts? Aren't you single? Or are you special since you been sparking that blind girl? It don't hurt your standing with—" Beldad's words were cut off midsentence as Josh lifted the man by his shirtfront so that only his boot tips touched the planks.

"Beldad, I'm going to tell you this just once: Your opinions about me are of no interest to me. But let me hear tell of you bad-mouthing Miss Callie just once, and not only will I thrash you within an inch of your life, but I'll tie a can to your tail and stone you out of town like the miserable cur you are! Now get out of my sight!" Josh let Beldad drop so abruptly that instead of landing upright, Beldad missed his footing and landed heavily, seat first, on the boardwalk.

417

"You better watch yourself, Roberts," snarled Beldad. "You'll be sorry you didn't listen to me. You'll see you can't treat me like this!"

Roberts turned slowly to stare down at Beldad, who for all his tough talk had not risen to his feet to speak his piece. "Should I consider that a threat, Mister Beldad?"

"A warning, call it. You'll be sorry!"

"Beldad, I'm already sorry I didn't run you out of town before now! Get out of here before I change my mind and start looking for the can and string!"

Beldad scrambled to his feet and made a quick exit in the opposite direction, cursing and muttering all the way.

✶ CHAPTER 11 ✶

Josh patrolled Garson's street for a few uneventful days. Then he looked up one morning to see Mont James sauntering toward him with a cat-that-got-the-canary grin on his face.

Before Mont could speak, Josh held up his hand. "Don't tell me; let me guess. You've unloaded all those spavined, jug-headed, death-on-four-feet critters on some poor unsuspecting greenhorns."

Mont's grin grew still wider, his eyes dancing with merriment. "All right, you're so all-fired smart—you tell me the rest."

Josh mused a minute, then continued. "And instead of making a down payment at Freeman's Mortuary, like they ought to before forking one of your widow makers, they paid in cash!"

Mont's smile fairly reached from ear to ear, but he only replied, "Now you're with it, brother. Preach on; preach on!"

"And, and . . . what else is there?"

Mont raised his eyebrows expectantly.

"You don't mean—you got more buyers than you had horses!"

"You can put a big amen to that, brother Joshua!" Mont dropped his exaggerated accent. "We sold every head out of this string, and we're heading back out for more!"

"That's great news, Mont. Will you and Tom and Nate be leaving right away?"

"Yes, but we're going home first. Tom's been missing Miss Emily something fierce. We've been on the dry side of those peaks for better'n a month now, and some things up yonder need tending to.

We figure to be back in two or three weeks and get another roundup and breaking done before the snow flies."

Josh stuck out his hand. "I hate to see you go, Mont. You and your family have been about the only ones in this town who aren't either crazy or scared or angry about something."

Mont grasped Josh's hand, looked directly into his friend's eyes, and replied, "Josh, you and me, we work around horses, and we know how tricky they can be and how ornery and how powerful. But sooner or later, they all come around to being broke to ride. How is that, do you figure?"

Josh wasn't sure where this twist in the conversation was leading, but he found himself nodding thoughtfully and answering, "I guess some horses figure out sooner than others that you're going to feed them as well as break them, and for a little cooperation they can get a lot of care."

Mont nodded. "And do we try to take all the spirit out of 'em?"

"No way. You just try to break their will to fight back, not destroy their spirit. Why, a horse with no spirit is as worthless as a nag that's never been broke, only in a different way."

"Exactly." Mont smiled.

"What do you mean, *exactly*? I don't know what you're getting at."

"You said everybody in Garson is angry or fretted or crazy. The truth is, they've never been broke; they're still fighting the bit and kicking the saddle to flinders."

"Broke? Broke by who?"

"Come on now, Josh. You told me your mama raised you in the church. You know what I'm driving at. The Lord Jesus is just waiting for a chance to care for them and teach them and take the fret out of their lives, but first they've gotta get their muliness broke down to size, so He can build up their good qualities from there."

"Yeah, I see what you mean. Just like breaking horses, huh?"

"Yep. Except for one little thing."

"What might that be?"

"When I go to break a horse, I don't ask his permission. But when God wants to make someone over, He can't even begin till they ask Him."

Josh scratched his chin. The idea had never occurred to him before. "Are you saying I need to ask Him?"

"Well, Josh, only you and the Lord Jesus know about that. But I know you're headed His way. God's got big plans for you, Josh Roberts, and He isn't through putting the school on you yet!"

Mont pumped Josh's hand again and nodded. "You be extra careful, Mister Constable. I want to see this town prosper and get civilized so they'll buy more horses. I figure the town needs you to guide it along." He slapped Josh on the shoulder. "If you need us sooner than a month, just give a holler and we'll come running. Be seeing you, Josh."

The stage from Mojave was running late. The connecting stage from San Bernadino was delayed, and the driver from Mojave had no choice but to wait. The connecting stage carried the payroll, some two thousand dollars in gold coin, for the Silver Rim in Garson.

420

The driver was a five-year veteran of this desert run. A short, stocky man with a loud voice and a swaggering walk, his name was Hurry Johnson. He enjoyed the task of guiding the four-up team of mules through the arid country. Much of the terrain was flat, allowing many opportunities for speed, and speed was what Hurry Johnson lived for.

Hurry was a great admirer of the exploits of Hank Monk and other line handlers whose daring—if not insane—driving had made them legendary. For all that he imitated of their style, Hurry didn't care about achieving fame; the chance to drive fast as often as possible was reward enough.

In spite of his emphasis on speed, Hurry was a skilled professional, constantly asking questions of the other drivers to improve his knowledge of the conditions of the road. But he was not given to worrying about what he considered idle speculation, so when he heard talk of Indian activity, he was skeptical.

"Them Mojaves ain't got grit enough to attack a stage with an armed driver an' guard. Their style is more pickin' on lonely old dirt-poor prospectors an' toothless dogs," he said.

He was told that some stretches of the trail toward the silver mining country were watched by Mojaves. It was not uncommon to see small clusters of Indians making their way from place to place, but they had never seemed to be concerned about the passage of the red and yellow coaches that spattered them with gravel and left them in the dust.

"Lately they been watchin' us, but it ain't like them to be movin' much in the heat of the day," he was told.

Hurry discounted all this talk. He knew stage drivers craved adventure. The plain fact was, most of the present bunch had grown up too late for much of the excitement in the West. Now the really long trips were all made by train, and even little out-of-the-way one-horse towns were getting civilized. Hurry figured that any talk of Indian trouble was a result of wishful but fanciful thinking. Anyway, speed was where real adventure could be found. "Ah—" he snorted— "I can outrun a Mojave any day."

His guard for this trip was a young man, Oliver de la Fontaine by name. Folks around said Oliver was too short by half for such a long name, but if they did make that observation they did so out of his hearing. Oliver was a slight young man of nineteen, but he had "killed his man" when he was only seventeen and was known to be a practiced hand with the Smith and Wesson he brought west with him from Boston.

For this trip he was carrying a shotgun, as stagecoach guards often did, but he still wore the S and W at his side. Hurry was impatient to be off, so when the inbound coach finally did arrive, he barely grunted in greeting before throwing the mail pouches and the payroll bag into the boot. He snapped its cover down and had it half secured when he was told that he also would have a passenger with some luggage.

Hurry ripped back the canvas with a violent yank that indicated how irritated he was. When the trunk had been deposited, he wasted no time in tightening the leather straps and buckles, then vaulted into his seat.

A kick to the brake lever and a slap of the reins and they were off, with Oliver making a grab at his hat and their solitary passenger being seated somewhat more abruptly than he had intended.

This was a good stretch of road to make up time, and Hurry proceeded to take advantage of it. The road skirted the mesquite- and yucca-covered foothills east of the Sierra Nevadas as it ran northward. The land was not flat, but the rises and washes were gentle enough to cause little loss of speed. Behind the coach rose a dust cloud twenty feet high that trailed them for a quarter of a mile as they sped along.

To reach the first stop at Weidner's was a matter of only an hour or so. The team was not changed here; they were just given a little water and a chance to breathe before the run was resumed.

The next hour contained both faster and slower passages. The road crossed deeper washes that flooded when the thunder crashed over the Sierra peaks. These canyons not only had steeper sides but sandy bottoms that slowed the team as resistance to the coach's wheels increased.

Slowing down was something Hurry did reluctantly, but he knew a driver who had dumped a coach in an attempt to use too much speed in one of these arroyos. Hurry hadn't particularly thought the wreck was a tragedy; what bothered him was that the driver had been fired and had been forced to leave this area to get work. So in the plunges into the canyons, Hurry used more caution than he really wanted.

These periods of slower travel were compensated by the times when the stage road ran through the alkali flats. Formed when the occasional flood burst out of the confining arroyos, the flats could be as much as a mile wide. The mineral-laden water that pooled in these areas was either absorbed into the soil or evaporated, leaving behind a crust of alkali salts that formed a hard, shiny surface on which almost nothing grew.

On these stretches Hurry was really in his element. He urged the team to greater and greater speed, and they responded till the coach fairly flew over the ground. A grin would break out on Hurry's features as if the force of the wind itself had pulled the corners of his mouth back toward his ears.

Oliver had ridden with Hurry enough to be nonchalant about

this breakneck charge across the desert. Passengers, on the other hand, were so often unprepared for the intensity of the rush that they remained unable to speak or relax their white-knuckled grips on their valises for several minutes after reaching Red Rock Station.

There the team was changed, and sometimes mail and passengers exchanged. The road was split at this point, turning aside toward Garson from the main track that continued on north to Indian Wells.

From the station eastward through Red Rock Canyon, Hurry's face resumed its normal, uninspired look. The twists and turns of the road as it followed the wash through sandstone ledges never allowed for the velocity Hurry craved. Passengers might enjoy the orange-and-pink formations and comment on the colorful bands stretched on either side of the road, but Hurry took no pleasure in sightseeing.

As the coach turned into the third in a series of S-shaped curves leading through the canyon, Oliver leaned over and observed, "You know, Hurry, I think I saw an Injun up top of that rock. Isn't this the stretch where Murchison said he saw those Mojaves?"

"I reckon. I never paid him no mind, anyways. What d'ya figger the Injun was doin'?"

"I don't know, but let me get Betsy here limbered up anyway," said Oliver as he took the shotgun out of its rest beside his seat and checked its loads.

"Hey, in there!" Oliver called to the passenger. "Look sharp! There may be some trouble up ahead. If you got a piece, get it ready."

The message produced more than just startled consternation, for in a moment a hand protruded from the driver's-side window holding a .45 caliber Colt.

The stage entered the next turn, slowing to a cautious pace, then speeding up as the corner was made and the way shown to be clear.

"'Twern't nothin' to it, after all," grunted Hurry. "Mebbe you had a speck o' dust in your eye."

✳ ✳ ✳

Oliver was about to agree when a rifle shot struck the seat between the two men, splintering the underside of the board. Oliver whirled to catch a glimpse of a Mojave on an overhead sandstone ledge just as he directed another shot at them. He returned one barrel of the shot-gun at the attacker, more in hope of spoiling the Indian's aim than of hitting him, then immediately emptied the second barrel at another Mojave on the opposite canyon wall. This time the blast made its mark as the Indian clutched his chest and tumbled forward off the rocks.

Hurry snapped the reins and cursed the mules into a burst of speed. They needed no urging as they caught the nervous excitement of rifle fire popping around them.

The passenger was firing now also, taking deliberate aim as well as he could from the pitching and careening coach. The sandstone walls seemed to have sprouted Mojaves; half a dozen were firing from either side of the arroyo. The passenger's last shot took out an Indian who was firing down on the coach but not before a .44 slug tore behind Hurry's left shoulder and dug a furrow down his back.

From the curse that burst from Hurry's lips and clenched teeth, Oliver knew the driver had been hit. "Shall I take the lines?" he shouted.

"I can drive with my teeth if I have to. Just you keep 'em offa me, an' I'll get us outta here." Other shots hit the coach as he spoke.

The fact was, the coach had already swept past all but the last pair of Mojaves. Although the occupants of the stage couldn't have known it at the time, the Indians had been unsure of their strategy and had relied too much on new weapons with which they were not yet very familiar.

Oliver fired his S and W at the last Indian on his side when both Mojaves leaped from their rocky perches toward the speeding stage-coach. One landed on top of the coach but was slung over the side as they jolted around a curve. The Indian caught himself just before being thrown off and began to pull himself back up over the side.

Oliver leveled his pistol at the Indian's head, but the hammer snapped on an empty chamber as he pulled the trigger. He instinctively reached for the shotgun that lay at his feet. Swinging it by the barrel, his gun stock's blow swept the Mojave backward and off the coach, bouncing him against the rocky wall and onto his face in the sand.

The other Indian, landing farther back on the stage's roof, did not attempt to attack either driver or guard. He had made his leap with a knife clenched in his fist, and he used it now to slit open the canvas covering of the boot.

After knocking one Mojave clear of the coach, Oliver had crammed two more shells into the shotgun and clambered to the roof. He was surprised to see the Indian crouching in the boot, throwing out the passenger's trunk and mailbag, then raising the payroll pouch to throw it off. At Oliver's involuntary shout, the Indian looked up, poised to throw his knife. Oliver's shotgun, no more than four feet away, blew him right off the back.

Hurry never let up on the mules until they had exited the canyon and put some miles of open space between themselves and the attack. Then he pulled up to rest the lathered and trembling team and allowed Oliver to examine and bandage his wound. The bullet had torn the flesh clear down to Hurry's hip, where it had glanced off a bone before exiting.

"Looks to me like this'll be more trouble to your sitting back in a chair than it will to your driving," observed Oliver.

"I coulda told you that," said Hurry through gritted teeth. "Ain't nothin' keeps me from drivin'."

"I can't imagine where the Mojaves got those rifles, but it was lucky for us they weren't too good at using them!"

"More'n that, it's lucky they didn't hit the mules. Likely they was tryin' not to hit 'em, so's they could drive 'em back to their camp and make a meal of 'em."

"Did you ever know these Indians to attack a stage before?"

"Never. Mostly they stay clear of folks that can fight back, but this bunch had a plan to take us out."

"Suppose they knew about the payroll shipment?"

"How in tarnation could an Injun know about that? That last 'un was likely trying to get whatever he could, since they couldn't stop us."

"You know, we were downright lucky. Helped to have that passenger shooting on your side of the coach."

"Ain't that the truth! Say, why haven't we heard from him?"

Oliver and Hurry looked at each other as the same thought struck them. Neither was surprised when Oliver opened the stagecoach door to find the passenger's lifeless body sprawled across the seats. Two of the Indians' .44 slugs had made their marks after all.

✳CHAPTER 12✳

Callie was sitting in her carriage, waiting for Ling Chow's return, when Fancy Dan walked up beside her.

"Miss Morris, a word with you, if you please?"

"Yes, Mister McGinty, what is it?"

"It never ceases to amaze me how you can tell in an instant who a person is by their voice alone."

"Is that what you wanted to tell me, Mister McGinty?"

"Why, no. No, it's not. I actually wanted to say—well, what I intended to ask was . . ."

"Come now, Mister McGinty, bashfulness is hardly your style," remarked Callie dryly. "What is on your mind?"

"You certainly are a direct person, Miss Morris; I like that. All right, I'll be direct as well. I'd like to call on you at your home, to get to know you better. You are a lovely and well-spoken woman, and I'd like to—"

"Thank you, Mister McGinty. I believe I understand your question. To be equally straightforward, your interest does not interest me. No, thank you."

"Ah, but, Miss Morris—may I call you Callie?"

"I'd rather you didn't, Mister McGinty."

McGinty continued smoothly, as if he hadn't detected the snub, "Miss Morris, I believe that I can offer you refined, intelligent conversation. What's more, I am a man of ambition. I expect to own a fine home in San Francisco, perhaps enter politics."

"And then what, Mister McGinty?"

McGinty's smoothness wavered. "What?" he demanded. Then catching himself, he said soothingly, "Pardon me, I didn't quite catch what you asked."

"Then what?" she repeated. "What are you doing that will outlast your saloon in Garson, your fine home in San Francisco, and even your ambition?"

In what was a most unusual circumstance for him, McGinty was momentarily speechless. He decided to ignore this baffling discussion and try a different approach. "Your friend Roberts may style himself a constable, but he's really just a sweaty blacksmith. He won't ever be able to treat you to the kind of genteel life you deserve."

This may have been straight talk, but it was entirely the wrong tactic to take with Callie Morris. She stiffened noticeably, and whether intentionally or not, she managed to turn so that the brilliant sunlight reflected off her smoked glasses directly into McGinty's eyes. He blinked and fidgeted uncomfortably, but she tilted her head to follow the sound, so that the irritation continued. "That is not even remotely any of your business, Mister McGinty. Now, good day to you."

"Miss Morris, you shouldn't be so hasty. After all, my attention might benefit your father. You do care about your father, don't you? Indeed, one might say that a disregard for my attentions could be, shall we say, *unpleasant* for your father."

Callie's remaining patience snapped at this poorly veiled threat. She stood in the carriage, her hand finding the buggy whip that rested at her side. She snatched the whip and snapped it into the air.

McGinty leaped back out of its way but not before the stinging lash caught his ear.

"Mister McGinty," she said slowly and deliberately, "do not threaten me or my father. And if you know what's good for you, never speak to me again."

At that moment Ling Chow hurried out of the hardware store. "What going on here? Miss Callie, what you do?" He climbed in beside her and took the reins.

"Ah, Ling Chow, Mister McGinty asked my opinion of something, and I was *giving it to him*." Callie flung the whip down on the leather seat.

McGinty, now that he was safely out of range, had recovered his aplomb. Holding a silk handkerchief to his bleeding earlobe, he sneered. "You shouldn't be so high-and-mighty, Miss Morris, and you *won't* be soon. If you're lucky, I might give you a job in my casino making change for gamblers. I guess even a blind girl could do that."

Callie turned her face from him. "Drive us home, Ling," she said through stiff lips. She could hear McGinty's mocking laughter behind her as the team stepped out smartly and drew the carriage up the street.

✵ ✵ ✵

"But what did he mean, Papa? How can he hurt us?"

"Hush now, child. He can't hurt us. He's just a no-good, rotten bully and a cheap crook with a two-bit way of talking."

"Papa, you're not telling me everything. How can he even think to turn us out?"

Morris sighed heavily and, taking Callie's hands in his, led her over to the settee. "All right, Callie, you deserve an explanation. Sit down here."

"First of all, McGinty has nothing on us, and you mustn't fret about it. But he has made an offer to the Golden Bear Mining Company to purchase the Silver Rim."

"Buy the Rim? But, Papa, you're a director of the Golden Bear."

"Yes, Callie, that's true. But I'm only one of many. You know the Rim's been losing money, and—well, McGinty's offer was substantial enough that the other directors have voted to consider it."

"Just like that? Without even thinking of us and all the work you've done?"

"Now simmer down, Callie. No, it's not just like that. The directors have agreed to give me a little more time to prove my belief in the quality of the ore the Rim can produce. Unfortunately, they're not willing to give me very long, and you know the setbacks we've been having."

"Yes, and I bet McGinty's behind them, too."

"I'm sure he's encouraged the talk of unrest among the men I laid off. But, Callie, he can't have been responsible for the loss of the payroll in the Indian attack. No, even McGinty wouldn't stoop that low."

"All right, Papa. You know, you shouldn't keep things from me. Anyway, I can always tell when you're upset. But how can I pray for you if I don't know what to pray about?"

"Lord love you, child, you're right. Let's both do some praying right now. If God is willing, we won't have any more trouble, and the Rim will make this town bloom—but it won't be by the likes of Fancy Dan McGinty running things!"

✦CHAPTER 13✦

Heading back to town on foot after another evening with Callie, Josh tried to analyze how he felt. Warmth flooded him, like the instant sense of heat when gray clouds part and sunshine bathes your face. The sensation felt unfamiliar, like waking up in a new place and not knowing for a time where you are. And it felt scary, like having the responsibility to care for something precious beyond measure. He was in love!

"Injun," he spoke to his horse, which he was leading behind him, "do you suppose everyone who's in love feels like this all the time? How do they ever get any work done?"

The horse nickered softly as if to reply, *Who knows? Wait and see, and enjoy the waiting.*

Josh shut his eyes and stood still, absorbing the night sounds, senses, and smells. He continued on down the road toward town, still walking and leading Injun. Riding would cut short the time he wanted to spend thinking.

He had just passed the turn in the trail that hid the Morris home from Garson when the buckskin whinnied again softly, then louder.

Off to his right, another horse answered! Josh couldn't have said why but instinctively he knew something was wrong, and in that knowing he reacted.

Josh swung Injun around on the lead rope, the horse prancing nervously. He slipped the straps of the greener and the cartridge pouch off the saddle horn, and as he thumbed back one hammer, something whistled just past his ear. A muzzle flash and report of a pistol came from the darkness.

Josh swung up the greener and fired from the hip as Pick had taught him, directly back toward the unseen attacker. Then he flung himself to the ground as Injun pounded off, back toward the Morris home.

A second shot and a third went over Josh's head as he lay on the ground. From the two flashes Josh could see that his attacker was circling to the left, apparently moving to get a clean shot at Josh's side.

Josh pulled back the other hammer, pointed the shotgun's muzzle along the road, and lay very still. An instant later his guess was proven correct as a boot crunched the gravel of the road not ten yards away.

Josh didn't wait for his assailant to fire but blasted off the second barrel, immediately rolling to the other side of the road as he did. His fire was met with an agonized shout and a wild return shot that ricocheted off a rock beside the road and went singing off into the dark. An instant searing pain, like a hot iron, leaped across Josh's forehead. A second later, Josh heard feet running clumsily and a continuous string of curses.

431

Joshua fumbled in the cartridge bag. His nervous fingers spilled three shells on the road, then closed on two more as he broke open the shotgun's action and replaced the spent ammunition with fresh.

Lying still in the slight depression beside the road, Josh could hear the retreating footfalls stop, then more cursing and shuffling as his attacker tried to get a spooked horse to stand still. The creaking of saddle leather suggested that the man, whoever he was, had succeeded. This was confirmed a moment later; hoofbeats retreated rapidly toward town.

Joshua stood slowly and felt himself grow dizzy. He put his hand to his forehead, and it came away wet and sticky to his touch.

From up the road came Morris' voice. "Joshua, are you there? Joshua, answer me! Ling Chow, have that rifle ready!"

"Ready, Mistah Mollis! Let Ling go fust!"

Josh called out to them, "It's all right. I'm here. Someone shot at me, but he's run off now."

Morris and the Chinaman hurried up, and as Morris stooped to light the lantern he carried, Josh could see a six-gun in his hand. The Chinaman was armed with a Henry rifle.

Morris stood. "Are you hurt . . . good *grief,* your face is all bloody! Sit down or, or . . . lie down! Ling, fetch the wagon. No, we'll carry you."

"It's all right, Mister Morris. It's only a scratch; I'm just a little dizzy. There, that'll do for now," said Josh, as he clamped a necker-chief over the wound.

Morris and Ling Chow walked on either side of Josh as they returned to the house.

Callie was standing in the doorway, her face a mask of worry and concern. She called out as she heard the returning footsteps, "Is he all right, Papa?"

Mr. Morris and Joshua exchanged looks that said, *She really cares* and *Let's not worry her.*

432

Morris said, "Yes, Callie, Joshua chased the other man off, and he's coming back with us."

Once inside the house, Josh was forced to admit to his forehead wound, and Callie immediately took charge. Leading him to the kitchen where she could get warm water, she instructed Josh to hold a clean compress on it while she washed the rest of his face. With strong, steady fingers, she gently traced the edges of the wound and announced with relief that it was indeed only a grazing.

Josh nodded thoughtfully. "I don't even think it's a bullet wound. A chunk of rock must have flown up from his last shot."

"Maybe—but, oh, Josh, *who* would want to *kill* you? It *could* have been a bullet!"

Josh reached up and took her slender hand in his. "Callie, I know that God is watching out for me. I've become convinced of that. As to who did it—that's exactly what I aim to find out!"

✳ ✳ ✳

The next day Josh made his way around Garson with his forehead bandaged, asking questions. He wanted to know who had been seen coming back to town with a fresh wound.

Among the merchants, no one knew anything or had seen anything unusual, and there was no reason to think they would cover up for anyone.

Dr. Racine examined the patch job Callie had done on Josh's forehead but vowed he'd had no late-night patients with gunshot wounds. "I'll sure let you know if anyone shows up. Any idea what sort of wound I should be looking for?"

Josh instinctively rubbed his forehead, which had a dull ache. "Whoever it was made it back to his horse all right and rode off, but his last shot was wild and he didn't fire again. I'd say it's good odds he's at least hit on his gun-hand side."

"Good enough. I'll be looking out for him."

Josh was hesitant to tackle the saloons. There he expected a less cheerful reception. If the attack was connected with the growing dispute among the miners, members of the so-called Working Men were less likely to be helpful.

Might as well start off with the place I know will be the least troublesome, he told himself. Turning his steps up the brush-covered slope, he entered the No Name Saloon.

"Welcome, my friend, welcome!" burst out Jersey Smith, his pointed beard bobbing as he spoke. "What have we here? I perceive some jealous female has attempted to scratch out your eyes!"

"Something like that, Jersey," remarked Josh, laying the greener on the bar top. "Can we visit quietly here for a minute?"

"Of course, my boy," agreed Jersey, lowering his voice. "Tell me what you need."

Josh recounted the story of the night before and ended by putting the question to Jersey about any man with a newly wounded right side or arm.

Jersey thought carefully before answering, then shook his mane of white hair. "No, I've seen some wounds but nothing of the sort you describe. Perhaps the ruffian has left town by now."

"I don't think so. I'm pretty certain he was acting on someone else's orders. They may try to get him out of town, but I was watching the road last night, and Dub Taylor's keeping an eye out today."

"He must be hiding somewhere."

433

"That's what I think, too. I'm hoping that where I find him will tell me who's behind this."

"I'll be happy to be of service any way I can, but I really doubt that he'd show up here. As you know, I'm opposed to the group of hoodlums calling themselves Working Men, so they don't frequent my establishment."

"I figured as much, but I don't want to jump to conclusions and overlook something."

Josh turned around slowly and surveyed the small saloon. The men were all quietly talking or playing cards. Most of them were married, and those who were single were not known as troublemakers. Josh turned back to Jersey with a wry smile. "What I really mean is that I put off going into the lion's den long enough. Thanks for your help." Taking the shotgun from the bar top, he left through the tent flap.

Josh squared his shoulders and took a deep breath. It was time to get down to serious business. He went first into the Chinaman's Chance. Immediately he felt some hostility in the sidelong glances and whispered comments that passed among the miners. Even though Josh had been well liked by all the miners, his position as constable with the full backing of the Silver Rim owner put him on the opposite side of the fence from the Working Men. Besides that, the fact that he was still employed while being a single man made for even more resentment.

No one knew anything about a wounded man, or if they did, they weren't saying. Josh located a few friendly faces to have a moment's conversation, but these men were subjected to intimidating stares for even giving the time of day to the constable. In any case, they added, they were moving on in a day or so to look for work in the mines around Independence.

That's just great, Josh mused, soberly shaking his head as he headed across the street toward Fancy Dan's. *Pretty soon the only single men left in Garson will be the ones who would rather drink and fight than do an honest day's work. I sure hope Mister Morris is right about that big vein opening up soon. This town needs some good luck before it boils over.*

Josh thought he saw Beldad looking out the door at the front of Fancy Dan's, but the face disappeared too quickly for him to be sure. One thing was certain—McGinty had been warned about Josh's approach. He stepped up to shake Josh's hand before he was completely through the door.

"Well, Constable Roberts, what brings you in this time of day? Say, I'll bet you're looking for information about that drunken sot who took a shot at you last night. How is your head, anyway?"

"My head's fine, Mister McGinty. I'm looking to find whoever that was last night, all right, but how do you know he was drunk?"

McGinty scratched absently at his smooth-shaven cheek. "Heh! Well—I don't know for a fact, of course, just guessing. But it must have been someone who'd had more than was good for him. Perhaps it was some cowboy nursing a grievance against you."

"Mister McGinty, what happened last night was an attempt at cold-blooded murder. I've divine Providence to thank that I'm alive today. Drunk or not, an ambush is not the ploy of an angry cowboy. This was more like the move of someone following orders."

"Perhaps you're right," agreed McGinty hastily. "In any case, how can I be of help?"

Josh was aware of the same hostile glances he had been subject to in the other saloon. There was an undercurrent of animosity that seemed to be directed at him personally—almost as if someone had been talking about him when he walked in.

When Josh spoke again, it was in a calm, quiet voice. "I'll just have a look around, if you don't mind."

"Not at all, not at all. Help yourself."

Josh made a slow circuit of the room, getting angry looks and muttered halfhearted curses, but seeing no one with the kind of recent injury he sought. He returned to McGinty, who was standing at the bar, sharing a private word with the bartender and smiling at something.

Josh stopped and took a good look at the slick saloon keeper, then remarked casually, "Guess I'll take a quick look upstairs."

McGinty reacted immediately. "Now, why would you want to do that? You can see I have nothing to hide. Besides, the activities

435

upstairs are no concern of yours, if you know what I mean." He gave Josh a broad wink and a leering smile.

"I believe I'll have a look just the same." Josh started for the stairs, and at the same moment the bartender, who had been arranging the bottles on a shelf behind the bar, knocked one over. It fell with a crash, amplified by its collision with a brass spittoon.

Josh whirled around, but the bartender merely lifted his palms and shrugged. Josh had his foot on the bottom step when a door at the head of the stairs opened, and one of the girls of the line came out, followed by Mike Drackett.

Drackett's voice boomed down the stairs, but it sounded somewhat strained. "What was that racket? Oh, it's you, Constable. Fall in the gaboon, did ya?"

The sneer with which Drackett addressed him made Josh bristle, but he forced himself to stay calm. "Where were you last night, Drackett?"

"Last night? My, my, ain't we gettin' nosy? Guess you could ask Irma here, ain't that right, Irma?" Drackett waved his right arm in a sweeping gesture.

The girl only nodded, her pale skin ashen against her bright red dress.

"Are you through pokin' in my private life, Constable?" This time the sneer was accompanied by his teeth gritting.

Without waiting for Josh's reply, Drackett hooked his right arm through Irma's elbow and began to tug the girl back into the room behind them.

"Just a minute, Drackett," called Josh sharply. "I seem to recall taking a Colt off you over at Jersey Smith's."

"Yeah? Well, what of it? I ain't forgot, you little—but you can see I ain't wearin' one now." Drackett moved his right hip and side into Josh's view and once again started to back up into the doorway.

"But, Mike," Josh corrected softly, "my recollection is that you are left-handed."

The girl called Irma screamed, as if some restraint had suddenly snapped. She pulled away from Drackett's grasp, stumbled, and fell to the floor, propelled by a rough push from her companion.

As Drackett turned involuntarily, his bloodstained left side and bound-up left arm came into view. So did the Starr revolver he wore in a cross-draw holster on his left side.

Drackett reached for the pistol as Josh fumbled with the stock of the greener. The upward angle was awkward for the sawed-off shotgun. It was a toss-up which man could bring his gun to bear first, but Drackett's side was stiff and he was not that good with his right hand.

The Starr hadn't even cleared leather when the .12 gauge's deafening roar sent all the patrons of Fancy Dan's diving for cover. Eight of the nine double-aught pellets found their mark, and Drackett was hurled backward through the doorway behind him and into the bed frame. His torso folded back onto the bed, his legs draped on the floor.

✳ ✳ ✳

"Lower away," hollered Dub Taylor to make himself heard over the ringing of single jacks and the puffing donkey engine whose cables drew the ore cars.

Taylor was on his way down to gallery number five to inspect the condition of the working face. The lowest level of the Silver Rim had finally been pumped dry, and just last night Beldad had personally set the charges to begin the excavation.

As he rode deeper into the mine, the heat increased noticeably, and the walls became slick with moisture. *This sure enough reminds me of the Consolidated in Virginia,* he thought. *Now there was a bonanza—three or four levels of good assay that anyone would be proud to work and then wham! Right in the middle of the hot, steamy water, the sweetest vein you ever saw. To think what they'd have missed if they'd never gone that deep!*

Far overhead, the operator of the cable saw the red-painted stretch of steel cords appear that marked the level of the opening to gallery number five. Slowing the descent of the platform, the operator brought the moving floor to a stop even with a rocky ledge.

Taylor stepped off and walked forward in the curious step-pause-step gait of the longtime hard-rock miner. Underground, men didn't rush about, or the candle in the tin reflector mounted on their heads would blow out. Moreover, many a man had lived through a narrow escape by listening to the creaking of timbers and the rumbling of earth in that brief delay between steps.

Taylor patted the sixteen-inch square box timbers that formed the framework of the mine's tunnels and shafts. Bending over, he paused to inspect the base of the timber that had been immersed in water the day before. It didn't appear to have been damaged, but for safety's sake it would need to be replaced. Dub wanted to see if work could continue on gallery five while new timbers were being put in. Beldad's blast the night before was intended to test the trustworthiness of the giant beams.

Beldad's shot, loaded and fired by him alone from much farther away than the miners usually worked, was also expected to reveal something else. If level five showed promise, then Morris could begin rehiring additional miners. If, on the other hand, it showed poorly, then work would continue on three alone, and the single men would still be without jobs.

The flickering light of Dub's candle lantern began to show pieces of rubble from the blast as he got nearer to the working face. As he turned a bend into what should have been a wider and higher gallery with a sloping mound of rubble ready to be cleared from the face, he stopped in consternation. The space was choked with debris. Boulders of all sizes blocked the passage and kept Dub from even seeing, much less reaching, the far wall.

"What is this?" he demanded of the heap of stone. "It looks like Beldad shot the roof instead of the face! He's completely blocked the gallery. We'll have two more weeks of work just to get it cleared!"

Taylor turned, still muttering to himself, angry to the point of distraction as he thought about how quickly he'd like to fire Beldad and then wring his neck or maybe the other way around. He was still disturbed as he kicked first one loose stone and then another. Why would Beldad do something so patently stupid and which benefited no one? Absentmindedly, Dub bent to pick up a chunk of rock.

He didn't even hear the hissing and crackling until he turned to see the flame moving up the cord to the ceiling of the tunnel ahead of him.

"Hey!" he shouted. "Hey! I'm in here!" He realized even as he yelled that the fuse was already burning too close to the charges to be pulled out in time.

A series of short, sharp concussions went off like brief claps of thunder. Dub was thrown against a rock wall but wasn't knocked unconscious. He had just enough time to raise his hands to his bleeding ears before twenty-five tons of ceiling fell on him.

⋆CHAPTER 14⋆

I say we lynch him—string him up."

"What cause did he have to blast old Mike thataway?"

"It was Mike who bushwhacked Roberts the night before; that's how he got that wound on his left side."

"Yeah? Says who? That's what Roberts wants you to think, ain't it? He's had it in for Mike ever since he came to Garson. Besides, who said Roberts got bushwhacked? Did anybody see the other feller? An' don't be handin' out that swill about Roberts bein' shot in the head an' all. A little bandage don't account for a head wound. How come *he* ain't dead?"

"But Drackett *was* shot in his gun arm—that's the only way Roberts could beat him at the draw."

"Who you gonna believe anyway—Mike or that bootlicker Roberts? Mike told me that somebody shot *him* from ambush."

"Hey, it coulda happened that way. What about the fellers who died suddenly? Like Swede—with his neck broke. In his whole life he never drunk so much he couldn't walk straight. How could he end up walkin' off a cliff?"

"Yeah, an' how about Dub Taylor? Mighty peculiar, that rock fall catchin' him all by hisself."

"Why would Roberts want to kill a foreman? I mean, they both work for Morris, don't they?"

"Yeah, well, maybe Roberts wants to run this whole town *and* the Silver Rim. I hear tell that since that blind gal is sweet on him, Morris'll do anything he wants."

"McGinty won't let 'em push us around. McGinty's as big a man as Morris, and he'll stand up to Roberts, too."

Beldad smiled contentedly and listened, while rolling a home-made smoke as he leaned back in his chair. He hadn't even had to stir this pot to make it boil. The out-of-work men were ready to believe the worst about Roberts. He was a handy target, since he represented both the management of the Rim and the law. All Beldad had to do was drop the suggestion that Roberts was looking for an excuse to murder Drackett, and the fuse of mob action was ignited.

McGinty will be pleased, Beldad thought, *and that spot as general foreman is as good as mine. You did good, Mike. You didn't amount to much alive, but you made up for it in your death!*

✳ ✳ ✳

"I think," remarked Fancy Dan McGinty with evident satisfaction, "that we've got everything coming our way now. Don't you agree, Mister Beldad?"

"Yes, sir, Boss, it sure seems that way—except for . . . except . . ."

"Oh yes, the loss of your job at the Silver Rim. Think nothing of it, Beldad, uh, *Mister General Foreman.* How does that sound to you?"

"Sounds great, Boss. But are you sure everything's been taken care of?"

"Second thoughts at this late hour? All right, Beldad, let's review: One, gallery five is buried under enough rubble that Morris and his men won't stumble on the big strike. But we can get it in operation in, oh, a week or ten days, since we won't waste any time on level three. Two, the Working Men are disrupting even the little production that the Rim still has, hastening the time when its stock will fall into my lap. Three, Pitahaya and his savages have gotten their promised rifles and will be able to take the next payroll shipment, no matter how well armed it is. That will be the finish of Morris, because none of his precious family men will continue working if unpaid. He'll be forced to concede defeat."

"Haven't you forgotten something, Mister McGinty?"

"I don't think so. What's that?" McGinty replied easily, pulling out his watch to examine its polish.

"What about Roberts?"

"Didn't I tell you, Mister Beldad? I'm sending up to Jawbone Canyon to bring back Logan."

"Miles Logan?"

"The same. The man they call Gates of Hell. And that, Mister Beldad, should put a finish to any concern we have with Joshua Roberts once and for all."

✷ ✷ ✷

"Josh, I've something I need you to do. I'll tell you now that I don't feel good about asking you, and I'll understand if you refuse."

"Mister Morris, I never went looking for this constable's job, but once I took it, I never figured to turn down something because it looked hard. Tell me what you need."

"As you know, we've got to get the next payroll shipment here at once, or the Rim is finished. McGinty will certainly own it, and he'll be able to run this town as he sees fit. I don't think either of us wants that."

At Josh's emphatic shake of his head, he continued. "I'm certain that the Mojaves are watching the line closely and waiting to attack again when they know the gold is there. So even if I could get a party of armed men to guard the stage, that would only be a signal to the Indians that here was a coach worth attacking!"

"But they wouldn't try to hit a well-armed party, would they? I thought a quick raid against no defense was more their style," Josh interjected.

"Up until the last attack on the coach, I would have agreed with you. But some things have changed. The Mojaves have figured out that the army is occupied elsewhere. They may be trying to get enough gold to retreat across the border to Mexico in between Apache-style forays. Even worse, they have gotten hold of some repeating rifles."

"Yes, so I hear. They must have stolen them from the prospectors they ambushed."

"That's what I assumed, but the stage driver and guard both say that as many as a *dozen* Mojaves were using them—poorly, I might add, but we can't trust poor marksmanship to continue. Besides, if someone is trading Winchesters to the Indians, the next coach may be facing twenty or thirty rifles!"

"What's the answer, then?"

"I've sent an urgent message requesting a detachment of cavalry be sent here at once. I have some friends in San Francisco with enough connections in Washington to get some prompt action. But 'prompt' in army terms means a couple of weeks, anyway. Right now, we need to pay these miners, or all work on the Rim will stop."

"What does all this have to do with what you said you had to ask me?"

"I want you to ride as scout for the next coach. There will be just the driver and guard on board. With you riding ahead to look for signs of ambush, you should be able to give the stage enough warning to turn around, avoiding a fight altogether.

"The Mojaves won't expect us to ship gold without a string of guards, so a second coach will be hitched up and surrounded by as many men as I can hire. It will proceed to the edge of the most dangerous stretch, then fake a breakdown. If the Indians are watching as closely as I think they are, they won't want to give away their position by attacking you when they think the gold shipment is following close behind."

Josh nodded pensively. "Sounds like it might work. When do you want to try it?"

"Just as soon as possible. Hurry Johnson and his guard have agreed to drive if you're the scout. Seems they've heard about your reputation for coolness."

"And we'll be leaving—"

"Tonight. Under cover of darkness. Going *away* from Garson, there'll be little chance of trouble with the Mojaves."

"All right, sir. I'll go make ready. Oh, one more thing. Do you think I could say good-bye to Callie before I go?"

A smile broke through Morris' weariness, and there was a twinkle in his eye. "I thought you might ask, son. She's waiting in the other room."

✳ ✳ ✳

"Boss, that stagecoach pulled out last night," reported Beldad to McGinty, who was shaving with an ivory-handled straight razor in front of a brass-framed mirror.

"So, what of it? We're not interested in coaches leaving Garson, only those coming in. Anyway, I've told the Indians that the next gold shipment will undoubtedly be heavily guarded. Now that they have the rest of the rifles, they're ready to attack at the first sign of valuables being shipped."

"Right, Boss. Uh—by the way, Roberts isn't in town, neither."

McGinty turned around with his face still half lathered. "*What?* How do you know?"

"Remember you told me to keep an eye on him on account of what we got planned for the Rim? Well, I had one of the boys ask if Mister Roberts was at breakfast yet, and that old potato-eatin' biddy—sorry, Boss—that Mrs. Flynn said he wasn't in the place and hadn't been there since yesterday afternoon."

"What? Hold on, Beldad; let me think." McGinty turned back to the mirror and absently resumed shaving. "It must mean something," he observed out loud to his reflection in the steamy glass. "Old Morris may be more subtle than I give him credit for. He wouldn't part with Roberts just to send him to hire some guards. He must know that Roberts' presence has been keeping the lid on things here."

Beldad knew better than to interrupt McGinty's reverie. Besides, he was inwardly cursing his stupidity for making a disparaging remark about the Irish. He was so involved with hoping McGinty hadn't noticed that he missed it when McGinty addressed him.

"Huh? What did you say, Boss?"

"Pay attention, Beldad. I think the time is ripe for all our plans to bear fruit. With Logan coming to town tonight, we're ready to shut down the Rim. By the time you get back, we'll have it all."

"Get back from where?"

"Didn't you hear anything I said? I want you to ride to Red Rock Canyon and tell the Mojaves not to be fooled by any guarded coach unless Roberts is with it. Tell them he'll be riding a buckskin horse and carrying a shotgun!"

✳CHAPTER 15✳

I'm sure sorry we had to let on to those men that they weren't really guarding a gold shipment. I'm afraid some careless word might get back to the Mojaves." Josh voiced his doubts to Hurry Johnson as they hitched up his teams at Weidner's.

"Naw, it ain't likely. Gettin' in two nights ago, jest hirin' them last night, an' leavin' this mornin'—I figger it ain't had time to get to them savages. Besides, you can't blame them for not wantin' to face Injuns totin' brand-new Winchesters for no twenty dollars."

"I guess you're right. But I wish we hadn't been here a day already. Are they ready to roll?"

"Same as us. They're gonna be just enough behind us that them Injuns will be watchin' both coaches. We don't want them to be hittin' us by mistake on account of not seein' the playactin'." Hurry's voice held a sad and regretful note.

Josh caught it and asked, "What's the matter? Don't you think it'll work?"

"Yeah, it'll work, I reckon. But to keep from gettin' ahead of them fellers, I'm sure gonna have to drive slow!"

✳ ✳ ✳

"What do you mean, stopping these miners from going to work? By what right are you trespassing on Silver Rim property?" Morris was shouting at a group of men who were milling around in front of the mine entrance. They included a line of men carrying weapons, led by a man dressed in black.

"Well, I represent the Working Men of Garson, and they have picked me to be their spokesman—"

"You?" interrupted Morris. "You're not a miner and neither are these others with you. I see some *behind* you who used to work for me. You men, what are you doing with these hooligans?"

The man in black laid his hand on the butt of his pistol with a confident air. Several others in the line did likewise but with less bravado. "I said I'm the spokesman, old man, so you'd best speak with me."

"All right, whoever you are, what do you want?"

"Are you prepared to give these single men, unfairly relieved of work, their jobs back?"

"Certainly not! Not only is it impossible for the Rim to support them now, but I would never give any man holding a gun on me a position in my mine—now or ever!"

"Then we, the Working Men of Garson, are prepared to see that no one else works either until we are treated fairly."

"We'll see about that! You just get—"

Morris' push forward and his brave words were cut short when the man in black drew his pistol and slammed its barrel into the side of Morris' head, knocking him to the ground.

"Tote his carcass out of my sight," the gunslinger ordered, "before I get really mad. And don't bother comin' to work until he either changes his mind or there's an owner with more sense at the Silver Rim. This mine is closed."

✻ ✻ ✻

Just outside the mouth of Red Rock Canyon, Hurry pulled his team to a halt. Oliver got down off the box to check the rigging as Hurry stepped around for a word with Josh.

Josh had been riding inside the coach, with his horse, Injun, tied on and trailing behind. He and Hurry had decided to travel this way to keep the weight off Injun's back and keep him fresher for the time when his speed might mean the difference between life and death.

"Right here's where that other bunch will have their breakdown," observed Hurry. "I figger there's a Mojave watchin' us right now, but all he'll see us do is put out an outrider." Hurry squinted back across the alkali flats to where an approaching swirl of dust could be seen. "In about five minutes, that Mojave'll be talkin' about a whole mess of men an' a coach with a busted wheel gettin' fixed right here outside the canyon. Soon as the guards get in sight, you can saddle up an' go to scoutin'."

Josh limbered the greener and checked its loads, thrusting some more shells into his shirt pockets from the cartridge pouch hanging from the saddle horn. He put the bit in Injun's mouth and flipped the bridle over the buckskin's head. Tightening the girth on the saddle, he untied the lead rope from the coach frame and mounted.

"I'll ride as far out front as I can so you can still see me. That will give you the most time to get turned if we've guessed wrong."

"Look sharp, boy. Them Mojaves ain't likely to show themselves, so you'll have to be right good. Just don't come back toward the coach for a chaw or nothin', 'cause if I see you turn around before we get through this canyon, you'll be eatin' my dust back to Weidner's!"

✳ ✳ ✳

When Morris came to, he was lying in the parlor of his own home being tended by Callie. A concerned and watchful half circle around him was made up of Ling Chow, Pickax, and Big John Daniels.

"My head," groaned Morris. "What happened?"

"Easy, Papa, just lie still," urged Callie.

Morris grimaced with the pain and clenched his jaw as if steadying himself. By the time he opened his eyes again he remembered what had happened. "What are the miners doing about this?" he demanded.

Big John shifted his great bulk uneasily. "They ain't doin' nothin', Mister Morris. They's scared. Scared of them hired guns."

Now Pickax broke his silence. "Scared is right! Especially by that black-dressed snake, Gates of Hell Logan. He's a coldhearted killer if'n ever there was one."

"But surely we can get enough men together to outnumber those thugs!"

"Yessir, we kin," said Big John slowly, "but—"

"But what?"

"There ain't nobody the miners will follow, leastwise not against Logan."

"I'll lead myself. I'm not afraid of Logan."

"Oh no you won't," said Callie firmly, pressing her father's shoulders back down on the sofa. "I won't let you go and get yourself killed. No mine in the whole world is worth that."

There was a tap at the front door. Ling Chow shuffled out to answer it, returning in a moment with his face set. Almost without moving his mouth he announced, "Mister McGinty here."

Fancy Dan stepped quickly into the room, doing a poor job of concealing his smirk as he looked at Morris' prostrate figure.

"What do you want, McGinty?"

"I heard about your unfortunate labor problem, Mister Morris, and I came to offer my assistance."

"Your assistance? You swine, you're behind all this if I know anything!"

McGinty held up a cautioning hand as Big John took a menacing step toward him. "Don't be hasty, Morris; hear me out."

"All right, John," Morris said to Daniels, "let's hear what this . . . this swindler has to say."

"It's plain that you cannot operate the mine. Your own people won't attempt to cross the line of the Working Men. Why, they're down in town right now, talking about how they haven't been paid and asking why they should risk their lives for you."

"They know they'll get paid. There's a replacement payroll on the—" Morris silenced himself abruptly.

"On the way now? Well, let's hope they don't run into any Indian trouble like the last time, eh? But even *if* they should get here with that payroll, these miners aren't going to challenge armed men for the sake of a few dollars." McGinty smiled briefly, coldly.

"Look, here's what I'm willing to do," he went on blandly. "I'm so confident that I can run this badly managed mine better than you that I'm willing to buy your shares of Golden Bear stock right now. That'll give me a place on the board, which I will happily relinquish to the other directors in exchange for clear title to the Silver Rim. How's that for fairness? To take over a failing operation in the midst of a labor dispute at a time when the town may be surrounded by hostile savages! You may call me crazy, but how does twenty-five thousand dollars sound, eh?"

Morris wavered for just a moment, weighing the offer. Then abruptly he made up his mind. "McGinty, get out of my house this instant!"

It was Callie who spoke next. She stood erect, facing McGinty as if her blind eyes nevertheless could see into his soul. "My father has poured his life into making this mine work and making this town a respectable place to live, to bring up families. Neither you nor your hired murderers will ever make us abandon the Silver Rim! Big John, show Mister McGinty to the door!"

McGinty was already backing up as the giant black man advanced. "You'll regret this," Fancy Dan snarled. Then he was gone.

"All right, Papa, now we know for certain who the enemy really is. What should we do now?"

"God bless you for your courage, child. Thank you for speaking out at just the right time, when my own courage was starting to fail. Now we need to pray for God to show us what is to be done."

"And pray for Josh's safe return?" asked Callie in a small voice, as if all the air had gone out of her slender frame.

"Yes, Callie, for that, too."

The plan must be working, thought Josh with grim satisfaction. *Either that, or I have to suppose those Indians have given up their taste for stagecoaches after one try. And that I just don't believe.*

The sandstone walls rose plain and barren into the windless afternoon. Their pace through the canyon had been steady but unhurried, Hurry reasoning that to race through its snakelike turns might result in a spill that could prove fatal in more ways than one.

If Pick is right about the fighting Indians—and he is about everything else in this desert—then the prickles on the back of my neck mean we're being watched right now. Josh was studying the buckskin's ears closely, but while they were in motion, flicking back and forth, the horse's attention seemed more on the route up the canyon than toward the rocks on either side.

In a few moments Josh understood why. He reined Injun to a halt as the echo of hooves coming toward him rebounded off the walls of the arroyo.

Josh glanced back over his shoulder; the coach was still coming along steadily. The guard was alert, scanning the cliffs to the sides and behind the coach, while Hurry watched ahead.

Nothing to do but keep on going, thought Josh. *If I stop here, Johnson will think something is wrong even before I know what this is all about.*

Pressing the buckskin close against the side of the canyon that had a slight overhang, Josh cocked the greener and went warily forward.

Around the next bend came a lone rider. He too studied the canyon walls, twisting nervously in his saddle. Paying so much attention to the sandstone cliffs, he failed to notice Josh's approach.

451

When he did look up and recognize Josh, he nearly spun the dun horse he was riding around. Mastering himself with great difficulty, he held out a trembling hand to halt Josh's progress.

Josh exclaimed, "Beldad! What are you doing here? Don't you know there's an Indian war on in these hills?"

"I-I-I . . . came to find . . . find you," stammered Beldad.

"Came to find me? Since when have you—?"

Just then the coach came into Beldad's view from around the last corner of the canyon before its walls opened out.

Beldad stood in his stirrups and shouted, "It's here! It's here, you fools—this is the coach you want!"

❋ ❋ ❋

Sotol had planted his ambush near the mouth of the canyon closest to the Garson side, hoping to lull the guards into falsely believing they had come through safely. He had let the first coach pass through without attacking it, so there was no indication given of the presence of his band. When Beldad approached from the Garson road Sotol hadn't recognized him, and Beldad hadn't yet gotten up enough nerve to call out to the Indians he knew must be lurking nearby.

Across the canyon from Sotol's position, a young brave jumped to his feet and began firing wildly. One of the first shots knocked Beldad from his saddle. He hit the ground calling out miserably, "Not me, you idiots! Not me!"

✳ ✳ ✳

Josh fired at the cliff face, knocking down the Indian with a blast of buckshot. Over his shoulder he saw Hurry snap the reins to make his break through the canyon, now only a short distance away.

Confusion reigned among the Indians. They had been advised not to fire until the band of guards arrived and to remain completely still.

The Mojaves began firing their rifles, but the Indian Josh had killed was the last brave before the mouth of the canyon; the coach had, in fact, passed all but two of the ambush positions.

The stage raced ahead, and Oliver began firing with good effect, his booming shotgun forcing two Indian ambushers to take cover behind the rocks. The other braves had only the rear of the speeding coach for a target.

Josh spurred Injun ahead, then jerked him to a stop beside Beldad. Instinctively, Josh leaped from the saddle to drag Beldad out of the road just before the coach thundered by. Then he draped Beldad across the saddle and, leaping up behind him, encouraged his horse after the stage. A few badly aimed shots rang out from the rocks, but they were soon out of range and danger.

At last the coach came to a halt, and while Oliver stood on the roof of the stage to watch their back trail, Hurry helped Josh load Beldad into the stage. He had been hit in the chest, and his breath came in short gasps.

Hurry looked at Josh and shook his head.

As they laid Beldad on the passenger seat, his eyes fluttered open, and he spoke to Josh with difficulty. "You . . . tried to save me. . . . I was trying to get you . . . killed!"

"By the Mojaves?" burst out Josh.

"McGinty . . . he and the Indians . . ." Beldad's back arched in a spasm of pain. His eyes widened, then glazed, and he was gone.

"You heard him, Hurry." Josh's voice was bitter, full of determination and anger.

"I sure did! I'd say we get on to Garson. McGinty's got a heap to answer for! And . . . look there!"

Josh whirled in the direction Hurry was pointing and exhaled a long gasp of air.

⋆CHAPTER 16⋆

"I say we can't wait no more," Big John Daniels declared. "The longer
we lets them gunmen stay, the tougher it's gonna be to get anyone to
go up agin 'em. Besides, them mining company folks is liable to take
McGinty's offer to buy the Rim just to get shed of all this mess."

"How many of them hired guns you figger there is?" Pick asked
Big John.

"Well, we seen ten, counting that Logan, but three of 'em ain't
really gunfighters. There could be more in the mine, but I doubt it.
I ain't sure how many more Working Men there are in Garson, but
they's just loudmouths an' out-a-work miners. They ain't killers."

"All right, then, let's go see what we can muster for our side. Lean
Duck, you stay here with Mister Morris an' Callie. Big John, you
an' me best split up an' spread the word. Tell 'em to meet at the No
Name in one hour."

⋆ ⋆ ⋆

At the prescribed time, at least fifty miners and townspeople gathered
at Jersey Smith's place. Two of the side canvas flaps had been tied up
and back so as to accommodate the crowd.

Most already knew the situation, but at Big John's call for action
there was an uneasy silence.

Finally a burly miner spoke up. "I'm right grateful to Mister
Morris for all he's done. But the reason I was still workin' is cause I

have a family. And that family would rather leave than have me dead. I ain't no hand to be facin' up to Miles Logan."

"Besides," said a single man, "I belong to the Working Men. I'm not sayin' hirin' those gunslingers was the right thing for McGinty to do, but this dispute's between him and Morris, right? I don't wanna get killed for either one of them."

When the man mentioned his connection with the Working Men, Big John started toward him with an upraised fist.

Pick stopped him. "Easy there, Big John. We don't want to start any fightin' here—that won't get no mine back."

"An' you so-called Workin' Men," Pick said, "you listen up an' listen good. That's your side there blockin' the road. Most of your group's there now, herded together like so many cows. You'd best choose up sides pronto. This ain't no time to be watchin' which way the wind blows."

A few men backed out of the group and, with furtive looks behind them, skulked off up the road toward the mine.

"All right, here's the plan," Pick said. "We'll divide into groups. Big John here'll lead one into the arroyo an' up the wash behind where them fellers is blockin' the road. The second group'll go up the road an' spread out along either side."

"Who's leadin' the second bunch, the ones goin' right into the teeth of them guns?" shouted a voice from the back of the crowd.

"Well," drawled Pick slowly, "it looks like I get that pleasant duty."

Shouts of "No" and "Sit down, old-timer" erupted from the group.

"Some of those men are friends of ours," said a tall man with close-cropped brown hair, "and the others are hired killers. How can we fight that? I say we try to parlay with them."

There were murmurs of agreement and nods.

"It won't wash," Pick replied. "Fancy Dan McGinty wants to keep the Rim shut down until he can take it away from Morris. I don't aim to let him do it."

"Then you'll get killed, old man," shouted another miner. "I haven't even been paid lately. Maybe McGinty could manage it better."

"Why don't you leave with them other skunks?" retorted Pick.

"Sittin' here jawin' ain't gettin' work for nobody. I may be old, but I ain't yella!"

"What do you say, Big John?" asked the tall man who'd spoken earlier.

"I say we got to be men an' stand up for what's right. If talkin' would fix it, then talkin's jes' fine, but I say we go ready to fight!"

"Enough said," rejoined Pick. "Nobody's twistin' your arm, but if you're comin' with us, get your guns an' let's go!"

Logan was lounging in the foreman's shack smoking a cigarette.

A hired gun rushed in to warn him. "You better come, Logan; we got trouble."

Logan took another drag on his cigarette and tossed it through the open door before leisurely getting to his feet. "Sonny boy, we don't got trouble; we *make* trouble. Ain't you figured that out yet?"

"Yeah? Well, there's a bunch of armed men comin' up the road right now."

Logan drew his six-shooter and spun the cylinder, then replaced it loosely in its holster. He casually checked the leather thongs that tied it down to his leg before sauntering after the nervous young gunhand.

"Well, well, what *have* we here?" Logan spoke to Pick, who had halted with twenty others about thirty yards from the mine property. "You're an even older old coot than the last old coot who came up here. Ain't there any young folks who know how to talk in this town, or are you all played out?"

"Logan, we come to tell you to get outta here. You ain't wanted in this town."

"Is that it? And if I don't choose to go—how do you propose to make me?"

"Me an' these—," Pick began.

Before he could finish, Logan shouted, "Let's open the ball," then drew his Colt and blasted point-blank, putting a bullet through Pick's stomach and another into his side as the old prospector collapsed.

Logan continued firing, joined by the other hired guns, until the miners and townspeople scattered to find hiding in the gullies and brush.

When the gunfire had ceased, Logan spoke again. "You men out there! Go on home, and there won't be any more killin'. Just don't cross me no more!"

A single miner came up behind Logan, who whirled around on him, the Colt pointed at the man's chest. The young man put both hands in the air and swallowed hard. "We didn't want no killing, Mister Logan. Not old Pickax, he—"

"Shut up before I plug you, too! If you ain't with me right now, then I'll shoot you down where you stand."

"But I'm not even armed," sputtered the miner.

"Then you best run on back to that mine so's I can protect you, little squally brat. Now git!"

Rifle fire from circling miners and townspeople began erupting from the brush. The young Working Man needed no further urging; he and the other unarmed dupes of McGinty crowded into the mine entrance.

"All right," yelled Logan, dropping to cover behind an ore car, "give it to them!"

The armed thugs who began firing had chosen their protection better than the attackers. From behind the walls of the mine buildings and heaps of timber and mounds of ore, hired guns fired with deadly effect.

One of the attackers rolled over, wailing and clutching his shoulder. Another staggered, holding his face in both hands, and fell over dead without making a sound. A third was hit in the hand.

None of the hired guns received so much as a scratch.

"Go on home—all of you!" Logan called out. "Unless you're itchin' to die. That we can oblige."

A crackle of rifle fire mixed with the popping of smaller caliber pistols came from behind Logan's position. One of his men grabbed his leg and rolled on the ground cursing. Big John's group had succeeded in getting up the wash unseen and began another attack.

"You five," ordered Logan, waving his pistol in a sweeping motion toward his gunmen on the front line, "keep those rock grubbers out there from movin' up while the rest of us take care of the others."

Members of Big John's party were shooting steadily from the lip of the arroyo, but Logan's men still had plenty of cover from which to return the fire.

Logan dashed from the ore car to a stack of timber. He fired three times over the stack, then retreated to calmly reload while a few shots struck the beams in reply.

Moving around the other end of the timbers, Logan dropped a miner who had just raised a rifle to his shoulder, then turned his aim toward Big John, who was brandishing a long-barrelled, ten-gauge shotgun. Logan's first shot clanged off Big John's shotgun as he brought it up across his face. The huge man fell heavily to the ground, trying to conceal himself behind mesquite scrub one-quarter his size. Logan was aiming another shot at Big John's head when the ten-gauge blasted, and Logan dropped quickly to his belly.

General firing continued on all sides. The miners and towns-people had the greater numbers, but the skill of the gunfighters was winning the day.

The pounding of hooves and the rolling, continuous creaking of a stagecoach at full speed drifted up from Garson between shots. The sound slowed but didn't stop, and the rushing noise continued right through town and up the hill toward the mine.

Hurry Johnson's rig rolled with such speed toward the entrance of the Silver Rim that men from both sides of the fight had to throw themselves out of the road to avoid being trampled. When Hurry pulled the team to a halt, the leaders reared at the sudden stop. Behind the coach rode Josh on Injun. He was shouting and waving his hat, but no one could understand what he was saying.

When the team had quieted and the crowd stilled, those who heard him were taken aback by the authority and urgency with which he spoke. "Stop this nonsense at once! Return to your homes; retreat to the mine buildings. Our only hope of survival is to band together."

"What? What are you talking about, Roberts?" One of Logan's men spoke up. "Is this some kind of cheap trick?"

"The Mojaves are preparing a full-scale attack on the town. At least fifty of them—maybe more!"

"That won't play, Roberts. Them Mojaves ain't got sand enough to make a try for a whole town!"

"That may have been true in the past, but now they're carrying Winchesters, and they're on their way here."

"Winchesters!" several gasped. "Where'd they get rifles from?"

"McGinty" was Josh's simple reply. "McGinty supplied them with all they'd need."

"My family! They're alone!" a miner cried out.

A single man from the entrance called out, "I'll come with you, Jim."

A stream of men exited the mine, running for their homes and weapons to defend the town.

"What about us?" asked one of the gunslingers, shifting allegiance to the constable.

"Stay here and keep the road to town open. If necessary, we may have to all retreat back to the mine."

Before Josh could continue, he noticed Pick's body lying face-down in the dust beside the road. His breath caught in his throat, and he leaped from the buckskin to cradle the old man's head in farewell. When he looked up, he asked bitterly, "Who's responsible for this?"

"Logan. Gates of Hell Logan."

"*Gates!* Where is he?" Joshua demanded.

Not even his own hired guns knew. In the sudden confusion at the entrance of the stage and Josh's announcement of the Indian attack, the man in black had taken the opportunity to escape.

✼ ✼ ✼

McGinty pulled a .32 caliber pistol out of his desk drawer at the pounding of footsteps up the outside stairs to his office. He held it leveled at the entry.

The door burst open and Miles Logan almost fell in, panting. "The jig's up, McGinty. We've had it."

"What do you mean, 'had it'? Do you mean to say that you let this rabble of town clowns and dirty grubbers run you out?"

"No," gasped Logan as he struggled to catch his breath, "they're on to us—*you,* I mean. They know about the Indians and the rifles."

"What? How can they possibly know that?"

"Because," sputtered Logan, gesturing toward the sound of feet running along the board sidewalks, "the Mojaves are comin' to visit, and they're bringin' your callin' cards with them!"

✻ ✻ ✻

"Josh." Big John Daniels spoke quietly. "Leave him for now. We gots a town to defend."

Josh made a pillow of his own hat and placed it gently under Pick's head. Then he rose slowly to face Daniels. "All right. Let's go check on the Morris home."

"Good idear," Big John replied. Then he told Josh how Logan had beaten Mr. Morris with the butt of his pistol.

Josh's jaw set grimly, the news giving him fresh determination to stop this madman.

✻ ✻ ✻

At the Morris home, the two men hadn't even reached the front step when Ling Chow came rushing out. He held a shotgun under one arm, but the other dangled at his side, blood soaking his wide sleeve.

"Mister Josh! God be thanked, you here!" the Chinaman burst out.

"What is it, Ling Chow? What's happened?"

"McGinty and man in black come here. They say they need . . . they need . . ."

"What? *Why* did they come? What did they say?"

"They say they need trade to buy freedom. They say no one follow till they send word or they will kill."

"Kill? Kill who, Ling Chow? You are making no sense."

Agitated and confused, Ling dropped the shotgun and grasped Josh's arm. "Why you not *understand*? They take Callie. *Callie!* They ride off in desert!"

"Callie!" Josh whirled Injun around, then stopped briefly to talk hurriedly with Morris before instructing Big John and Ling Chow in the defense of the house.

Morris himself lay on a couch with its back against an upstairs window, ready to defend the yard below. "Godspeed," he called hoarsely to Josh. "Please bring her home safely."

Josh nodded and was gone, pushing Injun to the limit up the winding trail that led past the Silver Rim and down through the canyons and washes to the desert floor below, even as the first sounds of gunfire drifted up from the town of Garson.

CHAPTER 17

As Josh rode furiously, his brain tried to sort out what he knew of tracking and what Pick had taught him of the desert trails. The thought of Callie's abduction and Pick's senseless death made him fearful and angry, and his heels dug into Injun's side, spurring him on to greater speed.

What's happening to Callie? pounded through his brain. He hardly dared think of the danger she might be in. He could think only of finding her, making her safe again. He forced himself to watch the trail left by three horses—two side by side and what seemed likely to be the prints of Callie's mare being led behind. If he thought of other things he feared he would miss a turn or mistake a sign.

Scanning the trail ahead, Josh was aware that Logan was too experienced a man to leave his back trail unwatched. So far, the kidnappers seemed to travel straight as an arrow. Intervening brush-covered hillsides blocked more than half a mile's view at a time. With each approach of the crest of a sandy hill, Josh skirted its rim so as to approach the back side from an unexpected direction. With no sign of any movement about, Josh regained the trail and rode on.

He knew they must go to water within another day; they could not be carrying a greater supply than that. He trailed them until darkness forced him to stop for the night.

Josh hobbled Injun and had a cold supper of jerky and hard biscuits from his saddlebags, washed down with water. He didn't want to take the chance of a fire revealing his position on the trail.

He could hear Injun contentedly chewing and rustling just outside the range of his night vision. Apparently the horse had found something to his liking, not returning to look for supper from his rider.

Josh took mental stock of his camp. His shotgun was at the ready and close at hand. Canteen and provisions were wrapped tightly in canvas and stowed beneath his saddle, secured against marauding pack rats. The saddle served as his pillow. Calling good night to his horse and breathing a prayer for Callie, Josh turned over, pulling half the tarp over his frame.

✳ ✳ ✳

The faintest ray in the east told Josh of the approach of dawn. He had slept fitfully and was eager to be off. Rubbing his eyes, a glance around revealed Injun standing not far off. In seconds he'd gathered his belongings together in a pile and was striding toward his horse, bridle in hand.

As he walked, he observed that the stems of thin grass that his horse had been grazing were supplanted in places by clumps of a gray, hairy plant with long, spiky leaves. Here and there stalks of white flowers stood above the gray-green foliage. This must have been the plant agreeable to Injun, because he had chewed it down to the ground in places.

At his call, Injun lifted his head, and Josh approached the horse and stroked his nose and head. "Come on, boy. Let's get movin'." The words, though spoken without urgency, had an unexpected effect.

Injun snorted violently and jumped sideways.

"Easy, boy, easy. What's wrong with you? You got the jumps about something? Here now, easy." Josh reached out again to stroke the horse's face and the animal appeared calm. *I wonder what that was all about,* Josh thought.

He flipped the loop of bridle over the horse's ears and began to place the bit in his mouth. Injun was trained to drop his head to allow the bit to be inserted, but he seemed to have forgotten this. He stood with his neck outstretched and his head held unnaturally high.

Josh returned to camp and poured water into his hat for the

horse to drink. After taking the water eagerly, the horse was more agreeable, letting Josh put the bit in his mouth. Leading him to camp, Josh smoothed the saddle blanket on his mount and secured the saddle. Then he tied his blanket roll behind the saddle and looped the strap of the greener over the horn on the off side. Tying the two canteens together, he hung them on the left side of the horn.

After a quick inspection, Josh jumped into the saddle and resumed the trail, hoping that Callie would be able to delay her captors as much as possible.

As Josh rode, the dawn breaking over the eastern hills began to light up the canyons and ravines to the west. From gray shadows, streaks of pink and orange began to appear as bands of brilliantly colored sandstone reflected the early morning rays. But Josh hardly noticed in his concern for Callie.

Soon the disk of the sun burst over the peaks. The warmth felt good on Josh's face, but it promised to be a very hot day. The night chill was nearly gone, and the sunlight had reduced the pale frost on the ground to white westward-pointing streaks shielded by the clumps of brush. In between the bushes, the ground was drying and beginning to steam.

Injun was still unusually agitated. His ears were constantly in motion, as if searching for danger nearby and confused at not finding it. His easy, ground-covering lope was interrupted frequently by sudden shifts to a bone-jarring trot. He could be urged back to the lope but would again break its gentle rhythm without warning.

After about an hour of this annoying pattern, Josh stopped the horse to inspect his feet. Even though he had not been limping, Josh thought perhaps a hoof was giving him trouble. He soon located and dislodged a pebble from the hoof, and when he mounted again, Injun seemed to have a smoother gait. Josh fretted over the delay, regretting the time lost from his pursuit.

Then all at once Injun shied violently, sending Josh sideways in his saddle, almost dislodging him. The horse made three jumps over clumps of mesquite before Josh hauled up on the reins and shouted for the horse to stop. With the halt, Injun stood shuddering in place.

Josh patted the horse's neck and spoke soothingly to him. The horse's shuddering subsided, and Josh urged him back on the path once again.

Suddenly something white caught Josh's eye on the trail. Drawing up alongside it, he recognized it as a woman's handkerchief. *Good girl, Callie!*

With another pat to reassure his mount, Josh climbed down to retrieve the scrap of linen, keeping his fingers entwined in the bridle.

As Josh breathed in the scent of Callie's perfume, the horse gave a lurch backward, tumbling Josh to the ground. He cried out in pain as his elbow struck a sharp rock and he lost hold of the reins.

Rubbing his elbow, he reached for the trailing reins, but at the same moment Injun whirled, lashing out with both feet and nearly connecting with Josh's face.

"Hey! Calm down!"

Again the animal was quiet, but as soon as Josh reached for the reins, Injun moved off, trotting a few more yards and stopping to look back at Josh.

Josh mused. The stop-and-go game continued for three more attempts, but no amount of coaxing, wheedling, or threatening would make the horse stand still for Josh to grasp the reins.

Josh stood in the middle of the trail at a loss to figure out the problem. Then he used another tactic. As soon as the movements of the horse's ears and tail momentarily stopped, Josh made a rush for the trailing reins. But at the exact moment his fingers touched the leather, he stumbled over a rock on the trail and fell face-first in the dirt.

The fall was fortunate, however, because Injun had at the same time aimed another kick at Josh, which whistled over the top of his head. Then the horse was gone, running flat out down the trail and disappearing over a small knoll about half a mile ahead.

The full horror of the situation washed over Josh. Not only had he lost all hope of overtaking Callie, but his bedroll, shotgun, and canteens of water were disappearing along with his horse, out of sight and out of reach!

The horse's abrupt departure left Josh some thirty miles from the nearest water. It would have been a hard day's ride; now it was going to be a punishing hike.

Josh could only hope the horse would stop to graze, enabling him to catch up somehow. At least he appeared to keep to the trail.

Nothing was to be gained by waiting, so he started off down the faint path. As he went, Pick's words echoed in his ears: *A man in the desert without horse or water is a dead man.*

When Josh topped the next rise he could see Injun, not a quarter of a mile away, grazing just to the side of the trail. He plodded on toward the horse, trying to plan his strategy as he went. *I need to come up on his left to have the best shot at grabbing those trailing reins,* he reasoned. *And I can't spook him before I get that close.*

He decided to mimic the horse's own actions as a means of putting the beast at ease. Each time the horse lifted his head to gaze around, Josh stood still and bent to the ground, even plucking a handful of the thin grass. Moving forward only when the horse grazed and stopping when he lifted his head, Josh was able to approach within a few yards of him. The next time Injun raised and turned his head, Josh shook a handful of the grass and called gently, "Look here, boy—see what I have for you."

The horse flared his nostrils suspiciously, and when Josh didn't move, Injun stretched his neck toward him.

Injun had been standing sideways to Josh's approach, but now he turned to face him directly. Stretching out his neck again he sniffed at the grass, deciding whether to investigate the offering.

Josh took a step closer and the horse snorted but didn't move. Extending the bouquet without moving another muscle, Josh stood completely still, silently praying.

Injun nudged the grass with his nose and took another step forward. Josh held his breath. If only he could wrap both arms around its neck, then secure the reins. The whole scene was so incredibly bizarre.

The horse pulled away, as if reading Josh's thoughts. Slowly, agonizingly Josh began to inch forward with the bundle of drying weeds, willing the horse to lean closer. He arched his left leg, fearing to step forward, lest he frighten the horse away.

466

At six feet apart Injun stopped. Josh gingerly pushed the fistful of drooping grass stems out. The horse stretched his neck to its greatest length, and then as if this were not safe enough, proceeded to nibble the weeds with only his lips. Injun's ears flicked nervously back and forth. A tremor began in his withers and ran down through his flank. *He's getting ready to bolt,* thought Josh anxiously. *It's now or never.*

As if reading his thoughts the horse exploded into motion, whirling to his left and pulling the reins out of Josh's reach.

Lunging for his neck, intending to hold on for all he was worth, Josh stumbled forward and Injun reared. A flailing hoof glanced off Josh's shoulder as he ducked to the side.

Josh leaped for the horse's side, thinking he could perhaps drag himself into the saddle. His hands felt the shotgun hanging from the horn, and he grasped it. The horse reared again, lashing out with iron-shod hooves and twisting to the left.

For a moment Josh could feel the horse being pulled toward him. Seconds later, the leather sling on the greener parted from the stock with a crack like a whip.

A wild flurry of flying hooves was followed by a buck that brought Injun's head completely to the ground. One murderous kick aimed at Josh's face and the horse was gone, pounding away to the west.

Josh was alone again, holding the greener with its dangling, broken strap.

⋆CHAPTER 18⋆

For two hours Josh tracked the horse into the relentless afternoon sun. Once he came within a hundred yards, but that was the closest point before Injun made another dash away.

Dear God, help me, Josh pleaded. *I'm back where I started. Will this time end up differently? Will I die in the desert? You have to save me, so I can save Callie. Please, God, for Callie's sake. . . .*

Josh continued to trail his only hope for survival into the dusty, still, desert afternoon. His mouth was dry, and the skin on his face became stiff and taut. The moisture was leaving his body. As lack of water in the blazing heat took its toll, his mind began to wander and his steps faltered.

He began to pick up small pebbles from the trail to put in his mouth to start the saliva flowing. In his delirium he found himself spending a long time choosing the stones. Hours passed, and Josh could feel his life ebb away with the moisture. A thick, pasty film formed on his palate, causing him to gag and retch.

The shotgun trailed over his shoulder by its broken sling, and the stock bumped against his back, causing increasing irritation. At one point he was tempted to whirl it around his head and fling it into the brush. He interrupted his frustration in time to allow the weapon to swing to a stop.

Then he tried to tie the end of the leather strap through the trigger guard to make a loop but found that his brain would not communicate the necessary steps to his fingers to tie a knot. He wandered aimlessly down the path, his feet keeping to the trail while his mind and hands fiddled with the problem.

A dry wash cut across the landscape in front of him. Its drab brown and ashen color blended in with the surrounding plain, and he didn't see it until almost too late. Half sliding, half swinging around a Joshua tree saved him from falling.

There, just below him in the wash and pawing anxiously at the sand bed, stood Injun. They both caught sight of each other in the same instant.

The horse whirled to run but was slower now, awkward and struggling. The relentless sun had taken its toll on his mount as well. The greener was already in Josh's hands. He instinctively brought it to a tight grip against his side, and his right hand thumbed back the hammer. There was a deafening roar and a cloud of bitter gray smoke.

Josh dropped the gun and ran into the gully, tumbling head over heels as he went. He came up next to the still form of Injun. A quick look told him that the double-aught had done its work—the horse had dropped down dead and never moved again. But in spinning, rearing, and falling, Injun had come down heavily on his left side. The double-yoked canteens had been crushed beneath him, and as Josh wrenched them free from beneath the carcass, the last drops were being swallowed by the thirsty sand.

Flinging himself face-first into the dust and gravel of the gully, Josh tried to suck life-giving water from the moist sand. He came up sputtering and retching as the harsh alkali soil burned his mouth and throat. The earth must have been even drier than Joshua, because it leeched the last moisture from his mouth, leaving him worse off than before.

Joshua knew he was in the most desperate situation possible. It was best that he act in anxious haste, because otherwise he might not be able to act at all. Remembering Pick's words, Josh reached into his pocket and drew out a small folding knife. With a crushed canteen held as a bowl under Injun's neck, Josh stabbed downward fiercely and slit the horse's throat. Bright red blood gushed out, flooding the canteen, Josh's hands, and the ground. After a moment's hesitation, he drank. Forcing down his rising gorge with difficulty, he swallowed and swallowed until the bowl was empty. The blood flowing from the dead horse was now only a trickle, but he refilled his improvised bowl. When it was full, he drank it all down again, every drop.

Josh looked at his gore-covered hands. Then he looked at the crimson pool shrinking rapidly into the sand and clotting into blackening clumps. His mind flashed a picture of how his face must look—mouth ringed with blood and chin and shirt spattered with it. He dropped the canteen and threw his hands up to his face in horror and revulsion.

Josh had to rouse himself from the desire to lay back and rest. He had to continue on in search of Callie. *Callie!* Her face flashed across his brain like lightning leaping to a peak in a Sierra thunderstorm. He had pursued the horse and the canteens for a whole afternoon, gradually forgetting why he was out in the desert in the first place.

God, I'm going crazy. I think I hear her voice calling my name.

"Josh, is it you? Josh, answer me!"

Callie! Then he heard McGinty and Logan. He *had* found them. Or was it the other way around?

"Ain't you a sight?" Logan chuckled. He casually drew his Colt.

At the rustling of the gun from its leather, Callie pleaded, "No, wait! Please don't hurt him!"

"Well, now, pretty lady, just since you ask," Logan replied. "I wish you could see your hero, gettin' hisself a fine drink of horse blood."

Turning to McGinty he added, "Shall we jest leave him out here to find his own way back? Maybe someone will rescue you, like the first time I left you in this predicament." He sneered at Josh.

"Gates." Josh groaned hoarsely, trying to make his brain, fuzzy with dust and sun, work. *How can I get Callie away?* he pondered.

"Let's get going, Logan. Bring Miss Morris and come on," ordered McGinty.

"You know, Roberts, it wasn't too smart of you to go blastin' off with that cannon yonder. Not with us sittin' just the other side of this gully. Not smart at all."

"I wouldn't be too sure about that," came another voice from the edge of the wash.

470

Rather than waste time looking to see who spoke, Logan spun on his heels and fired the Colt in the general direction. Such a move may have worked, had there been only one man to deal with. But *three* men stood on the rise.

Before Logan made a full turn, Nate Dawson's .45 cut him down and Logan's shot went wild.

Callie Morris screamed.

Tom Dawson never flinched. He kept his gun on Logan a moment longer, gesturing for Nate to walk cautiously down from the opposite side of the gully. He approached carefully in case the gunman was shamming, but Miles Logan was dead.

"Miss Morris, Tom Dawson here. Don't worry; everything's under control. Mont is holding a gun on Mister Fancy Dan McGinty."

Callie didn't wait any longer. She cried out as she ran toward Josh, calling his name.

"Here, Callie! I'm here, love!"

She flew to him, throwing her arms around his neck. Holding each other was enough.

Josh tried to hold her back, saying, "No, Callie, I'm all over blood!"

Callie stopped only a fraction of a second, and as Josh wiped his face on his sleeve, she scolded "Joshua Roberts, what's a little blood as long as it isn't yours?"

✳ ✳ ✳

"Come on, you two," Tom called after he figured an appropriate time had passed. "We'll take Mister McGinty with us while Nate and Mont bury Logan."

"I guess I can take Logan's horse," Josh commented. "He won't be needing it anymore."

"Sounds good," said Tom. "The others are a mite frisky, even for a salty old desert hand like yourself."

"Others?" Josh asked, looking around.

"Just up ahead," Tom indicated. "This wash leads up to the box canyon where we round up the mustangs before driving them to Garson. There's water there, but none of that loco weed for the horses to get into. Drives 'em crazy, you know."

471

✶EPILOGUE✶

"Y es, Papa, I'm just fine. Better than you, I think," Callie assured him.

"If you feel up to it, sir," urged Josh, "tell us what happened in the Indian attack."

"Wasn't anything to it at all," said Morris, his head wrapped in bandages. "Those Mojaves weren't expecting a whole town full of armed folks—and mad besides! For all their Winchesters, they couldn't stand up to the citizens pulling together and fighting it out like real soldiers. The only real damage done was by a fire. Quick work saved the other businesses but not before Fancy Dan's place was gutted. Anyway, I've heard that the army detachment is on the Mojaves' trail and will chase them clear to Mexico if need be."

"And the mine, sir—can you save it from being closed permanently?"

"That's the best part. I sent Sexton into the Silver Rim to see if those hooligans had damaged any equipment. He brought up a specimen of rock from gallery five's collapsed roof. You won't believe what he found."

"What's that, sir?"

"The sample assayed out two thousand dollars a ton! Sexton says it probably gets richer behind the rockfall. Of course, McGinty knew about the rich vein, and Beldad was working to keep it a secret till McGinty owned the Rim. I've already telegraphed the news to the other directors, and they're agreed: Everyone goes back to work."

"That's wonderful, Papa!" exclaimed Callie. "Now the town can grow—be a place to raise families and—" She stopped, blushing suddenly.

Both men laughed, and Callie joined in. "But you have to promise me one thing, Papa," she continued. "That the Rim will donate land and money to build a church."

"Whatever you say, my dear. Sounds like a very good idea to me." He turned to Josh. "Seem reasonable to you, Constable?"

"I think we still need a jail first," he countered.

"Why, Joshua Roberts, how can you say such a thing?" Callie protested.

"Well, actually I was just quoting what Fancy Dan McGinty is probably saying."

"McGinty? Why do you say that?" Morris questioned.

"Because he's out there right now, chained to that T-rail." Josh pointed out the window toward the bustling activity of the Silver Rim.

473

☀ DEAR READER ☀

We hope you've enjoyed these legends of the Wild West—tales of adventurous and courageous men and women who faced down danger, overcame impossible odds to triumph over their circumstances with God's help, and discovered the truth about what is most meaningful in life.

As you travel on your life's journey, you too will face numerous challenges that will impact your heart, mind, and soul. We'd love to hear from you! To write us, or for further information about the Legends of the West series (including behind-the-scenes stories and details you won't want to miss), visit:

WWW.THOENEBOOKS.COM

WWW.FAMILYAUDIOLIBRARY.COM

We pray that through these legends you will "discover the Truth through Fiction." For we are convinced that if you seek diligently, you will find the One who holds all the answers to the universe (1 Chronicles 28:9).

BROCK & BODIE THOENE

ABOUT THE AUTHORS

 **BROCK AND BODIE THOENE** (pronounced *Tay-nee*) live part of the year in the beautiful Sierra Nevada, in which their Legends of the West are set. Together they have written over 45 works of historical fiction. That these best sellers have sold more than 10 million copies and won eight ECPA Gold Medallion Awards affirms what millions of readers have already discovered—the Thoenes are not only master stylists but experts at capturing readers' minds and hearts.

In their timeless classic series about Israel (The Zion Chronicles, The Zion Covenant, and The Zion Legacy), the Thoenes' love for both story and research shines.

With the Legends of the West (gripping tales of adventure and danger in a land without law), The Shiloh Legacy and *Shiloh Autumn* (poignant portrayals of the American Depression), and The Galway Chronicles (dramatic stories of the 1840s famine in Ireland, the Thoenes have made their mark in modern history.

In the A.D. Chronicles, they step seamlessly into the world of Jerusalem and Rome, in the days when Yeshua walked the earth and transformed lives with His touch.

Bodie began her writing career as a teen journalist for her local newspaper. Eventually her byline appeared in prestigious periodicals such as *U.S. News and World Report, The American West,* and

The Saturday Evening Post. She also worked for John Wayne's Batjac Productions (she's best known as author of *The Fall Guy*) and ABC Circle Films as a writer and researcher. John Wayne described her as "a writer with talent that captures the people and the times!" She has degrees in journalism and communications.

Brock has often been described by Bodie as "an essential half of this writing team." With degrees in both history and education, Brock has, in his role as researcher and story-line consultant, added the vital dimension of historical accuracy. Due to such careful research, the Zion Covenant and Zion Chronicles series are recognized by the American Library Association, as well as Zionist libraries around the world, as classic historical novels and are used to teach history in college classrooms.

Brock and Bodie have four grown children—Rachel, Jake, Luke, and Ellie—and seven grandchildren. Their children are carrying on the Thoene family talent as the next generation of writers, and Luke produces the Thoene audiobooks. Brock and Bodie divide their time between London and Nevada.

For more information visit:

WWW.THOENEBOOKS.COM
WWW.FAMILYAUDIOLIBRARY.COM

THOENE FAMILY CLASSICS™

✪ ✪ ✪

THOENE FAMILY CLASSIC HISTORICALS
by Bodie and Brock Thoene
Gold Medallion Winners*

THE ZION COVENANT
Vienna Prelude*
Prague Counterpoint
Munich Signature
Jerusalem Interlude
Danzig Passage
Warsaw Requiem*
London Refrain
Paris Encore
Dunkirk Crescendo

THE ZION CHRONICLES
The Gates of Zion*
A Daughter of Zion
The Return to Zion
A Light in Zion
The Key to Zion*

THE SHILOH LEGACY
In My Father's House*
A Thousand Shall Fall
Say to This Mountain

SHILOH AUTUMN

THE GALWAY CHRONICLES
Only the River Runs Free*
Of Men and of Angels
Ashes of Remembrance*
All Rivers to the Sea

THE ZION LEGACY
Jerusalem Vigil
Thunder from Jerusalem
Jerusalem's Heart
Jerusalem Scrolls
Stones of Jerusalem
Jerusalem's Hope

A.D. CHRONICLES
First Light
Second Touch
Third Watch
Fourth Dawn
Fifth Seal
Sixth Covenant
Seventh Day
Eighth Shepherd
and more to come!

CP0064

THOENE FAMILY CLASSICS™

✪ ✪ ✪

✪ ✪ ✪

✪ ✪ ✪

✪ ✪ ✪

THOENE FAMILY CLASSIC AUDIOBOOKS

Available from
www.thoenebooks.com or
www.familyaudiolibrary.com

suspense with a mission